What Others Are Saying About *Last of the Nephilim. . . .*

Last of the Nephilim was absolutely AMAZING! Bryan Davis brings back characters that make you feel like you're meeting again with old friends, as well as bringing in new people, a different dimension, an old enemy, and an intense battle scene written only as Mr. Davis can.

—**Kurtis Enns** (Age 17)

This is an amazing book that has no bounds. It is so captivating and wonderful I didn't eat dinner one night. Of course, its spiritual level was off the charts, amazing. Mr. Davis has written the best book in the series yet, and I can't wait for the next one.

—**Dustin James** (Age 13)

Marvelous! A plot so stirring, . . . that it made me feel as if I was walking side by side with each of the characters. The depth of this book is unlike any other book I have ever read. A thrilling, hair raising, mouth gaping book! Mr. Davis has done it again!

—**Krista Culver** (Age 15)

Bryan Davis has once again captivated my mind in a fantasy world of good and evil. Opening this book is like opening a doorway into another world. You'll be rapidly turning the pages until you reach the end, only to find yourself wanting more. I had an incredibly hard time putting this book down, and you will too!

—**Mariah Holloway** (Age 13)

Last of the Nephilim is an exhilarating continuation of the amazing story that Bryan Davis has so expertly woven. With a spectacular plot and characters that leap off the page and wind into your heart, he has provided readers with another brilliant masterpiece to treasure.

—**Hannah Roberts** (Age 14)

Bryan Davis has outdone himself again! He seamlessly weaves the many developing storylines throughout the Oracles of Fire series, finally bringing them together. Tested and tried throughout their journeys, the characters grow in faith, courage, and love. If only there wasn't a year until the next one!

—**Madison Uhlenhoff** (Age 15)

I have read most, if not all, of the bestselling young adult fantasy books. There are rare times that one becomes more than reading, but a journey, an experience. Bryan Davis's writing raises the bar of his already excellent quality with *Last of the Nephilim.*

—**Justin Boyer** (Age 18)

This book was spectacular. It was full of excitement and suspense. Out of all the Oracles of Fire and Dragons in our Midst series, this one is by far the best. Once I started reading the book, I could not put it down, even to go to sleep.

—**Colby Bidwell** (Age 16)

This book was definitely worth waiting for. Soaring with dragons, fighting evil, and learning to trust God—I felt like I was really there. It inspired my faith in God and helped me in my walk with Jesus.

—**Karissa Dumbacher** (Age 10)

One of the most eye-opening books I have read, *Last of the Nephilim* justly conveys the ultimate sacrifice of laying down one's life for a friend in a way that no other book has portrayed.

—**Caleb Richard** (Age 15)

I am captivated by this story. It is full of adventure and suspense. Everything is so vivid when reading that it is like watching a movie.

—**Tanner Brotherton** (Age 15)

This book is AWESOME, definitely deserving of a place on my bookshelf. I read it under the covers after my lights were supposed to be out, it was so good! It wraps up where *Enoch's Ghost* left off, and I can't wait to read more of the adventure!

—**Adam Meyers** (Age 14)

I have read the entire series and rate this book as the best yet! The battles between good and evil are suspenseful and draw the reader closer to God.

—**Coleby Brotherton** (Age 14)

Who could not love this book? *Last of the Nephilim* is filled with action and excitement, making it almost impossible to put down. Readers of all ages will enjoy this excellent book.

—**Cory McGinnis** (Age 15)

This book is truly amazing! I couldn't stop reading it! *Last of the Nephilim* has to be the best book I've ever read, and it's a great addition to the masterfully-written Oracles of Fire series.

—**Keegan Pulz** (Age 13)

THIS BOOK ROCKS! I thought it was one of the most adventure-filled, plot twisting books Mr. Davis has ever done! This book will spin the world off its axis. It provides a wonderful springboard for the final book in the Oracles of Fire series.

—**L. A. Clark** (Age 17)

Bryan Davis's books are the best books I have ever read, and this one was no exception. Reading about Billy, Walter, Elam, and Gabriel inspires me to stand against evil and to trust God more for my life.

—**Josh Dumbacher** (Age 13)

The book was exhilarating, an honor just to read it. You'll be mesmerized, and you'll want to read it again and again.

—**Daniel Turkey** (Age 13)

Last of the Nephilim

Bryan Davis

Living Ink Books
An Imprint of AMG Publishers
Chattanooga, Tennessee

Oracles of Fire®
Last of the Nephilim
Copyright © 2008 by Bryan Davis
Published by Living Ink Books, an imprint of AMG Publishers
6815 Shallowford Rd.
Chattanooga, Tennessee 37421

ISBN: 978-0-89957-872-9
Second printing—September 2008
ORACLES OF FIRE is a trademark of AMG Publishers, Inc.

Cover designed by Daryle Beam at Bright Boy Design, Inc., Chattanooga,
    Tennessee
Interior design and typesetting by Reider Publishing Services,
    West Hollywood, California
Edited and proofread by Jeff Gerke, Dan Penwell, Rick Steele,
    and Sharon Neal
Map illustrated by Jim Brown, Clayton, North Carolina

Printed in Canada
14 13 12 11 10 09 08 –T– 8 7 6 5 4 3 2

Library of Congress Cataloging-in-Publication Data

Davis, Bryan, 1958-
  Last of the Nephilim / by Bryan Davis.
    p. cm. -- (Oracles of fire ; v. 3)
  Summary: When the Nephilim, a race of giants from ancient times, invade Second Eden, endangering the existence of that alternate dimension as well as every soul on Earth, the two Oracles of Fire, Sapphira and Acacia, and two young girls lead the battle to stop them.
  ISBN 978-0-89957-872-9 (pbk. : alk. paper)
  [1. Dragons--Fiction. 2. Demonology--Fiction. 3. Christian life--Fiction. 4. Supernatural--Fiction.] I. Title.
  PZ7.D28555Las 2008
  [Fic]--dc22
                                    2008014957

For those who spurn the whispered lie,
The doctrine binding hearts in chains;
For those who shout from rooftops high,
"Free indeed!" in loud refrains.

For those who trample underfoot
The broken bonds of fetters tossed;
For those who rise from ash and soot,
Forever cleansed, forever washed.

A story strange, a story wild,
That begs the reader to impart
The joy of life to man and child
To break the chains that bind their hearts.

Acknowledgments

Infinite thanks to my family for their inspiration and support. You are the reason I draw my sword.

Thank you also to the folks at AMG for their great work and leadership in the industry. Because of your vision, the fantasy genre is now accepted in our market.

Several of my faithful readers have aided me in writing this book, so I would like to mention a few of them and send my thanks.

Story collaboration and proofreading—Peter Blaskiewicz, L. A. Clark, Holli Herdeg, C.J. Giacominni, and Sharon Neal.

Map concepts—Catherine and Christian Johnson, Mary Tabitha Lumsden, Sarah Pratt, and Bekah Hagan.

AUTHOR'S NOTE

Last of the Nephilim is the third book in the **Oracles of Fire** series and is related to the **Dragons in our Midst** series. The numbers in the diagram below show the best reading order for the two series. Although the books are stacked vertically to indicate the chronological order of the storyline, they should be read in the numbered sequence.

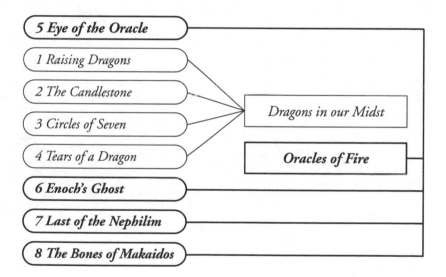

For readers unfamiliar with the previous books, I recommend reading the first six before this one. As a minimum, read *Enoch's Ghost*, including the recap at the end of that book. This story extends earlier adventures that will lead readers into a multi-dimensional land, a fascinating journey guided by the *Oracles of Fire*.

Mount
Elijah

Noah's Landing
(Northern Highlands)

Valley
of Shadows

Lilith's
Shallows

Singer's
Creek

Wolf
Hollow

Flint's
Village

Twin Falls
River

Birthing
Garden

Adam's Marsh
(Truce Zone)

Founder's Village
(Abraham's Village)

Dragon
Landing Field

Second Eden

CONTENTS

CONTENTS

x

ENOCH'S LAMENT

When darkness shrouds forgotten lands,
The souls abiding there lament
And ask the altar keeper why
The justice due has not been sent.

The persecutors had their day
In spilling blood, exacting toil;
So now expecting vengeance due
The martyrs cry beneath the soil.

"The underground still hides our eyes
And spills an evil band on Earth;
O grant our prayer to spring to life
O let us stem this wicked birth."

The oracle of fire lost
Must bear the sacred secret flame
And join the twin who weeps for her
And walks alone to fight the bane.

O God of Heaven hear my plea,
For I alone have seen this dread,
When giants thundered on the Earth,
Consuming hearts and minds like bread.

The lass who strides against our foe
Is brave indeed; her faith is rare.
But will the flame of wisdom burn
To keep her from deception's snare?

Allow me, Lord, to take her hand
In spirit, flame, or fleshly state
And lead her through the valleys where
Demonic spirits lie in wait.

Beneath the altar's seal I pray,
Where martyrs rest in holy gowns,
"O let me rise to crush the snakes
Or sleep until the trumpet sounds."

PROLOGUE

"Mardon, I know you don't enjoy being dead, but you must come to grips with reality."

From her seat on a flat rock, the lithe woman leaned over a stone table, the only furniture amid a collection of oddly shaped boulders draped by a black sky. Her movements troubled the red flame of a pewter-gray candle embedded in a hardened splash of wax on the table's surface.

Laying her hands over the intertwined fingers of the man sitting opposite her, she spoke with a breathy and ominous voice. "If you try to follow your giants to Second Eden, you will be swept into the Lake of Fire where you will burn with your father forever. Dead souls such as yourself cannot survive outside of Hades."

As the woman's long hair fell over his hands, Mardon caressed the ends between his thumb and finger but kept his eyes focused on a rope to his left, both ends of which had been tied to iron stakes, separated by perhaps twenty feet. The golden rope shimmered, quavering as if gently plucked by an invisible finger. A soft hum emanated and drifted to his ears in a warbling vibrato. It was a song of victory. It had taken him centuries to pull the two worlds together, and now a rope the thickness of a broom handle kept them in place. A huge man, one of Mardon's Nephilim, stood near one of the stakes, his muscular arms folded over his chest, one hand gripping an axe that rested on his shoulder.

"In order to carry out our plans, you must stay on Earth," she continued. "Because of your successful merging of Earth and Hades, no one there will even realize that you're dead."

Mardon returned his gaze to her. In the candle's waltzing glow, her skin took on a tone of blemished scarlet. "Mother, only Yereq and I are skilled enough to lead my giants. My father's dream to build a tower to Heaven will never be realized without one of us."

She pulled her hands back and sat up straight. With a red hood draping the shoulders of her red dress, she seemed covered by a scarlet shroud. After a few seconds of silence, a stern yet subtle growl escaped her crimson throat. "I understand Nimrod's dream far better than you do, and if you don't listen to me, not only will you never ascend to the gates of Heaven, you will also join him and your former mistress in eternal suffering."

"I will listen." His thumbs now pressing together, he nodded. "Go on."

A smile curled her lips, and, with a sparkle in her eye, her voice smoothed into a purr. "Yereq could eventually help us. He has a weakness we can exploit, but we must execute my plan with patience and careful deception. Without perfect timing, we will not be able to persuade the last and greatest of the Nephilim to join our forces. Yet, even if he comes to our aid, we must employ yet another ally, one who served a friend of ours for more than a thousand years."

"A friend of ours? Do you mean Morgan?"

She returned the slightest of nods. "I must carry on my teacher's work, and employing her servant will be of great benefit."

"But Morgan failed. Even after thousands of years of scheming, she failed."

"True. But I learned from her mistakes, and I have recovered her secret weapon." As she lifted a thin chain around her neck, a small crystalline egg elevated from her bosom, seeming to float in the air on its own. A light flickered within, but the candle's flame made the color impossible to determine.

She passed the chain to Mardon. The egg followed along, floating effortlessly across the table like a tiny dog on a leash. "In this state," she said, "the weapon is more powerful than ever. When the Bannister boy cleaved the candlestone, everyone thought Sir Devin dispersed into the sky, but his light energy had stabilized long before that event. Lord Lucifer guided him to me, and I gave him this new home where he will reside until we can safely resurrect his body."

Mardon draped the chain around his neck. The egg floated back and forth in front of his eyes as if surveying its new bearer. "What good can he do inside this crystal?"

She rose from her seat and walked toward the rope, gesturing for him to follow.

Keeping an eye on the crystal, he tiptoed along the flat stony ground. The egg hovered inches in front of him, keeping the chain slightly aloft. Now that they were out of the influence of the candle's flame, the crystal's inner light grew clear. Two tiny eyes glowed red within. A strange growl entered his mind, like the faint echo of a bad dream.

When his mother reached the giant, she took his axe and kicked the excess rope. With a quick chop, she cut it free from its stake. A loud hiss rose from each severed end, and both pieces flopped around like dying serpents.

She picked up the end that led to the coil, gripping it tightly to keep it from wiggling. "Enoch is mustering a new army, including the Bannister boy and his father and the former and current

3

dragons in the world. Sir Devin will help us locate them before they can all get to Second Eden. At the very least, we can put fear into their hearts and keep them in hiding."

Mardon glanced at the egg. It had moved to a point a few inches in front of his chin. The growl grew louder and seemed to come from within the crystal. "Haven't they lost their dragon powers?" Mardon asked.

"The Bannisters? Yes. As well as all the other dragons, except for Thigocia." She handed the axe to the giant and set the rope in Mardon's hand, pushing his fingers closed around it. "Though I haven't heard whether or not the girl, Bonnie Silver, has retained hers. Still, their current state matters little. It is their potential that we must arrest. Bonnie Silver will be your prime target. If you hold her, you control the boy, and without the two of them, Enoch's plans will come to nothing."

Mardon clutched the rope, much thicker now than when he had pulled the two worlds together. Warm to the touch, it felt alive in his grip. "I understand. What is my next step?"

"You will lasso one of their soldiers." She showed him a ring on her finger, an ornate gold band with a fiery red jewel. "Many of the former dragons and their offspring wear a symbol of their dragon essence, a rubellite ring. Whether they have lost their dragon natures or not, these gems still hold a remnant of that former glory. Devin, having lived within a dragon's skin, can detect and find the signal, no matter how faint. He is now a dragon-sniffing hound, and his victim, the Silver vixen, will not easily travel beyond the reach of his nose, especially since she has no knowledge that she carries the scent."

"And I am to use this to bind her," he said, passing the shimmering rope through his hands.

"In a sense. When you leave this place, the rope will become invisible, and it will stretch without tension and without limit. You are to attach it to Bonnie Silver's body and tie the other end to an anchor on Earth. Since she will eventually try to get to Second Eden, she will become the other anchor that allows you to bring the worlds together."

"Wouldn't it be easier to attach it to one of our giants? They would cooperate fully."

She nodded at the rope. "Tie it to yourself. You will see."

Keeping his eye on his mother, Mardon looped the coil around his waist and tied it in a loose knot. As soon as he let go, the knot tightened. Then, like a python, the loop constricted, tighter and tighter. He sucked in his stomach and jammed his fingers behind the rope. Straining against the painful, viselike hold, he pushed out his breath, but the loop tightened further. He couldn't draw in another gulp of air. Blood rushed to his head as he croaked, "Mother! Help me!"

She looked on with a stoic expression. "Uncomfortable, isn't it?"

He couldn't answer. The rope had slid up to his ribs, and the crushing pain forced him to his knees.

She took the axe again and chopped the rope. It immediately loosened and slipped down to his waist, writhing as Mardon gasped for breath.

She let out a sigh. "I'm afraid this rope has no fondness for corrupt souls."

Grabbing the severed piece, Mardon shot to his feet and slapped it to the ground. "Why did you do that?"

"So you will remember two things." She raised a finger. "One is that this rope will be docile only for a soul that is perfectly pure." As she raised a second finger, a scowl took shape on her face. "The second is that you must follow my instructions to the letter. Your failure to do so in the past led to your physical death and to your bungling with the second tower. I am in no mood for any further disobedience."

He picked up the coil of rope and nodded, trying to keep his own scowl from breaking through. "I will do what you ask."

5

She leaned the axe against her waist. "After you complete the attachment, keep little Miss Silver on the run for a while. The timing of her arrival in Second Eden must be precise. Make her think you simply want to kill her so she will never suspect your true goal. I'm sure with your knowledge of modern technology, that will be an entertaining game for you."

"Yes, it will." As the crystal floated in front of his nose, he gazed at its blinking eyes and smiled. "I can create quite a frightening nightmare for the little lady."

The growl strengthened again. A voice broke through in his mind, sinister and mocking. "That little lady, as you call her, is a demon witch. We will toy with her for a time, but in the end, we will remove her head and mount it next to the boy's. After all he has done to me, his head will be a prize ornament."

Mardon touched the crystal, now flashing with red light. "Mother, I believe he is speaking to my mind."

6

"As I expected," she said, "Devin has established a connection with your brain. The two of you will be able to converse silently."

Mardon stared at the two blinking eyes, scarlet and sinister. Would it be safe to try to probe it with his thoughts? Concentrating on the inner light, he spoke in his mind. *Can you hear me?*

"I can hear you," Devin replied, his voice now more genial, "and I have already read your unguarded thoughts. I'm glad to see that I'm working with an intelligent man who hates dragons almost as much as I do."

Then we will make a fine team. Mardon glanced at his mother out of the corner of his eye. She tapped her foot and let out an impatient huff. He would have to finish this conversation quickly. *What will be our first step in finding this demon witch, as you call her?*

"We will send some beasts of weaker minds to the Bannister home. That is her most likely place to hide. If that fails to scare out the witch, we will track her down using my dragon-sensing powers."

Mardon nodded and turned back to his mother. "This is very interesting, indeed. I am impressed with my new ally."

"And I suggest that you listen to him. His experience in hunting dragons is vast, and his mind is every bit as powerful as yours, so he will not take kindly to apathy, laziness, or cowardice."

"Laziness? Cowardice?" Mardon scowled. "Mother, I have persevered in my quest for thousands of years."

She laid a palm on his chest. "You have a soft spot in your heart for a certain spawn by the name of Mara, and it is this weakness that will tempt you to cower in the face of waging war against the dragon army, whether their soldiers are covered in scales and draconic teeth or fine hair and pretty young faces."

Mardon deepened his scowl and muttered, "She was an experiment. Nothing more. I could dispose of her as I did any of the other useless spawns."

"You will likely have an opportunity to test your fragile words. If you can generate the necessary violence against Bonnie Silver, perhaps you will succeed against the spawn when the time comes." Carrying the axe again, she sashayed back to the table and hovered her hand over the candle's flame, close enough to singe the skin of a normal human. "Because of their misguided loyalty," she continued, "Bonnie and her mother will separate themselves from the other former dragons, which will benefit our cause. I want you to capture Bonnie and obtain something for me."

Mardon grasped the egg and pushed it under his shirt. "Very well. What do you want?"

She lifted a finger, now partially blackened by the candle's smoke. "Cut off her finger and bring it to me with the ring still on it. That will be all we need to make the boy think we hold her and that we will harm her if he doesn't cooperate. If Enoch succeeds in gathering the other dragons to Second Eden, we will force them to give us their word that they will not join the battle. Then

7

we can release the girl and let her go to Second Eden to stretch our rope between the two worlds."

"This is all well and good. We will stop the dragons from interfering. But how does that help us win the war?"

As she rubbed her fingers together, sooty dust fell to the table. "With the dragons out of the way, *our* dragon ally will be able to complete the corruption of Second Eden so that it will be ready for the final merging with Hades and Earth. Such a union will open the portals to the Bridgelands for everyone. We can then amass an army that will attack Heaven's gate." She raised a slender arm and rolled her fingers into a fist. "If we cannot ascend to Heaven by invitation, we will take it by force."

"Corruption is clearly our first weapon, but has anyone in Second Eden succumbed to Lucifer's fruit?"

"Only one of Abraham's people," she said, raising a finger again, now free of soot, "but Abraham has successfully isolated him. We already have a plan to entice another one of his people, someone he won't be so ready to ostracize. Success is crucial, for that corruption will open the largest portal, allowing your giants to enter Second Eden. Yet, if that effort fails, there are other ways to ensure that there are no more sinless souls in Second Eden. Our alternative plan will be ready."

"And what is that?"

She lifted the axe with both hands and rested it on her shoulder. "To kill them all."

CHARRED BONES

The bones of the dead are a burden too great," Abraham murmured as he tramped through the dark cave. Carrying only two handfuls on this trip, his load was light, though only in a physical sense. The precious bones in his cupped palms meant more to him than the finest gold in all of Second Eden. He followed the glow of a lantern several paces ahead and continued his lament. "A great burden, indeed. Especially the bones of my son."

The lantern stopped. "Did you say something, Father Abraham?" a female voice called.

"Yes, Angel, but more to myself. When I get tired, I tend to mumble out loud." He caught up with the young lady, at least young in his view. Nearly every time he saw her, the image of her little body cradled in a birthing plant came to mind, and when he blessed her arrival as she lay in her mother's arms, he knew she would be someone special. Angel's one hundred thirty or so years in Second Eden had proved him right, but his own thousands of years in this world certainly skewed his perspective.

She was a lovely young woman, yet in his eyes, barely old enough to take an Adam, though she was already a widow with two children. Still, if ever he were to take an Eve of his own, Angel possessed every quality he could imagine wanting in a woman—courage, kindness, humility, and, above all, complete integrity and faithfulness. Her time of widowhood, according to their traditions, would expire in the near future, perhaps this week. She would have to select a mate very soon. Someone would be a blessed man, indeed.

He shook his head sadly. He would never be able to receive such a blessing. Even though he appeared to be the same age as the other adults, he was a founding father to all in this realm—the Prophet, many called him, or simply Father Abraham, certainly not a candidate to be anyone's mate. As Enoch had told him long ago, "Until the day fire consumes your body, you will not be able to take an Eve into your heart." He resisted the urge to heave a loud sigh. With their tradition of burning the slain warriors, it seemed clear that only death would break the millennia-long span of companionless leadership.

Angel raised the lantern, allowing the glow to illumine her smooth skin and braided blond hair. The shimmer of perspiration on her narrow face and angular jaw proved her hours of effort, though it seemed a garland of virtue, a testimony to her work ethic.

A sparkle floated near her eyes, then disappeared—her companion, shifting to the opposite side of her head to avoid the sudden light. In her other hand, she carried a long curved bone, perhaps a rib, blackened on both ends. The cave's fire had scorched most of Timothy's skeleton, but not enough to keep his loved ones from collecting every last piece.

Angel's eyes gleamed in the flickering lantern light. "Darkness will soon be upon us, Father. Shadows have likely already covered Candle and Listener, and the dragons will be anxious."

10

"Especially Albatross. He has not forgotten our last episode here." Abraham pushed onward, buoyed by Angel's urgent tone. When they reached the cave entrance, Angel blew out the lantern's wick, leaving only the failing light of early evening to guide their steps.

As soon as they passed through the yawning mouth, the distant sound of rushing water greeted their ears, yet it seemed to cast a hush across the small forest glade of grass and ferns that spread out like a skirt around the cave entrance. Oddly shaped bones littered the area closest to the cave—the flat bones of the shadow people who had faced their execution within the blazing light this tunnel had always, until recently, emitted.

Abraham closed his cloak and tied his belt. The breeze, colder than usual, gnawed at his clean-shaven face. With the season of death only days away, it would soon be time to grow his beard. It wasn't like the old days before the altered tribes formed—no seasons, no death, no pain, and no need for the prophesied warrior chief who would come to restore what was lost.

He breathed in the smoke-tinged air and allowed his eyes to adjust. Arching trees cast shadows over the garden of ferns that stretched to the edge of the deeper forest—the Forest of Erebus, so named for the terrifying blackness it concealed when night's shadows blanketed its soil. About five paces away, Candle—a handsome, twelve-year-old boy dressed in a sweatshirt and woolen trousers—knelt by a square animal hide, counting the many bones covering its leathery surface.

"One hundred and ninety four!" Candle turned toward Abraham, his brilliant smile framed by a dark brown face. His dreadlocks swayed as he added, "Do you have the rest?"

Abraham poured out several bones onto a clear corner of the skin. "A few. I think some are from his left hand." As he spread them out with his finger, he touched a sharp-edged fragment that looked like most of a thumb. "This one is broken," he said, picking it up again.

Angel looked over his shoulder. "Do we have the rest of it?"

"Not that I can see." He slid the fragment into a small pocket under his belt. "I will search for the rest when we have more time."

Angel brushed cave dirt from the knees of her riding pantaloons and sat on the long-leafed ferns that bordered their collection blanket. She laid her bone next to a loosely reconstructed rib cage. "I found another rib."

Candle positioned it to line up with the others. "Only one is missing now."

Listener, a little girl with nut-brown braids, plopped down next to Angel. Sitting cross-legged, she spread her corduroy jumper over her knees and laid a spyglass on her lap. With creamy white skin, rounded cheeks, and a button nose, she barely resembled her brother at all, except for her bright, inquisitive eyes. Cocking her head, she studied the collection. "You even found the ear bones!"

"Leave it to Listener to think of the ear bones," Candle said. "She's going to be a doctor, just like you, Mother."

Angel set her finger on top of an egg-shaped crystal that floated in front of Listener's eyes. Slightly smaller than a hen's egg, it sparkled, as if tickled by her touch, then zipped around and nestled behind the girl's ear. "The art of medicine is a noble pursuit," Angel said, "but we will allow her companion to guide her."

Abraham looked up at the darkening sky, now purplish in the glow of the rising Pegasus moon. "Prepare the dragons. The shadow people are no longer shy about roaming in this part of their valley, especially with only one moon tonight and its eclipse at hand."

"They're ready," Listener said. "Grackle behaved, but Albatross wouldn't let me buckle his saddle strap until I gave him a carrot." She aimed her spyglass at Pegasus. "May we watch the eclipse while we're flying home?"

"Without a doubt." Abraham pulled Angel to her feet and reached for one corner of the skin. "We can reconstruct the skeleton in the morning."

Angel and Candle helped him gather the corners to the center, making the skin into a bulky leather bag. As Abraham tied a leather strap around the opening and held it against his chest, his heart thumped. His own son, born as a dragon, perished twice as a human, now a bag of bones.

Angel brushed a tear from his cheek with a gentle finger. As a tear traced her own cheek, her lips trembled. "I loved him, too, Father."

He returned the favor, using his thumb to remove her tear. Her eyes, sad and sincere, spoke volumes—never hesitant to speak the truth, unashamed of her feelings, her heart as pure as the waters of the highlands. Angel was truly a symbol for all the people of Second Eden. Untarnished by the lies and deceptions of the original Eden, they knew nothing but truth and would be dismayed by any words spoken that harbored a shadow of falsehood.

13

Abraham firmed his chin. His people would never follow in Flint's footsteps. Not if he could help it.

Listener let out a thin gasp. "I see her!"

"Who?" Angel asked.

"The white-haired girl! The same one I saw before! She's wearing a white dress and a blue cloak. She's holding some kind of light in a dark place, and she's walking toward me."

"Could it be the tunnel?" Abraham gave Candle the bag of bones and strode toward the cave. "If she is the Oracle of Fire, she could well bring us news of the warrior chief."

"What of the shadow people?" Angel asked, following close behind. "The danger grows with every passing second."

He stood next to the face of the cliff, just to the side of the cave entrance. "Should we miss this opportunity to speak to the Oracle?"

"If I were the only one at risk," Angel said, "then no, but my children would be easy prey."

Abraham looked at Candle and Listener. They stood in the nearby ferns, now in deeper shadows as the arching trees shielded them from the bare glow of evening light, Candle with the bag drooping at his side and Listener still gazing through the spyglass.

"Shall I build a fire?" Angel asked. "The lantern is nearly out of fuel. The bone collecting took longer than we expected."

"Not yet." Abraham nodded at Listener. "What do you see now, little one?"

She kept her gaze locked through the spyglass. "The Oracle and a small girl are riding on a white horse, and a young man is leading them. Could he be betrothed to one of them?"

Abraham shook his head. "They come from a world with different customs. If there is a horse—"

"I see fire!" Listener cried.

Suddenly, flames erupted from the cave, a gushing stream that shot out and up into the sky, billowing into a trio of fiery blossoms that painted the trees in an orange hue. Then, as quickly as it had ignited, the river of flames vanished, yet not a hint of residual smoke hung in the air.

A glow brushed the sides of the inner cave wall with dancing ribbons of white light, brightening with every moment. The sound of clopping hooves drew nearer, then echoing voices made their way to the entrance.

"Acacia, I see something," a male voice said. "Maybe it's an exit."

"Or an entrance to something else," a deeper voice replied.

A female spoke up. "Dikaios, please stop for a moment. I'll lead with a brighter light."

"The Oracle," Abraham said as he leaned into the cave's opening. "I recognize her voice."

The horse hooves fell silent. Seconds later, the glow strengthened, steadily growing brighter as the hoof clops echoed once again.

14

A petite female form took shape within the light. Abraham backed away, whispering, "She is here."

Listener, now carrying the spyglass at her hip, sidled up to Angel and took her hand, wide-eyed and silent. Candle drew near as well, lugging the bag of bones through the ferns.

The light in the cave grew so bright, Abraham had to shield his eyes. The girl emerged, a brilliant white fire blazing in her palm. With hair that matched her flames, the girl stared at Abraham with dazzling blue eyes. A cloak of royal blue dressed her shoulders, its cape flowing behind her in the soft breeze.

With a quick puff, she blew out the flames. As a teenaged boy emerged from the cave, followed by a horse ridden by a little girl, the Oracle dipped into a low curtsy, her head bowed. "I am pleased to meet you, Father Abraham, founder of this realm." She straightened and looked him in the eye again. "I am Acacia, the Oracle of Fire who spoke to you in this cave."

Abraham fell to his knees and folded his hands. Angel did the same at his side, while Candle and Listener knelt next to her. Abraham bowed his head as he spoke. "I am honored to meet you, most excellent Oracle. Your presence here is a joy beyond words."

Laughing gently, Acacia motioned for him to rise. "You honor me too well. I am little more than a slave girl, born in the darkest of realms, yet lifted by grace to the highest of kingdoms." With a blue sparkle in her eye, she added, "But I'd like to stop talking like an uppity princess and just be friends, okay?"

Abraham straightened, giving a hearty laugh of his own. "Plain speech is welcome here." Angel, Candle, and Listener rose as well, each one staring at the visitors.

Acacia turned toward her fellow travelers. "This young man is Elam, son of Shem, grandson of Noah. Our valiant horse is Dikaios, sired by your moon's namesake, Pegasus himself. And last, but certainly not least ..." She reached for Dikaios's rider. The girl

15

slid off, and Acacia guided her to the ground. "This is Paili, my sister from the lower realms."

Paili, a girl of about eight or nine and draped in an oversized, hooded cloak, grinned, spreading her thin, pale cheeks as she dipped into a shallow curtsy. "I'm pleased to meet you."

Angel gave Abraham's cloak sleeve a slight tug but said nothing. He nodded at her, trying to signal that all was well. With the Oracle of Fire present, there was no need to be anxious about the coming darkness. He turned to Elam. "Young man, are you the warrior chief?"

Elam stepped forward, his dark brown hair whipping around in the stiffening breeze. Wearing a tunic with elbow-length sleeves, he rubbed his upper arms and bounced on his toes. "That's what I've been told."

Abraham took off his cloak, revealing his long-sleeved white tunic, and laid it over Elam's shoulders. "I am accustomed to our weather, so please allow me to do you this service."

Giving Abraham a thankful nod, Elam pushed his arms through the sleeves. "I hear you have been expecting me."

"We have been awaiting your arrival for a very long time." Abraham gazed at the young man's square jaw, firm chin, and deeply set eyes. He definitely looked like his father, Shem. "Do you know of the prophecy our people have sung together during our prayer vigils?"

"I do," Acacia said, "but I don't think Elam has heard it."

Elam shook his head. "No, but I'd like to."

"Very well. I will sing a portion of a longer psalm that relates to you." Abraham smiled at Angel, then looked up at the dark purple sky and crooned.

> The tunnel leads a warrior chief,
> A youth with mystery in his eyes,
> With flames he walks to burn the chaff.
> A child he leads to silence lies.

And once the hearts of gold he trains
Are drawn to lights of holy depth,
Then wielding swords they journey where
Corruption's harvest draws its breath.

When his final note faded, Abraham flapped his arms against his sides. "I hope I avoided damage to your eardrums."

"It was great," Elam said, "but what's the danger? Enoch told me I was supposed to come and help, but he wasn't clear about what I'm to do."

"The danger?" Abraham scanned the dark ground. "We are in the Valley of Shadows, the home of the shadow people, a race that makes up one of the altered tribes. They are likely already nearby, awaiting the darkness. But with your presence, perhaps they will not be bold enough to attack. Since you have no companion, they could well assume that you are the prophesied one."

Elam looked up at the sky. "It would be better to discuss the prophecy in a place of safety. If nightfall gives these shadow people courage, we should be on our way."

"Agreed. But getting back to our village presents a challenge. We have two dragons with two seats on each. We could manage to squeeze Paili in with Angel, and perhaps Acacia could ride with me, but you would likely make the load unbearable, and transporting the horse on a dragon is out of the question."

Dikaios blew through flapping lips. "I will carry Elam and follow the flight of the dragons. I am swift enough to keep pace."

"A talking horse!" Listener ran up and petted his snowy mane. "Do all horses talk where you come from, Dikaios?"

Angel stepped forward and gently pulled Listener away. "He is a warrior's horse, not a pet."

Dikaios bobbed his head. "True enough, good lady, but I am always pleased to let the little children come to me."

17

Elam guided Listener's hand back to Dikaios. "I see you found Enoch's spyglass," he said, touching its metal casing. "I once had it, but it fell from a bridge into a deep chasm."

"I found it in a strange bag." She ran her fingers through the horse's mane. "The bag was hanging from a branch high in a tree."

Elam looked up at the sky. "Very interesting."

Abraham patted Dikaios's flank. "I have no doubt of your swiftness, good horse, but you are lacking your sire's wings. The only easy route into or out of this land is by air. Even the shadow people have to attach themselves to large birds in order to cross the surrounding mountains, and they cannot escape by way of the river. We call it Twin Falls River, because it enters this valley by a steep waterfall and exits in a similar fashion, and, with the exception of eclipse nights, we guard that exit. So far they have been able to attack our village only in small raiding parties. If they could move en masse at night, we would not be able to fend them off."

"I don't think we have a choice." Elam brushed the shadowed ferns with his shoe. "We'd better get moving."

A dark hand shot up from the ground and grabbed Listener's ankle. She shrieked and tried to pull free, but it held fast. Abraham dove headfirst onto the ground, grabbed a human-shaped shadow, and wrestled it away from her. He then leaped to his feet, holding the shadow by its throat with its arms and legs flailing underneath. "Foul fiend!" Abraham growled. "I ought to—"

Another shriek sounded, this time from Paili. A dark form dragged her feetfirst toward the forest. She grasped for ferns and dug her fingernails across the ground, but to no avail.

Acacia pointed at a tree in the kidnapper's path and shouted, "Ignite!" Instantly a raging flame shot up the trunk. The shadow squealed. It released Paili and writhed in the ferns like a shriveling slug.

Abraham leaped ahead and kicked the shadow against the flaming tree, then, with an angry grunt, he threw the other one into the blaze. Purple sparks flew. Popping sounds and dying squeals filled the air. Like roaches skittering across a floor, dozens of shadows rippled along the ferns and scurried into the forest as light from the fire spread across the glade.

Acacia grabbed a hefty stick from the ground and lifted it high. "Flames! Come to my firebrand!" The end of the stick ignited with a bright orange flame. She passed it to Abraham and snatched up another stick that ignited the moment she touched it. "Lead us to safety!"

Waving his arm toward the sound of rushing water, Abraham shouted, "Follow me to the river!" He wrapped Paili in her cloak, scooped her up, and sprinted along a narrow path through the forest, swinging the burning stick back and forth as if cutting the underbrush with a machete. Seconds later, he burst into the open where a wide strip of beach sand bordered a swiftly flowing river. Chunks of ice floated in the churning current, knocking into each other as they tumbled along.

Two dragons, one white and one purple, stood at the edge of the water in the relative safety of the moon's light. Abraham dropped the flaming stick and whistled a "mount up" command at Albatross. As soon as the white dragon lowered his head, Abraham climbed his neck and set Paili in the second of two chairs attached to the dragon's back. His hands flying, he strapped her in with a leather belt. He then took a breath and placed a hand on her cold cheek. "Peace, little child. All is well."

He leaped down to the soft sand, and, as Angel led the others out of the forest, another firebrand in her grip, Abraham barked out commands. "Angel, you will fly Albatross, and we will try to fit Acacia in with you. Candle and Listener will take Grackle."

While Candle and Listener clambered up the purple dragon's neck, Angel hustled up the white dragon's. When she reached the top, she stood with one foot on her seat and one on the dragon's neck, her hands on her hips. "And you, Father?"

19

"I will guide the warrior chief out of this valley."

"But what of Adam's Marsh and the truce zone?"

"We will try to ascend the trail to the northern highlands."

"But the avalanche! You will have to—"

"No time to argue!" He pointed at the edge of the forest. A sea of shadows emerged, crawling rapidly toward them. He slapped Grackle's flank. "Fly!"

With a mighty leap and beat of his wings, Grackle launched into the air. Abraham reached for Acacia. "Come. You will take Angel's seat. She is able to sit higher on the dragon's neck."

Acacia shook her head. "I will stay with you. Without a light, you will never survive."

Abraham stared at her determined face. Who was he to argue with the Oracle? "Is there anything else we need to know before we send them off?"

"Yes." Acacia looked up at Grackle as he circled above. "Just before I left the Bridgelands, Enoch told me that the bones must be spread over your birthing garden immediately, and I will burn them at the appropriate time."

Angel dropped heavily to her dragon riding chair. "Burn the bones?"

"Enoch's word is never to be doubted," Abraham said. He let out a shrill whistle and slapped Albatross on the flank. "We need a shield, my good dragon. You know what to do."

Albatross beat his wings and rose into the air. As soon as he climbed to the tops of the trees, Angel guided him into a sharp turn, and he swooped toward the ground. A stream of ice gushed from his mouth and splashed against the beach, coating the strip between the forest and the river in a sheet of white.

His wings pulling madly against the air, Albatross swung upward and headed for the sky. As the two dragons shrank in the distance, their silhouettes flew across Pegasus, their dark wings flapping gently as they each carried two riders to safety.

"The ice will keep the shadows at bay," Abraham said, "but not for long." Heaving a sigh, he turned to Acacia. "I must say, your talent will be very useful in our battles."

"The shadow people are merely pawns." Acacia lifted her hand and whispered, "Give me light." A small fire erupted in her palm, a yellow blossom with flaming tongues for petals. "Your real enemy won't be frightened by my talents."

Abraham looked back at the forest. The shadows began to slither across the ice, so many, they looked like a slick of burnt cooking oil sliding their way. "Come," he said. "We will have to ford the river at a place I know. The shadow people on the other side likely are unaware of our presence. It will be a cold and dangerous crossing, but I am not willing to face ten thousand shadows, even with the Oracle's talents in our arsenal."

UNWELCOME VISITORS

"GHOSTS AND GHOULS TERRORIZE CITY!" Billy read the newspaper headline as he jogged toward his house. With swirling snow dancing all around, he halted a few steps before reaching the front porch and made a slow turn, scanning the deserted two-lane street and each nearby yard. With a few inches of snow painting the neighborhood white, spotting one of the dark hairy "ghouls" would be easier than it had been last night when several prowled the area.

These "Caitiff," as his father had called them, were the ugliest men he had ever seen. Earlier, when he viewed them from afar in the second circle of Hades, they had been hideous enough. Closer encounters proved that they smelled worse than they looked.

As his gaze passed by a rainwater drain at the side of the street, he noticed a dark splotch covering a bare spot on the pavement, the spilled blood of one of those freaks. His father had nailed it with his AR15, but the bullet in its chest only scared the apelike beast away. Now, gooey fluids lay in a black puddle that even snow wouldn't touch.

With no sign of new predators lurking, Billy scrambled up the snow-covered porch steps, unlocked the knob and deadbolt with separate keys, and breezed inside. The draft kicked up an envelope on the floor and carried it to the stairwell to the left.

After refastening the locks, he kicked off his boots and unzipped his thick jacket, revealing a navy blue "West Virginia" sweatshirt that overlapped his jeans' waistband. He checked the pistol in the jacket's inner pocket. Still secure. With a quick swipe, he snatched up the envelope and read the handwritten name on the front—*Jared Bannister, Personal.*

He turned it over. Sealed. No return address anywhere. Someone must have stuck it through the mail slot while he was at the Foleys' house. He squinted at the handwriting. With its elegant swirls, it seemed familiar, but who would drop off a message for his father? Dad was still home, so why wouldn't the delivery person knock on the door to make sure he got it?

He put the envelope in his back pocket and scanned the front page of the paper. A photo caught his attention, one of the "ghouls," a thin, hairy man with vampire-like fangs overlapping his bottom lip. He glanced up from the paper. He couldn't read while walking, at least not for a few more days. With the newly rebuilt house still unfamiliar, he had to check where he was going to keep from banging into anything. He nodded at the configuration—stairs in front on the left, foyer and kitchen straight ahead, family room to the right.

Shivering as he strolled past the family room, he slowed to look at the fireplace. The flames had dwindled to a few finger-tall orange tongues. Still glancing at the paper every few seconds, he ambled into the room and across the morning glow radiating through the front window. He grabbed the fireplace poker and, after rekindling the flames with a quick stir, studied the crackling logs, now not much more than ashen heaps. He'd have to get more wood soon, but the stack outside was still green and damp, much harder to ignite, especially without his fire breathing ability.

He passed his tongue along the roof of his mouth. No scales. No evidence of the dragon trait that had both hurt and helped him over the past couple of years. He looked at the ring on his index finger. A white gem mounted in the center stared back at him, the symbol he wore that proved what he had been and what he was now. He curled his fingers into a fist. It was all good. Being fully human was worth it.

Monique bolted into the family room and grabbed his hand. "Play checkers with me!" she shouted, her black mop of hair bouncing with her child-sized leaps.

Billy dropped the poker, scooped her up with one arm, and hustled her away from the window. Someone had opened the blinds. With daylight streaming in, it wasn't safe for her to be there. Faking a smile, he slowed his pace as he quick-marched toward the back of the house. "But we played fifteen times last night! Aren't you tired of it yet?"

With an impish grin lifting her lovely Asian features, Monique shook her head. "You're ahead eight to seven. I need to catch up."

Billy set her down and mussed her hair. "Get Stacey or Beck to play. They're upstairs with Mom. Or maybe Larry will play with you. I fixed his transmitter. He should be good to go."

Monique pouted. "Larry's no fun. I never win."

"Yeah. Supercomputers are like that. All brains and no compassion."

She locked her arms tightly across her chest, covering her green sweatshirt. "I wish Red would come home. She would play with me."

"Dad's supposed to hear from Walter or Ashley this morning. Maybe they'll give us an update on when Karen's coming home."

Monique clapped her hands. "Good!"

He followed Monique back to the stairs. When she had scampered out of sight to the upper floor, he marched back to the family room window and snapped the blinds closed. He'd have to remember to talk to the girls about security again. Until every Caitiff was dead, no children were safe.

Billy strode into the kitchen and laid the newspaper on the table in front of his father. "Same kind of freaks we got last night," he said, tapping a finger on the photo. He then pulled out the envelope and propped it on the newspaper so that *Jared Bannister* faced his father. "This was in the foyer," Billy said.

His father set down a steaming cup of coffee and tilted the envelope. With a Glock in a shoulder holster wrapped around his broad, sweater-clad chest and a scoped rifle leaning against the wall behind him, he seemed ready for a war.

His reddish-brown eyebrows dipped low. "This is Irene's handwriting."

26

Billy nodded. That made sense. Bonnie's mother would have familiar handwriting. It was a lot like Bonnie's.

His father flipped open the folded contents and read out loud. "A dark knight is coming quickly. The old plans are again in effect." His brow suddenly furrowed, and a familiar spark flashed in his eyes.

"A dark knight?" Billy repeated. "But the slayers are gone."

His father stared at the words, saying nothing.

After a few seconds, Billy added, "Aren't they?"

"Devin's henchman, Palin, is gone, but …" He folded the note and handed it to Billy. "Please burn this for me."

Billy took the page and wadded it up. "What did she mean by the old plans?"

"I think I know, but I'm not certain." As he looked at Billy, he stroked his chin. "Did you speak to your mother before you came in here?"

Billy sat in one of the seven empty chairs that surrounded the oval table and shook his head. His mother had asked him to check on Walter's sister, Shelly, while her parents were out of town, heading for Montana to meet with Walter. Everything was fine, of course. Shelly was too old to be a target of the Caitiff. Still, she was planning to come over to spend the night, just in case. "I didn't look for Mom when I got back." He squeezed the wad of paper in his fist. "Why?"

"The presence of a slayer is always bad news." His father leaned back and looked into the hallway, then slid his chair closer. "But there is more bad news."

Billy tightened his jaw and gazed into his father's deep brown eyes. "Okay. I'm ready. I think."

His father spun a cell phone on the table. "Remember Walter mentioning the Methuselah girl, the Oracle of Fire?"

"Yeah. Sapphira. He told me a lot more about her later."

"Well, she called while you were out. She said ..." He paused. Letting out a sigh, he turned and looked out the window, seeming to drift away into his thoughts.

Billy resisted the urge to drum his fingers. No sense in making Dad hurry. After so many centuries as a human, a few extra minutes to come up with exactly the right words probably seemed like nothing to him. Besides, if Sapphira called, she and the others were probably fine.

He followed his father's gaze. Outside, the mountains of West Virginia created a wintry backdrop, with bare trees poking through blankets of white. Snow had come early this year, forcing everyone to stay cooped up inside, another reason to feel antsy. With long-dead relatives suddenly showing up at people's doorsteps and hairy beasts chasing children through the streets, who wouldn't be scared spitless?

A knock sounded at the door. Billy sprang to his feet and withdrew his gun. His father snatched the rifle from the wall, and they hustled together toward the front of the house. Billy took his usual position five steps up the stairwell and shouted into the bedrooms

27

above. "Mom! Girls! Warning protocol!" He braced his pistol in both hands and aimed at the door. Now would have been a great time for his danger-sensing ability, but no use wishing for that to return. "Is it one of the ghouls?"

His father looked out the peephole. "Neither ghost nor ghoul!" He flung the door open, allowing a tall, gray-haired man and a teenaged girl to shuffle in, then closed it to ward off the snow that followed in their wake.

Bundled in heavy, ankle-length coats, the visitors brushed off thin layers of snow. The girl pulled down a hood, revealing light brown braids with blond highlights. "I apologize for my abrupt arrival," the man said in a dignified British accent as he shook more snow from his gray hair.

"Sir Patrick!" Billy stuffed the gun into his pocket and rushed to the door, extending his hand. "It's great to see you!"

Patrick enfolded Billy in a tight embrace. "A mere handshake is insufficient, dear William."

Billy relished Patrick's strong, lanky arms. The hug felt like one of Professor Hamilton's—warm, hearty, and genuine. To have the late professor stroll through the door would have been even better, but since that was no longer possible, Sir Patrick would do.

"We took an earlier flight," Patrick said, pulling back from Billy, "and my cell phone battery needs recharging, so I was unable to call." He shifted to Billy's father, and the two embraced for a brief moment before Patrick touched the girl's head with a gloved hand. "Of course, Shiloh needs no introduction."

Offering a friendly nod, Billy smiled at her. With those shining blue eyes, she looked so much like Bonnie her smile in return made his heart ache. He reached for her coat. "Here. Let me get that for you."

As she let the sleeves slide down her arms, Shiloh spoke in an accent that mimicked her father's. "Thank you so much. You're such a gentleman."

28

A flush warmed Billy's cheeks. As he hung Shiloh's coat in a side closet, he watched her out of the corner of his eye. She smoothed out the red blazer over her white, button-down blouse. With new jeans and walking shoes, she really looked sharp.

While Jared took Patrick's coat, Billy looked out the window at the side of the door. "Sir Barlow's out there."

"He is, indeed," Patrick said, reaching for the doorknob. "He was engaged in a conversation with the cab driver before we stopped. They were in the midst of exchanging war stories, so we left the two of them to collect the luggage."

As soon as he opened the door, a burly man with a thick mustache barreled in, carrying a lengthy box over his shoulder. Dressed in a red woolen sweater and thick knee britches that held a sword and scabbard at his hip, Sir Barlow set his gaze on Billy, his eyes twinkling. "I believe your expression here is, 'Santa Claus is coming to town.' But I'll wager he and his hoofed transports never carried packages such as this."

Billy leaned over to look outside again. A taxi cab lurched ahead, its tires sliding in the snow briefly before it roared away. Everything seemed clear. After hauling three suitcases in from the porch and sliding them next to the closet, he turned and shouted upstairs. "Mom! It's okay! Sirs Patrick and Barlow are here, and Shiloh, too!"

There was no reply.

"If your mother followed emergency protocol," his father said, "she took the girls down the back stairway to the computer room." He walked to an intercom unit on the wall and pressed three buttons. When the speaker beeped, he leaned toward it. "Everything's okay, Marilyn. We have some special guests. Want to come out and meet us by the fireplace?"

"In a minute," came the scratchy reply. "Monique fell and scraped her knee. I'm patching her up."

Billy lifted the box off Barlow's shoulder and hurried with it to the family room. As he laid it on a coffee table in front of the fireplace, the lid shifted and fell to the side. A beautiful sword lay on top of a blanket of crinkled white paper.

He grasped the hilt. He knew this sword, the replica of Excalibur he had used in training before he pulled the authentic one from the stone. Although only several months had passed since he last gripped this hilt, it now seemed like years. So much had happened since that day.

Raising the point toward the ceiling, he gazed at the etching of two dragons on the silvery blade and the ancient runes that bordered them near each edge. As he recalled the day he first learned the meaning of the odd letters, Professor Hamilton's voice echoed in his mind. *"This one says, roughly speaking, 'May the Lady's purity never depart from the one found worthy to draw the sword.'"*

Billy smiled. Leave it to Morgan to claim the purity label. She was so full of herself she probably pulled a muscle patting herself on the back. Still, the phrase was appropriate. In his mind, the Lady would always be Bonnie. No one could dispute her purity.

"I see that you have discovered your gift."

Billy spun around. Sir Patrick strode in, a wide smile on his face. Although his eyes seemed young and fresh, his gait revealed a much older man. Obviously his many years as a full-fledged human were catching up with him, yet with a wool sweater fitting snugly over his trim waist, he still displayed a youthful frame.

Patrick sat on the sofa's middle cushion and patted the one on his right. "Please, William. Sit, and I will tell you why I have brought this sword."

While Billy took a seat, his father, Sir Barlow, and Shiloh walked in. His father, still carrying the rifle, snapped open the blinds. "Better to let them see us with our weapons, at least until Marilyn and the girls come in."

"Indeed," Barlow said. "When it comes to those scoundrels, many a parent in my day used nightmarish legends to frighten children into submission." He lowered his voice to an ominous tone. "If you fail to obey me, young man, I shall give you over to Caitiff, and they will use your hair for a wig, your teeth for a necklace, and your eyeballs as fish bait!"

Billy laughed. "Did you ever use that threat yourself?"

"No, William. I was never blessed with a wife or children." Barlow sat on the floor near the hearth and prodded the fire with the poker. "But if I were to protect a child from the Caitiff, I think this rod could come in handy, especially when used in the proper place."

Shiloh sat on a plush recliner that faced the sofa, while Billy's father chose a space on the floor near Barlow. "I saw one of the ghouls down the street," he said, patting the rifle he kept at his side. "He was close to a neighbor's window, so I couldn't get a shot at him."

"Firearms will be of no lasting value." Patrick nodded at the sword in Billy's hand. "We should rely on the more tried-and-true method of relieving those villains of their heads."

Sir Barlow jabbed the air with the red-hot poker. "Slicing and dicing villains is preferred by knights two to one over shooting them with balls of lead."

Billy grinned at Barlow's antics. Ever since the gallant knight escaped from his centuries-long imprisonment in the candlestone, he relished every opportunity to use modern idioms, even when they sounded hokey. He was especially fond of using "the cat's pajamas," though he never seemed to understand what it really meant.

Billy lifted the sword a bit higher. "This was Prof's. Where did you get it?"

Patrick withdrew an envelope from his coat's inner pocket and showed it to Billy. "Charles left his will in the possession of the Circle of Knights. During the months between his locating you here in West Virginia and your subsequent journey to England, he altered his will and stored everything he left to you in this box.

31

Most of his possessions went to his daughter, Elizabeth, of course, but I think you will find some valuable treasures in here."

As heat surged through his ears, Billy rubbed the blade with his thumb. "He left this to me?"

"Who is more worthy?" Patrick removed the crinkled paper from the box, revealing spiral notebooks of various colors stacked haphazardly throughout.

"Some items," Patrick continued, "were on his person or at his lodging when he passed away." He lifted a gold chain from underneath one of the notebooks. An old-fashioned pocket watch dangled at its end, slowly twisting. As a jewel on its back plate caught the rays of the sun in each rotation, it sparkled. "You were likely far too busy to notice that this lay on the ground where Charles fell in battle. Fortunately, Sir Barlow's eyes were keen enough to spot it."

He laid the watch in Billy's hand and draped the chain over his arm. Billy placed the sword across his and Patrick's laps and closed his fingers around the watch. It fit perfectly in his palm. As his throat clamped shut, he couldn't bear to look at Shiloh. He would think of Bonnie again and how much they both loved Prof, and he'd cry for sure.

"And these," Patrick said, lifting one of the small spiral notebooks, "are journals. Charles was faithful to record his daily activities, including his efforts in finding you and your adventures together thereafter." He placed the notebook in Billy's other hand. "I perused his collection and gathered the ones that related to you." The aging knight gazed into Billy's eyes. "They are yours now."

Billy stared at the notebook's cover and imagined where the professor's hands had touched the worn edges. A chill crawled along his skin. Now the wise old teacher could speak to him once again, even from Heaven.

A loud thump shook the door.

Sir Barlow shot to his feet, a hand on the hilt of his sword. "That was not a friendly knock."

A window shattered. A long howl sounded from outside.

Billy and his father stood as one, Billy lifting the sword as he rose. Drawing his own sword, Sir Barlow rushed to the doorway. Billy kept pace. A hairy arm reached through a jagged hole in the glass next to the door and unlocked the knob.

As it released the deadbolt, Sir Barlow set his foot against the door. With a lightning-fast swipe, he slashed through the creature's wrist. Black fluid spewed from the arm as it jerked back through the hole. Its hand splashed in a puddle and wriggled like a decapitated snake.

Barlow tried to refasten the deadbolt, but the door flew open and knocked him to the side. A thin, hairy man in a dirty loincloth burst in, grasping his bleeding stub of an arm. As ten more crowded in behind him, each one snarling through long, pointed fangs, he raised a club and lunged toward Billy.

Billy swung the sword at the lead Caitiff and whacked its head off. So much for barging in with a club.

"Catch!" Barlow yelled. He flung his sword to Jared, lowered his shoulder, and plowed into the pack from behind, steamrolling them with his hefty body. As they toppled forward, Billy and his father severed heads and limbs until only one Caitiff remained alive, quivering as he lay on the floor in a widening puddle of thick, dark blood.

Jared pressed his sword's point against the Caitiff's throat. "Tell me, foul beast. Why did you come here?"

The dirty-faced creature trembled violently and let out a plaintive howl.

Pushing the sword, Jared cut into the Caitiff's flesh. "I heard one of your kind speak just last night. I know you can talk."

33

The Caitiff raised a finger and pointed at Shiloh. She stood near the fireplace next to Patrick, firmly embraced in his arms. "We saw the girl," it squeaked. "We wanted the girl."

Jared glanced at Shiloh, then back at the Caitiff. "She is just one. Why did so many of you attack? And why are all of you in a little town like Castlewood?"

The creature tugged nervously at his loincloth. His fangs dragged so heavily against his mouth, his lips began to bleed. "She has the scent … the scent of the circles. I must … I must take her."

The Caitiff pushed his body up with his hands, but Jared slammed his shoe against his skinny chest, pinning him. "Why are you in Castlewood?" he yelled. "Answer me!"

"Let me stand." The Caitiff pointed at one of his fellow attackers. "And I will show you something."

Jared moved his foot away, but kept his sword close to the creature's throat. "Very well."

The Caitiff struggled to his feet and pushed his fingers into the loincloth of the dead body next to him. He withdrew a flattened scroll, about six inches long and tied in the middle by rough twine.

Jared snatched it away and handed it to Billy.

After ripping off the twine, Billy unrolled the dirty, wrinkled page. Odd lettering had been scrawled in a single line from one end to the other. "I have no clue what this says."

Sir Barlow leaned over his shoulder. "The script is from my era, but my reading skills were quite poor in those days."

Jared took the note and looked it over. "Hmmm … It says, 'The devilish witch carries the odor of Hades. Take her, and you will be set free from your wretched state.'"

"Hades?" Shiloh said. "Well, I was certainly there long enough, but I hope I don't still smell like that place."

"True." Jared crushed the note in his fist. "But you're not the only one who has been in Hades. If the slayer is looking for Bonnie, these stupid beasts wouldn't know—"

The Caitiff screamed and pushed Jared to the side. "I must have her!" He lunged at Shiloh but stopped in mid-leap. The end of a poker protruded from his back, its red barb partially blackened by the Caitiff's blood.

Patrick held the other end, his face twisting in rage as he lifted the beast farther off the ground. "Nothing from the bowels of Hell will ever touch my daughter again!" He threw the poker, sending the Caitiff sprawling backward.

Barlow hacked its head off, then turned away as the stench of its fluids joined that of the others littering the floor. "Phew! We will need more than Lysol to rid the carpet of this foul odor!"

Jared nudged the Caitiff's body with his foot. "They were already dead with regard to their lives on Earth. If the legends are accurate, when the dead residents of Hades die again in that realm, their bodies and fluids will disintegrate, and their souls will pass to the Lake of Fire."

"I hope it happens before Mom comes in here," Billy said, holding his nose.

Jared nodded toward the rear of the house. "With all the commotion, she probably stayed in the computer room."

"Then let's go there. This place reeks."

After cleaning his sword, stowing it with the journals, and picking up the box, Billy and his father led the others through a hallway to the back of the house. Jared pushed a key into a dooknob but didn't turn it. "Son, I need to tell you the bad news before we enter." He let out a long sigh and glanced at each person in turn. A low hum reverberating from within the door made the air feel heavy, even prickly.

Billy shuddered. Something was wrong … very wrong.

Finally, his father spoke in a near whisper. "As I told you, Sapphira called earlier. Karen, our valiant little warrior, died in the battle against the Nephilim. According to Sapphira, Karen literally saved the entire planet."

A painful lump lodged in Billy's throat. He imagined the cute redhead and her freckled face the day he first met her on a wintry mountain. Her voice played in his mind. *"So,"* she had said, snow flecking her fiery-red bangs, *"I'm supposed to believe that you're a dragon? Human and dragon in one body?"*

Billy let a tear drip from each eye, unashamed. He hadn't merely lost a fellow warrior; he had lost a sister whom he had grown to love dearly.

He scanned the others. Tears passed down Shiloh's cheeks as well as Patrick's. Barlow's eyes glistened, and he shook his head sadly. "We will all miss that feisty lass. She was a corker."

"Your mother knows about Karen," Jared said to Billy as he turned the knob, "but your sisters don't. We will tell them in due time."

Still carrying the box, Billy swiped his sleeve across his face and forced a fake smile as they entered the computer room. A high ceiling and bright lights greeted their eyes, as did his mother sitting at a desk in front of Larry the supercomputer, a collection of metal boxes and glass enclosures covering most of the wall on the left and rising to near the ceiling. Red letters flashed on the largest of five flat monitors on Larry's outer panel. His stoic voice, more human than mechanical, interrupted the hum of his cooling fans. "Marilyn, an intruder has breached the perimeter. My sensors indicate an unusual odor, suggesting a skunklike presence."

Marilyn rapped her knuckles on the panel. "It's just Jared and Billy. Get a clue."

"Clue collected. Jared and Billy are now registered in my database as skunk apes."

Three girls—a blonde with Nordic features, a dark-skinned brunette, and Monique—rose from their cross-legged positions on the carpet, abandoning the scattered pieces of a Monopoly game, and followed Marilyn as she shuffled wearily toward the door. Red blotches on her cheeks gave evidence of a recently scrubbed face, and a wide bandage on the side of her neck, partially hidden by her shoulder-length light brown hair, provided a painful reminder that she had recently been the victim of a dog attack. "Jared? Is everything all right?"

"We survived." Jared took her in his arms, kissed her tenderly, and turned her toward their guests. "Marilyn, I'm sure we have room for everyone, don't we?"

She smiled. "Of course. The more the merrier."

Billy felt tears forming again. His mother's smile was mechanical, pain-streaked. With three frightened girls gathering behind her, the picture seemed more tragic than ever. Karen had been her daughter long enough to become a true part of the family. His mom's heart ached, but she couldn't afford to let on to the other girls, not while the Caitiff were still lurking. They were scared enough already.

Patrick bowed. "The merging of Earth and Hades is a rather lame excuse for leaving England, isn't it?"

"Any excuse will do for friends to come together." Marilyn waved her hand, fanning her husband. "Did you men wallow in a pig sty?"

Jared wiped a splotch of Caitiff blood from his hand to his shirt. "Those monsters aren't exactly the cleanest—"

"Alert!" Larry called out. "Incoming message from Ashley."

Billy hustled to the computer desk, slid into the swivel chair, and looked at the monitor on Larry's panel. "Can we get her onscreen?"

"The bandwidth allocation from her handheld computer is inadequate for full-motion video. I will bring across still photos as a background for her voice."

After blinking once, the screen showed a picture of Ashley, her hair blowing back into Walter's face as he sat behind her. A sword hilt protruded from his back scabbard, the real Excalibur.

37

Another female sat in the rear, a dragon's spine between her and Walter. Billy studied her features, long auburn hair and piercing eyes framed by a face much like Ashley's. Although they had never met, from Walter's description, she had to be Ashley's sister Abigail, the former dragon, Roxil.

"Who's on the console?" Ashley's voice seemed wind-blown and agitated.

Billy grabbed a headset, slipped it on, and adjusted the microphone in front of his lips. "It's Billy. Go ahead, Ashley. I have you on headset and external speakers. Mom and Dad, Sirs Patrick and Barlow, Shiloh, and our sisters are here."

The others gathered behind him and watched the screen. The photo changed, the same scene shifted to one side to show part of a dragon's wing. Only half of Ashley's face was visible now. With her dampened brown hair plastered against her cheek, she seemed ready to blow it out of the way. "My mother's going to try to create a portal to the Bridgelands," she said. "Arramos did it, so she thinks she can do it, too. Once we go through, I don't think we can contact you anymore."

"What's the hurry?" Billy asked. "I thought you were going to wait for Sir Patrick."

"Yeah, I know. I sent Larry an e-mail. That'll explain everything."

Jared stepped up to the desk. "I already heard from Sapphira. She says the portal at the top of the turbine is still active."

"True," Ashley replied, "but that roof was too small to use safely, especially since one of us is a dragon. When you and Billy and Patrick and his knights meet Sapphira in Montana, she can transport you from the turbine."

"No more time to talk!" a male voice shouted. "See you later, Billy! We'll— "

Static drowned out his words, though the monitor still displayed the previous scene, half showing the dragon and half showing Ashley, Walter, and Abigail. Somehow, the blend seemed appropriate.

Billy clenched his fist and whispered, "Knock 'em dead, buddy!"

"Ashley is no longer within range," Larry said. "I will show the final photo and print out an e-mail Ashley sent immediately before her call."

As the printer hummed, Billy stared at the new photo, Ashley and Walter leaning forward, their hair shaded orange in the glow of a stream of fire that spun in a tight cyclone to their left. Thigocia was probably flying in a circle and creating a ring of flames as she attempted to construct the portal. Walter's face beamed. Ashley's showed her fierce determination. Abigail's expression mimicked Ashley's, her brow low and her lips in a flat line as she held on to Walter.

Billy loosened his fist and slapped his palm lightly on the desk. If only he could go, too. Fighting side by side with Walter again would be awesome.

As if reading his mind, Jared laid a hand on Billy's shoulder. "Adventures await all who follow the narrow path, son. We have plenty to do here."

Sir Patrick held up the printed page. "I should say so! Ashley's e-mail is most interesting, indeed!"

"Will you read it out loud?" Billy asked.

"Certainly." Patrick waved a hand. "Everyone please gather comfortably. The message isn't overly long, but I'm sure our conversation about it will be considerably longer."

Billy got up from the computer seat and let Shiloh take his place. He dragged a hardback chair from a worktable and slid it next to his mother. He smiled at her, arching his eyebrows much higher than normal, hoping to get a response.

One corner of her lips twitched upward, but every other line in her face sagged. Billy's father approached her from behind and

39

rested his hands on her shoulders, gently kneading her muscles. While Monique nestled in her lap, Stacey and Rebecca knelt on the floor at either side, quietly fidgeting. Sir Barlow eyed Sir Patrick as he paced back and forth across the computer room.

Stroking his chin, Patrick read the e-mail. "Dear Billy and whoever else is reading this, here's what's going on. Walter might have told you about this creepy old guy who sat with me during the airplane ride to London. Well, he suddenly appeared again when I was being chased up a stairwell from Hades by a giant with a missing leg. Turns out he wasn't just a creepy old guy. He was Enoch, the prophet from the Bible. Pretty weird, right? Anyway, while Abigail and I went down to get a waffle at the motel room buffet, guess who was refilling the waffle batter. Yup! Enoch, himself! He told us the key to separating Earth and Hades was in another world called Second Eden. He needs every dragon and former dragon to come and help with a war that's about to start there. He also asked for Billy, Barlow, and the other knights, something about including the heirs and friends of King Arthur in the great battle."

Patrick looked up at Billy. "Edmund will arrive later, but Newman was not able to accompany me because of obligations with the museum in Scotland. Had I known of the need, I would have insisted. Of course, Fiske and Woodrow are still recovering from broken bones, but I could call upon Standish, if necessary."

"Sure," Billy said, nodding. "Is there more in the e-mail?"

"Quite a bit." He looked down at the page and continued. "I know you're busy with a bunch of hairy fiends from Hades, but we have bigger problems to worry about. There are at least ten giants called Nephilim roaming around in Montana, and an overzealous genius named Mardon probably still has big plans for them. My theory is that this dragon named Arramos wants to use them in that war I was talking about. So, if we want to do the David and Goliath thing, rid the world of hairy monsters, and save

40

another world with a single stone, let's all go to this place called the Bridgelands. Enoch says the portals will lead us there, and then someone will guide us from that point on. Call Sapphira and tell her when you can meet her and Gabriel at the top of the mountain in Montana where I used to live. Larry has the GPS coordinates. I hope they're accurate. My handheld computer is on its last legs battery-wise, so I'm not sure I can trust it. I pray that it lasts long enough to send this message. Anyway, tell Sir Patrick that he should recognize Sapphira and Gabriel. They haven't changed a bit. I hope to see you soon. Ashley."

"So we fly to Montana." Billy stood up. "Can we all fit in *Merlin*? We have more seats in the new model."

His mother shook her head. "I have to stay with the girls. They can't be involved in a war. I can manage without the men for a while."

Jared reached for his wife's hand. "I told you that I would never leave you again."

"Thank you for remembering." She kissed his knuckles. "You have to go. There's just no other option."

Raising a finger for each person, Billy counted. "Okay, so there's me, Dad, Sir Patrick, Sir Barlow, and ..."

"And me!" Shiloh said. "I'm an heir to King Arthur. Well, an adoptive one, anyway."

"Okay, that's five." He turned to his father. "What about Bonnie and her mother? Any chance of finding them?"

He shook his head. "It would take too long to get a message to them. When we were hiding from the slayers, we had ways of communicating, but it often took months, even years, to get our messages across."

"This is the Internet age, Dad. There's got to be a faster way."

"What do you propose, son? Post a coded message on a fantasy blog? Irene wouldn't know to look there. We have to use the old methods."

41

"What methods?"

His father sighed and nodded at Sir Patrick. "It would be better if you explained it since you set up the system."

Setting a hand on Billy's back, Patrick spoke in a serious tone. "It is impossible for you to comprehend how secretive we had to be. Over the centuries, the slayer picked us off one by one until only Jared, Irene, and I remained. Even though we exercised extraordinary care, Devin was able to track Irene to Montana and Jared here to West Virginia. Such was his obsession and prowess. Yet, although he knew where I lived, Morgan forbade him from killing me. She wanted me alive to continue her blackmailing schemes."

"You mean to use Shiloh as a hostiam?" Billy asked.

"Exactly. If a slayer is stalking Irene and Bonnie, any form of communication could well endanger their lives. I think it best if we take this journey without them. Perhaps Enoch will unite us later."

Billy clenched his fist, imagining Devin's throat in his grasp. "But could any slayer be as crafty as Devin? Whoever this new slayer is, he's probably just a wannabe without any experience."

"Are you sure this is a new slayer?" Patrick asked. "How do you know he isn't Devin himself?"

"I cracked the candlestone Devin was in. He's nothing but a bunch of sparkling light now."

"Yet he survived a similar fate in the past."

Billy's heart thumped. Patrick was right. After Devin came out of the candlestone as a weird energy monster, Excalibur sent him away in a swirling cyclone of energy. Somehow Morgan was able to put him into the body of Clefspeare, but who could have reconstituted him this time? "I guess you're right. Maybe the former dragons really are in big trouble."

Patrick gave him a grim nod. "I know how to reach Legossi in a safe way, so I will send her a note immediately. I also secured a hiding place for a few other dragons in Europe, so I will ask Larry to store and secure those addresses. Perhaps I can call upon Legossi to warn them for us. Still, there are others we might not be able to contact without compromising security. For them, including Hartanna, I will use our safest form of communication, though it is also the slowest. We have rented post office boxes in every major region of this country as well as in England. I will instruct one of the members of the Circle of Knights to write a letter addressed to each one. They will be sent from various locations, and, of course, the message will be in code using a method we dragons devised long ago."

"That sounds pretty safe," Billy said, looking at his father. "How often did you check the box in this region?"

"To us," his father said, "time was not a major factor. I cannot speak for the other dragons, but I checked mine once each year."

"Once a year!" Billy moaned. "We can't wait that long!"

"I wish I could give you better news." He draped an arm over Billy's shoulder and pulled him close. "Bonnie's presence could well cause Irene to check hers sooner, but if she believes Devin is on her trail, she might not come out of hiding at all."

Swallowing hard, Billy looked up at his father. Still a few inches taller, his protective stance reassured him. It was as if Jared Bannister maintained the power and presence of Clefspeare. "Who will stay to protect Mom and the girls?" Billy asked.

Patrick looked at his watch. "Sir Edmund should arrive before nightfall, but I'm not sure we should wait for him. Marilyn will be safer if all former dragons vacate the premises."

"Edmund would be the perfect guardian," Barlow said. "As his captain, I hereby order it."

Billy pulled free from his father and picked up a phone on the desk. "We'd better let Sapphira know when we're coming."

"She has Walter's cell—speed dial nine," his father said. "When I was last in Montana in dragon form, I flew over the mountaintop Ashley mentioned. There's plenty of room to land our plane."

43

Billy looked at the phone's keypad. "What time should I tell her?"

"Probably late morning to midday tomorrow."

"Can't we fly all night?" Billy asked. "We can take turns."

His father shook his head. "We'll fly as far as we can tonight and finish in the morning. I don't want to land on that mountain in the dark."

"Got it." He punched the numeral nine and raised the phone to his ear. "But if what I hear about Sapphira is true, she could light up that mountain like it was daytime."

44

CHAPTER

RETURN OF THE RING

Walter tightened his grip around Ashley's waist and clutched a handful of her sweatshirt. "Do you think they heard that last message?" he called.

"Can't tell," Ashley said. "My computer lost the connection."

Walter looked at the mist-covered screen in her hand. "Should you try again?"

"I think the battery's finally given up the ghost." She lowered her head, sending her hair into a frenzy. "Time for a portal dive!"

Flames shot from Thigocia's mouth and nostrils as she bent into a hard left turn. The fiery arc tightened until it became a spinning wheel that funneled downward into a tornado. Her wings fanned and twisted the flames, making them spin faster and faster. As she continued to pour a river of orange into the vortex, the opening at the top widened.

Clouds within a few feet of the spin streamed into the funnel, ripping a hole in the fabric of the sky. The rift expanded into a black chasm that dipped toward the vortex, an expanse of nothingness at least the width of a dragon's wing.

"Here we go!" Thigocia shouted. "Hold your breath and hang on!"

Ashley stuffed her handheld computer behind her jeans waistband and gripped a protruding spine. Folding in her wings, Thigocia dove into the void.

Walter took a deep breath and held it as the surrounding air faded to black. Now floating in cold darkness, he slowly exhaled, keeping as much air as possible, but after a minute or so, his body craved oxygen. He tried to suck in air, but nothing would enter. As his chest muscles clutched painfully, he felt Ashley's abdomen tighten. Abigail's hands trembled around his waist. If they didn't break out of this vacuum in a few seconds, they would faint and fall off.

Finally, a rush of air breezed in. Walter took in long, deep breaths, soothing his aching lungs. Ashley's abdomen relaxed, as did Abigail's grip. Light filled the skies, and down below, a field came into view, a wide expanse of green grass dotted with purple and yellow flowers that bordered a dense forest.

Walter patted Thigocia's scales. "Way to go! You did it!"

Her wings beating the fragrant air, she curled her neck, bringing her head near her passengers. "I apologize. The lack of oxygen lasted longer than I remembered."

"It still doesn't make sense," Ashley said. "No air, but enough pressure to keep our bodies from exploding."

Thigocia snorted plumes of smoke from her nostrils. "There are two things you need to learn, my dear. One is that the laws to which you are accustomed on Earth might not hold true here in the Bridgelands." As she descended, she straightened her neck and aimed twin red beams at the grass below.

Walter grinned. Thigocia was baiting Ashley to ask about the second thing she needed to learn, but either Ashley didn't want to bite or her newly awakened mind-reading skills had already given her the answer.

After a few seconds, Abigail piped up from behind, shouting into the wind. "What's the second thing?"

Thigocia spread out her wings and flattened her angle as she swept parallel to the meadow near the forest's outer tree line. As soon as she landed in a graceful slide, she reached her head toward them again. "The second thing is to always trust your mother."

She lowered her snout to the ground, creating a staircase with her neck. Ashley, Walter, and Abigail stepped across the oddly angled ridges until they could jump safely to the ground.

Abigail stopped for a moment. She adjusted her jeans, tucked in her T-shirt, and pulled the hem of her thick woolen sweater over her belt. "I am not accustomed to pants yet. During my time as a human in Dragons' Rest, I wore dresses."

"I hope you're a quick study," Ashley said. "Dresses aren't very practical when riding a dragon."

Walter quickly checked his jeans, shirt, and sweatshirt, a dark gray one with a Glacier National Park logo on the front. No use being the only one looking like a bum. He then stooped and passed a hand through the grass. As soft as silk and as green as emeralds, it seemed unearthly.

"Because it *is* unearthly," Ashley said. "I think we're in the Bridgelands."

Walter straightened, trying not to scowl. "This mind reading of yours might get annoying after a while."

Ashley's brown eyes sparkled in the warm sunshine. "Don't fret, Walter. I pick up your thoughts only once in a while, mostly images, really. An occasional word or two pops up, but nothing for you to be ashamed of." She smiled. "Your thoughts are ... well ... sweet."

"Thanks." Walter pressed his lips together. "I think." He dug into his pocket. "Speaking of sweet ..."

Ashley tried to peek. "Did you bring candy?"

"My MP3 player." He pushed the earbuds into place and set the player to its radio setting. "I got it when we stopped at Wal-Mart. Just thought I'd check for any stations."

"Don't you know where we are? What do you think you'll find? A Top 40 countdown of hymns from an angelic choir?"

"That's the point. I wanted to make sure we really made a jump. When I had my cell phone, I used that to check, but since I gave it to Sapphira, this is all I have. No stations means we're not in Montana anymore." After scanning the frequencies, he shook his head. "Not a sound."

"Well, unplug yourself and put it away. We all need to keep our ears open."

"Sure thing." He popped out the buds and slid the player into his pocket. "But you never know when it might come in handy."

Abigail untied the strap of a backpack from a spine near Thigocia's tail. As she bent over to check its zipper, a clear bauble dangled from a thin chain around her neck. Walter watched it swing back and forth, the egg crystal that Sapphira had formed out of the diamond-like shards that had fallen from the sky when Ashley's and Abigail's father gave his life for them. He glanced at Ashley, but hers wasn't in sight. She was wearing it earlier, so it was probably hidden under her shirt.

Abigail pushed her arms through the backpack straps and hiked it up. "I see a jagged line in the distance that interrupts this meadow."

"Trees?" Walter asked. "Hills?"

Thigocia folded her wings in tightly. "It is a chasm bordered by a rocky ridge. I noticed it on the way down."

"That would suggest a river at the bottom," Abigail said. "A water source is a good find. We only have enough for a couple of days. If we don't locate Enoch soon, we will have to refill our bottles."

Walter pointed at the horizon. "If water is over there, then why did we land here?"

"I sensed a presence." Thigocia's triangular ears twitched. "I thought it best to investigate."

"Danger?" Walter asked.

"I did not detect it using my danger senses. I picked it up by smell." Thigocia sniffed the air. "It is an old memory, very old."

"A human smell," Ashley said. "But I can't pick up a name from your mind."

"Because I cannot identify it." Thigocia sniffed again. "It is not Enoch … or Timothy."

A voice called from the trees. "Thigocia, your senses are as sharp as ever."

Walter spun on his heels. An old man shuffled out of the forest, slightly bent as he pushed a wrinkled hand through his wispy white hair. Dressed in a gray cloth robe that covered his legs down to his ankles and his arms to his elbows, he wobbled back and forth in a lively gait.

Thigocia bowed her head. "A pleasure to see you again, Glewlwyd. How many years has it been?"

As soon as Glewlwyd joined them, he stroked Thigocia's neck three times. "Let us not count years, good Queen of the dragons."

Walter grimaced. Glewlwyd's voice sounded like a cross between a squeaky door and a complaining Siamese cat, all scratchy with a touch of growling.

Glewlwyd splayed his hands and continued. "When the number of centuries I have seen eclipsed the number of fingers on my hands, I forsook the practice of counting. Years are like days, days like minutes. Time seems rather meaningless now."

Thigocia tapped the end of her tail on the ground twice. "In the days of Arthur, Glewlwyd rode me into battle on a number of occasions. He is a gatekeeper during times of peace, but all

49

able-bodied men had to go to war when called upon, especially those who could ride dragons."

"My dragon riding days are long gone. When I died, it had been forty years since I had even seen a dragon. Their transformation into humans made us bereft of a great and noble race."

Walter shuddered. Just a few feet in front of him, a dragon and a dead man were having a conversation. Not exactly an everyday occurrence, but stuff like this was becoming more and more normal all the time. He extended his hand. "Well, I'm pleased to meet you, sir. I'm Walter."

"I know who you are." Glewlwyd shook his hand heartily. "You are the descendant of Arthur, the son of his body."

"Yeah, I guess. At least that's what someone told me."

"And he would be correct." Glewlwyd patted him on the back. "I sense that you have not traveled to the Bridgelands to stand around and talk to a decrepit gatekeeper. Shall we discuss your business?"

"I am searching for Enoch," Thigocia said. "We saw him from Earth, and we assumed he could tell us what happened to my mate."

"Well, that is quite a feat. Enoch rarely travels far from Heaven's Altar, so your eyesight must be keen indeed." Glewlwyd made a circle with his fingers and placed it in front of his eye. "Did Elam let you borrow Enoch's prophetic spyglass?"

Ashley stepped forward and began her characteristic rapid-fire explanation. "We looked through a portal created by Mardon's giants when they tried to merge Earth with Heaven, and we could see Enoch, Acacia, and Elam standing on a field much like this one. I also saw a vision in the sky that looked like my father, Timothy … or Makaidos … burning up. We think he died, but we want to know for sure, and we want to find out if there's any way to take his body home, or whatever's left of it."

As Glewlwyd lowered his hand, the lines in his face turned downward. "Makaidos was a fine dragon king and was sorely missed during my final years on Earth. I honor him highly."

"Then can you help us find him?" Ashley asked.

"I will tell you what I know." He extended an arm and pointed across the grassy expanse. "I sent Elam to the bridge not long ago, and now you tell me that he has found Enoch. I have also met Acacia, a lovely white-haired girl with sparkling blue eyes. She accompanied my friend Joseph who was carrying a woman who appeared to be dead. Yet, I have not seen King Makaidos. No, not in this realm."

"He might have been in human form," Thigocia explained. "His human name is Timothy."

Glewlwyd shook his head. "I have no recollection of a man named Timothy, but if you wish to inquire of Enoch, I suggest that you follow Elam's path. The bridge is treacherous, but holy ones are able to cross, though sometimes through great suffering. Yet, I do not know how to advise a dragon. The bridge would never hold you. You could attempt an air crossing, though I fear it might well be impossible. It is not called Zeno's Chasm for no reason."

Walter pondered those words. The name *Zeno* sounded familiar, some Greek guy who—

"He was a Greek philosopher," Ashley said. "He described a paradox that claimed you can never reach any given point, because you always have to go halfway there first, and there are an infinite number of halfway points, and each one of those can't be reached, because—"

"Stop it!" Walter pressed his hands against his head.

"I know. It's contrary to observed fact. I was just trying to explain—"

"No!" Walter lowered a hand and pointed at his skull. "I mean stop reading my mind."

51

"But I didn't. I just assumed you would want to know."

"You assumed I *didn't* know. How would you feel if I did that to you?"

After a few seconds of silence, Ashley dipped her head. "You're right. I'm sorry." Now with a solemn countenance, she turned to Glewlwyd and extended her hand. "It was nice meeting you, Sir. Do you have any last-minute instructions before we head for the chasm?"

"Indeed I do." He pointed again toward the horizon. "Be sure to cross by way of the bridge. Other travelers have told of a different passage, but I strongly advise against seeking it. If you search in the wrong direction, you will never be able to find the bridge again."

"How can that be true?" Ashley asked. "You could just follow the edge of the chasm back to where you started."

Glewlwyd chuckled. "Young lady, you have parroted Elam almost word for word. You must learn that this world is very different from your own. Your knowledge of the physical laws of your realm could very well be a hindrance rather than a help in this one."

"That sounds familiar." Thigocia set the tip of a wing on Ashley's back. "Doesn't it, my dear?"

Ashley gave her a sly wink. "I can't imagine why."

"Familiar or not," Thigocia said, "I have seen many strange things here. We should trust this knight's counsel and fly to the edge of the chasm, then decide what to do when we get there. Perhaps from the air, we will be able to see the safest passage."

Glewlwyd raised a knobby finger. "Another way is likely to exist, but I exhort you to heed my warning. If it is Heaven's Altar you seek, the bridge is the only way to arrive at that destination. All other paths are far more treacherous than they appear. The bridge, however, will never let you fall as long as you are a follower of the Christ."

"Even if you jump?" Ashley asked.

A sad frown wilted the old man's face. "I have no answer for that. I cannot imagine anyone wanting to leap into the chasm."

"Just asking. I'm an analyst, so it's hard to imagine a bridge having a will of its own. It really can't keep you on it if you don't want to be there."

"I will not argue the point, young lady, but again I warn you to beware of assumptions that arise from your earthly under standings. Perhaps the bridge would allow an insane fellow to leap from its grasp. I cannot say." Glewlwyd wrapped his arms around himself tightly. "But as long as you hold on with all your might, the bridge will never let you fall."

Irene closed her laptop computer and sat back in the motel room's desk chair. No Internet. Not even dial-up. Shaking her head at herself, she slid the computer into its pack. She should have known. With a slayer on their trail, civilization might be inaccessible for quite a while.

Now sitting in darkness, except for a ribbon of light peeking through the gap between the curtain and the window, she listened to the sounds of the two-lane highway that served as a front porch for this rural flophouse. A car buzzed by from left to right, then a rumbling truck from the other direction.

After the whining of tires on pavement faded in the distance, silence ensued, blanketing the room as if having a sound all its own. The rush of blood pumping through her ears blended with gentle breaths, her own as well as Bonnie's as she slept in one of the nearby beds.

Soon, another truck droned along the highway, but this one slowed down. Its headlights flashed across the curtain, and the engine died away. Irene stood and edged toward the window. Apparently a tired driver couldn't endure the hundred miles to the next oasis and decided to pull into this rundown motel. But he was about to be disappointed. Although there were vacancies, a sign on the office window said no check-ins after midnight.

53

A door slammed outside. Standing inches away from the curtain, she longed to learn who would be traveling the lonely highway—a married couple on a honeymoon, a family on a cross-country trek with children sleeping in the back, or a businessman lost after a wrong turn back at Route 45—but she resisted the urge to peek outside. The last time she investigated a noise in the night—another night when Bonnie slept peacefully in bed—proved painful beyond words. To this day, the image of a sword plowing into her stomach sent shock waves through her nerves, replaying the most horrible physical pain she had ever endured.

She leaned closer to the window. Maybe she could just nudge the curtain to the side enough to see. Using her nose, she pushed it an inch. Her Ford Expedition, rented the morning before, sat in the space directly in front of their window, but, with the small gap, little else came into view.

54

Letting out a yawn, she walked back to her chair, checking her glowing watch. Five after one in the morning. Sleep was always a luxury when running from slayers. Now it was impossible, especially under these circumstances. This time it seemed that ghosts chased her instead of flesh-and-blood humans.

As she watched Bonnie sleep, a more recent memory flowed through her mind, their reason for being on the run. After their harrowing adventure in the battle against the Watchers back in Maryland and her own transformation from dragon to human, she and Bonnie had decided to go away for a while, a vacation at a ski lodge in the Pennsylvania mountains. Irene sat again and watched the memory play, somewhat fuzzy and distorted, with faces and voices the only clear input.

Laughing, Bonnie tossed a popcorn kernel into Irene's open mouth. Irene caught it and chomped down. "Mmmm! I haven't had popcorn since I died!"

Huddled in blankets, Bonnie handed her a red and white box, spilling a few kernels onto their laps. "Take as much as you want. I'll start the movie." She pointed a remote at the television and pushed a button. "I guess you haven't seen any of the Narnia movies, have you?"

Shaking her head, she spoke through a mouthful of popcorn. "Let it roll!"

The television flashed on, but instead of images from the DVD Bonnie had inserted, an animated portrait of Devin wielding a sword took over the screen. As sinister and nightmarish as ever, the evil knight approached the foreground and pointed his sword.

"Put down the popcorn, Demon Witches, and listen carefully. This is not a recording. I see the box you're sharing, the red and white one on the older witch's lap, and the mugs of hot chocolate poised at your feet, one yellow and one blue. Be careful not to kick them over when you run." As they sat riveted in their seats, he laughed loud and long. "And you will run. If you stay at this lodge, I will kill you in your sleep, and when you leave, I will chase you to the ends of the Earth. And every night as you try to sleep, remember that I will have already found you, and I will sneak into your lair and slit your throats."

The television flashed, and the opening scene from the movie began to play. Irene leaped to her feet. "Grab your suitcase! I'll get mine! Just stuff all you can inside. We have to run!"

As the memory faded away, Irene sighed. They had been running ever since.

She stared at the ticking second hand on her watch, now showing ten after one. Another glow, ever so faint, caught her eye, something near her finger. She lifted her hand. The light followed. She touched it with her other hand and felt the slick surface of the gem in her ring—the rubellite she had worn before she became a dragon again. Now glowing with a barely perceptible white aura, it brought

55

back another recent memory, the day she found the ring after reading a note her husband had entered in his journal before he died.

As soon as she started growing, I pulled off her ring, knowing
it would strangle or perhaps even sever her finger. Even then, I
could barely get it off. Soon, her swelling muscles ripped her
clothes to shreds, and I had to cut away the collar and waistband
to keep them from constricting her rapid, shallow breaths. The
clothing, of course, I discarded, but I put the ring in my briefcase's
zippered pocket.

Finding the briefcase proved difficult. Since it had been buried
by rubble in the mountain collapse, she had to search for hours,
but recovering the symbol of her dragon life was worth it. When
she finally unearthed the briefcase, the outer shell had broken
apart, but the inner pocket still held the ring, safe and sound.

She caressed the smooth gem. What could the glow mean?
The white shade, of course, proved that she no longer had dragon
essence, but why it would emit light was a new mystery.

She glanced over at Bonnie, just a lump in the darkness. She
slept soundly … quietly … peacefully. This new danger didn't
seem to faze her. In fact, she seemed invigorated by it. All the dangers she had faced had instilled her with a longing for adventure.

A gentle knock sounded on the door. Irene froze. Who could
it be? Of course, Devin wouldn't knock. He was neither polite nor
anxious to give away his presence.

She rose slowly and looked through the door's peephole. A
white-haired man, shivering and blowing white puffs as he bundled his heavy coat together, stood on the walkway in the glow of
a parking lot streetlamp.

Irene checked the chain. It seemed good and strong, at least
strong enough to stop an old man. Opening the door an inch or
so, she pressed her mouth close to the crack. "Who are you?"

"My name is Enoch." He backed up a step and spread out his coat, revealing a dark belted robe. "As you can see I am unarmed."

"Enoch, the prophet?" She narrowed the door's opening. "Why should I believe you?"

He held a small object close to the door's opening. "Because of this."

She focused on his fingers. It was a gold ring with a mounted gem. "A rubellite?" she asked.

"Not just a rubellite." He pushed it through the opening. "Examine it closely."

She plucked the ring from his hand and flicked on the standing lamp next to the door. As she rocked the gold band back and forth under the light, she took note of several features. The dark red gem had at least three major cracks, and the mounting seemed loose. And was that an inscription in the band? She held it closer to her eyes, forming the tiny words with her lips as she read them silently. *To Hannah. Now I am Autarkeia.*

She blurted out the last word. "*Autarkeia?*"

A quiet sigh drifted toward her from Bonnie's bed. "Mama? Are you okay?"

Irene flicked off the light. In the sudden darkness, she couldn't see if her daughter was sitting or still lying down. "Everything's fine, Bonnie."

"Is someone at the door?"

"An old friend. I'll tell you about it in a minute." She slid the chain off, swung the door open, then pulled it nearly closed again behind her as she stepped outside.

Enoch closed his coat and smiled. "I assume you deduced where it came from."

"*Autarkeia* means contentment." She held up the ring. "This was my father's."

"Excellent. I'm glad you remember."

57

"But I heard his rubellite shattered after the dragons exited Dragons' Rest and made their choices."

"It was destroyed, but it was temporarily restored to him in another world."

She sucked in a quick breath. "Then is he alive?"

"I'm afraid not, my dear," he said, patting her hand tenderly. "It's a very long story that will have to wait to be told fully." He touched the gem with his fingertip as if anointing it. "After the end of his life in the other world, I recovered the gem from the remains of an inferno. It was quite a chore piecing it back together and polishing it, but I think it is functional once again."

"Functional?" She laid the ring in her palm and stared at it. "What do you mean?"

"As a dragon who served mankind with all his heart, Makaidos sometimes longed to be human himself, but he had to learn to be content with whichever form God deemed better. Since he learned that lesson well, and since he was the king of the dragons, God bestowed on his rubellite the power to give him a choice to keep his dragon essence or become fully human. Now, I am asking you to take it with you. There will come a time when you will have the opportunity to make it available to him." He covered her hand, and the ring, with his hand. "You, too, have such a ring. As I'm sure you have learned by now, the blessing of contentment often opens the door to wider opportunities."

She pressed a finger against her chest. "Do you mean that I could become a—"

"Dragon again?" He nodded. "If that is your choice."

Irene backed away a step. "I ... I don't want to choose. I don't want that responsibility."

"Life is filled with choices we don't want to make." Enoch pulled her closer and whispered. "And what does Bonnie want? What would make her content?"

"She's already content. She decided—"

58

"Shhh." Enoch pressed two fingers over her lips. "I don't want to know. It is crucial that you reveal her current state to as few people as possible."

As he drew his fingers away, she raised the gem closer to her eyes. "So do we look at it to make a choice?"

"That gem, as well as yours, must be energized in a way you will not understand. You might not know that an Oracle of Fire stood within that gem and created a covenant veil. The two witnesses cried out, 'Jehovah Yasha,' to ensure that all imprisoned dragons who passed through believed in the saving power of the Maker's Messiah. Once a gem is energized, the same transforming power that once infused Makaidos's gem will be stored within." He withdrew a curved bone from underneath his coat. "This is a rib. Even as God used one of Adam's ribs to fashion a helpmate, he will soon use one of Timothy's to create helpers for him."

As Irene reached toward the bone, her hands trembled. "This is one of my ... my father's bones?"

"He sacrificed himself to save Roxil and Ashley, and in the fires of rebirth, his bones are now filled with the power to regenerate. This, in combination with the gem, will harness the transforming power."

She took the bone, but her hand wouldn't stop shaking. "How does it work?"

Enoch glanced at the highway. A semi barreled along, close enough to add to the breeze after it passed. "It is cold, and time is short, so I cannot explain everything. When you see one of the Oracles of Fire, give the bone to her, and I will tell her how to use it. I would give it to her myself, but I can't assume which one will accept the task. Neither of the Oracles wishes to return to the place where you must hide.

"Also, have Bonnie wear her backpack at all times. I repeat, it is important that you hide whether or not she has wings. As I said, even I don't know, and I don't want to know."

59

Irene nodded. "I understand. We haven't told anyone yet, not even Billy."

"You should also leave at once." He reached into a deep outer pocket and handed her an electronic gadget that looked like a flat walkie-talkie. "This is a GPS mapping device. It has already been programmed to direct you to Timothy's former home in Montana. You should go there with all haste, and I will try to make sure an Oracle of Fire meets you with further instructions."

Irene backed up again, pushing the motel room door open behind her. She tried to keep her voice as calm as possible, yet loud enough to communicate urgency. "Bonnie. Get packed. We have to go right away."

Through the darkness, Irene could barely see Bonnie's seated form on the bed. "What's wrong?" she asked.

"I'll explain on the way." As she turned to Enoch, Irene slid the ring into her jeans pocket and took the GPS unit. "It's a long way to Montana. It might take a couple of days."

"All for the best," Enoch said. "I will need some time to collect the Oracle and perhaps another helper."

"Another helper?" She squinted at him. "Who?"

"I will not say at this time in case she declines. Her role would be exceedingly dangerous, so I will make no demands." Enoch pulled his coat together and fastened its buttons. "Let us be off. A dark knight is coming quickly."

"Yes. I already sent a note to Jared saying the same thing. When slayers are near, decisive action is our ally." Irene kissed him on the cheek. "God be with you, good prophet."

4

CHAPTER

PEGASUS DARKENED

Elam walked at the back of the line, Abraham taking the lead, with Dikaios in between, Acacia riding his bare back. The horse's coat shimmered like diamond dust in the moonlight as they trooped along the river's edge against its flow. With the moon now eclipsing, the surrounding forest grew progressively darker, making it impossible to detect any shifting shadows at the tree line.

Acacia kept a blossom of flames in her palm, switching hands when her arm grew weary. From time to time she would kindle the flame into a larger fireball, allowing a quick scan across the sandy beach from the river to the forest. This worked well until the heat became too much for Dikaios, though he merely snorted to indicate discomfort.

Soon, Pegasus blinked out. A blanket of darkness spread across the valley, a heavy, stifling darkness that carried a new wetness. Elam held out his palm but felt no raindrops. Able to see little more than Acacia and her flame, and Dikaios and Abraham at the edge of the glow, he maintained the pace, though his shoes felt heavier every second.

After another minute or so, Abraham stopped and held up his hand. When the others halted, he sniffed the air. "The mists have come. We must make haste. The river will rise very soon."

"The mists?" Elam asked.

"I will explain in a moment." Abraham reached for Acacia's arm. "Please dismount and illuminate the river. I think we have arrived at the crossing point."

As she slid down, Abraham focused on Elam. "Unlike in your world, no rain falls here. Whenever Pegasus eclipses, great mists rise from the fountains of the deep and fill the air. They provide water for the plants."

Elam listened to the river's flow, picking up the sounds of ice chunks colliding, but darkness shielded the water itself. "And how does the river rise?"

While Acacia extended a huge fireball over the rushing noise, Abraham peered into the glow. "In the mountains, there are springs that gush in towering geysers at the time of eclipse, filling enormous reservoirs that feed this river." He set a sandaled foot in the water, cringing for a moment before stepping in with the other. "It takes a few minutes for the rush to reach the waterfall that feeds this valley. That is why nothing grows on the surrounding beach. Each month, the flood strips away everything."

Elam rubbed his shoe along the sand. "*Everything* is right."

Abraham leaned over and peered at the opposite shore, now barely visible in Acacia's light. "Yes, I believe this is Lilith's Shallows. We should cross at once."

Dikaios tromped into the water. "All three of you may ride. I am a strong swimmer."

"There is more to avoid than just high water, my good horse. An ice boulder flowing at this rate could break your bones. I was thinking we would have to find stones or fallen trees to build a bridge of some kind, but our time is short."

Acacia stepped out into the river. "Then I will go first." Raising two handfuls of flames, she shouted, "Increase!" The balls of fire instantly tripled in size. Her eyes shining blue and her white hair blowing in the breeze kicked up by the river, she slowly waved each hand in a circle, making the flames spread out into a ring. Then, as she brought her hands down, she pulled her arms in against her sides until her entire body erupted in an inferno blaze.

With orange tongues shooting skyward, she waded into the river. Clouds of steam boiled all around, enfolding her in white. With fire constantly flashing within, she looked like a thundercloud drifting across the churning expanse.

A cacophony of booming sizzles and pops drowned out the sound of rushing water. Acacia stopped in the middle of the river, faced the current, and spread out her arms. The current bent around her on each side, but most of the water rushed upward in a billowing cloud of steam. "Go!" she yelled, barely audible in the chaos.

63

Elam leaped ahead, crossing the first third of the channel in swiftly flowing shallow water. As he neared Acacia, he tried to see through the cloud, but it was no use. Heat from the steam nearly scalded his skin, and the water that passed between her legs bubbled as it flowed over his shoe tops, radiating intense heat into his toes. Even with all the sizzling, Acacia's labored breaths reached his ears. She was tiring. How long could she hold out?

He took leaping steps the rest of the way. Dikaios followed, then Abraham, who looked like a human jumping bean as he bounced through the boiling water.

As Abraham reached shore, he called out. "Come, dear Oracle. We are all safe."

The cloud that enveloped Acacia turned slowly and drifted toward them. The flames within the mist ebbed. The sizzles ceased. As the steam thinned out, her twisted, blazing face clarified, revealing her agony.

Standing on the shore, Abraham extended a hand. Elam sloshed into the shallows and reached as far as he could. A dozen or so paces remained, but with each of Acacia's labored steps, her surrounding heat shield grew closer, hotter, baking Elam's skin. He couldn't grab her if he wanted to, and she couldn't turn off her flames. Not yet.

Suddenly, a deafening rush sounded from upstream. "The flood!" Abraham cried. He dashed into the water, and, just as an enormous wave crashed over Acacia, he dove for her.

Something yanked Elam's shirt. Flying backward, he could barely see the avalanche of water dousing Acacia's flames as Abraham threw his arms around her. They disappeared in a spray of steam and foam.

Elam splashed backward in waist-deep water, the rushing current pushing him downstream while another force dragged him out of the flow.

64

When he reached safe ground, he jumped up and pivoted. Dikaios stood next to him, panting. "Get on my back! We must make haste!"

Elam leaped on and grabbed his long mane. Dikaios bolted into a frenzied gallop. Only a bare glow from Pegasus, now showing a yellow sliver, gave any hint of the river's presence. The roar of raging water, however, guided his thunderous hoof falls.

The flooding river forced him to veer to the side. Trees raced by on the right, close enough to touch. The reemerging Pegasus painted shadows in the branches that seemed to reach out as they sped past.

Elam strained to see the water. Dikaios had finally matched the river's pace. He let out a wild snort and leaped into a faster gallop. Well ahead on each shoreline, two shadows took shape, rocky promontories that jutted into the river. Whenever they reached that point, with no beach to follow, the chase would be over. Elam tried to focus on the stony barrier. Did it signal a waterfall? The river's exit channel from this land of shadows?

A hand protruded from the river's boiling surface, then another, yet too far in front and moving too fast to allow for rescue. Dikaios snorted again. Obviously he saw them as well.

As they closed the gap, Elam leaned forward, sliding his hands through Dikaios's foaming withers, and shouted into his bent back ear. "We'll never make it! The rocks!"

"I see the rocks! Just hang on!" As the hoofbeats thundered even louder, Elam grabbed two fistfuls of the horse's mane and pressed his body against his muscular neck. The rocky towers loomed, now only seconds away. Pegasus brightened. The hands sank in the watery tumult and disappeared under a swirling rush of icy rocks.

With a loud whinny, Dikaios leaped. His glistening body arced over the churning water, and he splashed forelegs-first into the flood.

Buried to his waist in a wild rush of water and foam, Elam squeezed his eyes half-closed to ward off the icy spray. To his left, a head of white hair popped up, then rolled under the tempest. It surfaced again, this time with blue eyes shining and a wide mouth gasping for breath.

Acacia! Clutching the mane with one hand and clamping the horse's body with his legs, Elam reached toward her, but she disappeared again, buried by foam.

Dikaios lunged with his head, snapping the water with his teeth, but his jaw resurfaced empty.

Once more, Acacia bobbed up. Elam threw himself into the water and grasped for something—a hand, an arm, her dress—anything. His hand touched a wad of strings. He clenched it with his numbed fingers and pulled, swimming furiously for Dikaios who now held Abraham's collar in his teeth as he battled the raging river.

Pulling his limp, wet load, Elam thrashed with his free hand. Finally, he latched on to Dikaios's mane. He looked back at his hand, now clutching a fistful of white hair. He pulled, bringing

65

Acacia's head above water. She gasped for another breath and flailed her arms, but he couldn't risk letting go to catch her hand. He just had to hang on until—

Suddenly, the water gave way underneath. Their bodies followed, three humans and a horse plummeting into darkness. Elam let go of Dikaios and wrapped his arms around Acacia. Two seconds later, they splashed down. Their bodies knifed into a deep pool, water so numbingly cold, it stiffened his body and locked his joints.

The waterfall pushed them farther down. Thousands of tons of water pounded the surface above and created a plunging current. With Acacia now limp in his rigid arms, he fought back, kicking his pain-racked legs into motion.

His lungs ached. With water pressing into every cavity, he pushed back to keep from drowning. How could Acacia possibly survive, now unable to battle the chilling pressure of the life-robbing pool?

The moon's glow rippled on the surface. Only a few body lengths to go. His lungs demanded air. He screamed inside, *Just hang on! We're almost there!*

Kicking with all his might, he caught a current that swept him away from the downward blast. Then, with one final heave, he broke the surface and sucked in air. He dove under and set both hands on Acacia's back, pushing from underneath to raise her head above water. As he kicked for shore, he couldn't tell if she was breathing, but he had to keep going.

Finally, his feet touched bottom. As he trudged toward land, he regripped Acacia, threading his arms around her waist again as he rose up out of the pool. With both bodies soaked and heavy, including Abraham's saturated cloak that had stayed clasped around his shoulders, he had to slide his shoes across the slippery ground, lurching with each frozen leg.

About thirty feet away, Dikaios dragged Abraham to shore, walking backward as he pulled on his collar.

Elam laid Acacia on a bed of gravelly sand and covered her with his body, hoping their combined heat would keep them from freezing to death. Kneeling, he set his ear close to her mouth. No sound, but the roar of tumbling water made it impossible to know for certain.

He laid his head on her chest. Again, no sound. No rise or fall. Not even a shallow breath.

"Dikaios!" Elam had to scream to overcome the roaring waterfall. "Help me!"

The rumble of hoofbeats signaled the horse's approach. "Abraham is breathing," he said, "but I fear he will not be alive for long if he remains exposed to the elements."

Shivering violently, Elam stripped off the wet cloak, slung water from his hair, and looked up at Dikaios. "Find shelter! Leaves! Wood! Dig a hole! Something!"

As Dikaios galloped away, Elam pressed the heels of his hands against Acacia's sternum and pushed several times, simulating the rhythm of a heartbeat. He slid over to her head, pinched her nose, and breathed into her mouth, but his body shook too hard. He could barely force any air into her lungs.

He pushed on her chest again, counting through watery coughs. "Ten ... eleven ... twelve ..."

He lunged back to her mouth and breathed through her cold blue lips, glancing at her chest as he huffed. It rose, but less than an inch. He clenched a fist. It wasn't working! He had to breathe harder! But was he even doing it right?

Pressing on her chest again, he lifted his head. "I need help!" he shouted. "She can't die! She just can't!"

Pegasus stared at him, its pockmarked yellow disk motionless in the purple sky. Hot tears warmed Elam's cheeks. Did God hear?

Was this dimension so different that God might not listen to prayer?

Elam continued his resuscitation efforts, alternately pushing air into her lungs and collapsing them again with a series of hefty shoves. How long could he keep going? Could he ever stop? Just give up and let her die? With more hot tears flowing, he gritted his teeth. Never! He would never give up! She had to live. She just had to.

After what seemed like an eternity, hoofbeats sounded again. Elam swung his head around. Dikaios galloped toward him, a dark man riding tall on his back with only one hand on the horse's mane as they tore across a flat field. His other hand clutched a bag of some kind, but darkness veiled any details.

As soon as they slid to a stop at the river's edge, the man jumped off and pushed Elam's shoulder, knocking him down. "Give space!" he grunted as he dropped his bag and knelt at Acacia's side.

Elam scrambled to his feet and glared at the man's back, but he shivered so hard, he couldn't talk.

"I found him while searching for shelter," Dikaios said. "I will explain more later. Take the blanket from my back and cover Abraham."

Elam touched the man's shoulder and finally managed to spit out, "Breathe ... breathe into her mouth."

The man didn't turn. "I know this."

"Cover Abraham!" Dikaios pushed Elam with his head. "Now!"

Elam jerked the blanket from the horse and jogged toward Abraham, glancing back every second to keep an eye on the stranger. So far, he seemed to be doing nothing, only staring at Acacia.

He laid the rough material over Abraham's trembling body and tucked it in at the sides, pressing down on him with his own body to offer what little heat he could. Thirty feet away, the stranger withdrew something from his bag while Dikaios looked on. A light sparked, but the stranger blocked the source.

Now certain he had helped Abraham all he could, Elam jumped to his feet and hurried back, his legs heavy and his shoes squishing on the hard ground. When he arrived, he touched Dikaios's neck and looked at the shadowy figure looming over Acacia. With careful hands, the man pushed Acacia's cheeks together, puckering her lips, and inserted the end of a flexible reed into her mouth. A flame burned at the other end of the hoselike plant that probably measured a half inch in width and two feet in length. "Hold lips," the man said without turning.

Still shivering, Elam knelt and pressed Acacia's lips around the reed, keeping it in place. The man pushed the reed deeper until it stopped, probably because it had jammed against the back of her throat.

"What will this do?" Elam asked.

The man said nothing. Tipping his head back, he laid something small and round on his tongue, then, leaning toward Acacia again, he opened his mouth wide and pushed the flaming end of the tube inside. Closing his lips around it, he puffed out his cheeks and exhaled. A glow passed through the reed, as if thick radioactive liquid eased downward within the shaft.

Elam shook even harder but managed to keep his fingers around Acacia's lips. What was that stuff? Did this guy who barely croaked a full sentence know what he was doing? He glanced up at Dikaios. Calm, as usual. Not a hint of emotion. Clearly he already realized the obvious. They had to let this man try to save her. What else could they do?

As the stranger pushed the liquid, smoke blew out from his nostrils, dense and black in the light of the moon. Finally, when the glow passed through Acacia's lips, heat radiated into Elam's fingers. It would be only a second or two before the liquid, whatever it was, came out the other end.

Suddenly, Acacia's head jerked. Her arms stiffened. The skin around her mouth grew so hot, Elam's fingers stung, but he kept them in place. He tried to catch any hint of change in the man's expression. Was it time to let go? Was it working? Yet, the man kept a stoic face.

Finally, with a hefty blow, he forced the remaining liquid through the reed and jerked it out of Acacia's mouth. Her skin grew blazing hot. Tiny sparks sizzled across her hair and erupted into tongues of fire.

Elam lurched back and blew on his fingers. The fire in Acacia's hair spread to her face, then across her chest and arms. Yet, her dress and cloak didn't burn, and not a trace of smoke rose from the inch-high flames. Her bosom suddenly arched up. Her eyelids flashed open, and her wondrous blue irises reflected the moon's yellow face. She shivered hard, making the leaflike firelets wink out across her face and clothes.

70

The man slid back and let out a grunt. "Unusual girl."

"Then she's going to be all right?" Elam asked. His trembling began to subside in the warmth of Acacia's blaze.

"If fire normal for strange girl ..." He gave a firm nod.

A stuttering voice broke in. "She's an ... Oracle of Fire ... Greevelow."

Elam looked for the source. Abraham staggered toward them, the blanket draped over his shoulders. "We are ... pleased that you ... could help."

Acacia, tongues of fire still arcing across her hair, pushed against the ground and rose to a sitting position. As she turned to gaze at each face, she blinked. "Is everyone okay?"

Elam took her hand. It was warm and dry. "I think so."

"Your hair is wet," she said. "You'll freeze." As her fingers lit up with a soft white glow, she combed them through his hair. The massage felt heavenly. Warmth surged through his body, loosening his rigid limbs. She lifted her other hand and whispered, "Give me light." A handful of fire erupted in her palm, brightening the area and spreading warmth throughout their huddle.

Greevelow pinched the hem of Acacia's cloak and sniffed it. "Oracle from Enoch?" he asked, turning to Abraham.

"She is." As Abraham crouched close to Greevelow, his shivering eased. "We appreciate your help, especially in light of the conditions of our truce. Although we are far from home, we will gladly follow the river and avoid your master's lands."

Greevelow stared at Abraham. Now illuminated by Acacia's flame, his features clarified. His nose, bulbous and shiny, still emanated twin trails of wispy smoke. Blinking his two enormous black eyes and furrowing his ebony brow, he nodded. "This is wisdom."

"May we stay here until we are warm and dry?" Abraham asked.

Greevelow nodded but said nothing.

"I assume your people saw you leave with the horse. Will they ask questions?"

"Questions? Yes." He pointed at himself. "Answers? No."

Elam searched for a trace of a smile on Greevelow's face, but his lips stayed taut. Every word eked out as if measured with a micrometer, and he seemed even more miserly with his emotions.

Greevelow picked up his bag, rose to his feet, and walked away. Out of the darkness, his voice rode the cold wind. "Keep blanket."

"Do you want a ride home?" Dikaios called.

Only a grunt drifted in on the breeze.

As the roaring flood began to recede, Elam and Abraham plucked armfuls of reeds and piled them on the newly exposed sand. "Better to be close to the noise," Abraham said, "in order to mask our conversation."

Acacia drew her body into a cross-legged position and held out two cabbage-sized balls of fire. With an underhanded toss, she threw them onto the reeds. The flames crawled across the wet fuel,

71

sputtering and smoking, but they soon caught hold and created a modest blaze. Dikaios edged as close as he could, and Elam and Abraham joined him and Acacia to complete a circle around the fire.

"Well," Acacia said. "I didn't even get a chance to thank him."

"All for the best." Abraham stood and laid the blanket on Dikaios's back. "The lowlands people are not accustomed to polite words. They don't consider them necessary."

"I gathered that." Elam rose to his feet and pulled his clothes away from his skin, flapping the material to help it dry. "So what now?"

Abraham pointed toward the waterfall. "I had hoped to cross the mountain ridge bordering the north side of the Valley of Shadows in order to exit into the highlands, a region of hills and mountains we call Noah's Landing. We would have come out just south of Mount Elijah and cut across the alpine territory of my own domain. It seems the river had other ideas and deposited us in Adam's Marsh.

"Still, this shouldn't delay us too much. Ascending the ridge with all the shadow people around would have forced us to wait until dawn, and camping near the river would have been perilous. Now, we can depart whenever we feel warm, dry, and rested."

Dikaios shook a spray of droplets from his mane and pulled the blanket off his back with his teeth. Ambling closer to Acacia, he extended his head and dropped the blanket at her feet. "For the lady."

Elam scooped it up and laid it over her shoulders as he watched the flames' reflections in the horse's eyes. No doubt Dikaios had the same questions. Now that everyone had a chance to settle, it was time to ask them.

Finding a stiff reed half-buried in the sand, Elam scooped it up and poked a glowing ember. "Now that we have a little time, can you tell me what's going on? If I'm a warrior chief, what kind of war am I supposed to help with?"

"A fair question." Abraham draped his cloak over a stick he had pushed into the ground. "I already sang Enoch's prophecy. Was there a part you didn't understand?"

Elam chuckled. "Merlin used to sing poems a lot like that one, and they weren't always easy to interpret. Sometimes he would explain them, and sometimes he wouldn't. But I don't even remember enough of the one you sang to raise a question."

"Quite understandable. Enoch sang it to me at the dawning of every day, so it is embedded in my mind. I will repeat it for you, but without singing. After that frigid swim, I don't think I could hold a note without shaking it to pieces." He cleared his throat and spoke in a low tone.

> The tunnel leads a warrior chief,
> A youth with mystery in his eyes,
> With flames he walks to burn the chaff.
> A child he leads to silence lies.
>
> And once the hearts of gold he trains
> Are drawn to lights of holy depth,
> Then wielding swords they journey where
> Corruption's harvest draws its breath.

73

When he finished, he shifted his cloak a half turn to dry another portion. "It seems that Paili is the girl who will silence lies. How you will do that is a question I should ask you, and what the other phrases mean will likely become clear as time presses forward, but I will first tell you of another prophecy that explains the coming war.

"Our world is unlike yours in many ways, but the pertinent difference is that our Adam ..." He tapped himself on the chest. "... never fell to temptation. And I don't have an Eve, so the possibility of succumbing in that manner did not exist. My people are born in plants that grow in our birthing garden, and they come into the world clutching companions, crystal eggs that float around their heads and always stay quite nearby. You probably saw them with Angel and her two children."

Elam nodded. "I did. Very interesting."

"A companion is a living conscience, a moral guide that cannot be suppressed by the mind or twisted to conform to outside influences. It is incorruptible, and it creates a spiritual attachment with a person's soul."

"So that's why Angel seemed so ... so perfect, I guess you could say. Her companion helps her stay flawless."

"Indeed. And Angel is the finest example you can name. If a woman could possibly live as a saint without need of a companion, Angel would be that woman. Yet, I doubt that she would want to try." Abraham touched his forehead with his fingertip. "You see, when they hover close, they are able to speak to the mind, thereby helping my people escape corruption all their years until ..." He took in a deep breath. As he let it out slowly, he turned the cloak again even though the side toward the fire hadn't had time to dry. Tears sparkled in his eyes. He sat still and watched the flames for several seconds, saying nothing.

Acacia slid her hand into his. "You lost someone close?"

Wiping his eyes with his sleeve, he nodded. "One of our people rebelled. His name is Flint, a young man I had taken on as an apprentice, hoping he would help me as a judge over our growing population. Since he was highly intelligent, he became very knowledgeable, but he bristled at my authority. When he defied me in public, I had to send him away to prevent his attitude from spreading."

"That must have been very painful." Acacia pulled his hand toward her and kissed his knuckles. "And your heart is still broken."

"No doubt." After another moment of silence, Abraham's frown deepened. "Yet far more painful than a broken heart, this rebellion changed our world. Soon after Flint left, the shadow people appeared in the valley, and other humanlike creatures emerged in

74

the marsh and allied themselves with Flint. Not only that, many of the beasts that already existed here became aggressive toward us, when in the past, we could walk with any lion or bear as you would with a faithful dog. Fortunately, with the rebel gone, my people could live without his influence threatening their innocence.

"Still, I don't know how long that will last. Enoch gave me another prophecy that I have shared with only a few, mainly my army's general and the widows of soldiers killed in battle against what we call the altered tribes. Shall I recite that one for you, as well?"

"Yes," Elam said. "Please do."

Acacia nodded. "We would be honored to hear it."

"Very well." Closing his eyes, Abraham lifted his head and spoke with a vibrant voice.

> For what was lost to be reborn,
> Bestow your blood and breath.
> To bring to life a dragon shorn,
> Bequeath your willing death.
>
> The birthing fields will spring anew
> When seeded by the bones;
> Companions dark will flash with light,
> When dragons rise from stones.
>
> A slave girl from another world
> Will call a warrior hence;
> A dragon slain will rise anew
> And come to your defense.
>
> While shadows dress the virgin soil
> Before the moon gives light,
> The girl calls forth the garden's fruit,
> Then day will rule the night.

They carry gems of ruby red,
A dragon's essence stone;
The resurrecting power ignites
When ruby meets the bone.

Beware the dragon from below
Who sings a siren song
And calls an Eve from Eden's twin
To twist the right to wrong.

The liar comes and breaks the seal,
Constructing stairs from Hell;
A war erupts and those corrupt,
Will call her to rebel.

76

Her words will send a dagger forth
And separate the skies;
Then down will come the rain of Earth
In water, death, and lies.

The judge can render just desserts
When criminals stand trial;
He offers death or life in shame,
Forever in exile.

Yet mercy comes, the gavel slips
From Father's righteous hand,
And tears, remorse from broken hearts,
Will make the guilty stand.

And only one can save her life,
A man who lost his scales.
A sacrifice to win his wife,
If love is to prevail.

A bone, a stone, meeting atone,
A dragon born in flame;
A shield to wield, marching to yield,
The dragon sheds his shame.

When he finished, Abraham took in another deep breath and once again turned his cloak, his cheeks dripping tears.

Elam, Acacia, and Dikaios said nothing for several minutes. Elam let the words sink into his mind. Paili was obviously the slave girl who would call for a warrior, but who could the liar be? How could the liar's words start a war?

He poked the fire again with his reed. "Do you have any idea who the liar is?"

"Only that the pronouns in the prophecy indicate a woman, though that might be a poetic device. But even if I knew, I'm not sure how to stop someone who wishes to lie. I could use persuasion, but little else would be effective. And once the lie is uttered, the damage would be done. I would do nothing to stop the ramifications."

"Even if the result would lead to war?" Elam asked.

"Even then. You see, Enoch has since told me that my role is to create an environment in which no one should ever choose to lie. As I said, I can try to influence the potential liar with verbal persuasion, and I'm confident that I would be able to do so, but I would not use force. In fact, I would hope the lie would be spoken publicly. If one of my people still wants to lie, even in the face of full exposure, the guilt would be his and his alone ... or hers, perhaps. That way, no one would be able to question her banishment."

"Banishment?"

Abraham's face reddened, and his voice grew sharper. "I assume you heard the prophecy. Only two punishment options are given—death or exile. A seed of corruption must never take root among my people. I banished the rebel. I will banish any liar. As

77

you say in your world, 'A little leaven leavens the whole lump of dough.'"

"I see." Elam nodded slowly. Maybe it would be best to change the subject. Abraham's emotions seemed as fragile as eggshells. He reached over and patted Dikaios on his neck as he lay on his belly. "So, what happened when you found Greevelow?"

Dikaios bobbed his head. "Since this is a land of grass and marshes, I was unable to locate any trees or leaves. I noticed fire-light, so I galloped toward it and found a village of huts. Two men sat near the fire, and both jumped to their feet when they saw me. I explained our dilemma, but neither man reacted in the slightest. Finally, I asked for someone at least to help us revive Acacia. Greevelow nodded at the other man, pointed at the closest hut, and said, 'Get bag. Not tell Flint.'"

"Flint?" Abraham's eyes lit up. "Are you sure?"

"Quite sure. The other man entered the hut, walking much more slowly than I had hoped, and returned with a third man who handed Greevelow a bag."

"I wonder if Flint saw you," Abraham said.

"They did not introduce me to anyone named Flint." Dikaios blew through his lips and shuddered. "But another man walked by asking questions about me, and the three answered with little more than grunts. If that fourth fellow was Flint, I am glad not to have met him. He had the eyes of a demon."

"Yes … I know." Abraham stroked his chin. "Go on."

"After that man walked out of earshot, I asked Greevelow to ride me. He threw his sitting blanket over my back and mounted me like a seasoned warrior. I returned as quickly as possible, and you know the rest."

Abraham stood and grabbed his cloak from the stick. "Did you notice where Flint … I mean, the demon-eyed man, was when you left?"

Dikaios bobbed his head. "He entered a larger house, one of bricks and mortar. After that, my focus was on finding my way here. The moon is brighter now, but the marshes have few landmarks."

"When you explained our dilemma, did you mention my name?"

"To the first two men, yes. I hoped that they might know you and be more willing to hurry to our aid."

Abraham waved a hand at the fire. "Acacia, can you lower the flames?"

She blew a whisper at their campfire. "Settle." The fire crackled and died to a smoldering mass of embers.

"Are you trying to avoid Flint?" Elam asked.

Abraham glanced from side to side, then leaned toward him, lowering his voice. "It is not his presence I fear. We have no weapons save for the Oracle's flames, but that will do little good against arrows shot from dark marshes."

79

CHAPTER 5

BINDING THE HARNESS

Sapphira, shivering in the bitter cold breeze, crept toward the giant's body. Without a hint of movement as he lay sprawled out on top of the generator roof, his face charred black and his legs sliced through at the ankles, he had to be dead, but she didn't want to take any chances. Too many strange things had happened lately. A mangled giant coming back to life after being electrocuted and having his feet chopped off wouldn't be the strangest.

Pulling her sweatshirt's hood over her head, she looked up and scanned the sky for Gabriel. Since she perched near a dimensional portal, her vision had sharpened, enabling her to see across miles of Montana scenery—snowcapped mountains, highways threading the passes, and houses nestled in the folds. It was all truly beautiful.

After a few seconds, she spotted him. He flew high above, battling the breeze and circling as he searched the area for any sign of the other giants who had helped this dead one create the power grid.

Now that the sky had returned to normal, blue and sun-drenched, the view of Heaven seemed like a dream. Yet it was only days ago that the very roof she stood upon had been the anchor point for a connection between Earth and Heaven, a connection of electricity, fire, and spiritual power that had nearly destroyed Earth and the Bridgelands, the region separating Heaven from the created worlds.

As Gabriel descended, she stooped at a splotch of blood where Karen had fallen. After the little redhead had cut off the giant's feet, ending Mardon's plans to build a new Tower of Babel, she hit the concrete at this spot, gashing her forehead and spilling her precious blood before she died.

Sapphira dabbed the blood and rubbed her finger and thumb together. Still tacky. How strange! It should have dried long ago. Touching her finger to her forehead, she bowed and prayed in a whisper. "Father in Heaven, let this anointing remind me of the great sacrifice your faithful witness made at this altar. I am thankful that she now knows how pleased you are with her as she basks in the warmth of your holy light and luxuriates in the splendor of your loving embrace."

As she rose to her feet, Gabriel landed, flapping his wings to steady himself. Breathing heavily, he touched her forehead, a grin breaking out on his youthful face. "New kind of makeup?"

Sapphira smiled. "Just a symbol. I want to be at least half as brave as she was."

"I know what you mean." He nodded toward the power plant's dam, barely visible over the wall that once supported the roof. Water poured through the spillway, creating a low roar. "I saw a bunch of huge footprints. The giants must have congregated over there, and a trail leads to the highway, but with all the pavement, I couldn't figure out where they went after that. I guess we won't be able to report anything new to Sir Patrick when he gets here."

Sapphira pushed on the dead giant's arm with her foot. "Should we do anything with this one? When they finally decide to reopen the plant, finding him here might give someone a heart attack."

"I don't think so." Gabriel twitched his nose. "Just another monster. The merging with Hades kind of made Earth a big Halloween party. They might be getting used to it."

She looked out over the devastated power plant—its ripped metal roof, partially collapsed cinderblock walls, and scorched machinery. There was no way they could clean up everything, but maybe they could dispose of the Naphil's carcass. At least that would forestall some of the investigation. "We could roll his body off and burn it on the turbine room floor." She snapped her fingers and opened her palm, displaying a grapefruit-sized flame in the middle. "It would be a snap."

"Maybe." Gabriel knelt and wedged his hands under the giant's body. Grunting as he pushed, he looked up at the sky. "We should have asked Thigocia to haul him down there before she left."

"Thigocia?" Sapphira extinguished her flame and joined in, matching his grunts. "Don't you call her 'Mother' or 'Mom'?"

"Not yet. I knew my mother as a human for thirteen years, so it's hard to say 'Mother' to a dragon."

Exhaling heavily, she stood again. "I could try to transport him. We could see where this portal goes now."

"I thought we were going to wait for the Bannisters and Patrick and his knights." Gabriel sat back on his heels. "If we had Sir Barlow here to help us, we could roll this lug off the side and not have to risk a portal jump."

She touched her jeans pocket where she had put Walter's cell phone. "Billy said they'll fly out on their airplane today, but they won't get to the mountain until morning."

"Can you get a quick look through the portal and come back if it isn't safe?"

83

She shrugged. "I don't see why not. I've done it before."

"Then let's go together." He stood and reached out a hand. "Just like in Dragons' Rest."

"I hope not like that." As she rose with his pull, she looked back at the dead giant. "I guess we'll have to straddle him to make sure he comes with us."

Gabriel spread his legs and set a foot on each side of the massive torso. "No problem."

"Easy for you to say." She moved down to the giant's thighs and matched Gabriel's pose. "I'm shorter than you are."

Grinning, he patted her on the head. "Okay, short stuff. Let's light up the skies."

Sapphira lifted her hands and shouted, "Give me light!"

New flames burst from her palms and covered her hands and wrists. She waved her arms around, making the fire swirl until it transformed into a ring of flickering orange. As she lowered her hands, the ring descended in a swirling curtain that surrounded her and Gabriel, like a cocoon spun from an inferno. When it reached below their knees, it spilled out over the giant. The flames crawled along his body and coated him in a fiery blanket.

Heat bathed her skin, raising prickles that made her shiver in spite of the warmth. A few seconds later, the flames thickened and flashed brighter, as if refueled. She furrowed her brow. That was so strange. She hadn't pushed more energy through her hands, and the flames were usually ready to die away by this time, not strengthen. This was supposed to be a glance, not a plunge.

She looked over at Gabriel. Sweat trickled down his cheek. He gave her a "what's going on?" kind of look, but all she could do was shrug. She had already slowed her arms, but the flames just kept growing.

After almost a full minute, the fire thinned out and vanished. They stood on a grassy meadow filled with colorful wildflowers. A warm breeze replaced the bitter wind and bathed their bodies in a fragrant aroma. On one side, the meadow stretched out for miles, grass as green as emeralds decorated with pools of brilliant blue. On the other, a bright blue sky filled their entire view, as though the meadow ended abruptly at a sheer cliff. Yet, it looked solid, like a wall painted to resemble the horizon.

Sapphira narrowed her eyes. Everything seemed brighter, fresher. "I think this is the place we saw from Earth, the place Elam was when Karen cut down the tower."

"You mean this is Heaven?" Gabriel asked.

"I'm not sure." She stepped away from the giant and reached toward the wall. "I think they were standing right in front of this."

"Wait!" Gabriel leaped for her and pulled her back. "Maybe you'd better not do that. Remember all the lightning that shot out from it?"

She stepped away. "I guess you're right."

He walked her back to the giant and prodded its body with his toe. "So should we leave this bad boy here, or what? I don't think Heaven's janitors would appreciate us leaving our trash behind."

She touched the giant's shoulder. Something seemed different. His body now lay curled in a fetal position. Could the transport have repositioned him somehow? "We'd better not. Maybe we could—"

"Sapphira!" Gabriel pointed at the body. "His feet! They're attached! And where did he get the sword and scabbard?"

She jumped to the spot where the giant's legs flattened the grass. His pants had ridden up a few inches exposing his bare ankle. There was no sign of the sword's severing blow. And a scabbard now hung from a belt strapped to his back, the hilt of a sword protruding from the end.

With a long moan, the giant shifted and stretched out his arms.

Sapphira and Gabriel jumped back. The giant turned his head and faced them. Squinting, he rose to a sitting position. "I have

85

dreamed of my beloved Sapphira many times," he said with a yawn, "but this is the most vivid of all."

Sapphira edged closer. She stared at the giant's bearded face, his bright eyes, and his gentle smile. Shivers ran across her body as she whispered, "Yereq?"

Gabriel pulled a dagger from his belt. "Are you sure it's Yereq?"

"Of course I'm sure. Put that knife away." She stooped and ran her fingers through the giant's thick hair. "Wake up, sleepyhead!"

Yereq climbed to his feet and looked down at them from his staggering height. "I'm getting the impression that this isn't a dream."

Gabriel looked up at him, wide-eyed. "I'm starting to hope it is."

"Oh, don't be silly, Gabriel." Sapphira reached up and threw her arms around Yereq's waist. "You're alive! I can't believe you're really alive!"

"My sweet angel!" He picked her up, wrapped his long arms around her, and spun in a circle. "I've dreamed of doing this for centuries!"

Sapphira laughed. The beautiful landscape swirled, a thousand colors stretching out into lovely ribbons of green and blue and yellow and purple. His powerful arms held her fast, arms of love that would never let her go. As he slowed his spin, she closed her eyes and laid her head on his shoulder. "Oh, Yereq! My precious spawn!"

He set her down, keeping her hand in his. Sapphira teetered. The world kept spinning, but she laughed again as her giant kept her from falling. When she finally recovered, she pulled away and set her hands on her hips, cocking her head as she stared up at him. "My, how you've grown!"

"You fed me well, my little gardener." He raised his arm and flexed his bicep. "Worm guts made me big and strong."

Sapphira giggled and spun around to Gabriel. "Isn't he amazing?"

"Uh ... yeah." Gabriel's smile trembled. "That wasn't the word I was thinking, but ... yeah."

"So," she said, looking up at Yereq again, "what happened? How did you get here?"

Yereq shrugged his massive shoulders. "I do not even know where 'here' is, much less how I arrived."

Sapphira reached for Gabriel's hand. "Can you tell him? I'm smiling so much my cheeks hurt."

"Yeah. ... Sure. ... If I can figure it all out myself." Gabriel cleared his throat and took a step closer to the giant, still gawking at him. "I think we're at a place in Heaven, or at least nearby. We saw it from Earth when Mardon tried to lasso Heaven and bring it down, but we messed up Mardon's plans and killed one of the Nephilim. When Sapphira and I were trying to see if we could transport him, you know, to kind of clean up our mess, it was like you took over his body, and we all showed up here." Grinning, he stretched out his wings. "I guess that all sounds too weird to be true, especially coming from a guy who looks like me."

Yereq let out a belly laugh. "After battling demons at the very shore of the Lake of Fire, your story seems tame by comparison."

"The Lake of Fire," Gabriel repeated. "Not exactly the best place for a vacation."

"The worst of all places." Yereq stooped, glancing between Sapphira and Gabriel as he continued. "Just before I blacked out, at least twenty demons confronted me, so close to the lake, the sulfur fumes curled my nostril hairs, and the heat in the sand radiated through my boots."

Sapphira painted the images in her mind as he told his story, a sea of blackness with a dark red sky and skinny naked devils thrusting pitchforks at her beloved giant. "What did you do?"

Yereq waved his arms back and forth. "I swung my sword in every direction. I whacked off a few hands and feet, but they

87

pushed me closer and closer to the lake. The liquid fire lapped against my boots and ignited them."

Sapphira looked down at Yereq's feet. Black scorch marks covered the heels of his boots, and a hole in each one exposed his skin.

"So I just leaped into the demons, kicking and punching and hacking, but when one of them stabbed me in the leg, I fell over and hit my head on something." He rubbed the side of his head, wincing. "I suddenly felt at peace, as if all my battles were over. Soon, I heard the warble of my little songbird, asking me to awake."

Gabriel touched the sheathed dagger at his belt. "Fighting demons is a dream I'd want to wake up from. That's for sure."

"It wasn't a dream," Sapphira said, pointing at Yereq's boots. "We must have pulled him out of that dimension when we transported."

"And left the dead one behind?"

"I suppose so." Sapphira slid her hand into Yereq's. "Back in the mobility room, I saw your body. I listened for your heartbeat. I know you were dead."

"It is true," Yereq said, nodding. "When I died, I was transported to the shores of final judgment. I met Walter there, and we battled a few demons together, but after he left, one of the angels who guarded that realm told me I would soon be going back to Earth. He said something about Earth and Hades combining, so, even though I was dead, I could exist there."

"Well, we're not on Earth right now," Sapphira said, "but we have to go back there and meet some people on a mountaintop."

"Yes, I remember that now."

"You remember?"

"The angel spoke of things I knew so little about, it was difficult to piece it all together." He pushed his hand through his hair and scratched his head, speaking slowly, as if trying to remember the exact words. "He said all the former dragons must be gathered to battle, and to regain their fire and mail, they must go to a mountaintop I would soon visit and be transported to another realm. He also told me that I would become the guardian of the tomb, whatever that means."

Sapphira touched her chin and looked skyward. "Guardian of the tomb ... I have no idea."

"In any case, he said to gather a pocketful of soil from the place of my awakening and keep it until I learn what I must do." Yereq pushed his fingers into the lush turf and peeled back a patch of deeply rooted grass. Then, digging into the soil, he collected a handful and transferred it to his pocket. "I suppose that will be enough."

"More than a pocketful for most people." Gabriel drew closer to Sapphira and the giant. "I guess it's time to do the fiery transport thing again. Maybe we'll find out more when we get to the mountain."

"You bet." Sapphira raised her hands and, locking her gaze on Yereq, shouted, "Give me light!"

89

While Irene disappeared in the inner darkness, Enoch backed away from the motel door. Seconds later, the latch clicked, and the chain slid across its bracket. As he turned to leave, the room's curtain pulled aside slightly, and Bonnie's face appeared in the narrow opening. She smiled and offered a little wave, making a necklace of colorful beads sway across the front of her frilly nightshirt.

Enoch paused and gazed at her lovely blue eyes and beautiful smile, a countenance that allowed a glimpse into what she had proven to be, an even lovelier inner spirit.

He returned her smile, nodded amiably, and hurried into the parking lot. The portal from Heaven's Gate had dropped him off far behind the motel. He had chosen to appear deep in the woods to keep from alerting anyone in the vicinity, so now he would have to march with all speed to get back to the portal in time to meet Sapphira. Since Irene and Bonnie knew what to do, the little white-haired Oracle was next in line to receive her set of instructions for the divine plan.

When he reached the corner of the building, he glanced back at Irene's room. In the parking space directly in front, a man had climbed on top of her rented SUV and appeared to be tying something to the luggage rack.

Enoch hurried back, raising a finger as he ran. "You there! What are you doing?"

The man looked up. His eyes shot open wide. He leaped to the pavement and dashed away in the opposite direction, far too fast for Enoch to chase.

Slowing as he approached the SUV, Enoch looked all around. No sign of the man anywhere. Either he was quicker than a jackrabbit, or he had hidden somewhere close by.

Enoch raised up on tiptoes and examined the luggage rack. Nothing there. He pulled on the passenger door handle. Although the door was locked, the lights inside flashed on, enabling him to scan the seats and floorboards. A Wendy's cup with a protruding straw sat in a cup holder on the driver's side, and pillows and blankets lay strewn around the folded-down area in the back. Other than that, the inside looked safe, no sign of tampering.

The motel door's chain slid again. Enoch hurried to an old car parked a couple of spaces away and ducked behind it, but he allowed himself a peek over its rusted trunk.

Irene bustled out first, leaving the door open. Carrying a travel bag in one hand and the straps of a small black purse in her teeth, she pressed a key fob with her free hand as she quickstepped to the SUV.

Bonnie ran out the door, her eyes darting from side to side. Her blond-streaked locks waved in the cool breeze as she pulled a hefty suitcase along on its wheels. When she let it bump down to the parking level, her backpack entered the street-lamp's glow.

Enoch nodded. Good girl. Obviously she had followed her mother's instructions. Still, if she had wings, she likely wouldn't be out in public without her backpack anyway.

While her mother closed the motel room door, Bonnie opened the SUV's rear access and heaved the suitcase inside. She then slung open the front passenger door and got in, but she paused and touched her chest, a perplexed look wrinkling her face.

"What's wrong?" Irene asked.

Enoch shuffled closer to listen.

Bonnie brushed her hand against the front of her sweatshirt. "It's weird. It feels like spider webs or something, but I can't see anything."

Irene brushed her own hand across the embroidered lion on Bonnie's sweatshirt. "It's nothing. Close the door. We have a long way to go."

"Aren't we going to check out?" Bonnie asked.

"I left the key in the room, and I prepaid."

With a quick tug, Bonnie closed the door. The engine started, and the SUV backed out, then shot away into the night.

Enoch waited behind the car for a moment. Now that he was out of sight, would the man who tried to tamper with their vehicle return? A few seconds of silence passed, then a man emerged from the shadows of a side corridor. He held both hands in front of him as if grasping a fishing pole, though there was nothing in his grip.

Inching as close as he dared, Enoch squinted at him. The man turned his way for a moment, giving Enoch a glimpse of his spectacles and thinning white hair. Something else appeared in the streetlamp's glow, a sparkle of light that floated around the man's head.

91

Enoch rose slowly to his feet and cleared his throat. "Mardon, why are you here, and how did you acquire a companion?"

Mardon froze in place, still holding to his invisible fishing pole. He just stared at Enoch and said nothing, while his companion flashed red and hovered next to his cheek.

Enoch took a step closer. Could Mardon have a weapon? He seemed too frightened to be dangerous. But what might the companion be telling him to do? How could a prisoner of Hades acquire something that only residents of Second Eden were allowed to have?

"Son of Nimrod," Enoch said, raising his voice, "I ask again, what are you doing here?"

Releasing his grip with one hand, Mardon reached into his pocket and withdrew a gun. Holding it shakily, he pointed it at Enoch. "Please ..." His voice matched his trembling hand. "Please come no closer, or I will have to shoot you."

Enoch stepped back and raised his hands. "You have no reason to fear an unarmed old man. I merely saw you on top of that SUV and wondered what you were doing."

The companion flashed red over and over. Mardon scowled at it. "I will not shoot him! He has not been aggressive."

Enoch eased a foot forward and reached out his hand. "Mardon, come with me. I can arrange to have you released from that companion. It will not enslave you ever again."

"Stay where you are!" Mardon hissed. The companion flew up to his nose and strobed at a frenetic rate. Its light flashed in his eyes, making him blink wildly.

"Please, Mardon," Enoch called, taking another step. "Why make things worse than they already are? A tower of pride will not lead you to Heaven. It will only hasten your ultimate destruction."

Mardon gritted his teeth and shouted at the companion. "I don't have to listen to you! I am not your slave!"

A light blinked on inside one of the rooms, and a man looked out the window. He quickly snapped the curtain closed.

Enoch took yet another step. "Is your companion telling you not to explain your presence here? If so, perhaps you *should* tell me to prove you are not enslaved to it."

Mardon re-aimed the gun. "I am no fool to be baited. I will keep my own counsel."

Taking two steps back, Enoch lifted his hands again. "Do what you must, Mardon, but let it be known that you have been fully warned."

The companion flashed brighter than ever. Pointing the gun into the air, Mardon slapped a hand over his ear. "Stop it! You're splitting my brain in half!"

As a siren wailed in the distance, the companion dimmed. Mardon swiveled toward the sound, his eyes widening. "The rope!" He batted at the air for a moment, then, dropping the gun, dove to the ground. After brushing the pavement for a moment with his hands, he grasped something invisible. Breathing a sigh, he rose to his knees and pulled, as if winding a rope into a loop over his shoulder.

As the siren grew louder, Enoch lunged ahead and scooped up the gun. "What are you holding?"

Mardon scowled again. "Can't you see? I'm a madman playing with an imaginary rope." He released the rope with one hand, grabbed the companion out of the air, and stuffed it back into his pocket. "But I suggest that you leave. The authorities are more likely to be sympathetic toward an empty-handed madman like me than toward a Bible-movie reject holding a gun."

Enoch looked down. With sandals on his otherwise bare feet, he didn't quite fit in with the modern crowd, especially in cold weather. When he looked up again, a police car's flashing lights came into view well down the highway. He slid the gun under a

93

car and strode toward the rear of the motel. As he turned the corner, he glanced back. A woman dressed in red appeared in the streetlamp's glow.

He whispered her name. "Semiramis?"

Just as the police car roared into the parking lot, Semiramis raised her arms and threw something down to the pavement. An explosion of sparks and smoke enveloped her and Mardon, and when the breeze cleared the area, they were gone.

Enoch turned and hustled around the building and into the woods. The presence of Semiramis meant trouble and plenty of it. If she had conjured some kind of magic rope, who could tell how she and Mardon might be using it?

He found his portal, a shining aura, shaped like an oval and standing upright. As he stepped into its radiant embrace, he took a deep breath. Maybe Bonnie wasn't as safe as he had thought. It was time to journey to Montana and make sure she entered the mines without interference.

94

W alter shuffled to the precipice and looked over the edge. The face of the cliff below plunged straight down, a sheer drop as far as the eye could see. The cliff on the opposite side, maybe half a mile away, did the same. The two walls seemed to join at the bottom of the deep chasm, an illusion created by a glimpse at apparently infinite lines.

The view seemed to waver, then swing back and forth. He pressed the toes of his shoes against the ground to keep his balance. The chasm was so deep ... so amazingly deep. Something drew his attention, movement so far down it was almost imperceptible. He leaned over, reaching. Something drew him closer, something—

A strong hand yanked on his shirt. "Walter!"

He stumbled backward but kept his balance. With a quick spin he found the source of the pull. "Ashley?"

"It looked like you were about to fall in," she said. "Something must have been messing with your mind."

A sudden surge of wetness covered his body—cold sweat. He swiped his sleeve across his forehead. "Yeah. It was weird. Thanks."

Ashley tugged on a rope tied at the top of an upright metal pole anchored at the edge of the chasm. "Seems strong."

Walter pulled a rope hanging parallel to Ashley's. The two lines ran across the long gap, making up the top supports of a suspension bridge that spanned the chasm.

He knelt and pressed his hand on the first of hundreds of narrow planks that tied a lower pair of parallel ropes together. It moved downward an inch or so but held fast. Reaching out farther, he pushed down on the second plank. A crack in the center broke open. The heel of his hand punched through, but he jerked back before he lost his balance.

Straightening his body, he looked up at Ashley. "Not a good idea."

They looked out over the chasm. A strong wind beat against the bridge, whipping the lowest part of the arc into a galloping swing.

"Definitely not a good idea." She crossed her arms over her chest. "But what do we do about Glewlwyd's warning? We can't ignore it."

Walter rose to his feet and looked up at the pale blue sky. Thigocia soared high above. She seemed to be about a third of the way across the chasm, yet flying toward them and descending rather than attempting to cross as she had said she would. Abigail rode high on Thigocia's neck, her body straight and her shoulders back. She seemed to be having the time of her life.

He scanned the edges of the precipice in each direction. To the left, the elevation rose to three times his height. Pointed towers of stone blocked his view of what lay beyond. To the right, the

95

ground ascended even higher with massive boulders strewn around in haphazard fashion.

As Thigocia's winged shadow passed over their bodies, Walter spied something at the edge of a boulder, something red. He hissed at Ashley. "Someone's here."

Ashley pivoted toward his line of sight. "Are you sure?" she whispered. "I didn't sense any thoughts but yours."

He took several steps to his right, hoping to improve his angle. The red figure appeared again but quickly jerked out of sight.

"Who's there?" Walter shouted.

A trembling feminine voice called out. "It is I, Semiramis."

"Why are you stalking us?"

A pretty young woman, maybe twenty years old, peeked out from the side of the boulder. She pulled back a red hood, allowing silky brown tresses to fall over her shoulders. "I am not stalking. I want to speak to you, but I fear the approaching dragon."

Walter looked up. Thigocia seemed to be making a final sweep across the chasm as she closed in. "The dragon won't hurt you," he said. "She's a friend of ours."

Lowering her head as if dodging raindrops, Semiramis scooted toward them. Her cloak's red cape swept the air behind her, revealing a matching velvet dress that draped her legs almost to her bare feet. When she came within a few paces, she stopped and laid a palm on her chest. With sleeves covering most of her narrow hand, she patted herself as though she were calming her heart. "I was so frightened. I have heard of dragons, but I have never seen one in these lands."

Walter squinted at her. "Do you live here?"

A smile spread across her lovely face, allowing shallow dimples to form in her cheeks. "Oh, yes. This is my home. I am the guardian of Zeno's Chasm."

Ashley set a hand on her hip. Walter didn't have to read her mind to interpret her skeptical posture. Since she couldn't pierce this lady's thoughts, she probably concluded that Semiramis meant trouble.

"Guard the chasm?" Walter asked. "Are you afraid someone will steal it?"

Semiramis's lips curled upward. "I perceive a jest, my lord, for no one could ever steal such a chasm. I am here to ensure that no one tries to navigate the bridge. It is far too dangerous."

"I can believe that." Ashley moved her arms back over her chest. "Why don't you just cut the ropes and be done with it?"

"I have tried to destroy the bridge in many ways, but no blade is sharp enough to slice those ropes, no hands are strong enough to uproot the support poles, and no pick is hard enough to break the bedrock that holds them in place. All I can do is warn travelers not to cross. Many have ignored my call and have fallen into the chasm."

"What's at the bottom?" Walter asked.

Her head tipped downward, and her voice lowered to a whisper. "Lucifer's Lair."

Ashley scrunched her eyebrows. "Lucifer? As in the devil?"

"No, my lady. We in the Bridgelands have named the land below Lucifer's Lair, because it is governed by a cruel king who wantonly murders all who oppose him. If you were to fall into the chasm, you would transport into his kingdom. His loyal subjects would enslave you, and any covert rebels would never trust you. There would be no place for you to hide."

A rush of wind beat down from above, throwing Semiramis off balance. Walter caught her by the hand and pulled her upright. "It's just the dragon's wings," he said. "Nothing to worry about."

Seconds later, Thigocia landed in a galloping slide on a nearby patch of grass, her ears twitching as she came to a stop.

"Thank you, my lord." Semiramis eased away from Walter's grasp. "I am not worthy to be rescued by you. It is I who must serve you."

Walter's fingers tingled. Her touch had sent a mild electrostatic charge of some kind into his body.

Abigail dismounted. As she and Thigocia approached, Walter reached for Semiramis again. "Don't be scared. Her name is Thigocia."

She dodged his touch and bowed. "Greetings, great dragon. I am Semiramis, guardian of this chasm. I trust that you have come with good news about an alternative crossing."

"I tried to fly to the other side," Thigocia said, "but after I reached the halfway point, I seemed unable to get any closer. I detected no headwinds, so the mystery remains. I decided to search for another route, but the chasm remained deep as far as I could see."

Semiramis touched her chin with her finger. "How strange!" she said, her lips pursing into a comely pucker. "I know of an easy passage, and I hoped to lead you there."

Ashley rolled her eyes but said nothing. Again, Walter knew that look. She didn't trust Semiramis, not in the least.

"My human friends have been charged by Glewlwyd to use the bridge," Thigocia said. "I assume that I must find another way."

Semiramis nodded slowly. "Glewlwyd is wise, to be sure, but have you asked yourself why he stays on this side of the chasm? He fears the bridge, and he distrusts me. Such lack of faith will keep him here forever."

"Elam crossed," Ashley said with a huff. "We saw him through a portal. He was at Heaven's Altar."

"Ah! The son of Shem! I remember him well, for he is the only one ever to cross successfully. I heard later from Glewlwyd that he had eaten from the tree of life, thus protecting him from death. If you have also eaten the fruit, then by all means use the bridge." She covered a gentle laugh with her fingers. "I should have known that those in the company of a dragon would be unusually gifted. Forgive me for not recognizing you as ageless ones."

Ashley clutched her stomach and pulled Walter's sleeve. As he drew close she whispered, "I sense something."

He replied in a low tone. "Are you sick?"

"No. Just an excuse to talk to you privately."

"Do you sense something dangerous?" Walter kept an eye on Semiramis. With her head tilted to one side, she seemed perplexed but not annoyed.

"Other minds ... getting closer. One thinks clearly. The others are dense and stupid."

"Any idea who they are?"

"I see images. The intelligent one is thinking about Mardon."

"The Nephilim?"

She nodded. "We'd better cross right away. I don't want them around while we're on the bridge."

"Good thinking." He looked again at Semiramis. "Shouldn't we warn her about the Nephilim?"

"No. Just trust me."

As Walter stepped back, he nodded at Semiramis. "We have to get going. I think something in the air is bothering Ashley." He added in his mind, *Thoughts of stupid giants are in the air.*

Abigail untwisted a cap on a water bottle and handed it to Ashley. "Are you sure you're well enough to cross?"

Ashley took a sip and extended the bottle. As Abigail grasped it, Ashley drew it back, forcing Abigail to step closer. "Play along," she said, barely moving her lips.

Abigail took the bottle and hustled back to Thigocia, obviously whispering something to her as she put the bottle in the backpack tied to one of her spines.

Ashley pulled Walter. She staggered slightly as she approached the bridge. "Gotta go," Walter said. "Nice chatting with you."

"Travelers!" Semiramis called, raising a hand. "Please hear me. The bridge is fraught with danger. Even youthful, vigorous Elam crossed with extraordinary effort. In this young lady's condition,

LAST OF THE NEPHILIM

you will never make it. Please, just stay with me a little while until she has recovered."

"Thanks all the same." Walter steadied Ashley at the edge of the chasm, then let go and stepped onto the first plank. Grasping the side ropes, he shifted his weight forward. He kept his focus on the opposite side, trying not to think of the miles of empty space below, and stretched his leg over the broken plank. He shouted to compete with the cross breeze. "If it'll hold me, it'll hold you two, so just watch where I step."

"And the dragon?" Semiramis asked, raising her voice as well. "How will she cross?"

Walter glanced back, twisting while holding tightly. He had no clue how to answer.

Thigocia stretched out her wings. "I will fly in an orbit over their heads. At the very least, I can protect them along the way. If they can make it, perhaps I can."

"Very well." Semiramis bowed her head. "Good journey to you. I will climb one of the higher ridges to watch and pray for your progress." With a wide twirl of her cape, she turned and strode away. Within seconds she disappeared behind the boulder.

Standing on the first plank, Ashley touched Walter's back. "Better hurry. They're getting closer, and the smart one wants to kill."

CHAPTER

A Voice Within

Angel unfastened Paili's belt, then leaped from her seat and landed in the grassy meadow with a soft thump. Candle and Listener clambered down Grackle's outstretched neck and hustled to her side, Candle holding up the bag of bones with both hands. "Shall I take these to Father Abraham's hut or keep them for our mantle?"

Angel touched the bag but paused. It would be wonderful to keep just one bone, maybe a little finger as a way to remember Timothy. Would it be so bad to put everything else in the garden and save one—

A flash of light caught her eye. Her companion floated around to the front of her face, a red flash strobing in its egg-shaped crystal. The eyes blinked at her, and its words melded with her thoughts. *Did the Oracle give you permission to keep a bone?*

Angel shook her head. *But she did not say I was not allowed to keep one.*

If you really believe she did not intend for every bone to be included in her command ... The companion's light dimmed. *Then so be it.*

Nudging the companion with her finger, Angel spoke out loud. "Your message is clear, but must the scattering in the garden be carried out during night watch hours?"

"Mother?" Candle held up the bag again. "The bones?"

She waited a moment to see if the companion would reply, but it hovered quietly for a second, then floated down and sat on her shoulder. Finally, she nodded at Candle. "Leave the bag with me. Make sure Paili gets down safely, and take care of the dragons."

While Listener crawled under Grackle's belly to unfasten the seat harness, Candle helped Paili climb down Albatross's neck. "Did you enjoy your ride?" he asked.

Paili, wearing a long-sleeved white dress and thick leggings, rubbed her arms. "I lost my cloak, but it was fun."

Angel picked up the bag and peered down a wide path through the forest that opened into the moonlit village. A young woman walked around one of the huts, stopping for a moment to look at the dragon landing area where Angel stood. She waved and then continued her stroll, followed soon thereafter by a young man.

Smiling, Angel shook her head. Emerald would never accept this suitor. She was very selective, and he was far too young. Yet, could a widow afford to be so picky? Most thought not, but Angel knew better. Emerald's good Adam fell in battle shortly after her own did, and now she and Emerald remained the only two widows in Abraham's flock who had not taken a new Adam. Was it wrong to believe that no man could live up to the memories of their departed loves? Probably not. Such thinking didn't cause her to doubt the goodness of any man. It was just that none could ever be as good as Dragon. He was the best of the best.

"Acacia told us to spread the bones over the birthing garden," Paili said.

102

Angel shook herself out of her trance and looked down at Paili. Her furrowed little brow meant business. "Thank you for the reminder, fair visitor. I was lost in my thoughts."

"That's okay." Paili turned toward the village and narrowed her eyes. "I'm supposed to say something after the bones are spread out, but now that Acacia isn't here, I'm not sure what to do. Maybe I should wait for her."

"The Prophet, that is, Father Abraham, taught us that delayed obedience is disobedience. If you know what you are to say, then I see no reason to wait." Angel tightened her grip on the bag of bones and took Paili's hand. "Come with me."

Paili stroked Angel's smallest finger. "That's a pretty ring. What kind of gem is it?"

"This?" Angel lifted her hand and pulled off the ring. "I call it a changing stone." She held it close to Paili's eyes. "See? It's red now. It was white before." She put it in Paili's hand. "You may borrow it, but please take good care of it. I would like it back."

103

Paili slid it over her index finger. The second it passed her knuckle, the gem turned white again. "Where did you get it?"

"I was born with it on my thumb. No one knows why." She took Paili's hand again. "Let's go." As they hurried toward the village, Angel called behind her. "Candle! Listener! Finish caring for the dragons and meet me in the garden."

After reaching the village, Angel and Paili strode quietly down the deserted street, a stone path wide enough for five people walking side by side. Illuminated by lanterns hanging from poles at twenty-foot intervals, there was no concern about stumbling over one of the potted plants that lined the street.

Angel glanced at the modest huts on each side, some built with stones, others with clay bricks. Although this wasn't her village, many of these homes were familiar, places her parents visited many times when she was Paili's age. Even as a young adult of one hundred thirty-three, she still called on her childhood friends occasionally.

But now wasn't a good time for socializing. She had to hurry through the streets unseen and—

"Angel?"

She halted and spun around. "Emerald?"

A slender form emerged from the shadows, tiptoeing into the lantern's light, her green eyes shining. "Cliffside is arranging a betrothal meeting with my father."

"Oh?" Angel said. "Is that good news or bad news?"

"Bad news." Emerald glanced behind her, then lowered her voice. "I do not know what to tell Cliffside."

Angel looked down at Paili and pointed at a lantern a few paces away. "Please wait under the light."

Taking Emerald's arm, Angel led her into the shadows near the edge of the street, whispering. "What's so difficult? Just tell him you don't wish to be betrothed to him. Or let your father tell him."

"I prefer to avoid hurting his feelings. Maybe I could tell him I will choose permanent servitude status. That is allowed for widows who pass the allotted time."

Angel searched for Emerald's companion but couldn't find it. It must have nested in her hair. "I had no idea that you had servitude in mind. That's a noble choice."

"But servitude is not my choice. I want to be married, just not to Cliffside."

Angel set a hand on her forehead. "Emerald, you're confusing me. It sounds as if you want to speak words to Cliffside that aren't in your heart."

"I know!" Even in the shadows, her eyes seemed to glitter as they widened. "Something happened today that has never happened to me before, but I have been fearful of telling anyone."

"You have no need to fear me. I have no authority over you, and we've been friends for many years."

Emerald glanced left and right before focusing on Angel again. She leaned close, whispering so softly, Angel could barely hear. "I met a talking dragon today in the field beyond the birthing garden. It was so strange. He seemed more shadow than solid, as if he had no substance."

"Like a spirit?" Angel asked. "As in the stories the Prophet has told at campfire?"

"Yes, and he asked me why I seemed downcast. I had heard the Prophet's stories about talking dragons being wise and good, so I told this dragon of my dilemma. He suggested that I avoid hurting Cliffside's feelings by telling him a lie. He called it a white lie, whatever that means."

Angel tried to repeat the word "lie," but her lips tightened. She couldn't bear to say it. Although the word itself had passed into her ears before, it came only during worship lessons, in tales about other worlds and the dangers of forbidden speech. She never dreamed that any of her people would consider uttering a real lie.

"Emerald," she replied slowly, "I hope you haven't taken this notion seriously. Speaking words that aren't in your heart is wrong. Not only that, it would get you banished ... or worse."

Pulling in her bottom lip, Emerald glanced around again before continuing. "The dragon said if no one knows of the lie, then banishment would never come. Wouldn't it be better to speak kind words that are not in my heart, words that would not injure Cliffside's feelings?"

Angel shook her head hard. "Feelings are not as important as truth. If you dare to bring such shame on our people, I will reveal your plan to the Prophet myself."

Emerald's face drooped into a pitiful frown. "I believed you to be my friend. Your harshness makes me think otherwise."

"I *am* your friend. That's why I give you harsh words. They will keep you out of danger." Angel stood on tiptoes and scanned the village. Not a soul stirred except for Paili, still waiting patiently near the lantern. Angel raised a finger close to Emerald's face. "Do not listen to that dragon again. Whoever he is, if he is tempting our people to lie, he doesn't have goodness dwelling within."

Emerald nodded. "I will think about it."

"Think about it?" Angel turned Emerald to the side. "Where is your companion?"

Emerald backed away, a hand over her pocket. "It is …"

"In your pocket?" Angel grabbed Emerald's wrist and pulled. The ovular crystal leaped out of the pocket and zipped in front of Emerald's eyes, flashing wildly.

With every flash, Emerald's head drooped an inch until her chin nearly touched her chest. "You're right. I'm ashamed that I would consider such a foolish idea."

As if sighing, the companion's light slowly faded. It floated to her ear and buried itself in her hair.

"I apologize," Emerald said, her gaze lifting toward Angel. "I have set my standards for a man so high, while I, myself, am so low. I am such a foolish child, I actually dreamed I could be—" She pressed a hand over her mouth.

"Could be what?"

Emerald let her fingers slowly fall away from her lips. "The Prophet's Eve."

Angel whispered sharply. "Father Abraham's Eve?"

With a slight nod in return, Emerald shuffled back. "I have said enough foolish things. I will go now."

Angel watched Emerald's companion push out of her hair and rub against her ear. What might it be saying? A word of comfort? That such thoughts weren't so foolish?

A familiar tickle in her own ear raised goose bumps. Angel's companion was ready to speak to her mind. *Verbal compassion for Emerald would be appropriate, Angel, for ideas such as hers have also entered your thoughts.*

Very true, Angel replied. *What woman would not want to be Father Abraham's Eve? He is the wisest of us all. Yet, aren't such thoughts foolish? He has told the elders that he can never take an Eve.*

Her companion floated up to her eye level. *Were those really his words?*

In a manner of speaking. He quoted a prophecy about burning in flames before he could take an Eve. We all interpreted that as "never."

Quite reasonable. As her companion floated back toward her ear, its whispered voice faded. *Still, foolish or not, compassion is in order.*

Very well. Angel touched Emerald's arm. "Don't think yourself foolish, my friend, when you yearn for a wise Adam. The Father of Lights is pleased when we desire wisdom to surround us."

Emerald allowed a trembling smile to break through. "Thank you."

"When I go to the garden, I will tell Cliffside of your dilemma. His feelings could still be injured, but your temptations will be eased."

Before Emerald could answer, Angel hurried away and reached for Paili's hand. "Come. We must go with all haste."

The two ran into the village center, dashed around a low circular berm that enclosed a plot of grass, a small courtyard with a bell on a pole standing in the middle, and headed down the street on the opposite side. One man standing near a door to a hut gave them a curious glance but remained silent.

When they reached the end of the street, Angel and Paili slowed their pace and quick-marched through the forest that marked the boundary between the village and the birthing garden. As soon as they approached the clearing, a man stepped in front of them, tall and broad-shouldered. With a thin mustache and beard dressing his stern expression, Cliffside looked more vicious than he really was. "Greetings. What brings you to the garden at this hour?"

Out of breath, Angel lifted the bag of bones and stepped into the moon's glow. "I am on a mission. I have to—"

107

"Ah!" His face brightened. "Angel of Peace Village. Your children have already entered."

"Yes, Cliffside. I have been sent by the Oracle of Fire herself to deliver this to the garden."

"By all means." He squinted at the bag. "May I ask what this is?"

She tried to offer a smile, but it felt weak on her lips. "You may ask, but I will not answer. I have not been given leave to reveal the mysteries of the Oracle. Perhaps when she arrives, she will explain it to us all."

Cliffside stepped away from the path. "Very well. I will be patient."

Just as she lifted her foot to continue, Angel stopped and reached for his hand. "You are a patient man, dear Cliffside, but I have something to tell you that will test your patience further."

His brow furrowed, but he smiled and nodded amiably. "Speak, Angel. I fear no words from the lips of a friend."

As she rubbed her thumb along his knuckles, she tried to strengthen her own smile, but her lips wouldn't obey. "Emerald is so concerned about injuring your heart, she cannot bear to tell you that she doesn't want to be betrothed to you. I volunteered to tell you in her stead."

His smile withered, but after a second or two it perked up again. "If she cares so much for my heart, then her love for me is real. It is merely dormant and needs to be awakened."

Angel gazed into his hopeful eyes. How could she argue with him? She had neither the will nor the time to engage in a debate. And now Emerald's desire not to hurt this fine man's heart became as real as the charred bones weighing down her bag and the sacred duty that awaited her. "I will make an effort to speak to Emerald again and relay your thoughts. For now, I must do the Oracle's bidding."

"I thank you for your kindness," Cliffside said, waving her on.

Angel studied him again. The innocence of pure virtue glowed from within, honest, trustworthy, serene. Emerald truly needed to rethink her doubts.

She touched his arm. "When you patrol the garden, you will see what we have done, but you must not disturb our work. I have the Prophet's orders."

He bowed. "Your word is as good as his, my lady."

"Come, Paili." Angel took her hand and marched across the grassy field, the wide expanse between the narrow forest and the garden. With Pegasus still high, a yellowish glow illuminated the rows of plants only a dozen or so paces away. Now that they were out of the forest, the cold breeze blew unhindered from the western border of the field where Hilidan and Zera, two massive fir trees, stood guard as gate standards for a head-high wall. The leaf pairs in the garden, enclosing precious fruit in their praying hands, waved slowly back and forth as if greeting the visitors with silent blessings.

Following a path between garden rows, two small figures ran toward Angel and Paili. "Mother!" Candle called. "What caused your delay?"

"Matters of the heart, but all is well." When they gathered at the edge of the garden, she set the bag on the path next to Candle and stooped in front of Paili. "Is there any instruction as to how the bones should be spread?"

Paili nodded. "Enoch has given me many words for this world, and most are in song." She closed her eyes for a moment, then looked up at the moon, humming softly before singing a lilting melody.

> Scatter them near, scatter them far,
> Scatter them to the wind.
> Better to trust, better to hope,
> Better than plans of men.

109

After opening her eyes again, she pointed at the bag. "I think we just throw them into the garden."

"But what of the plants?" Angel asked. "A miscast femur could damage them."

Listener touched Angel's hip. "Mother, Paili's words are from Enoch. If he says to scatter them and trust, then all will be well."

"A sentiment of true faith," Angel said as she lovingly caressed Listener's cheek. "Do I have a second companion now? One who walks like a little girl yet speaks as a sage?" She unraveled the bag's strap and spread out the skin, then scooped up two handfuls of smaller bones and faced the garden.

As she looked out over the swaying plants, she imagined the little baby each one held in its grasp. Maybe some already clutched a companion and were being taught the laws of the Father of Lights, preparing them for birth in a climate of cold, now enhanced by the bitter winds of rebellion in both man and beast.

The thought of new companions brought back the image of Dragon's once dormant companion as it rose to claim Timothy as its new charge. She smiled at the mental picture, yet sighed at the irony. Now she would cast his remains into the garden that brought soul and conscience together, a man stripped of flesh joining with the dust of the earth that the Great Father used to fashion his body.

"Dear Timothy," she said, her voice quavering, "in the name of the Father above, and in obedience to his command, I scatter your bones to the soil of new birth."

With a great heave, she threw the bones as far as she could. As they flew, the moon shone on them, bathing their white shapes in a yellow glow. A fresh breeze collided with the bundle and sent the smaller bones flying in every direction. When they disappeared on the surface, she reached for one of the larger bones in the bag. "Come children. This is a sad chore, but a necessary one."

As Candle and Listener gathered bones, Paili sang again, this time in a mournful tone.

Forsake me not, O God of love,
And ne'er forget my tomb.
I lie and wait in cold, dark earth,
A melancholy womb.

After a few minutes, the job was done, except for one final bone. Paili lifted it, a femur, scorched and cracked. Reaching back, she heaved it into the air. It swung around three times and fell to the ground with a dull thud.

As the wind played a soft whistle, Listener took Candle's hand. He reached for Paili's, linking the three children as they looked up at Angel. "What now?" Candle asked.

Angel joined in and formed a circle. "We obeyed the Oracle, so our task is complete." She looked up at the sky, then shifted her gaze to the distant hills, rolling contours on the dark horizon that signaled higher terrain far beyond. Even with the aid of a son of Pegasus, how could Father Abraham and the others possibly arrive before dawn? And if they had to scale the northern boundary of the Shadowlands, who could tell how long their journey might take? Was the Oracle's presence necessary for this scattering of the bones to have an effect? Did this rite they performed have something to do with the warrior chief and Father Abraham's desire to rid the world of the altered tribes?

She jerked up the empty skin, grasped Candle's shoulder, and looked him in the eye. "Fly Grackle to our village," she said. "Take Listener and Paili with you. Give them each a bowl of warm soup and put them both in Listener's bed."

His shoulders drooped. "Yes, Mother. As you wish."

She set a finger under his chin and lifted his head. Smiling, she added, "After I speak with Emerald, I will come home, and

111

you and I will fly Grackle together until we find Father Abraham
and the others."

Candle leaped into the air and let out a whoop. He rounded
up the girls, and the three hurried toward the dragons' launching
field.

As they faded into the darkness, Angel turned her gaze back
to the sky. Pegasus had passed its zenith. In about two hours it
would set, and without a second moon they would have to search
over a land of shadows, the desolate highlands, and maybe even
the forbidden marshes in complete darkness. She shivered and
rubbed her arms. And every minute of that search would take
place in the bitter cold of the approaching season of death.

B illy sat back in *Merlin III*'s copilot seat and opened one of
Professor Hamilton's notebooks, a light brown one with
"Notes for William" in block letters on the first page. With the airplane's headset on, and the volume control turned just loud
enough to hear background static, the propeller's buzz barely
seeped into his ears.

He glanced at the passengers behind him. Shiloh, sitting in the
first row's aisle seat, leaned against her father's shoulder, asleep. Sir
Patrick's head lay propped against the window, his mouth open as
he slept. On the other side of the aisle, Sir Barlow stared out the
window, wide-eyed. He had already made a thousand comments
about the scenery below, but now he just gazed quietly, apparently
mesmerized.

Billy settled back again. With Dad at the controls, hundreds
of miles to go before they reached Montana, and everyone else
occupied, now would be a good time to read this notebook.
Although the inscription on the title page had piqued his interest,
the thought of actually turning the page sent chills up his spine.

Reading Prof's words would be like listening to a ghost, as if
the professor himself would lay a hand on his shoulder in the same

gentle way he always did and once again provide the kind of wisdom he had dispensed so many times before. An emotional catharsis would be sure to follow, a crippling state he wanted to avoid in order to keep his wits about him. Still, with a few uninterrupted flight hours ahead, maybe he could recover in time for the adventure that lay in store.

He turned to the first page of notes and read the lovely script.

William, I plan to use this notebook as a collection of all my journal entries that concern you in particular. I will transfer them from my other journals along with enough context to allow for comprehension. My hope is to give this to you when our adventures together come to a satisfactory conclusion. If, however, I suffer an untimely demise, I have already included instructions in my will that bequeaths all my journals to you, save a similar collection that I am making for my daughter, Elizabeth.

I trust that these notes will help you understand more about the history behind my search for you as well as the deep, abiding love that developed as a result of our friendship and the many adventures we had together. I will never forget the day I handed you Excalibur on the floor of a collapsing underground laboratory and asked, "What now is your weapon?" I am sure that you will never forget your reply.

"Truth," Billy whispered. "Truth is my sword."

And when I asked, "What now is your defense?" your answer sang in my ears as the loveliest melody ever to play in heaven's choir.

"Faith." Billy swallowed down a hard lump. "Faith is my shield."

And now, William, as a child of the King of kings, I trust that you understand how our fellowship will never end. Even if we part at the end of our journey, we will meet again at heaven's gate, and we will rejoice together in the light of our savior, Jesus Christ. May the Lord bless you with wisdom as you turn the page and relive these adventures.

Billy took a deep breath. Tears were already welling. As he wiped them away with his knuckle, his father glanced over at him but said nothing. He just nodded and shifted his eyes back to the front.

After turning the page, Billy began reading about Professor Hamilton's meeting with the Circle of Knights when they commissioned him to search for Arthur's heir in West Virginia. Page after page flew by, each one generating new tears as they retold tales of sword battling, crossbow shooting, and dragon riding. Although each tale was familiar, the professor made them come alive once again and create fresh images in Billy's mind, this time from the scholarly bard's point of view rather than his own.

In addition to the lively accounts, the professor had also provided illustrations of many new discoveries along the way—a pencil sketch of Clefspeare along with detailed anatomical notes, a map of the Circles of Seven based on Billy's description, and two photographs of Excalibur taped to a page showing each side of the great sword. Next to the photo, the professor's careful lettering described many of Excalibur's features, including the two fighting dragons etched into the blade. In giving details about the hilt, he noted a peculiar concern.

114

According to every ancient description I was able to find, the hilt's ornate wood contained three embedded gems, two of which were clear crystal, perhaps diamonds, and one red gem, usually described as a ruby. Yet now after my experiences with dragons, and since Morgan gave Excalibur to King Arthur hoping it would be used to slay dragons, I wonder if the red gem might have been a rubellite. All three gems exist in my replica, two clear and one red, as expected, though all three are glass. As the photographs clearly show, there are two gems on one side of the hilt and an empty depression on the other, yet no third gem. Is the red gem missing? Perhaps it fell out in battle long ago, or even in one of William's recent battles. It seems impossible to know.

Billy read the date the professor had written next to the photos. Apparently he had taken them shortly after their Circles of

Seven adventures, probably the night they roasted marshmallows at the campfire.

Flipping the page, he continued with the fascinating entries. One in particular caught his eye, a poem centered on the page, set in the familiar quatrains that Merlin always used, along with a similar rhyme and meter scheme. It was as if the professor wanted to mimic his prophetic ancestor.

The virgin bride arose to fly
And found the faith to soar;
The child of doubt has cast aside
His fears forevermore.

And now the two are prophesied
To join their hands as one,
To stand at holy altars high
And kneel before the Son.

A vow, a pledge, a promise made
That never has an end,
When words of love bind knight and maid
To make forever friends.

A witness there I long to be,
The one who sings the rites,
Who blesses two to make them one
And spiritually unites.

And when the virgin lifts her veil
To give her knight the seal,
Let angels sing; let demons wail;
Let all the holy kneel.

And then forever will I rest,
My labors at an end,
And seeing all my efforts blessed,
To God will I ascend.

Billy bit his lip hard. The poem was too sad for words. Obviously Prof wanted to be there to see him marry Bonnie, even preside over the wedding, but he died too soon. To write with such vision and passion, the professor's hope had to be consuming, maybe even an obsession. His years of searching for Arthur's heir would come to its conclusion through the fulfillment of the ancient wedding prophecy, and now he wouldn't be there to see it.

Sighing deeply, Billy read on. When he flipped toward the back to read the most recent entries, the handwriting changed, darkening somewhat and becoming less readable.

William, I am addressing you directly from this point on. This is a new entry, not one copied from another journal. As you know, I have long been interested in genealogies, so I traced yours quite some time ago when I began researching your past. Although the fact that your father's ancestry was a dead end, so to speak, because of his dragon heritage, I was unable to account for a similar obstacle in your mother's line. It seems that her father, a certain Marshall Peters, arrived in the States from England just a few years before she was born. Yet, when I searched for his records in my own country, I was unable to locate anything that would lead me to his ancestry. When we next talk, I should like to ask you more about your grandfather. If he is still living, perhaps I can find the opportunity to converse with him myself.

Billy turned the page. The remaining three or four were blank. He pulled off his headset and turned to his father, holding up the journal. "Prof mentioned Mom's father."

"Marshall?" His father slid his own headset down and draped it over his shoulders. "What did he say about him?"

"He was wondering about his ancestry. Any ideas?"

Shaking his head, his father squinted at one of the instruments on the panel. "I never met him. Even when I married your mother, we were unable to contact him in England to ask him to come to our wedding. We learned about his death through a telegram when you were still pretty young. It was quite a mystery."

"Mom must know more. Couldn't she check into his past?"

"Not really. He left home when your mother was only five. She remembers that he was a stern father but loving in his own way. When he left, she never heard from him until he visited while I was away on a multistate flight. You were only six at the time, so you might not remember. After that visit, the telegram was the only contact we ever received."

Billy nodded. "I remember him, sort of like in a dream. He was kind of strange ... really strange, I guess. But he helped me learn to draw. I still remember him teaching me how to draw a dra—"

Heat surged into his ears. A flood of images, like ghosts with warped faces, flashed in his mind's eye. An ancient book, *Fama Regis*, lay on the table in his old living room, before their house burned to the ground. A hand, his father's hand, opened it and turned to a drawing of a dragon in combat with a knight. The furious eyes of the dragon seemed to glow, yet they were little more than white dots in the center of a red pupil. This memory echoed the reality of his first glimpse of the ancient book. When he had gazed at the picture, he had noticed a striking similarity between the artist's style and his own, especially in the dragon's eyes.

His father cocked his head. "What's wrong?"

"My grandfather taught me how to draw a dragon."

"Okay. Why is that important?"

"You told me the pictures in *Fama Regis* were drawn by ..." He swallowed through his tightening throat. He couldn't spit out the words. A new image seared his mind, this one with sounds that brought back the nightmares of a hundred nights. A man lay in a

117

field of snow, his body blackened by fire and his fist clenched around Billy's coat. His face half melted by the inferno Billy had created, he coughed through his dying words. *"You're just like me, boy. You kill to get what you want."*

As the scowl burned in his memory, it morphed into the face of the man who sat next to him at a kitchen table, sketching a dragon with a white dot in the center of its pupil. *"Just remember, all dragons are evil,"* he had said. *"Draw them if you wish, but only as the conquered enemy of a knight in shining armor."*

Suddenly every image vanished. As blood rushed away from his head, dizziness made him wobble in his seat.

"Billy?" His father leaned over and prodded his shoulder. "Are you okay?"

He shook his head. "My grandfather was …" He stared at his father, barely able to form the word. "Palin!"

CHAPTER

INTO THE DARKNESS

Walter took a deep breath and set one foot on the outer edge of a plank and the other foot on the opposite side. Sliding his clenched fists along the upper ropes, he strode forward. With the wind whipping the bridge violently as he stepped farther out, shouting instructions wouldn't make sense. Everyone just had to follow his lead, ride out the gusts, and hope for the best. Fortunately, their added weight helped to settle the sagging span, but would they make it sag too much and snap one of the ropes?

After a few minutes, they managed to safely cross at least a hundred planks, putting them well out over the chasm. Every few seconds, a winged shadow crossed their path. Flying low with her claws extended, Thigocia seemed ready to snatch anyone who might get blown over a support rope or fall through a broken plank.

A sudden gust batted the bridge to one side. Walter braced his legs. Ashley and Abigail gasped. When it eased back to the center, Walter exhaled and looked back. Both women hung on with rigid arms and white knuckles.

"You guys okay?" he shouted.

Abigail nodded, her face taut. Ashley did the same, adding a cry that carried a hint of fear. "Walter, we can't do this. It's only going to get worse."

"Should we get Mother to carry us?" Abigail called. "Drop us off at the farthest point she can go?"

"And then climb off her back and hop onto the bridge?" Ashley asked. "Impossible!"

Abigail shook her head. "She can pick us up with her claws one at a time and—"

Thigocia's roar echoed all around. "Nephilim!" She zoomed back to the cliff where at least five Nephilim had gathered. Two of the giants grabbed the bridge's upper ropes, one on each side, and began swinging the entire span back and forth.

"Brace yourselves!" Walter shouted. The bridge flipped on its side and whipped up into the air. Ashley and Walter toppled over a support rope, but they hung on, dangling as the bridge swayed over the chasm.

Abigail lunged for them, but her foot broke through a rotting board. Her bottom smacked down on a secure plank, keeping her from falling through. She latched on to Ashley's collar, then to Walter's. "Mother!" she screamed. "Save us!"

Gasping for breath, Walter tried to pull up and watch Thigocia at the same time. She shot a burst of fire at each Naphil, hitting them in the legs. As they tried to slap out the flames, she swooped low, then bent around. Her tail slapped the first giant off his feet. The second one grabbed her tail with one arm and hung on to the bridge's support pole with the other.

Thigocia's momentum swung her around, bringing her back toward the waiting hands of two more Nephilim. They each grasped a wing. One grabbed a mainstay and wrestled her to the ground. The other caught the leather webbing and ripped it through.

Thrashing to get free, Thigocia whipped her tail and shook the first giant loose. She beat her good wing, but the other giant held fast. Setting his feet, he thrust the mainstay against his leg, snapping her wing with a loud crack.

Thigocia bellowed and clawed the giant's face. Spraying fire all around, she broke free and lumbered to the edge of the cliff. As she hesitated, the giants closed in, but just as one leaped for her tail, she jumped, beating her wings against the fierce wind.

Half of her broken wing flapped hopelessly while her torn wing barely held enough air to keep her aloft. Still, she pushed forward.

Walter regripped the rope and tried to swing up, but it was no use. "Hang on!" he shouted. "Your mother's on her way!"

Panting, Ashley nodded. "I see her. But she's hurt."

Abigail leaned back, using her weight to keep them from falling. "Have faith! Glewlwyd said the bridge won't let us fall if we just hang on!"

The Nephilim grabbed the ropes again and jerked the bridge into a wild swing. Ashley screamed. One of her hands lost its grip, and she flailed wildly. "I'm losing it!"

Abigail let go of Walter and yanked Ashley higher. "Mother! Hurry!"

"I'm coming!" With fiery spittle leaking from her mouth, the great she-dragon closed in, but her elevation diminished with every second. "I'll fly under you. You'll have to drop to my back."

Walter grunted. "But the extra weight will—"

"Let me worry about that!"

"We have to hang on!" Abigail cried. "Trust the gatekeeper!"

Red-faced, Ashley groaned. "I can't let Mother fall into the chasm by herself!"

Just as Thigocia's head passed several feet underneath, Ashley jerked free from Abigail's grip and let go. She fell to her mother's back, narrowly missing a protruding spine. Thigocia dipped downward. Straining every sinew in her muscular wings, she bent into a tight turn and headed back for another pass, still dropping in elevation.

The bridge jerked again, throwing Abigail against the side rope. As she struggled to her feet, balancing on the sides of the broken plank, Walter shouted, "Jump! Before she gets too low!"

She squeezed between the upper and lower ropes, then, timing Thigocia's approach, she leaped, her arms spread as if she were reliving her dragon past.

Reaching for Ashley's outstretched arms, Abigail missed her aim and smacked face-first on Thigocia's shoulder. She clawed at her mother's scales, slipping inch by inch.

As Thigocia wheeled around to pick up Walter, Ashley flattened her body, looped her arm around a spine, and groped for Abigail's hand. Their fingertips touched, but it wasn't enough. Abigail slid off and plummeted into the chasm.

122

Thigocia roared. Fire spewed from her mouth and nostrils. As she folded in her wings and began to fall, Walter let go of the bridge. He twisted into a vertical dive and reached out, hoping to catch hold of the dragon before she dropped out of sight. Just as Thigocia turned into a full dive, he caught her tail and wedged his arms between two spines.

As she plummeted, he fell with her, reaching for each spine in succession, climbing down her body as if scaling a ladder in reverse. Farther ahead, Ashley hung on tightly. She glanced back and gasped, then reached out a hand toward Walter and yelled something, but the buffeting wind snatched her words away.

Deeper in the chasm, Abigail's body flailed, but they gained no ground. She had to be at least two hundred feet lower, much too far away for them to catch up. Walter struggled against the wind, forcing himself to let go of one spine as he lunged for another. He set his feet on the edge of a scale to steady himself, making the rest of the downward climb easier as he stepped on scale after scale.

When he reached Ashley, he grasped her wrist and rode her hefty pull until he was able to seat himself in his usual riding spot, though plummeting into a seemingly bottomless chasm was anything but usual.

Falling faster and faster, seconds passed, then minutes. The rocky faces of the chasm's sides sped by, blurring as they accelerated. As light from above faded, their surroundings dimmed. Soon, the depths below grew dark and enfolded Abigail's body in a pool of blackness.

Elam set his hands close to the smoldering embers, though they were barely warm enough to keep his body from freezing. He had again donned Abraham's cloak, which helped, but a blazing fire would have done wonders to keep out the chill. No matter how many times Acacia relit the damp marsh reeds as she tried to maintain a low fire, they merely flared and died away. Not only that, Acacia had spent her last ounce of energy and could barely light a stick, much less create a blaze.

Still, as Abraham had indicated, a bright fire probably wasn't a good idea for wanderers in a strange land. It would be best to stay undetected as Pegasus made his slow descent toward the horizon.

Abraham rose to his feet and whispered, "We should go. The floodwaters are low enough now, and darkness will soon cover our movements."

Elam listened to the rushing water. Indeed, the noise had subsided. Yet, it was probably enough to drown out their footsteps and keep them from giving themselves away. Not only that, even in total darkness, they would be able to follow the river's path without a problem.

123

As he rubbed out the embers with his shoe, Elam returned Abraham's whisper. "I get the impression that Flint hates you. Would he really kill you?"

Abraham seemed unwilling to answer. He just stared at the moon with sad eyes.

Elam helped Acacia onto Dikaios's back and covered her with the blanket, now dry and reasonably warm. She leaned over and hugged the horse's neck. "Thank you, Dikaios. I think I am completely flamed out. I hope you don't mind me being such a burden."

"Fret not," Dikaios said. "I am here to serve you and Elam."

Elam touched Abraham's back. "Shall we go?"

Nodding his head sadly, Abraham turned toward him. "Yes, we must go."

They walked over the mushy sand to the river's edge, Abraham leading the way with Elam close behind. When the rush of water rose to an angry roar on their left, Abraham slowed and allowed Elam to come alongside.

"I think the river will mask our conversation," Elam said, "so we might as well use this time to get me up to speed."

"Up to speed?" Abraham smiled. "That's an idiom I haven't taught my people yet."

"You teach your people idioms?"

"They have invented some of their own, to be sure, but I also delight in teaching them. You see, I have watched your world for centuries through a portal viewer called Enoch's Ghost, so I am well acquainted with your customs. We have even adopted some of your technological advances and your speech patterns. Yet, you will soon learn that we are very different in many ways."

"How so?"

"As I mentioned before, our world was a kind of paradise, much like your Eden. Yet, we had no tree of knowledge of good and evil, no forbidden fruit, no serpent who would tempt either Adams or Eves in this world. Because of this, you will likely think my people are naïve, perhaps even dangerously so. Still, we have endured many tests and tempters in the form of nonhuman creatures who come here when there is a rift in the Bridgelands, and those experiences have shaken the innocence of my people."

Elam glanced back at Dikaios to see if he was listening, but it was too dark to tell. "A rift in the Bridgelands? How does that happen?"

As they came to a dip in elevation, the river's rippling song heightened. They stepped gingerly down the trail, now stony rather than sandy. "According to Enoch's Ghost," Abraham continued, "there is a great chasm spanned by a bridge."

Elam had to hurry to keep pace with the longer-legged man. "I know all about that bridge."

Abraham's voice rose a notch. "Have you crossed it?"

"With great difficulty, I assure you."

Something rustled to their right. Abraham stopped and raised his hand. Elam and Dikaios halted while Abraham scanned the marshes, his neck craned as he listened.

Elam stood on tiptoes to see over the scrubby bushes lining the flood basin. Only the sound of water trickled into his ears.

Turning back to the others, Abraham muttered, "Muskrats." Returning to his march, he spoke again, but he lowered his volume, now frequently peering into the reeds. "It seems that the Father of Lights has allowed the Bridgelands to be used as an entryway into Second Eden. An evil deed committed here opened a crack, and Enoch prophesied that if another one of my people ever commits such an act, it will open a new rift to allow entry of the greatest evil we have ever faced. The chasm is a natural portal to our land, but no evil can pass through it unless a specific evil act opens it."

"Did Enoch say what kind?"

"Indeed. There is one act that I have spoken against ever since the first child came to this world in the birthing garden. My people always speak the truth. If we believe that true words will hurt someone's heart or endanger a life, we will remain silent rather than invent a falsehood. If a lie should ever proceed from the lips of one of my people, the great evil will come through the chasm. That's why I told you earlier that if a lie occurs, the damage would already have been done."

Elam raised a finger. "So you *do* have a forbidden fruit."

"In a way, yes, but ours is different. Adam and Eve fell together, suffered together, and laid the foundation for their children to follow. If one of my people were to lie, it is important to ensure that he or she suffers alone."

"Wouldn't the corruption spread to everyone else? Lies have a way of giving birth to more lies."

"I'm sure you have seen corruption spreading like a disease," Abraham said, "but it isn't really like an infection. No one becomes corrupt because of the sins of another. They cannot catch it by mere exposure or by birth. All people choose for themselves." Abraham stopped again, his voice fading as he stared into the marsh. "That's why my people have two safeguards. I told you about the companions, and the people also have me to look to for guidance. Since I am the founder of the realm, and my people are naïve about the ways of wickedness and inexperienced in dealing with the forces of evil, they often ask me for counsel when they have to venture into the regions occupied by the altered tribes or if one of the fiends violates our borders."

Elam slowed his pace for a moment to let Dikaios and Acacia catch up. "Are you two doing okay?"

"All is well," Dikaios said. "Please continue. I find your conversation intriguing."

Acacia, her fair face glowing in the light of the moon, nodded. "I'm tired, but I'm listening. Don't get too far ahead, though. I can barely hear you."

Abraham slowed his pace. "Do we have eavesdroppers?" he asked, showing a weary smile.

"The best kind." Elam stepped up to Abraham's side again, risking a slightly louder tone. "So if something happened to you, your people would be without an experienced leader."

"Experienced? You could say that. I witnessed many great evils while in your world, and Enoch helps me from yet another realm, so, yes, my people's reliance on me is heavy, and I take great risk every time I leave the village. Even now, I feel anxious at being gone for so long. Still, I have learned to rely on Valiant." He held up a pair of fingers. "There are two communities. Mine is called Founders' Village, and Valiant is the leader of Peace Village. He is a wise man and my best warrior. If something were to happen to me, my people know to look to him for counsel."

Elam held up his hand, halting Dikaios. When the horse caught up, Elam whispered. "I heard something. Did you?"

Dikaios bobbed his head. "I think so, but ask the Oracle. She has a better vantage point."

Looking up at Acacia, Elam set his hand to his ear, hoping to signal his question.

She leaned over, keeping her voice whisper quiet. "I see moving reeds, but there is a wind."

Dropping to a crouch, Abraham waved his hands at them. "Stay low."

Elam wrapped his arms around Acacia's waist and hoisted her down. While they squatted near Abraham, Dikaios settled to the cold ground, now hard sand once again.

Something zinged through the air. A thud sprang up from the ground nearby. Another zing. Then a splash.

"Arrows!" Abraham waved a hand again, signaling everyone to get lower.

127

More zings. More thuds and splashes. Abraham fell to his seat, an arrow protruding from his lower leg. He bit his fist to stifle a grunt.

Elam braced Abraham's back. Acacia looked on, her blue eyes wide in the moonlight.

The arrows ceased. More rustling sounded. Suddenly a man broke through the thicket, his arms raised, showing that he had no weapon. Then, pressing a finger to his lips, he crouched with them.

Elam stared at the man's wide white eyes. Greevelow! What was he doing here?

Greevelow grasped the arrow's shaft and broke it off, leaving a few inches protruding from Abraham's leg. The snap of wood made him stop in mid motion and perk up his head.

Elam listened with him. No sound but the never-ending rush of water.

Apparently satisfied, Greevelow bent close to Abraham. "Must flee. Attack comes."

"Why did they stop?" Elam asked.

"Arrows found you." He reached into the thicket and withdrew a long wooden shaft with a barbed metal end. "Spears kill you."

Angel folded the bag and held it close to her face with both arms. She took in the aroma, a combination of leather and charred bones. Yet, there was something more, a familiar smell. She pressed her nose against it and took a long sniff, then raised her head and exhaled slowly. Yes, it was Dragon, her long lost Adam. Even three years after his death, this skin still carried his manly scent.

He had used it many times to cover his pillow, preferring the feel of leather under his head rather than the sheets she had spun and sewn from tufts of marlyn fur. It had taken her weeks to capture enough of the speedy rodents, but their soft coats made it worth the trouble for most of the villagers.

Smiling, she hugged it to her chest. Oh, if only those days could return! Running in the rabbit fields, laughing and playing with the children, teaching Candle how to build a rabbit trap, comforting Listener during her nights of torment and pain.

She sighed. Yes, those lovely nights, having him near as she drifted off to sleep, hearing his contented breaths after a hard day's work. What bliss that would be! No more cold, lonely nights, no more drying tears of children bereft of his strong, masculine presence.

She lowered her head and shuffled away from the garden. It wasn't to be. The Father of Lights had so decided, so it was up to her to be content and—

"Angel?"

She spun around. Dragon's voice? She closed her eyes and shook her head. No. It couldn't be. She was just exhausted. She was imagining things.

"Angel? I am over here."

She gasped. It was his voice! She crept back toward the garden. "Dragon? Is that you?"

"Yes, my love. I have returned."

A dark silhouette walked along a row in the garden, coming toward her with an outstretched arm. "A miracle of the scattered bones. You have been praying for my return for these three years, and your faith has been rewarded. Timothy held my companion when he died, so when his bones were spread over this soil, the birthing garden was able to regenerate my life." He stopped at the edge of the grass. "I have missed you, my love."

Her heart pounding, Angel ran toward him, but he held up a hand. "Come no closer."

She stopped, panting, her lips trembling. "But why? I don't understand." She reached out her hands. "My arms ache for you."

"If you touch me now, all will be lost. I cannot set foot out of this garden until my resurrection is complete."

"What is left to resurrect? I see your head, your chest, your arms and legs. Even your feet make impressions in the earth, so you are not a spirit."

"I walk in the valley of dead souls, and the lord of that valley told me that the scattering has opened a door to this world. Yet, I can come only when it is dark. Since the moon's glow is ebbing, I am safe, but if I were exposed to the light of day, I would evaporate, and if we made contact, I would be forced completely into your world and would remain in this vaporous state forever."

Angel's entire body quaked. Her knees knocked together as she tried to keep her balance. "What ... what must we do to complete the resurrection?"

"What you were planning to do. Find Father Abraham, the warrior chief, and the Oracle. Bring them here."

She clasped her hands. "Yes! Yes, of course! They will be glad to know that you are back. They will—"

"No!" He lifted a hand again. "You must not tell them that I am in this state. They will not believe you. Only bring them here. The little girl who sang will sing again to bless the garden in the presence of the Oracle." He spread out his hands over the garden's soil. "She will invoke the name of Makaidos, king of the dragons, in order to resurrect him from these bones. But you must get her to change the name and ask for me instead."

"Change Makaidos to Dragon?"

"To maintain the meter of the poem, she should say, 'the dragon.'"

"I see," she said, nodding. "Three syllables."

"Correct. It is a very simple task."

"How will I convince Paili to make the change? Resurrecting Makaidos is the very mission she and the Oracle have come to accomplish."

"This will only delay the return of the great Makaidos. He can be resurrected at the next eclipse cycle. I have spoken to him in the valley of souls, and I assure you that he agrees with this plan. But you must get the participants here before the second moon comes back into phase, or it will be too late."

"Second moon?" Angel tilted her head toward the sky. "It rises the night after next."

Dragon lifted two fingers. "So you have today, for it is now early morning, and tomorrow, as long as the girl can sing before midnight, for that is when Phoenix rises."

Angel extended two fingers of her own and stared at them. Two days would be plenty of time to find Father Abraham and the others, but what could she say to cause Paili to change her song without revealing Dragon's plan?

Edging even closer to him, Angel gazed into his lovely eyes. Now she could smell him again, that wonderful aroma she had so longed for on many lonely nights.

With her eyes half closed, she pursed her lips and spoke in the playful singsong voice she had often used at romantic moments. "It will be much easier if I could tell them that my handsome Adam will come home to me if they change the name."

His face remained stoic. "As I said, they will not believe you, so you should tell them that while Father Abraham was gone, you peered into Enoch's Ghost. Tell them Enoch himself commanded the girl to change the name to 'the dragon' instead of 'Makaidos.' Since Makaidos was the king of the dragons, that label is appropriate."

Angel's mouth dropped open. "Tell them I looked into Enoch's Ghost? Why?"

"Simple enough. You were seeking their whereabouts in order to aid your search."

Her companion buzzed into her line of sight, flashing red. *Such a statement would not be true! You cannot do this!*

131

Dragon chuckled. "I can easily guess what your companion is saying, and she is right, of course; the statement would not be true. But it will be true by the time you speak it if you peer into Enoch's Ghost and ask for help in locating Father Abraham."

The companion flashed again. *Do not plan to speak what is not yet true. Let the passage of time prove events before you implant them prematurely in your mind.*

Angel stepped to the side to look past the companion. "I can see how consulting Enoch's Ghost will become true, but how do you know Enoch will tell me to change Paili's song?"

"I cannot guess what Enoch will tell you, but no harm will come if you say that he gave you my instructions."

The companion rushed back and forth, its light blinking wildly. *This man has no companion and speaks from a pit of despair, so he is influenced by his sorrows. Whether or not immediate harm comes is not your deciding factor. Saying something that is not true is a violation of our law. That should be enough to keep you from falsehood.*

Angel knitted her brow, searching for a floating companion around Dragon's head. There was no sign of one. "You are asking me to speak a ... a lie!"

He set a hand over his heart. "I have learned much in the valley of souls. Although Father Abraham is a wise and noble teacher, there is much that he doesn't know. While truth is the best choice in almost every case, telling a lie is an option in desperate times. Our enemies are willing to deceive us, so we would not be wise to ignore a powerful weapon."

"But Father Abraham and the others are our friends, not our enemies. Why would you want me to lie to them?"

"No doubt, they are our friends. But a lie is not only a weapon; it is a shield to protect life. If one of the shadow people trespassed into our home at night and demanded to know where Candle and Listener slept, would you tell him they were sleeping peacefully in their room?"

She clenched a fist. "Of course not. I would not speak a word to the fiend."

"Then he would merely search for them and eventually find them. Yet, if you told him they were visiting a friend in another village, he would slither away and accost you no more. Such is the power of a well-placed lie."

Once again the companion flashed. *Trust in the Father of Lights. Falsehoods are the path to darkness. If you—*

"Would you please silence your companion?" Dragon said, his voice spiking. "We cannot discuss this if it continues to interrupt."

Angel wrapped her fingers around her companion and, swallowing hard, placed it in the pocket of her pantaloons. As she held her hand over the opening, it pushed and prodded her leg, but after a few seconds, it became still.

"I ..." Angel swallowed again, but the lump in her throat wouldn't go away. "I will look into Enoch's Ghost, but I do not know if the prophet will speak to me."

"If he doesn't speak, then you should search for Father Abraham without his help. You were going to do that anyway." Dragon sighed and reached out his hand. His fingers passed by her cheek, an inch away, stroking the air tenderly. "I apologize for being so adamant, my love, but this is a critical hour. We cannot allow emotions to blind us. We cannot allow allegiance to unexplainable rules to erect obstacles to our reunion."

As she drank in Dragon's dark eyes, Angel's heart thrummed. How could she possibly question her Adam, her protector, her love? Since Makaidos would eventually be resurrected, surely it was the right thing to do. Father Abraham would understand, at least eventually. Once Dragon came back, he could explain everything, just as he did tonight. All would be well.

She licked her lips, dry and cracked. "I ... I'd better go now. When Pegasus sets, it will be harder to search the highlands."

He smiled. "Yes, my love, and Flint's Marsh, as well."

133

"Flint's Marsh?" She cocked her head. "Do you mean Adam's Marsh?"

"Yes. Of course. I was merely referring to the fact that Flint now controls that area."

"But would Father go there? Would he risk facing Flint's arrows?"

"Ask Enoch." He turned toward the twin fir trees at the edge of the field and angled his head upward. "If he doesn't speak, I recommend flying over the marsh. Following the river is the easiest route from the Valley of Shadows, and Flint sleeps without knowledge of Father Abraham's journey, so that would be a good guess. If you go there first, you can search all of Flint's territory before dawn."

"In the darkness? Without Pegasus, it will be like looking for a raven hiding in the Shadowlands."

"You are witty, my love." He turned back to her, smiling. "Watch for Acacia's fire. Eventually they will need light and warmth."

"How do you know about Acacia? I just learned of her gifts—"

"Shhhh …" He raised a finger and hovered it over her lips. "I learned much in the valley of souls." He then pointed toward the village. "Go now. The sooner you complete your journey, the sooner we can be in each other's arms."

Angel turned and hurried away, glancing back every few seconds to see if Dragon watched. He was there, his handsome form waiting patiently, but when she neared the bordering forest, darkness veiled his body.

She focused straight ahead, ignoring her desire to search for him again. With little moonlight now, she could easily trip on protruding roots, so it was better to pay attention to what she was doing.

As she approached Cliffside, still standing guard at the boundary, she pressed her hands together and hurried on. Her prayer posture would let him know that she was on a mission and couldn't afford the time to stand around and chat. With a smile and a nod, she breezed by him and hurried into the deserted street. Father Abraham's home would be the third one on the right, the adobe hut with the thatched roof and a red dragon painted on each side of the entrance.

She set her hand on the door and pushed. Unlocked, of course. The shadow people feared his dwelling, and none of his own people would dare enter without his permission … She set a foot inside. … Until now.

She pushed the door behind her, but not enough to close it fully, and crept to the back of the room, a combination bedroom and study with a table near the back wall that held Enoch's Ghost. Its red glow provided the only light, but it was enough to guide her way. When she reached the table, she set her hands on the weathered wood and peered inside the ovulum, a clear crystal at least ten times the size of her companion.

She pressed her hand over her pocket. *My companion!* She reached in and took it out, setting it on her palm as she tried to find its eyes. The red glow washed over the little egg. Its eyes blinked, then stayed open, looking at her.

What's wrong? she asked it in her mind.

It blinked again but stayed silent.

Angel flicked her head toward her shoulder. *Go on, then. If you're not going to talk, you can sit up there.*

The companion stayed on her palm, tipping slightly to the side.

Too tired? She wrapped her hand around it and pushed it back into her pocket. *Then rest there.*

She closed her eyes and drew in a deep breath. Heaviness weighed down her heart. The room seemed darker, colder. Even the air seemed thicker, and she noticed the odor of unwashed clothes for the first time.

135

Shaking her head, she cast away the annoying feelings and leaned closer to Enoch's Ghost. Inside, red mist swirled, veiling anything that might lie deeper. She whispered, "Enoch? Are you there?"

The cloud suddenly twisted, as if blown by her breath. She drew so close, her lips nearly touched the glass. "Enoch? Can you hear me?"

This time, the mist coiled into a tight, spinning cylinder, clearing the inside, and as even that disappeared, the face of an elderly man began to materialize, taking up half of the crystal.

Angel gasped. "Enoch?"

The old man smiled. "Is this Angel of the Village of Peace?"

Her throat tightening, she could barely squeak out, "Yes. It is Angel."

His brow furrowed, and his smile diminished, yet his voice remained gentle. "Why are you in Abraham's hut? Is he nearby?"

136

"No, good prophet. That is why I am here. He is on a journey home from the Valley of Shadows, but he has no dragon to ride. I want to search for him, but I need guidance."

He nodded. "Your motivation is noble, yet I wonder at the wisdom of entering his home uninvited."

She cleared her throat, strengthening her voice. "Father Abraham has given us no law about his home. The requirement of an invitation is merely custom. Are not customs to be swept aside in a dire situation?"

"Not necessarily." His image magnified, drawing his eyes closer to the surface. Like a pair of knives, they seemed to pierce her own eyes and cut into her soul. As he shrank again to his original size, his lips stayed flat. "It is a dire situation, but that is not the only reason you have come."

Angel clenched her hands together and twisted her fingers. "You are wise, good prophet. Must I tell you all my reasons?"

Lowering his gaze, Enoch shook his head. "Search the kingdom of Flint, especially along the river's path. Abraham's danger is great, as is the danger to all his company."

She bowed her head, almost touching the table. "Thank you, dear prophet! Thank you!"

As she turned, Enoch called out, "Angel!"

She spun back. "Yes?"

His lips parted, but, after a moment of silence, they closed.

Angel set her hand on the side of the glass. "Whatever you have to say, good prophet, I am ready to hear."

"Are you, really?" With a heavy sigh, he added, "What you must do, do quickly."

She cocked her head to the side. "Because of the danger?"

His face faded away along with his voice. "Because of the cost."

Enoch's Ghost darkened. Even its red glow faded away. Only a street lantern spilling light through the partially open door gave the room any illumination. Taking careful steps, she found her way back outside and closed the door.

137

Again assuming the prayer posture, she hurried past the village's central circle, but, seeing no one around, she lowered her hands and ran. When she neared the end of the street, someone cried out. "Angel!"

She halted and spun toward the voice. "Emerald? Why are you still awake?"

Emerald emerged from the shadows, her eyes bleary. "I have been waiting for you. Did you speak to Cliffside?"

Angel peered into the dragon launching field. Albatross was still waiting. "I told him that you did not wish to be betrothed to him, but I fear that I did little to discourage his affections."

Emerald's brow lifted. "Was he hurt?"

"If you care so much for his feelings, why do you turn him away?"

Emerald's companion floated near her eyes. Blue light flashed as it rocked back and forth in the air.

Angel grinned. "Your companion is laughing, isn't she?"

Nodding, Emerald gently poked her companion with her finger. "I am getting a friendly, 'I told you so.'"

"Yes, they are quite good at that. When mine wants to—"

"Where is your companion?" Emerald searched both sides of Angel's head. "In your hair?"

Angel gulped. She touched her pocket but didn't look down. "I … uh … I have to hurry. Enoch himself told me to act quickly."

She leaped into a run, not daring to look back as she dashed into the launching field. When Albatross saw her, he whistled and lowered his head to the ground.

"I know. I know." Angel clambered up his neck and plopped down in her seat. "I'm late, but I had to talk to some people."

As he stretched out his wings, Albatross whistled again.

"To my village." Angel buckled her belt. "Don't worry about a rough ride. Just get me there as fast as you can."

As they ascended, the bitter wind flapped her clothes. She shivered but didn't bother to ask Albatross for heat. The flight would be short enough to keep from freezing. Still, it wouldn't be short enough to keep from considering the hundreds of thoughts that pushed into her brain. If her companion were still talking, she knew what it would say. Remember the prophecy? *Beware the dragon from below who sings a siren song and calls an Eve from Eden's twin to twist the right to wrong.*

She blinked away welling tears. Could her Dragon be the dragon from below? That seemed impossible. He was good and kind, a perfect Adam and the best father in all of Second Eden. He …

A cold lump swelled in her throat as the words rolled through her mind. *Second Eden … Eden's twin. A dragon from below.*

She shook her head hard. It couldn't be. It just couldn't. Father Abraham had taught her so many times to hold fast to what she knew, to cast aside dark doubts that contradicted what she had learned in the light. Dragon couldn't possibly be evil. A hundred years of watching his gallantry had proven that over and over. No one could possibly have an evil heart and hide it for so long, especially from his Eve.

Letting a smile break through, she took in a deep breath from the cold, biting air. Settling the truth in her mind felt good. She would never doubt her Adam again.

8

CHAPTER

A Hole into Hades

B illy looked over at his father in the pilot's seat. Although the revelation that Palin was his grandfather had sent shivers up and down his spine, his father hardly reacted at all. He just looked straight ahead, nodding slightly without a word.

The propeller's buzz droned on, the only sound in the cabin. Outside, the tops of clouds whipped by, misty protrusions from the thick bank below. A few clipped the wings and gave them a bump. Nothing serious. Just enough to remind them that their final descent could be a little rough.

Billy looked back at the passengers. Had they heard about Palin? Although Sir Patrick and Shiloh continued their naps, Sir Barlow fixed his gaze on him. With crimson cheeks and bulging eyes, he seemed ready to blurt out a typical Barlowism, but he, too, stayed silent.

Closing Professor Hamilton's journal with a slap, Billy jerked up the headset and slid it back over his ears. "Do we have any death march music?"

"Death march?" His father dipped his eyebrows. "Just because Palin's your grandfather?"

"Well, yeah." Billy glared through the window. How could he explain what he felt? When he first learned he had dragon blood, it took him a long time to figure out it wasn't so bad, that the dragons were the good guys and the slayers were the bad guys. Now, not long after losing his dragon essence, he discovers that he has slayer blood, and there was probably no way to get rid of that.

"I know how you feel," his father said. Now staring straight at him, he showed Billy his hand. "What do you see?"

Billy scanned the back of his hand from the tips of his fingers to his wrist, but noticed nothing unusual, just skin covered with reddish brown hair. Yet, a line of lighter skin wrapped one finger near the lowest knuckle, a sign that something had once shielded it from the sun.

"I'm wearing your ring." Billy touched the pearly white gem mounted in a gold band on his own finger. Since his hands had always been narrower than his father's, the ring slid up and down easily. "Is that it?"

"My father never gave me a rubellite, so I had to find one for myself." Pulling his hand back, he looked forward again and pushed the yoke slightly. The airplane dipped into a gentle descent and broke into the blanket of clouds. A wall of white vapor slammed into the windshield, blinding them, and the plane began to shake. "Do you remember who my father was?" he asked, raising his voice slightly to compete with the vibrating airplane.

Billy nodded. He spoke the name *Goliath* in his mind, but decided to stay quiet for a while. With his father now busy flying only by the instruments, it was better to just sit and think. Although he wasn't sure what Goliath looked like, an image appeared in his mind, the sketch Palin had used to help him learn to draw a dragon. He knew, of course, that Goliath was the first rebel dragon, the one who started the war between their race and

142

humans and whetted the slayers' appetite for killing. Because of Goliath, King Arthur listened to shrill cries of fear and allowed the slayers to hunt down and slaughter the supposed evil dragons, but they wouldn't stop there. And that's why Merlin had to step in and transform eleven faithful dragons into humans, thus beginning the race of anthrozils.

As thoughts of so many deaths coming at the hands of Devin and Palin flowed through his mind—Bonnie's father, Ashley's parents, and Professor Hamilton—Billy gripped the journal on his lap. His fingers tightened around the edge as a new image formed in his mind, the lifeless gray face of his beloved teacher. He lay unconscious after being thrown off Devin, who, while in dragon form, had tried to murder everyone in his path. The professor, riding on the dragon's back, had pulled the slayer away, a heroic act that eventually cost him his life.

"I see that you understand my point," his father said.

Billy turned toward him. They had broken through the clouds and were now flying over a landscape of high mountains and plunging valleys. With smooth sailing ahead and a quieter cabin, they could speak without interruption. "If you mean Goliath's rebellion caused a whole lot of trouble, then, yeah, I understand."

"Not exactly." Shaking his head slowly, he pushed *Merlin* into a steeper descent. "I have lived for centuries with the knowledge that my own father was a murderer, a lying rebel who caused horrendous pain and suffering for untold thousands. If not for him, there would have been no war, no Devin or Palin and their bloodlust, and dragons might still be living freely, even today, in peaceful harmony with mankind. My father was the demonic dragon who ruined everything, and that thought tortured me for centuries."

"But you're nothing like him. You're ..." Billy let his voice fade. He wasn't sure how to put it into words.

"That's exactly my point. The sins of a father are the father's alone. What the sons do is their own choice. It took me a long

143

time to learn this, but now I understand that I didn't inherit guilt from my father, only the mess he left behind."

Billy settled back in his seat. His father was right. If he could live with being the son of the dragon who caused all this grief, surely it wasn't so bad being the grandson of a slayer.

"Ahem."

Billy turned. With his brow arched high, Sir Barlow seemed anxious to speak. "Yes, Sir Barlow?"

"May I interject something into your conversation?"

"Absolutely." And Billy meant it. What man living today could possibly know more about both Goliath and Palin than the captain of King Arthur's guard?

Sir Barlow leaned in between the two seats and set a hand on Billy's shoulder. "Your father is correct. Goliath was the cruelest beast I have ever encountered, but I will avoid dwelling on that; my battle with him is little more than a high-flying tale. Yet Palin was quite different. He was the most dedicated squire you can imagine. His lust for killing dragons was troubling, to be sure, but he was zealous for what he believed to be right. He was a gentleman with ladies and children and a superior swordsman. His dedication to Sir Devin, though misguided, exemplified loyalty more perfectly than any storybook legend. May I suggest that your grief should be limited to the loss of his soul, that you should not allow the punishment he is likely suffering now to punish you as well? Let his life be a lesson, not a cruel whip for your own back."

As the knight's thick fingers slid away, Billy grabbed his wrist. "That was beautiful, Sir Barlow. Thank you."

Barlow's eyes gleamed. "Well, I had a fair amount of time to put the words together. I hope they helped."

"Everyone buckle up," Billy's father said as he surveyed the ground. "Apparently, the GPS coordinates weren't as precise as I had hoped, but we should be close. Look for a mountain with a grassy dome and a big hole at the top."

144

"A big hole?" Billy asked.

"Walter told me the story over the phone. After the giants climbed up out of Hades, the ground collapsed and made a deep crater all the way down to something called the mobility room. But I didn't understand it all. Walter gave me the details so fast I couldn't keep up."

"Yeah. I know what you mean. Talking on the phone with him is an adventure in itself." As the plane skimmed over the mountaintops, Billy searched each one. Trees covered most of the lower hills, and jutting rocks topped several of the taller mountains. So far, only one grass dome, but it had a two-story brick house and no crater.

A female voice piped up. "Could that be it?"

Billy lurched around in his seat. Shiloh and Sir Patrick were both looking out the window. "I didn't know you were awake," Billy said.

Still clutching her father's hand, she smiled. "Ever since that first big bump." She pressed her finger on the window. "See that mountain just past the one with the rock formation that looks sort of like a face? I think it has a grass top."

Billy swung back around and looked out his own window. "Yeah. I got it marked. And that dot in the middle could be a hole."

His father turned the yoke. "We're on our way."

After a few minutes, they arrived at the mountaintop and circled a couple of hundred feet over its cap of brown grass. A deep pit scarred the middle, taking up over half of the dome.

Billy whistled. "That crater's going to make it tough to land, Dad. Not much room for an airstrip."

"Remember when I landed on our street back in Castlewood? I had to dodge power lines, trash cans, and two dogs. I can handle this." He pushed the plane into a steep dive. "Hang on."

Billy clutched his armrest. His heart thumped. This risky landing would be another shot of adrenaline, a great rush, but exhausting all the same.

145

Like a stone flying toward their faces, the ground hurtled in their direction. Billy instinctively reached for his own yoke, but drew back. He had landed *Merlin* several times before, but not like this. Dad was in control.

The plane suddenly jerked upward. Billy's back pressed against his seat. The landing gear bounced heavily, and their momentum pushed them forward, but with the plane's body angling up, they couldn't see the pit. His heart pounded faster. Sweat dampened his shirt. They had to be getting close. There just wasn't that much room.

Finally, they slowed and turned sharply. As Billy's window shifted to face the chasm, he looked straight down into its depths. They had missed a plunge by mere inches.

Grinning, he unbuckled his belt and tossed it to the side. "What were you so worried about, Dad? That was a piece of cake!"

"Me? Worried?" He shot a grin back at Billy. "Just keeping you on your toes."

146

After they stopped, Billy hustled back, pushed down the rear passenger door on the plane's right side, and extended the airstair. A bitter wind swept in, biting through his clothes. "Everyone bundle up!" He grabbed a pair of gloves from the nearest seat along with his sweatshirt, slid them on, then hustled down the stairs.

Breathing white puffs into the crisp air, he surveyed the land. With a huge hole in the center of the snow-speckled brown grass, the domed top looked more like a volcano cone than a typical peak in the Montana highlands. The scarred meadow stretched out a few hundred feet in diameter, bordered by trees all around, some evergreen and some void of leaves.

He leaned back against the fuselage, waiting while everyone else put on their cold-weather gear. A few birds flitted about, and the tops of trees swayed, but no other movement caught his eye.

Sir Patrick stepped off the plane next, followed by Shiloh, both wearing coats. "A rather desolate place, isn't it?" Patrick asked.

Billy nodded. "Do you see Gabriel or Sapphira anywhere?"

"They should be quite easy to identify. A boy with wings and a girl with white hair are not exactly commonplace."

"Especially wandering around out in the middle of nowhere." Billy pushed his hands into his sweatshirt pouch and shivered. Even his gloves weren't enough to ward off the frosty air. Walter had warned him about the mountains of Montana, but he had said they were as cold as Morgan's heart. Now he would have to tell Walter that Morgan's heart would put earmuffs on if she came out in this weather. He grinned as he imagined Walter's response. *That's very heartwarming, Billy, very heartwarming.*

Her hands deep in her pockets, Shiloh marched toward the pit. "I wonder if there's a way to get down there?"

"It seemed empty when I looked into it," Billy said, "but I guess it won't hurt to get a closer look."

Sir Barlow lumbered down the stairs, rocking the airplane before landing with a thump on the ground. He fastened his jacket, a downy-lined leather one with a coat of arms embroidered on the front. "It is as cold as ..." He touched a finger to his chin. "Let's see, what is an appropriate idiom?"

"Cold as Morgan's heart?" Billy asked.

"I was thinking 'as cold as a lonely night,' but, yes, your idiom works quite well."

"Speaking of Morgan ..." Billy turned back to the plane. His father had just stepped out and was coming down the stairs. "Dad. Any cell service here? We'd better call Mom and ask her about Palin."

He pulled a cell phone from his pocket and looked at the display. "No. Nothing."

Sir Patrick withdrew his phone. "Use mine. It's charged now, and I have international service via satellite."

As Billy punched in the phone number, he watched Shiloh peeking over the edge of the hole. The phone trilled in his ear twice before his mother picked up.

147

"Hello?"

"Mom, it's me. Listen. We made it to Montana, and we're waiting for Sapphira and Gabriel to show up, but on the way I was reading some stuff in Prof's journals, and it made Dad and me think."

"Thinking is good." A hint of laughter flavored her voice.

He grinned at his father. "Yeah. We're men of action, but we got kind of bored and decided to think for a while. Anyway, when was the last time you heard from your father?"

"My father? Why do you bring him up?"

"Please just hang with me for a minute, and I'll explain."

After a few seconds of silence, she spoke with a hesitant tone. "Well, he visited us back when you were little, but I never heard from him after that, at least, not directly. We did get word that he had died."

"Was there a will? Did he leave you anything? Is there a last known address?"

"Slow down, Billy. One question at a time."

"Okay." Keeping his eyes on Shiloh as she walked around the hole's perimeter, he tried to formulate a good question. "If someone contacted you about his death, then there must be a way to trace him. Do you have any letters from him?"

"Billy, my father left my mother when I was little. I barely knew him at all. He never called, never wrote, didn't leave a forwarding address, and I threw away the telegram that announced his death."

"So one day he just showed up at our house out of the blue?"

"Exactly. Your father wasn't home, but I let him in anyway. I didn't think he meant us any harm, and I didn't want to try to kick him out, at least not by myself."

"Was he mean? Aggressive?"

"Not really aggressive, just kind of strange, sort of a wide-eyed fanaticism about him. He kept talking about dragons, cracking jokes about them that weren't funny at all, and asking me if I had seen any lately. He even pulled out a drawing of one."

"A drawing?" He raised his eyebrows at his father. "Sort of an example? To help you know what he was looking for?"

"I suppose, but you saw it and asked him to show you how to draw one. So while the two of you were in the kitchen, I called Walter's dad. A few minutes later, when I saw Carl walking up, I sent you to your room, and Carl showed my father to the door."

Billy stared into space, murmuring. "Palin was checking us out. He and Devin were already suspicious of Dad."

"Palin? Devin?" Her voice grew so loud, Billy pulled the earpiece back. "What are you talking about?"

Sir Patrick reached out his hand. "May I?"

"Mom, I'll let Sir Patrick explain." Billy gave him the phone and strolled toward Shiloh. As he walked, he listened to Patrick's voice fade behind him.

"Marilyn, it is essential that you tell me all you remember about your father's situation in England. My people can research ..."

When he arrived at the pit, Shiloh was leaning over the edge, too far in Billy's estimation. The urge to take her hand was almost overwhelming, but he held back. She was experienced enough to know what she was doing.

Her coat, flat against her back as she bent forward, seemed so strange. After getting accustomed to seeing Bonnie with wings, either outstretched or hidden in a backpack, this mirror image of her with a different profile was hard to get used to.

The last time he had seen Bonnie, she had asked him if he wanted to know the color of the rubellite in her ring. Red would have signaled that she still had her wings, while white would have proven that she had given them up. He had decided that it didn't matter, and he never had a chance to find out.

Now, several days after she and her mother left to "get to know each other again," he wanted the answer. With all that was going on, they might need a girl with dragon wings, so maybe keeping them would have been the right choice. Still, with all the media hounds searching for her, he couldn't blame her for wanting to get rid of them. Ever since she left, she hadn't answered her phone or returned any messages. Obviously, she had intentionally dropped off the face of the Earth.

"What's so interesting down there?" he asked.

Shiloh straightened, her hand stroking her chin as she walked around the perimeter. "Let me show you."

As Billy followed, Shiloh pointed at the grass. "There are quite a few human prints here and there, but wait until you see this." She halted and stepped inside an impression in the dried mud, a print twice the size of a normal foot. "They start at the very edge and lead to the forest, but I can't see any way for someone to get into or out of the hole."

Billy peered into the pit. "Tough to scale sheer walls."

"A dragon probably has prints this big, but these are human."

He reached for her hand. "C'mon. Let's report to the others."

When they arrived back at the plane, his father broke off a conversation with Sir Patrick and turned toward him. "Find anything?"

Billy set his hands two feet apart. "Only footprints this big."

"The Nephilim," Sir Patrick said. "Ashley mentioned them."

Shiloh hugged herself and shivered. "If what she said is true, knowing they might be around somewhere gives me the creeps."

"Billy," Jared said, "Patrick made a call to England. One of his knights will investigate your grandfather and report to your mother. Larry will help by searching electronic databases and analyzing a recording that one of Ashley's computers picked up when Palin was in her underground laboratory. Maybe Larry can match the voiceprint with something online to help us track down Palin's former home. Then maybe clues we find there will lead us to the identity and whereabouts of this new slayer."

"If he *is* new." Billy couldn't resist flashing a grin. "After all the years you had to run from him, now we have the technology to turn the tables."

"That's true. And now it seems clear that he had tracked me to West Virginia much earlier than I had thought."

"Yeah. I wonder why they gave up until recently." Billy had his suspicions, but he didn't want to voice them. Not yet. Maybe they looked elsewhere because he hadn't acquired any dragon traits when Palin visited. Not only that, Dad was gone, so Palin couldn't make a positive ID. He probably had seen Dad back when he and Devin fought in the throne room centuries ago, and since Mom knew better than to have photos of Dad sitting around the house, Palin had to go away without proof. Still, Devin did come back later, so his clues must have kept leading to Castlewood, West Virginia, and the Bannister name.

Sir Barlow stepped ahead of Billy and pointed at the tree line. "I see movement in the bushes near that stand of oaks."

"I see it, too." Billy ran that way, keeping his eye on the spot. A boy emerged from behind the trees, followed by a girl.

As the breeze whipped the girl's white hair, she smiled and ran to meet him. "Billy!"

When they met, she wrapped her arms around his waist and laid her head against his chest. "I'm so glad to see you again!"

Billy touched her lightly on the back. This girl was much more affectionate than he had expected. "Again?" he asked.

She pulled away, her cheeks turning red. "Oh! That's right. You couldn't see me before."

As the boy approached, a pair of wings spread out behind him. "She means inside the Great Key," he said, extending his hand. "She and I were there and set up the covenant veil for the dragons."

151

Billy shook the boy's hand. "Billy Bannister."

"Gabriel. My last name changed so many times, I'm not sure which one to say. But I watched you as an invisible energy field for long enough, I feel like I know you."

"An energy field?" Eyeing Gabriel's wings, Billy let out a whistle. "I think I need to get up to speed on a lot of stuff."

Sapphira took Billy's hand, smiling up at him as if she were his little sister. He squinted at a red spot on her forehead. Was it blood?

"There won't be much time for getting up to speed," she said. "We have to open a portal to the Bridgelands. According to Yereq, we're supposed to transport all the former dragons up there."

"Yereq?" Billy asked.

"Yes, he's—"

"Well, what do we have here?" Sir Patrick called as he approached. "A boy with wings and a girl with white hair?"

Gabriel ran to meet him. "Patrick!" While the two hugged, Billy's father and Sir Barlow joined the group.

152

"Ah, yes!" Barlow said. "Reunions are always such a pleasant sight."

Sapphira stepped around Billy and looked at the airplane. "Where's Bonnie? Didn't she come with you?"

He stuffed his gloved hands back into his sweatshirt pouch. "She and her mom went into hiding. We got a note about a slayer chasing them, so we might not be able to get in touch with them for months."

"Oh." Sapphira's brow creased. "That's terrible!"

Gabriel nodded toward the woods. "Well, we can't replace Bonnie, but we do have a giant-size surprise for you." He set a hand on Barlow's sword hilt. "But don't be too surprised when you see him. He's a friend."

Sapphira grinned and cupped her hands around her mouth. "Come on out!"

A man, nearly as tall as one of the smaller oaks, walked out from behind the tree line.

Sir Barlow gasped. "By all that is holy!"

"This is Yereq," Sapphira said. "He's going with us to the Bridgelands, the same place Walter and Ashley and her mother and sister went."

Gabriel reached as high as he could and patted Yereq on his shoulder. "Yep. The bad guys have giants, so the good guys need one, too."

"If such a man can handle a blade," Barlow said, "then he will be a great asset indeed!"

Yereq drew a long sword from the scabbard on his back and held it out in front of him. "During frightful days of darkness, I have been practicing on demons who are both fast and clever. I'm looking forward to using it in the light."

Billy surveyed all the travelers—himself, his dad, two knights, two girls, a boy with wings, and a giant. "So how do you propose to get all of us to this Bridgelands place?"

"With our solar-powered portal maker," Gabriel said, nodding at Sapphira. "She just whips up a firestorm and off we go."

Sapphira smiled demurely. "I've never transported this many people. I might have to take two or three at a time."

"That's a lot of back and forth," Gabriel said. "Are you sure you have enough firepower?"

"I won't know until I try." She raised a finger and spun it in the air. A tiny flame encircled the tip, like an adhesive bandage made out of fire. "I feel pretty strong."

"I have an idea," Patrick said, signaling for everyone to gather around. When they had made a tight huddle, he spoke in a solemn tone. "My idea is a very dangerous one. If it works, we will have a great advantage in the other realm. If it doesn't work, then we will be, as the idiom says … toast."

153

CHAPTER

9

GROUND ZERO

Ashley's voice pierced the darkness, stretching out in a lamenting call. "Abigail!"

Still plunging, Thigocia bent her neck, bringing her head toward her two passengers. Her scarlet eyebeams looked like high-powered lasers as they swept the black void. "She is not in sight," she yelled. "But I see the ground. Hang on."

Walter stretched his arms around Ashley and grasped the spine in front of her. Her fingers overlapped his. With his chest against her back, he could feel her muscles grow tense as Thigocia thrust out her injured wings.

Suddenly, her scales pushed into his backside. Like a ten-ton weight, momentum slammed down their bodies. Walter locked his elbows, trying not to crush Ashley, but the weight pressed so hard, his chin dug into her back. She screamed. Thigocia roared. With a slow twist of his neck, Walter turned his head until his cheek lay against Ashley's sweatshirt. Seconds later, her scream died away, and the pressure eased.

Walter pulled his body back and helped Ashley straighten. As the rushing air calmed, her heavy breaths eased into a long sigh. "I think my heart is in my throat," she said.

"I think I spit mine out."

As Thigocia circled in a wobbly horizontal flight, her body lurching up and down in time with her faltering wings, her eyebeams scanned the land below.

Walter spotted a few dim lights behind a stand of trees. Could it be a campground? Or maybe a small neighborhood? Would there be enough light to help them search for Abigail?

A large yellow moon hovered in the sky near the horizon, but it looked different, bigger somehow, and its face didn't match the familiar pattern of seas and craters.

He patted the scales next to his leg. "Do you see her body anywhere?"

The eyebeams jerked up and landed on Walter's chest. Thigocia spoke, her voice low and laboring. "Not yet. ... I will try to land ... where Abigail must have fallen. I am ... too injured to continue an aerial search. "

Walter grimaced. Thigocia seemed angry about the "body" question. But there was no way Abigail could have survived that plunge. If she still had her dragon form, the fall wouldn't have been a problem, but they were going a couple of hundred miles an hour.

Landing on the run, Thigocia beat her floundering wings against the ground until she came to a full stop.

Walter sat up straight and looked around. When they descended below the surrounding treetops and land contours, the moon slid out of sight, darkening the region. The field of grass Thigocia had used as a landing strip was just a vague mass of gray. About a stone's throw from where she stood, the ground changed to a darker hue and seemed to be cut into rows.

"Looks like a garden," Ashley said.

"Maybe." Walter leaped off, bending his knees to absorb the impact, but they buckled. He rolled on the ground but sprang right back up.

"Are you all right?"

"Yeah." He lifted each foot in turn. "But my legs feel like wet noodles. Better go down the scaly staircase."

As Thigocia lowered her head, her eyebeams kept moving across the landscape. "It is a garden," she said, "but I have never seen plants like these."

Walter pushed his legs forward until he reached the edge of the furrowed ground. Stretching out over many acres, several plants lined the tops of the tilled ridges. He knelt and examined the closest one, a calf-high stalk with two large leaves pressed against each other, leaving an air pocket in between.

"What is it?" Ashley knelt beside him. Her trembling voice gave away her fear. "See anything?"

"It's just some kind of cabbage." He touched something white and rigid near the garden's edge. "A bone?"

"Looks like it." She pointed farther out into the garden. "More bones."

Walter followed her gesture. Beyond the closest plants, in a circular section where nothing grew, the dirt had been disturbed, as if someone had recently buried something. Could Abigail's body be over there? He jumped up and threaded between two rows, dodging the plants, until he reached the circle. He dropped to his knees again and felt the mixture of soil and small bones.

After a few seconds, Ashley caught up and leaned over his shoulder, touching his back. "It looks like something wallowed here."

"The dirt's loose and warm, too warm for how cold it is here."

She waved her hand over the disturbed area. "It's a circle, maybe eight feet across. That's kind of big for a wallowing animal, except maybe a dragon."

Walter looked up at her. "Are you thinking Abigail landed here?"

"Where else?" She set her hands on her hips and turned in a slow circle. "But she couldn't have just gotten up and walked away."

Walter imagined Abigail crashing to the ground and her bones flying all over the garden. He cringed at the thought. It was just too morbid. It didn't make sense, anyway. These bones had been scoured clean.

"Look at this." He pointed at the center of the circular area. "There's another plant, a little one. If she had landed here, she would have crushed it."

Ashley walked to the plant and knelt next to it, careful not to step on the bones. She touched the top where the leaves met. "I guess you're right. This plant is pretty much exactly in the middle."

Thigocia called from the edge of the garden. "What have you found?"

Walter scooped up a handful of soil and jogged back to where the dragon sat. Holding his palm open, he lifted the soil close to her snout. "Smell anything familiar?"

As she took in a long sniff, her beams flashed red. "Roxil?"

A man's voice broke through the darkness. "Who goes there?"

"Uh-oh." Walter brushed his hand against his jeans. "I think the farmer's coming. I hope he's not afraid of dragons."

A lantern bobbed toward them. As it drew closer, the shape of a man, tall and wide, appeared in its glow. "No dragons are allowed here," he said, waving his hand back and forth. "The landing zone is on the other side of the village." He jumped over Thigocia's tail and looked at the garden. "Are my babies safe?"

"We didn't land on the plants," Walter said, "if that's what you mean."

"Good." The farmer wiped his sleeve across his brow. With the lantern close to his face, his thin beard and mustache became clear. "Now please take this dragon to the other side of the village."

Walter pointed toward the lights in the midst of the trees. "Is that the village?"

"It is." The farmer looked that way. "My name is Cliffside. I will alert whomever you have come to visit. The emergency must be great for you to arrive at this hour."

Thigocia flashed her eyebeams on the man's chest. "Did you see a young woman here in the last few minutes?"

Cliffside staggered back. "The dragon spoke!"

"Uh ..." Walter glanced at Ashley. "Yeah. She's been talking for a long time."

Thigocia's beams grew brighter, and her tone deepened to a growl. "I repeat. Did you see a young woman here?"

Cliffside's voice rattled. "Angel was here earlier. Are you looking for her?"

"No. Her name is Abigail." Her eyebeams locked on something floating near the man's head, an ovular crystal about the size of a small hen's egg. It hovered in front of his eyes, flashing a blue light.

"What's that?" Walter asked, pointing at the egg.

Cliffside made a shushing sound and pushed the crystal down to his shoulder. "My companion, of course. It suggests that I invite you to sunrise prayers where we will ask everyone about your missing friend."

"When is sunrise?" Ashley asked.

Cliffside pulled a chain from his trousers pocket and caught a small glass ball dangling at the end. He aimed it at the sky and looked through it. "Maybe two hours."

"This is a dire emergency," Thigocia said. "My daughter fell from a great height and likely landed somewhere nearby, but she is nowhere in sight."

"Your daughter? I'm so sorry!" His brow suddenly wrinkled. "But you were looking for a young woman, not a dragon."

"It's hard to explain." Walter pointed at the garden. "We were thinking she might have fallen in there, but we couldn't see everything in the dark."

159

"I will search with my light." Holding the lantern in front of him, the man ran along a row, hopping gingerly to avoid the bones. As he turned in a circle, the glow spread across every section. After a minute or so, he ambled back to the field. "Something has disturbed the newly plowed area, but I saw no woman, and no plants are crushed or missing. In fact, there is a new plant. I will have to prepare a growth chart for it and arrange the lottery."

"The lottery?" Ashley asked.

"Yes, of course. The parent lottery." He smiled. "There will be another happy couple before the day is over."

Walter extended his hand. "I'm Walter. She's Ashley, and the dragon is Thigocia."

"I am pleased to meet you." Grasping Walter's hand, Cliffside shook it clumsily. "The Prophet taught us this custom only recently. It is a pleasant greeting."

160

Walter pulled away from Cliffside's crushing grip. "Well, we're sorry about landing in the wrong place, but Thigocia's pretty upset about losing Abigail. In fact, we all are, so if there's anything you can do to help, we'd sure appreciate it."

"You have a strange way with words, Walter, but I think I understand. I will ring the bell immediately and call an emergency session." Cliffside began walking toward the lights in the forest. "Follow me, please, but I fear there will be no room for the dragon."

Walter turned to Ashley and Thigocia. "I guess we have no choice."

"I think you're right." Ashley crossed her arms and sighed. "I'm sorry, Mother."

Thigocia spread out her wings. The end of one dangled while the other displayed a rip through part of the membrane. Her voice stayed near a low growl. "If I can fly at all, I will continue the search. When your meeting is complete, look for me here." Her ears rotated, one independent of the other. "Something is desperately amiss, a strange threat I cannot describe."

She leaped into the air, beating her damaged wings furiously. As she roared in pain, gusts of wind whipped Ashley's and Walter's hair into a frenzy and bit through their clothes. Rising in a slow circle, Thigocia soon faded into the darkness above.

Ashley shivered and edged closer to Walter. "We'd better get going," she said.

"Yeah." He laid his arm over her shoulders. "It *is* getting cold."

"That's not what I mean." She peered into the garden. "I keep thinking I see something moving out there."

"Probably just the wind."

"Maybe. But I sense another mind around here somewhere, and it's not Abigail. I can't pick up any details, but it feels dark and dangerous. That's really what's making me feel cold."

Marilyn tapped her keyboard while watching the flat-screen monitor on her desk. After adjusting her headset microphone, she spoke into it. "You got all that, Larry?"

"Affirmative. One moment please."

She looked up at the largest flat-panel screen mounted on the side of Larry's outer wall. A stream of lines scrolled from bottom to top, far too fast to read.

"Your search criteria are now loaded. Would you like the results in print format?"

She tapped a pencil eraser on the page of an open journal. "Yes, and a spreadsheet on my screen, too. I want to make notes on every record you find."

"Because I must rely on outside data sources, the results may take several minutes. When the search is complete, I will give you an appropriate signal."

"Thank you." Marilyn closed the journal and rested her palm on top of its worn leather cover. "Do you have any hits on your local database?"

"I have many popular music titles in my database. Do you want me to play one for you while you wait?"

"No, Larry. By *hits* I mean data records that match the criteria."

"New definition of *hits* recorded for future use." The word flashed on Larry's monitor, its font color changing from black to blue to red. An animated book labeled "Dictionary" walked up to the word, opened to a page marked "H," and sucked it in. "To answer your question, nothing in my local data matches. I found several men by the name of Peters in three of the cities you entered, but when I added the street addresses, each potential match was eliminated."

"Can you give me two spreadsheets? One with all the men named Peters and another with only the exact matches?"

A file cabinet appeared on the monitor. A drawer sprang open, and two folders fell to the bottom of the display area, spilling papers from within. "The hits from my local data for all men by the name of Peters in the specified cities are now on your screen. While you are perusing these, in keeping with the adventure Ashley recently completed, I will play 'Stairway to Heaven' on my synthesizer using an accordion and bagpipe blend."

Marilyn jerked off her headset and laid it on the desk. As tinny music sounded from the earpieces, she leaned over and spoke into the microphone. "Just give me a visual signal when you're done with the search."

She spun her chair halfway around and checked on Monique. With her cheek resting on a rag doll, she had fallen asleep in the middle of a circle of stacked building blocks. Marilyn called toward the open door that led to the rest of the house. "Shelly? Can you hear me?"

"Coming!"

A few seconds later, Shelly popped through the doorway, both thumbs busily punching buttons on her cell phone. Dressed in loose red pajama bottoms and a baggy long-sleeved T-shirt, she

162

stopped near the desk, not bothering to pull her gaze away from the phone's screen. "What's up?"

"Are you texting your parents?"

"Yep. They made it to D.C., but they're hitting the sack. Dad'll start checking on your genealogy in the morning."

"Did you thank him for changing their flight?"

Shelly nodded. "He said it's no problem. With Walter flying off to Never Never Land, they didn't have any reason to go to Montana now."

"That's a relief." Marilyn swiveled her chair toward Monique. "Can you take Pebbles to bed?"

"Sure thing." Shelly looked up from the phone, her eyebrows rising. "Anything else? You want coffee or something?"

"I think I'll need it. And please take a cup to Sir Edmund, too."

Shelly glanced at the only window in the room, a large square one next to Larry's end wall, but an air handling unit took up most of the opening, and closed blinds covered the rest. "Is our faithful knight still outside?"

"He insists on patrolling the perimeter." Marilyn stood and separated two of the slats with her fingers. "I don't get it," she said, peering out. "He can't stay out there all night."

"A knight out all night," Shelly grinned at her joke. "Maybe it has something to do with being a knight, you know, the whole gentleman thing. He doesn't want to be in the house alone with only females around. I'm sure Larry and Gandalf don't count as males in his book."

"That might be true." Marilyn ran her finger over the slats, closing them again. "Any ideas?"

Shelly gave her shoulders a light shrug. "Appeal to his valor? Tell him we will be too scared to sleep if he stays out there?"

"I know I'd sleep better if he came inside. It's worth a try."

163

"I'm on it." Shelly scooped up Monique and carried her toward the hallway. "Two cups of extra strong java, and my best frightened little girl impression, coming right up."

As Shelly closed the door behind her, Marilyn turned her attention to the spreadsheet on her desk screen and scanned the rows of data. The third entry showed a Marshall Peters, but his street address didn't match anything her mother had recorded in her diary. Mom had saved all her letters from her late husband, so she wouldn't have erred so badly in recording his address. Still, the city matched one of her entries, Missoula, Montana, the same town Hartanna had settled in years ago. That couldn't be mere coincidence.

She opened the journal to the back page and withdrew a photo from its inner pocket. Holding it up, she gazed at the man and woman posing in front of a fireplace. The man held a little girl in his arms. Wearing a frilly blue party dress and patent-leather shoes over white lacy socks, the curly-headed toddler had to be less than two years old.

Marilyn touched her own hair. Those curls had straightened long ago, but the birthmark on the girl's exposed calf proved her to be a much younger version of Marilyn Bannister, or, rather, Marilyn Peters at that time.

Focusing now on her father, a short, muscular man with a closely trimmed goatee and curly hair, both as black as his narrow eyes, she let her memories wander. When her father had visited about ten years ago, he was clean shaven, and his youthful appearance had startled her. After thirty years of aging, he should have had wrinkles and gray hair, but he seemed to be as young as the man in the photo. At the time, she had attributed his appearance to hair dye and facelifts, but she hadn't let him stick around long enough to find out. His probing questions had raised lots of red flags, so when she asked Walter's dad to show him out, making him leave seemed like the best option. After all, how could she trust a father who had abandoned his family?

Soon, her thoughts drifted to a time she saw Palin, the dragon slayer. At Dr. Conner's office suite at the University of Montana, Palin had grabbed Billy, pressed a dagger against his throat, and dragged him out of the office. She and Walter fought him in the hallway—lunging, punching, kicking. Every memory seemed like a split-second frame from a movie. Dark facial hair of some kind obscured Palin's face, and streams of sweat and blood glistened on his cheeks. But the images flew by too quickly. All she could think about at the time was grabbing the dagger that was cutting her boy's throat, getting him away from that monster with the …

She held a hand to the bandage on her own throat and finished her thought. *Get him away from that monster with the dark eyes!* She pulled the photo closer. Could it really be true? Up to this point, her effort was just a computer search, a sleuthing expedition. Now she had thrust a shovel into her own father's grave, digging toward his coffin while glancing around in the darkness to make sure no ghosts were lurking.

A clock on the wall gonged several low tones, tolling the midnight hour. She slid the headset on again, just in time to hear a bagpipe whining the final measure of "Stairway to Heaven." Cringing at the notes, she spoke into the microphone. "Larry, can you drill down that Missoula entry? What's the date, and where did the data come from?"

A calendar appeared on the larger monitor, its pages flipping through the months. When it reached November, the number eleven flashed red in one of the thirty date squares. "November eleventh, nineteen-eighty-two. I obtained the data from a criminal records search. Apparently Mr. Peters violated local traffic laws by driving eighty in a fifty-five zone. He never paid his ticket."

"Can you bring the address up on a map?"

"One moment." A digital rendering of Missoula appeared on the screen with a red pushpin graphic in the northeastern quadrant. "The pointer indicates the vicinity of the traffic violation, but the home address is not in the mapping database. The address he gave to officers could be erroneous."

She leaned close to the screen and searched the area surrounding the pushpin. "But he must have shown the police a driver's license. Even if that had a fake address, he would've had to show proof of insurance to get it. Let's concentrate on this guy and see if we can track him down."

"Affirmative. My external search is almost complete. I will transform into a digital tracking hound momentarily." The map faded, replaced by a cartoon hound sniffing through a pile of haphazardly stacked papers.

Marilyn laughed. The dog looked remarkably like Hambone, the blue tick hound that had helped them track Jared to his mountain cave when he was in dragon form.

A knock sounded on the door leading to the hallway. "Mrs. Bannister?"

Marilyn pulled off her headset and swung around. "Come in, Edmund."

The door pushed open. Edmund eased in, carrying two steaming mugs of coffee. "I hope I am not disturbing you. The lass said you would sleep better knowing I am inside, so I wanted to let you know I am here." He handed her one of the mugs. "Is there any way I can assist you?"

"As a matter of fact, there is." She held up the photo, taking a sip of her coffee as he looked at it.

"A family portrait?" he asked.

She set down her mug and nodded. "Do you recognize the man?"

Pinching the corner of the photo, he drew it closer. "He seems familiar, to be sure, but I can't quite place him."

"Think back to your days as King Arthur's confidante. Who else stayed by the king's side?"

Edmund's brow arched up. "Ah! Yes! Now I remember. This man looks very much like the king's scribe, the one who also acted as Devin's squire, the ignoble Palin."

Marilyn took the photo and, looking at it again, sighed. "I was afraid of that."

"Afraid? Is something amiss?"

"Not really. I just learned something that troubles me. There's nothing you or anyone else can do about it."

"Very well." Walking backwards, he bowed his head. "If you no longer have need of me, I will check the door locks and retire to William's bedroom."

"Thank you, Edmund. Good night." When the door closed behind him, Marilyn slid the headset back on. A sniffing sound filled her ears, matching the animated bloodhound on the screen. She adjusted the microphone again. "Almost done, Larry?"

"I am compiling your data as we speak."

The hound dug a hole and vanished. Seconds later, the spreadsheet returned, black characters on a white background, with the first several rows in light blue. An identical spreadsheet appeared on her desk screen as well. She set her finger on one of the blue cells. "Why did you highlight some of these, Larry?"

"Those records are related to the Marshall Peters in Missoula, oldest to newest. Since the first two have their origin in England, I suggest that you use them to dig further."

She picked up a phone on the desk. "What time is it in Scotland?"

"Shortly after six in the morning. No offices are likely to be open."

167

She pulled a slip of paper from her pocket and read the hastily scrawled digits. "Sir Patrick gave me Sir Newman's phone number. My guess is that he is an early riser."

"At least he will be one today."

She pushed her headset down around her neck and cradled the phone at her ear. After punching in the numbers, she waited through the trills. "I guess he must be asleep, it's—"

"Hello. Newman here."

"Sir Newman. It's Marilyn Bannister. I'm sorry to wake you up."

"Oh, I wasn't sleeping. I was feeding the fish in our moat. I very nearly dropped my cell phone in the water when it vibrated. I thought a fish had jumped into my coat pocket!"

"How is the museum going?"

"Splendidly! Once we repaired the castle turret, we conducted a bit of theatre for the museum patrons, a knight rescuing a damsel in distress from the turret window. I played the knight, but I had a bit of trouble climbing down the ladder with the damsel. You see, she wasn't exactly a petite young lady, and we fell from several rungs up. The crowd thought it was part of the act and applauded with great enthusiasm. At the next day's show, the crowd doubled, so we have fallen from the ladder at every performance."

Marilyn held her fingers over her mouth, stifling a laugh. "Aren't you afraid of getting hurt?"

"That was a concern, so we installed rubber padding at our point of impact, but if we don't time our fall properly, and the lady lands on top of me, I do get a bruise or two."

"Sounds painful. Listen. Do you have an e-mail address?"

"Yes. Newman at Hinkling Manor dot com."

She jotted down the address on a notepad. "Great. I'm sending you some data about a man named Marshall Peters. I think he's really Palin. Sir Patrick said you could help us track down where he lived in England."

168

"I know a few people in London who could help us, but I cannot get there myself until late this afternoon. It is a fair drive from Glasgow, if you'll remember."

"Yes, I remember."

"I don't mean to pry into your business, Mrs. Bannister, but I need to know what we're looking for."

"Of course you do." She picked up the photo and propped it against her monitor. "We think Devin is on the prowl again, so we're looking for any clue to help us find out who could have captured and reconstituted his energy."

"And that person might lead you to Devin himself."

"Exactly. We want to find him, before he finds us."

A Face like Flint

B oy wake."

Elam blinked open his eyes. Greevelow stood over him like an ebony tower in muddy trousers.

"Move now." Greevelow nodded toward Abraham lying at Elam's side. "Wake others." He strode away into a curtain of reeds. "Return soon."

Elam sat up. The first rays of dawn spread across the soupy air. Thick fog had settled in, filling his clothes with moisture and bringing a new chill. With Elam, Dikaios, Abraham, and Acacia sleeping in a huddle, everyone had kept warm through the late night hours, but now they would have to get up and face the journey. This search for Abraham's home had become a long series of starts and stops, ducking and hiding, and dodging arrows. After about two hours of sleep, they would have to start the process again, but now without darkness to cover their presence.

He looked at Abraham's leg. The broken end of the arrow still protruded from his skin just below his calf. Greevelow had made a salve from various weeds and applied it to the wound, but he had solemnly warned him not to pull the arrow out. The barbed end would rip his muscle. A doctor would have to push it through when he arrived home.

But where was home? In order to escape the archers, Greevelow had insisted that they leave the river's path and cut straight through the marsh. They had left the comforting sounds of rushing water, a constant noise that had covered their footsteps and hoofbeats while guiding their way, and now without it, Elam felt lost and exposed.

"Abraham." Elam prodded his side. "Greevelow says it's time to go."

"Very well." Abraham sat up and stretched, his eyes darting around. "Where *is* our elusive guide?"

"He said he'd be back soon." As Elam rose to his feet, the top of his head brushed the foggy layer. Since they had chosen a high mound as their bed, his elevation allowed him to see over the tops of the stalks that dressed the expansive marsh in green.

Short trees with skinny branches of smooth yellow bark grew here and there, most of them marking places where the ground rose out of the shallow lake, a clear-water sea that spread for miles across the seemingly endless flat terrain.

"We'd better wake up Acacia and Dikaios," Elam said.

"I am awake." The horsy voice rumbled next to Abraham. "But I think my legs are not yet responding."

"I know that feeling well," Abraham said. He slid over and massaged one of Dikaios's legs. "How many years have you seen, good horse?"

"I passed my second millennium a few decades ago."

"Two thousand years!" Elam shook his head. "Are you related to the colt Jesus rode into Jerusalem?"

Dikaios flapped his lips. "*He* was a donkey. *I* am a horse. Yet, since I once served the Messiah's family in another way, I came to be owned by him later."

While Dikaios struggled to his feet, Elam stooped next to Acacia. She lay on a pillow of twisted weeds, her white hair spread over tiny red blossoms that had withered overnight. Mud spattered her blue cloak and white dress, now torn at the sleeve and at the bottom hem where it brushed her thin ankle. Darker mud caked her bare feet, like form-fitting earthen shoes, certainly not proper attire for a prophetic oracle.

He passed a hand across a strand of hair, pushing it away from her eyes. With her lips slightly parted and her fingers loosely intertwined, she resembled a praying angel.

He sighed. And she looked so much like his beloved Sapphira … too much. Leaning close, he whispered. "Acacia. It's time to go."

"Hmmm?" She blinked, then looked at him with her beautiful blue eyes. "Did I oversleep?"

"No. You're fine." He slid his arm under her back. "You're still exhausted. I'll give you a boost onto Dikaios."

As she rose to her feet, her gaze fell on Abraham's wounded leg. "Abraham should ride," she said. "I'll be fine."

"I'm sure he can carry you both." Elam turned toward Dikaios. "Right?"

Dikaios limped toward them. "Of course. I have borne as many as three, though one was quite small."

Acacia shook her head. "Look at you! Your legs are as stiff as boards." She crossed her arms over her chest. "Whether or not Abraham chooses to ride is up to him. I will walk."

"Fair enough." While helping Abraham mount, Elam kept his eyes on Acacia. "Are you strong enough to make fire?"

She opened her palm and stared at it. For a moment, nothing happened, then, as she furrowed her brow, a ball of fire slowly grew at the center. "There you go, but I'm not sure how long—" The ball suddenly exploded in a tiny spray of sparks that arced to the ground and sizzled. "Hmmm," she said, scowling at her hand. "I guess I needed more rest."

Elam flapped his damp shirt. "I was hoping I could dry off. If we had a—"

"Quiet!" Greevelow parted the reeds and ascended their mound. "Follow! Now!" He then ran through the same gap he had entered.

Dikaios reared up and shot after him. Elam took Acacia's hand and broke into a rapid trot, making sure she could keep up. She pulled her hand away and pumped her arms. Although pain streaked her brow, she seemed able to match his stride as they kept about ten steps behind Dikaios.

Even with Abraham riding, the great horse had no trouble as he cantered over the marshy terrain, threading the narrow gaps between patches of reeds and sloshing through mud and water that sometimes rose a third of the way up his legs.

Acacia's cloak flowed behind her, catching air and creating drag. While keeping his pace, Elam reached over, unhooked the clasp, and wadded the cloak into a ball under his arm. Acacia blew him a kiss and smiled, her eyes as bright as ever.

Elam caught the kiss and looked at his hand. He wanted to wiggle his fingers, the symbol he and Sapphira had often used to show love to each other. But he couldn't. Not to Acacia. Sapphira's sign was too sacred to share with another. He just smiled back and touched his cheek.

After three full minutes of running, warmth spread across Elam's skin. Light broke through the fog in intermittent holes, revealing a rising sun that painted the reeds in a wash of dappled yellow. He glanced at Acacia. Puffing quietly as she ran, she had kept up brilliantly, but now she seemed to favor a leg, the same one Morgan's serpent had bitten so long ago.

Finally, Dikaios slowed to a stop. Elam and Acacia caught up just in time to see Greevelow duck into a thick stand of reeds.

"Where's he going?" Elam whispered up to Abraham.

"He didn't say. He just held up his hand for us to stop, then you saw him leave."

Elam slowed his breathing, turning in a circle to take in the brightening marsh. Now standing in a lower area, a relatively clear spot with ankle-deep water, the taller reeds blocked his view, keeping him from seeing much of the expanse. In one direction, smoke rose into the sky. Could it be a sign that Flint was near?

He touched Abraham's hip and whispered. "You have a better view from up there. Can you see where that smoke's coming from?"

Abraham shielded his eyes. "I see only smoke. ... No! Reeds are moving! Coming this way!"

Greevelow burst through the wall of reeds, carrying a spear. He crouched low and touched his lips, signaling for silence. Abraham slid quietly off Dikaios and held on to the horse's neck, while Elam squatted next to Greevelow. Acacia limped over and sat down in the water, obviously unable to crouch without pain. Elam spread the cloak over her back and refastened the clasp.

Rustling sounds came to Elam's ears, first directly in front, then to his left. He let his eyes dart from place to place, searching the grass stalks for any sign of movement.

An odor drifted into his nostrils. Was it a skunk? Rotting flesh? Acacia wrinkled her nose but said nothing.

Greevelow lifted his spear as if ready to attack, but he slowly lowered it again. He reached over and touched Acacia's ankle, now swollen. He then turned to Abraham and looked at his torn trousers where the arrow shaft protruded from his leg. As his frown deepened, he shook his head.

Elam stared at this odd fellow. Without a single word he had communicated his concern that they wouldn't be able to escape from Flint this time.

Rising to his feet, Greevelow whistled a long warbling call, then spun around and set the point of his spear at Elam's throat. "Surrender!" he barked.

Elam stiffened. Acacia gasped. Abraham whisper-shouted, "What are you—"

"Silence!" Greevelow whistled again.

175

Another whistle rose from the marsh, echoing Greevelow's, then another. Soon dozens of whistles surrounded them, and the marsh grass rustled furiously.

As the spear's point pricked his skin, Elam swallowed. One voice in his head shouted, *"Traitor!"* Another voice shouted back, *"He's pretending!"* But the point of that spear didn't feel like an act. One wrong move, and this play would be over.

Heavy footfalls sounded, getting closer by the second. Dikaios jerked Acacia off the ground with his teeth and swung her around to his back, then took off in a wild gallop. In a splash of water and mud, Dikaios was gone.

The reeds parted directly behind Greevelow, then all around. At least twenty men tromped into the clearing, each one carrying a long spear and whistling the same warble.

"Extend your arms forward!" Abraham called as he struggled to his feet. "It's the sign of surrender."

176

Clenching his fists, Elam pushed his arms out in front of his chest. A long-haired white man dressed only in loose breeches crossed Elam's wrists, pressed the backs of his hands together, and bound them with a prickly vine. The tiny thorns dug into Elam's skin, stinging him with every wiggle beneath the tight handcuffs.

A shorter man, dark, bald, and dressed in similar garb, bound Abraham's hands in the same way. Yet, Abraham showed no signs of pain as the man yanked the vine tight and raised a fist. "We capture fox!" the man crowed.

While the band of half-naked men whistled again, Greevelow pulled back the point of the spear, releasing the pressure on Elam's throat. Elam quickly scanned each of their captors. Strangely enough, only one resembled Greevelow in build, facial shape, and skin tone. Most of the others looked pale and thinner, a few with yellowish hair, and two others with no hair at all, either on their heads or on their chests.

Suddenly, the men fell silent. Another man strode out of the weeds, making deliberate splashes with each emphasized step. Blond and pale, this man stalked toward them in high-top laced boots, thick zippered pants, and a long-sleeved button-down shirt. When he came upon Greevelow, he snatched the spear. "Excellent work. We will release your son when we get the fox back to our village."

The man thrust the spear into the mud and stood face-to-face with Abraham. "Father," he said, emphasizing the name with a sneer, "it is a pleasure to see you again."

"Flint?" Abraham squinted at him. "Is that really you?"

"Were you expecting someone else ... *Father*?" Flint spat on the ground. "Or do you forget all your children when they go astray?"

"It's just that your countenance has changed so much." Abraham held out his hands. "Release me, and I will embrace you. Slap me on the cheek, and I will turn the other. Kill me, and I will die saying that I love you."

Letting out a scornful laugh, Flint stooped next to Abraham's leg. "Words that mask your true feelings amount to the same as lying, don't they?" He grasped the shaft of the broken arrow. "And we both know that lying is strictly forbidden." With a quick thrust, he shoved the arrow the rest of the way through and snatched it out from the other side.

Abraham gnashed his teeth and grunted, but he didn't cry out.

With blood dripping from the point, Flint raised the arrow next to Abraham's face. "Hiding your pain, Father? Are you trying to deceive me into thinking that didn't hurt?" He grasped one of Abraham's bound hands and drove the arrow into his palm.

"Ahrg!" Abraham bit his lip. Breathing heavily, he squeezed his eyes shut.

Flint ripped the arrow back out and let it drop to the water. "That's a little better, but when we get back to our village, I will give you more lessons in expressing your true thoughts."

177

Elam wrestled against his bonds, but the nettlelike vine stung him mercilessly. "What do you want, you coward?"

Flint plucked the spear and set the side of the pointed blade against Elam's cheek. "Is this little man your promised warrior chief?" He laughed again, this time gesturing for his company to laugh with him. They joined in, some adding whistles and indistinct catcalls. "What a shame that Enoch is unable to find a real man among his followers. He had to send a sacrificial lamb. It's almost comical how your heroes are always the ones who end up dead."

With a twist of his wrist, Flint turned the blade, scraping it along Elam's cheek. Elam winced but held his tongue. The sharp edge dug into his face. Blood trickled to his chin and dripped to his chest then to the water at his feet.

"Tell me," Flint crooned, "who is the pretty girl who was with you? I would like to get to know her better."

Elam spoke through clenched teeth. "If you tried, you would drop dead."

"Drop dead?" Flint lowered the spear and drove it through Elam's shoe, slicing through the gap between his toes. "Perhaps you would like to keep your toes and tell me why."

Elam leaned over. As his blood dripped down the shaft of the spear and onto his captor's hand, he raised his head slowly. Something odd dangled at the bottom of a thin gold chain around Flint's neck, a small egg-shaped bauble, glassy, yet cloudy. Elam lifted his gaze and glared at this demon's evil blue eyes. "You would drop dead because worms like you are easily toasted."

His lips parting slightly, Flint's eyes widened, but only for a moment. Then, as he slowly withdrew the spear, his smile returned. "Thank you for that most informative answer." He turned and began to walk away, but he suddenly whipped back around, swinging the spear. The shaft slammed against the side of Elam's head and knocked him off his feet.

Elam splashed face-first into the water. He writhed in agony, clawing at handfuls of mud, barely able to shift his head in order to breathe. Pain roared from one side of his skull to the other, then down his spine. His arms and legs tingled, and his vision dimmed.

He felt the point of the spear against his back. As a ringing buzz clogged his ears, Flint's voice pierced the static. "It would be an easy victory plunging this through his heart right now, wouldn't it, Father?"

"What do you want, Flint? Tell me, and I will do what I can. Just let the boy go."

"Is he really your warrior chief?" Flint laughed once again. "Tell me, Father. I know you won't lie, but if you don't answer at all, I will impale his heart after three draws of his breath."

The sharp point dug into Elam's back, but he couldn't move. Spasms throttled his chest. He wanted to hold his breath to slow the count to three, but he couldn't control his lungs.

Flint's voice rose in dramatic fashion. "One ... two ..."

"He is!" Abraham cried out. After a few seconds of silence, he spoke in a trembling whisper. "He is the warrior chief."

The point lifted. Elam exhaled long and hard. He tried to push up, but a hefty shove sent his face splashing back into the mud.

"Now tell me, Father. If I let this runt you call a warrior chief go running home to his mama, will you cooperate with me?"

"What kind of cooperation do you have in mind?"

"A ceremony that only you are qualified to perform. If all goes according to plan, I will need to keep you alive in order to carry it out."

Abraham sighed. "I will go with you, but I ask that you send Elam with a message telling my people when you will let me go home."

"Easily done. I need to keep you here only two more days. Then my allies will come."

"You remember the prophecies well," Abraham said. "To the greatest detail."

179

"I had a demanding teacher."

The pressure on Elam's back lifted. He turned over, his head still pounding as he sat up. In his crippled vision, Flint's face drifted in and out of focus.

Flint withdrew a dagger from his belt and sliced through Elam's bonds. "I don't think I have anything to worry about. In his condition, he will take at least two days to get home, if he gets there at all."

Elam massaged his lower arms. The nettle had raised itchy red welts and swelled his wrists.

Abraham limped heavily toward Elam, keeping his eye on Flint. "Will you give the warrior chief a guide?"

Flint grabbed Elam's shirt and yanked him to his feet. "I will point him in the right direction. If he has the sense to maintain his heading, he will find his way."

180

"He doesn't know these lands," Abraham said. "How will he survive?"

Flint swept his boot across the water. "There is plenty to drink, and the fruit of the bitternut tree is edible this time of year." With a quick thrust, he slung the spear at a squatty tree about thirty feet away, cleanly piercing a small black fruit and impaling it against the tree's slender trunk.

Trying not to show any surprise at Flint's expertise, Elam eyed the fruit. Thick liquid oozed out, painting a purple stripe on the yellow bark. He concealed an inner shiver. His heart had almost suffered the same fate.

"If its skin is black," Flint continued, "you may eat it. If it is red, it will kill you. Now take the spear and go in the direction I threw it. You will need it if you come upon any muskrats."

Angel patted Grackle's neck and whistled into the wind. The dragon banked left and descended just above the foggy layer. "You search on that side," she said, pointing to her right. "I'll look over here."

Riding in the seat behind her, Candle's voice barely overcame the sound of rushing wind. "I can finally see the ground."

Angel scanned the marsh below. Indeed, with the sun now surfacing above the horizon, the fog was burning away, revealing the vast field of reeds, short trees, and motionless water. Her first pass earlier in the night had proven futile, not a hint of movement or light except in Flint's village, and her later flight over the northern highlands had yielded only a very frightened pair of hunters from her own village. The father and son had tracked a giant boar to a plateau, and their campfire had brought Angel and her dragon diving down in a flurry to investigate.

Angel laughed to herself. The two had reminded her of Dragon and Candle when they went out on the traditional father-and-son initiation, a dedication time for a boy's tenth birthday. The hunters' looks of surprise and then delight would be etched in her mind forever.

With light spreading across her field of vision, a new surge of energy buzzed through her body. Now maybe she'd be able to find Father Abraham, but she couldn't afford to fly close to Flint's village again. Without the cover of darkness, she'd be a target of his warriors' arrows.

She blinked her weary eyes, stifled a yawn, and focused on the swiftly moving ground below. The river was nowhere in sight. She must have shifted to the inner sector, far away from Father Abraham's most likely path. She would have to bend to the east for quite a while to—

"I see someone!" Candle shouted.

Angel jerked around. "Where?"

Candle pointed behind them. "Back there. We passed him."

"Father Abraham?"

He shook his head. "Younger. Hurry. I think he's in trouble."

Elam raised his spear, aiming at a pair of snarling beasts that blocked his path, the only gap in the reeds that would keep him going in the direction Flint had indicated. He could opt to escape through another gap, but similar growls from within had warned him to stay away.

When Abraham and Flint had mentioned muskrats, he had pictured two-pound beaverlike rodents he could shoo away with the shaft of his spear, but these bear-sized balls of fur and fangs seemed to want him for breakfast, and they didn't flinch at the sight of his weapon.

It seemed as if they had a strategy. Staying a few feet apart from each other, one would lunge a step, then draw back, baiting him. Yet, if he threw or thrust his spear at it, he'd be easy prey for the other one.

"You can't outsmart me," Elam said, growling to intimidate them.

As if prodded by Elam's words, one of the muskrats charged. Elam dodged and jabbed as it shot past, but he missed. The other lunged low and snapped at his leg. He leaped over it and sprinted toward the gap in the reeds, but tripped in the mud and toppled forward into a slide. Water and mud splashed into his face and jetted up his nose. Twisting, he flipped to his back, thrusting his spear upward just in time to clip a muskrat's side with a glancing blow. It splashed to the ground, yelped, and scampered away.

The other muskrat leaped on Elam's chest, clamped on to his unguarded wrist, and dug in with needle-sharp teeth.

"Arrrgh!" Elam thrashed his arm, but the snarling rodent hung on. Screaming in agony, Elam slid his hand up his spear and jabbed at the muskrat's side, but he didn't have enough strength to pierce its tough hide.

Finally, he jerked the beast closer and bit its nose as hard as he could. As soon as its jaw loosened, he wrenched his arm away and leaped to his feet. Then, blood dripping from his fingers, he ran, splitting two stands of reeds.

182

After splashing through a narrow channel, he broke into a clearing but stopped in his tracks. In the middle of the twenty-foot-wide shallow pool sat at least fifteen huge muskrats, all with their beady eyes trained on him.

Elam gulped. He spun around. The first two had followed and blocked the way out of the clearing. Now with only one spear and a wounded wrist, he would have to dodge, jab, or even dance his way past the whole lot of them.

As the first two lowered their heads and prowled toward him, the other fifteen slinked through the water from the other side and spread out, surrounding him in a tightening circle of snarls and gleaming teeth. Elam searched for a gap on the other side of the clearing. If he pole-vaulted over the smallest one, he could—

Suddenly, something clawed his back. His shirt tightened. The ground shot away from under his feet. Still clutching his spear, he looked up. Purple scales blocked his vision, purple scales and ... wings? A dragon?

A woman's voice called from above. "Hang on, Elam! We'll find a safe place for Grackle to land!"

"Angel! Great timing!" Elam flinched at the pain of the dragon's claw as it dug into his shoulder, but he stayed as still as possible. Better to bleed now than to be a meal for muskrats.

He scanned the brightening marsh. When would she find a safe place? There was nothing but water and grass for miles, and wandering muskrats here and there. It was a good thing those hungry rodents were morning feeders. Facing them in the middle of the night would have been deadly.

In the distance, the land rose into a meadow of browning grass. He searched for hoofprints, hoping Dikaios had been speedy enough to outrun and leap over the predators. Yet, he found no sign of a horse anywhere.

As soon as they reached the field, Grackle descended and set Elam down, but not as gently as he had hoped. He fell headlong

183

into a wild somersault and slid through the grass on his bottom. When he came to a stop, he jammed his spear into the ground and pushed himself to his feet. The dragon landed several paces in front of him, beating its wings and scampering on its short, muscular legs.

Candle leaped off first, jumping from his seat all the way to the ground. Wearing a broad grin, he hustled to Elam's side and grabbed his free hand. "You can take my seat. Mother says I get to ride on Grackle's neck!"

"Thank you. That would be better than—"

"You're bleeding!" Candle jerked away and shook blood from his fingers. "My mother is a doctor; she'll know what to do."

Yawning as she walked, Angel approached. She reached for him with an open hand, a look of distress in her eyes. "You're hurt!"

She touched his cheek, making him wince. He couldn't figure out what hurt the most—his cheek, his wrist, or the dragon claw wound on his back. "I'm okay," he said with a nod. "Did you see Dikaios or Acacia or Father Abraham?"

Her brow shot upward. "I was going to ask *you* where they are."

"Flint captured Father Abraham, but Dikaios and Acacia escaped. Flint set me free to find the way on my own."

Angel looked out over the marsh. "Flint is challenging us. He craves a war, but he knows he cannot win if Father Abraham is here to lead our people."

"Won't his abduction cause your people to rise up in anger? Doesn't Flint fear an army fueled by rage?"

Looking back at him, Angel shook her head. "Without the Prophet here to call for Enoch's help, my people will be like dragons without riders. They won't know what to do."

"Will Flint attack?"

"Not today, I think. He is likely to reestablish his alliance with the shadow people and attack with all his forces under the cover

184

of night. Whether he could be ready by this evening, I don't know."

Elam cast his gaze back over the marsh. Flint said he had to wait two days for his allies to come. Did he mean the shadow people? Maybe. But how could anyone know whether or not Flint was telling the truth? He also might have been lying, hoping Abraham's people wouldn't be ready for an immediate attack. Either way, wouldn't it be better to prepare for them to show up sooner?

"Is there any chance of rescuing Father Abraham before nightfall?" Elam asked.

Angel shook her head. "No raiding party could penetrate the marshes. Even from the air with the five dragons willing to carry us, we would be too few."

"Then we have to get ready." Elam clenched his fist and strode toward Grackle. "Come on. There's no time to lose."

Angel grabbed his sleeve. Nearly falling as he spun back toward her, he wrapped his bloody fingers around his spear and leaned on it. "Yes?" he asked.

She gazed into his eyes. "You are truly the warrior chief we have awaited for so many years."

He nodded. "I appreciate your confidence. I hope I can—"

"No!" she cried, a large tear streaming. "You don't understand. When I first saw you, I feared that Enoch sent a boy to do a man's job. I doubted you. I thought we would have to wait for another." She gripped the spear, wrapping her fingers tightly around his as she drew her face closer. "But now I see a fire in your eyes and wisdom beyond your years. I watched you face more than a dozen wild muskrats, and you proved yourself a warrior as strong as Valiant himself." She wiped her tear, then pulled so close her cheek brushed against his. As she nuzzled his ear, she whispered. "You are *my* warrior chief, and I will fight with you to the death."

185

Goose bumps crawled across his skin. He let her stay close for a moment, unsure of how to react. This culture's affectionate ways felt good, but they would take some getting used to.

"Okay," he said, pulling back. "First we have to find Dikaios and Acacia. Then we should see about talking to Enoch."

"May I suggest consulting Enoch first? Perhaps he can tell us where the great horse and the Oracle are." She covered her mouth with her fingers. "But who am I to tell the warrior chief what to do?"

Elam tried to keep a straight face, but a grin broke through. "Make all the suggestions you want. I'm new at this warrior chief business."

CHAPTER

HEALING FIRES

Ashley marched into a field of grass, her arms stiff at her sides and her fists tight. Walter followed a few paces behind, looking back at the village before focusing on Ashley again. Since she was in her mad-at-the-world posture, it was best to stay quiet. They had already searched for her mother back at the spot they had last seen her. Now the dragon launching field was the only place they knew to look. At least this was the only option the villagers would suggest.

When Ashley reached a point about a hundred feet into the field, she looked up into the sky and called out, "Mother! Where are you?"

Walter cupped his hands around his mouth and shouted, "Thigocia! The meeting's over! We have some information!"

"Information?" Ashley repeated. "You call what just happened 'information'?" She reached into her hair and grabbed two fistfuls. "Ohhh! Those people practically drove me crazy! I wonder how they even dress themselves without consulting 'the Prophet'!"

Walter stuffed his hands into his pockets and shrugged. "I can't say I blame them. We're strangers. We wear odd clothes. We brought a talking dragon. Why should they tell us what they know about their garden?"

Ashley let out a huff and flapped her arms at her sides. "I know. I know. It's just that it's life or death. Abigail is missing, and now so's my mother. If either one needs healing, I can help. But I can't heal what I can't see."

Walter reached back to his scabbard and touched Excalibur's hilt. "I guess I should test the beam. It didn't always work in Hades."

"Right. We might need it for healing and as a weapon."

Walter withdrew Excalibur and lifted it toward the sky. As he gazed at its point, something dark appeared close to the horizon, flying erratically. "Is that a dragon?" he asked, aiming the sword at it.

188

Ashley stood on tiptoes. "I think so, but it's darker, maybe even black. It isn't my mother."

They watched the winged form draw closer and closer. Soon three riders took shape, one high on the neck and two in seats strapped to the dragon's back. They circled once, then, as Walter and Ashley backed toward the edge of the field, the dragon, purple and smaller than Thigocia, landed in a flurry of wings and churning legs.

As soon as the dragon lowered its head, the passenger on its neck, a black boy with bright eyes and a wide smile, scampered down the stairway and hurried toward the village. "I'll run for help!" he called without turning back.

A woman and a teenaged boy began to dismount, both half staggering.

Walter rushed over and extended a hand toward each of them. They gladly accepted his help as they stepped off the dragon's neck. The boy looked like death warmed over. With blood oozing down his cheek and fingers, and a nasty laceration showing through a rip on the back of his shirt, he had to have been the loser in a fight with a bear ... or worse.

Stifling a yawn, the woman curtsied. "Welcome, stranger. I am Angel. The boy who ran into the village is my son, Candle. You must be from a distant village, for I do not recognize you."

"Very distant," Walter said, "but it's kind of hard to explain. We—"

"Walter!" Ashley marched straight to the boy and touched his wounded cheek. "It's Elam!"

"Oh, yeah!" Walter patted his back, careful to avoid the slice in his shirt. "Sorry. I only saw you once when that giant lassoed Heaven, and you don't exactly look yourself now."

"It's okay." Elam smiled, but his weariness showed through in his sagging shoulders. "Where's Sapphira?"

Ashley massaged his wound lightly. "She'll be coming later. At least, we hope she will, and with more helpers."

Elam's head sank. "I hope so, too." Suddenly, his eyes lit up, and he laid his fingers over Ashley's. "What did you do?"

Ashley pulled her hand back. "Does it feel better?"

"Yeah. A lot." He dabbed the wound, now smaller and oozing less blood. "The cut's still there, but the sting is gone."

"What happened to you?" Walter asked Elam. "Were you in a fight?"

"Just some big muskrats and a sadistic guy with a spear, but that can wait. Acacia, Dikaios, and Abraham are missing, so we came here to consult Enoch."

"My sister is missing, too," Ashley said, "and the people here said someone named 'the Prophet' could ask Enoch where she is. But why can't we ask him ourselves? The people were pretty mysterious about it, something about talking to an egg, but when I heard that, I just shut down. I felt like I was in the middle of a nightmare."

189

Angel raised her fingers to her lips, hiding a smile. "The egg is Enoch's Ghost, Father Abraham's ovulum. Since he was not born here, it is the only companion he has."

"Too much information!" Ashley laid her palms on the sides of her head. "My brain is about to choke. I need to—" She jerked her head upward. "I sense something … a strange call. … Distressed. … Urgent."

Walter searched the sky. Flying low across the meadow, a dragon closed in on the field, its wings faltering as it descended.

Ashley pointed. "Mother's coming!"

Thigocia beat her wings against the cool breeze, tossed back and forth as if unable to combat the crosswind. A blue cloak and white hair flowed behind her passenger, but the girl's face was hidden. She was leaning her cheek against a spine, both arms clutching it loosely.

"The Oracle, Acacia, is riding," Angel said as Thigocia extended her claws for a landing, "but she appears to be hurt."

"Come on, Mother, you can do it!" Ashley angled her body, as if mentally guiding Thigocia to bank left to keep her white-haired passenger from falling. She landed heavily, her mangled wings beating hard as she tried to keep her balance. Acacia wobbled. With her eyes blinking wearily, she tipped over and tumbled down Thigocia's side.

Elam lunged and caught her in his arms. The sudden load made him stagger backward, but Walter and Ashley braced him before he could fall. Elam let Acacia down to her feet slowly, making sure she could stand on her own.

Heaving for breath, Thigocia pulled in her wings and settled to the ground. Puffs of black smoke punctuated each labored word. "I found the girl … and her horse … surrounded by men with spears. I recognized her … caught her up … knocked the men out of the way. … The horse escaped … A man jabbed … a spear into me. My wings were insufficient to avoid it." She rolled partway to the side, revealing a wide gash in her unprotected belly.

"Mother!" Ashley bolted to her and laid her hand on the wound. As she scooted on her knees to brace her body under her mother's belly, sparkling blood oozed between her fingers and dripped to the ground. "Can you tell how bad it is?"

Thigocia wagged her head back and forth. "It must be bad. … I have no energy … to heal myself." Her red pupils flashed, then faded. With a thump, her head dropped to the ground.

"Walter!" Ashley yelled. "Light up the sword!"

"Stand back, everyone!" Walter drew out Excalibur and lifted it high. He concentrated on the blade, sending the usual mental energy, but it merely glinted in the sunlight. Letting out a loud groan, he shook the sword. "It's not working!"

Ashley pushed the sides of the wound together, but blood continued to flow. "What can we do? My touch isn't helping!"

"Another energy source." Walter pointed the sword at Acacia. "Can you whip up a fire like your sister can?"

"When I am healthy." Acacia gave him a weary nod. "I will try."

Ashley waved frantically. "Come over here and wrap your arms around me."

Taking wobbly steps, Acacia obeyed. She draped her body over Ashley's kneeling form and reached both arms around her. "Like this?"

"Yes. Now turn on your fire. Just a little at first. I don't know how it's going to affect me."

"A little might be all I can manage." Acacia took in a slow breath, then let it out in a whisper. "Give me light."

Starting at her hands, a rippling fire spread along her arms, then across her body. The flames seemed weak, no more than a half inch high, but they soon covered Acacia's dress and cloak, as well as her dirty face and legs.

As the flames spread over Ashley's clothes, she gasped. Her eyes opened wide. Heaving and exhaling in rapid bursts as the fire coated her body, her face tensed. Her hand pressed tighter against her mother's wound. After a few seconds, a weak white light emanated from her eyes. She moved her hand out of the way and rotated her head to shift the light to the deep gash.

Acacia groaned but said nothing. The flames flickered. No longer covering her feet, the line of fire receded up her legs and faded from her face.

Ashley's eyebeams coated the wound. The blood sizzled and hardened to black ash. Slowly, ever so slowly, a scab eased over the cut. Ashley's legs jerked. Her entire body trembled, shaking Acacia as well, but she kept her eyebeams in place.

Finally, with a slight popping sound, her beams blinked off. She pushed away from her mother, and with Acacia still hanging on, she toppled to the side. The flames died away as the two bodies sprawled across the ground.

In a flash, Walter and Elam were at their side. Walter slid his hands under Ashley's back, while Elam dropped to his seat and pulled Acacia into his arms.

As Elam brushed Acacia's hair back from her face, she gave him a weak smile. "I think she's okay," he called.

Walter gritted his teeth. "Ashley's still smoking!"

Thigocia opened her eyes and tried to lift her head. "Move her into the clear where the breeze will cool her."

When he had pulled Ashley well away, Walter laid her on her back and began fanning her face. With her eyes loosely closed, she wheezed through half-second shallow breaths.

"Anyone have any water?" he asked, turning toward Angel.

Angel waved at a group of four women who had just stepped onto the field, led by Candle. "Birdsong! Greenleaf!" Angel shouted as she knelt at Ashley's side. "Fill a tub from the spring! Hurry! I will meet you at your hut."

Two women turned and ran back to the village, while the other two hustled to join Angel. With curiosity-filled eyes they bent over and looked on.

"I have heard of such fever," Angel said, "but only among the marsh people." She looked up at the new arrivals. "Carry her to the tub. Remove her clothes and cool her with wet cloths before setting her in the bath. We don't want to shock her."

One woman picked up Ashley's feet, while the other lifted her under her arms, and the two carried her toward the village.

Candle stayed behind and touched Angel's hip. "The men are gathering a search party. May I go with them?"

"I will ask Valiant if you are old enough. For now, stay here. I might need you."

"Yes, Mother." Candle sat in the grass and stared at a glass egg rocking back and forth on his palm. "I will wait for your word."

Angel laid her hand behind Walter's head. "You should go with your Eve. She will probably awaken when she is put in the water, and if you are not there, she might be frightened. I will see to the others."

Heat flowed into Walter's face. What did she mean by "Eve"? As he tried to figure out how to answer, he glanced at Thigocia. She had raised her head and was now testing her legs. Elam and Acacia stood side by side watching her. They all seemed fine. "If I'm not there," he finally said, "Ashley might be scared, but if I *am* there, and she's ... well ..."

Angel set her cool fingers on Walter's cheek. "This redness in your face. Is it shame?"

"Not really. Just embarrassed at the thought of being around when she's ... you know."

"Uncovered?" she asked, cocking her head.

"Well ... yeah."

Her brow wrinkled. "Are you not her Adam?"

"Her Adam?"

193

She tapped her foot on the ground and looked down at Candle. "What was that word Timothy used?"

"Husband," Candle said, rising to his feet. "And they say 'wife' instead of 'Eve.'"

Angel raised a finger. "Oh, yes, her husband."

Walter slid his hands into his pockets. "Well, no. Where I come from we don't usually get married this young."

"I see. So you *are* from another world." She took Candle's hand and walked toward Elam and Acacia. "I was wondering why you had no companion."

Walter stayed near her side, just a step behind. What could she have meant by "companion"? Obviously she didn't mean Ashley, but, if he asked, it would probably make the situation more confusing than ever.

When Angel reached the others, she massaged Thigocia's neck. "Father Abraham has told me about talking dragons, but you are the first I have met. I have many questions, including why Ashley called you her mother, but if you truly are her mother, I'm sure you want us to see how she is faring before I satisfy my curiosity."

"You have spoken well," Thigocia said. "I do want to know about her recovery." She narrowed her eyes to a pair of slits. "Your manner of address reminds me of a dear old friend, actually a relative of mine, but we can speak of that later, as well."

Angel smiled. "I have no dragon relations, but I love every dragon I have ever met." She walked over to Thigocia's wing and raised a loose flap. "We have people who mend dragon wings. Since you are larger than our passenger dragons, I doubt that you can navigate our streets, so I will send a leather worker out to you. Maybe by then he can bring word of your daughter's condition."

A weak whinny sounded. Elam and Walter spun toward the call. A white horse plodded toward them, its head down and its coat striped with long red marks.

"Dikaios!" Elam ran to the horse and threw his arms around its neck. As he pulled back, he brushed Dikaios's mane up over his withers, revealing a deep gash. "What happened?"

As the two walked toward the rest of the company, Dikaios spoke in a low voice. "After the dragon rescued Acacia, I had a violent disagreement with a large contingent of muskrats. While trying unsuccessfully to negotiate terms of peace, Flint's men caught up and reintroduced me to their spears. Fortunately, they became preoccupied with the muskrats, allowing me to excuse myself. One of the muskrats tried to go for a ride on my back, and it took quite a while to discourage him. When I finally succeeded, I looked up in the sky and watched the dragon transfer Acacia from her claws to her back. I was so impressed, I decided to follow its path."

Elam grinned and rubbed an uninjured part of Dikaios's coat. "Did you work on that explanation all the way over here?"

"Yes." Dikaios winked at him. "I thought I would mimic your penchant for understatement."

Angel clapped her hands twice. "With the exception of Father Abraham, all are accounted for. Valiant will want to send the search party immediately, but even if they find Father Abraham from the air, they will not be able to rescue him." She set a hand on Elam's shoulder. "We need our warrior chief to devise a plan to bring him home."

Elam took in a breath and exhaled loud and long. "Okay. Let's go talk to Enoch's Ghost."

Standing atop the turbine next to Yereq and Gabriel, Sapphira whipped the fiery cyclone above her head into a frenzy. As she swirled her arms, she followed the sound of a buzzing airplane engine and spotted *Merlin* closing in directly in front of her. "Okay," she called. "Boost me up."

195

Yereq ducked below the fire and wrapped his huge hands around her waist. Suddenly, she flew upward until she was suspended a dozen feet above the turbine. Her head entered the eye of her firestorm for a moment, but as she continued waving her arms, it ascended and spun furiously around her hands.

She reached down with her bare feet, trying to locate his shoulders. When she finally planted them firmly, she called to him. "When I say 'Now,' I'm going to jump and cover all three of us with the flames. The portal column should stay in the air long enough for the plane to fly into it."

"At your command," Yereq said. "I will make sure you land gently."

Gabriel called from below. "And I'll be here to catch you, just in case."

As the plane drew near, using her enhanced vision, she could see Billy and his father in the cockpit, both looking right at her through their windshield. She took a deep breath and held it. She had to time this just right. Once she lowered the portal column, she might not be able to see the plane at all.

She brought her arms down. The ring of fire descended, making a flaming cocoon around her body. The sound of whipping flames drowned out the buzzing propeller, and the plane faded into a miragelike apparition of swirling orange. Pulling her arms in at her sides, she closed her eyes, now relying on her memory of *Merlin*'s speed, and counted. Five … four … three … two … one … "Now!"

She leaped off Yereq's shoulders. With Yereq's hands again around her waist, she drifted down. Her body slid out of her cocoon, and the flames continued to spin above her. As soon as her feet touched down, she thrust her fiery hands upward again, trying to weave a connection to the cyclone. The airplane blasted into the flaming wall, its landing gear barely sweeping over their heads. Like a toy twisting in a tornado, *Merlin* spun with the cyclone. As orange sparks launched in arching splashes, the wings melted away, then the fuselage, until the airplane and the portal disappeared.

Sapphira clasped her hands together, snuffing her fire. She looked up at Yereq. He looked back at her. He reached down one of his meaty hands and took hers. "I am sure they are all right. They just went to the other world without us."

"Yeah," Gabriel said. "An airplane couldn't possibly burn up that fast."

"We'll soon find out." Sapphira pulled away from Yereq and raised her arms. "I'll just make another portal and—"

"No!" A new voice shouted from somewhere below. "You must not."

Sapphira lowered her hands and walked to the edge of the platform. A man waved from the turbine room floor. With her eyes still sharp, she had no trouble identifying the newcomer, a man she had recently seen from far away as he stood at Heaven's Gate. "Enoch!"

As the plane raced toward the twisting fire, Billy grabbed the hand rests and tensed his muscles. "Just a few seconds! Everyone hang on!"

He looked back. Sirs Patrick and Barlow had copied his pose, but Shiloh sat comfortably, her hands loose on the rests. "This should be fun!" she said with a smile and a wink.

"Yeah, right." Billy wheeled to the front. "As fun as a hot foot!"

His father gripped the control yoke, his knuckles white. "She jumped! I'm cutting the engine!"

As the propeller's buzz died, Billy held his breath. The flames splashed against the windshield. The airplane jerked to the right, but then settled. Instead of bursting out on the other side or spinning in a fiery carnival ride, they seemed to float in a sea of orange. Suddenly, as if kicked from behind, they blasted out of the cone and into the clear.

"Restart!" Billy called.

His father revived the engine. The propeller whirled up to speed, and the plane coasted over the new scenery with ease.

Billy looked out the side window. The power plant, the dam, and the river had all disappeared. Now only a vast green meadow spread out below, dotted with lush trees and coated with a multi-colored blanket of wildflowers.

He pumped his fist. "Woo-hoo! We made it!"

His father flopped back in his seat and whispered, "Thank the Maker!"

"Praise the Lord!" Shiloh called from the back. She turned to her father. "It worked! You were right!"

"Yes, my prediction was accurate," Sir Patrick said as he mopped his brow with a handkerchief. "But I must say, I had my doubts."

Sir Barlow squeezed as far as he could into the cockpit. "Any sign of the white-haired lass and her friendly giant?"

Billy's father turned the yoke. "We're swinging back now to have a look."

Billy leaned forward and scanned the ground, searching the colors for a telltale spot of white. As they descended, however, the greens, purples, reds, and yellows that swept past them underneath gave no hint of white, or the other obvious feature, a man nearly as big as their airplane.

After several passes of silent scanning, his father finally said, "No sign of them. We'll have to land."

As they descended, Billy looked at the GPS monitor. A warning light said that the receiver had lost contact with the satellites. He settled back in his seat and let out a long breath. They really were in another world.

Elam followed Angel into the humble abode, passing between two dragons painted on the exterior wall. Leaving the door open to allow light into the room, he stayed just a step behind her as she tiptoed forward.

She stopped for a moment, then dashed to the back of the hut and slapped her palms on a table. "Where is it? It was here last night!"

She dropped to her knees and searched the floor underneath. "It's clear glass, the shape of an egg, and the size of a small cantaloupe."

Elam crossed his arms and scanned the area, his gaze hopping from a blanket-covered cot at the right side of the room, to an oval throw rug next to the cot, to a solitary hardback chair close to the table, to a well-worn kneeling altar at the left. "I've seen one before. Red mist inside, right?"

She banged her head on the table, let out a yelp, then crawled out, her hand massaging her scalp. "Yes. That's exactly right." As she rose to her feet, she pointed at him. "You didn't take it, did you?"

"Not me." He raised his hands and backed away. "I haven't seen one in years."

She closed her eyes and shook her head. "I'm sorry. I'm just so confused, I'm not thinking straight."

"How about Flint? Or one of the shadow people?"

"It's too big for the shadow people to carry. They can barely manage one of our companions. And as long as Flint's holding Father Abraham, I don't think he would risk leaving his prisoner."

Angel scooted over to the cot and flipped up the thin, straw-stuffed mattress. While she looked through the blankets, Elam ran a finger along the table, making a line in the dust. Near the back, a round stand sat on the weathered wood. It, too, had made a slight path through the dust, as if someone had pushed it when taking the ovulum. As his eyes adjusted to the dimmer light, something else came into view on the table. Was it writing?

He stepped to the side, allowing light to spill over the table. He stooped and looked at it again, this time at an angle. The writing became clear—*For Sapphira.*

199

Picking up the stand, he walked over to Angel. She flopped down on the cot and blew a shock of hair out of her eyes. Tears welled, sparkling in the light from the doorway. "I'm the last one who saw it," she said, her voice breaking. "I came in here uninvited."

He sat next to her and set his elbows on his thighs, propping the empty stand in his fingers. "Don't worry. I know where it is."

"You do? Where?"

He smiled, partially because of Angel's cry of relief and partially because he knew why his old friend had taken the ovulum. "Enoch has it."

She pointed at the floor. "Enoch walked right into this room?"

"Apparently so. He wrote a note for me in the dust on the table."

"But why would he take it? We need his help so desperately! And why would he leave? He could have stayed and given us advice."

200

Elam got up and reached for her hand. "Enoch's ways are mysterious, but my guess is that he wants me to rely on what I have already learned, and he knows someone else needs the ovulum more than we do."

CHAPTER

NEW JOURNEYS

Gabriel flew down from the turbine, carrying Sapphira. As soon as her feet touched the main floor, she broke free from his embrace and ran into Enoch's waiting arms. She pressed her cheek against his tunic and breathed in the aroma of worn leather. "Oh, Father Enoch! It's so good to see you!"

His strong hand patted her back, and his friendly voice rose above the sound of the nearby waterfall. "My dear girl, it is a delight to finally be with you after all these years."

As she rubbed her cheek against the rough tunic, she squeezed even tighter. "I'll never forget how much you helped me! Never!"

"Well, now I need your help." When Gabriel joined them, Enoch gently pushed Sapphira away and waved at Yereq, who was climbing down the last few rungs of the ladder. "Come, and we'll sit together so the four of us can talk at the same level."

When they had all sat down on the floor, the wind eased, and the sun's warming rays washed over them. Enoch took Sapphira's hand and looked at her palm. "Your power is quite remarkable, young lady."

"Young lady?" Sapphira grinned. "Father Enoch, I'm thousands of years old."

"And I am older still, so I claim the right to call you young." As he released her hand, his laugh lines smoothed out, and his eyes seemed to deepen with his tone. "It is because of your many years in the darkest of dungeons that I call for your help. You have successfully delivered the necessary warriors for the initial battle, but now I ask you to protect a warrior who will be needed later."

"So I have to stay here on Earth?"

"In a manner of speaking. You see, since Earth and Hades have united, you don't have to leave this realm at all."

A slight lump grew in her throat. "Do you want me to go back to Hades?"

"As I said, you are already in Hades, but you will have to go—"

"To the underground mines?" Her voice pitched higher. "But why?"

"I am sending you and Yereq to protect a very special person. A slayer is chasing her, and without your help, she will likely fall into his hands."

"Is Bonnie the special person?"

Enoch smiled. "Your many years have allowed you to figure out my thoughts very easily."

Sapphira tilted her head downward and intertwined her fingers. She had been in those caves for thousands of years, while her time spent in freedom had seemed like seconds, and most of those seconds had been filled with danger. Now Enoch, the great prophet who had given her so much, the bard who had introduced her to Elohim and had taught her how to dance with God, wanted her to return to that awful, horrible, dark place.

As the image came to mind of her hovel, a gloomy dugout in the rock that held her little cave of a bed for hundreds of years, tears welled in her eyes. It was so lonely, especially after Elam left, and now ... now when she thought she would get to go up to

Heaven's Gate and be with him … to touch him once again, see him smile, hold his hand …

Finally, the tears flowed. "But why, Father Enoch? Why can't Bonnie find another place to hide? She's been able to stay away from slayers before."

He rubbed her back tenderly. "The slayer is the crafty Sir Devin. You see, he never died on Earth. He was transformed into light energy, and a dark, magical power has given him a physical residence as well as a new ability that allows him to track Bonnie wherever she goes."

She lifted her head. "Except for the mines?"

Enoch nodded. "Except for the mines. And since you know the mines so well—how to find food and water, how to maintain your faith even after years of darkness, and how to see through spiritual windows to know when it is safe to depart—you are the only one suitable for this task."

"Spiritual windows? I thought the portals between Earth and Hades wouldn't work anymore, since the two realms combined."

"Those portals are closed, but a physical hole to the underground is still passable on the mountaintop."

"Then what good is hiding there? The slayer can follow us."

Enoch shook his head. "Only Yereq is strong enough to climb down the walls of the chasm to the old mobility room, and the tunnel from there to the mines has collapsed. He can dig it out and close you in again. Then he will stand guard for as long as it takes and supply your provisions as you need them.

"Would you do that?" Sapphira asked, looking up at Yereq. "Even if it takes years?"

Yereq blinked his huge eyes. "For you, I would stand guard for centuries."

"Good for you." Gabriel patted Yereq on the back. "You're the coolest giant I've ever met. Well … you're the *only* giant I've ever met, but I'm sure you're the coolest."

Sapphira took Yereq's hand and kissed his thumb. "Gabriel's right. You're amazing." She then turned to Enoch. "So if there are no portals, how can I look through spiritual windows?"

Enoch leaned to the side and reached into a pocket. He withdrew a glass egg the size of two fists.

"The ovulum!" Sapphira reached for it. "I thought it was destroyed!"

He laid it in her hands. "This is not the one you had, my dear. It came from another land. It was misused by someone there and, quite frankly, had become too much of a crutch for the people it helped. I give it to you now so that you can watch the proceedings in Second Eden. Soon ... relatively speaking, of course ... you and Bonnie will be called upon to go there."

"And Yereq?"

"Oh, yes. And Yereq. As the last of the Nephilim, at least the last here on Earth, his services will be indispensable."

Sapphira gazed into the ovulum. Inside, the image of a dim room appeared. A woman had lifted a thin mattress on a cot and was looking underneath. A young man walked into the scene, and he and the woman began talking, though their voices didn't come through. As the two sat, Sapphira brought the egg closer and stared at the young man. "It's Elam!"

"He is in Second Eden, doing my bidding."

She held the ovulum against her chest and caressed the glass. "Will I get to go to him?"

"Perhaps. It's too early to tell."

"But don't prophets like you know the future?"

"We report what God intends to do, but we don't see the future, at least not as one views an object with his eyes. God will complete his purpose on Earth and in Second Eden, but who will live and who will die along the way?" He shook his head sadly. "I do not know."

Sapphira looked at the ovulum again, but the inner image had faded away, replaced by red mist. Still, the portrait of Elam's face stayed in her mind—determined, yet serene, as usual. Always with his mind on his task, he was never distracted by his emotions. If the desire for the two of them to someday unite coursed within him as powerfully as it did in her, it had to be overwhelming at times. Yet, he seemed content to wait.

Letting out a long sigh, she firmed her chin. "I can do this." She looked at Enoch's wise old face. "For you and Bonnie, I'll do anything."

"Very good, my child." Enoch raised a finger. "One more caution. It seems that Devin's new talent is linked to being able to locate sources of spiritual light energy. If you use your fire-making power too often in the mines, he could well track you down. And if he believes he knows where Bonnie is, no giant will be able to stop the army he will amass in his mad obsession to kill her."

"So Bonnie has light energy?" Sapphira asked.

"Oh, yes. She carries it with her, and it's crucial that she keep it, even if she discovers it is leading a slayer to her. I believe, however, that hers will be weak enough in the depths to be ineffectual as a ... a homing device I suppose you could say."

"If I can't use my power, will we always be in the dark?"

"I think it will be safe to use your hands or a lantern until you orient yourselves, but after that, you should use only the light of the ovulum and the magma river."

Sapphira took in a deep breath. "That will make it much harder."

"Indeed it will. That is why you, as one who has endured a much longer trial in those caves, must be Bonnie's comfort, for I expect you to be there for a considerable amount of time. At the end of this journey, I believe you will come out far stronger, wiser, and more prepared for your battle. And if not for you joining the effort against the evil forces, Second Eden would not survive, and Earth and Hades would stay merged forever."

"Okay. What do I do first?"

205

"Bonnie and her mother will meet you at the mountain site. I know it's a long walk, and you're tired, but Gabriel and Yereq will help you, and you should have plenty of time."

"I'll fly her all the way there," Gabriel said, "but is there anything else you want me to do?"

Enoch gripped his shoulder. "You will be an excellent shuttle service for those going to the bottom of the mobility room hole. After that, however, I have no expectations. You are free to serve as you wish."

"I could stay with them down there." Gabriel shrugged. "I mean, I know I'll be the only guy in the gaggle, but I can find a private little cave to sleep in. I don't have anywhere else to go."

Sapphira took Gabriel's hand. "We'd love to have you. I know just the place for you to stay."

"I hope to have one other person join you," Enoch said. "Like you, she has suffered greatly, so I will not coerce her in any way. If she is unwilling, we will have to change our plans dramatically, but I believe she will come without question. When you are all settled in the underground hideaway, I will appear to you in the ovulum and give you further instructions."

Sapphira cradled the ovulum in her palms. As she gazed again into its red mist, Enoch continued. "I must go now to guide the other warriors to battle. As long as you hold firmly to what you know, you will be able to endure."

Billy swept a shoe through the grass. Nothing but colorful wildflowers, crystal-clear pools, and pristine forests as far as the eye could see. Sure, it was beautiful, but he didn't come here to see the greatest landscape job in all creation. They needed Sapphira, and she wasn't anywhere in sight.

Sir Barlow joined him and waved an arm toward the scenery. "A magnificent view! I tell you, if the white-haired lass is right, and this is merely Heaven's porch, then I think my eyes could not stand the glory of Heaven itself."

Billy smiled at the noble knight. He was a true gentleman without a trace of deception ... or subtlety. His centuries in the candlestone must have been torture, but they obviously taught him a lot about appreciating freedom.

"It really is beautiful, that's for sure." Billy nodded toward a point where the grass suddenly ended. "I'm going to see what's over that cliff."

As he walked toward the edge, he kept his eye on Shiloh as she sat cross-legged in the grass, the warm breeze blowing back her braids. With her eyes open wide and her face tilted toward the sky, she seemed content to drink in the beauty. As usual, nothing fazed her, not a hair-raising collision with a fiery cyclone, a sudden appearance in another world, not even the disappearance of the only person who could possibly get them back home.

Her father stood next to his father, the two of them examining a series of scorch marks on one of the airplane's wings, but since it had flown around this place and landed without incident, the damage couldn't have been too heavy.

When he neared the edge of the grass, he slowed down. Something didn't look right. The blue sky that signaled the sudden drop-off seemed odd, not transparent, but rather more like a painted wall, yet so well constructed that it appeared to have depth.

He turned back. "Hey, Sir Barlow! Check this out!"

"Yes, William," the burly man replied as he marched toward him. "Did you find something strange down there?"

"More like up here." As he set his palm close to the surface, a slight tingling sensation ran along his skin. He jerked his hand back. "That's weird. It feels like it might be electrically charged."

Sir Barlow drew his sword. "Perhaps a light touch will reveal the truth without causing undue harm."

As he set the point near the barrier, a narrow vertical line split the blue canopy, revealing a brilliant light, so bright, Billy had to shield his eyes.

Sir Barlow staggered backward. "I didn't touch it! I swear it!"

The rift widened to at least three feet. Then, a human figure emerged from the light. As the gap closed, the radiance faded, leaving an elderly man wearing a leather tunic tied at the waist with a narrow rope. Sandaled and sporting calf-length breeches, he looked like a character out of a Bible drama.

Billy extended his hand, but he couldn't keep it from trembling. "I'm Billy Bannister."

The man took Billy's hand and shook it heartily. "I am Enoch, prophet of the Most High. I'm glad to meet you, son of Jared."

"Enoch?" Sir Barlow dropped to one knee and bowed his head. "I am most honored to meet you, sir. I have heard stories about you ever since I was just a lad."

"Is that so?" Enoch touched Barlow's shoulder. "The Bible says little about me."

As Barlow rose, his mustache lifted, revealing a wide smile. "Yet there are many stories in other books, incredible tales of wonderful adventures."

"Incredible?" Enoch pursed his lips and nodded slowly. "Yes, perhaps to many they are."

"Speaking of incredible tales," Billy said, "Ashley told me she met you while running away from a giant in a stairwell from Hades."

"A true tale, and a harrowing one."

"I was wondering how you know my father's name? Did she mention it?"

Enoch waved his hand. "I will have to tell you someday after our adventures are complete. What is important now is your mission, and I must guide you to Second Eden as soon as possible."

Billy nodded toward *Merlin*. "We flew our airplane here. Will that help?"

"Without a doubt. I'm impressed by your ingenious plan to bring it to the Bridgelands."

"It was Sir Patrick's idea," Billy said. "He and Sapphira figured out how to do it."

"Ah, yes." Enoch patted Billy on the back. "The noble gentleman is downplaying his role. Yet, you are the one who suggested the engine stoppage. Without that approach, you would have shredded the portal and perhaps burned the airplane. Your cleverness will be essential as you go to war."

Billy suppressed the urge to grin. He really was pumped about how everyone worked together. "Ashley mentioned the war," he said. "We have to battle some giants, right?"

"Come." Enoch strode toward the airplane. "I don't have an Oracle of Fire here to open the tunnel portal to the Valley of Shadows, but you wouldn't want to go that route, anyway. There is another path."

As Billy and Sir Barlow followed, Billy wondered at the prophet's words. Tunnel portal? Valley of Shadows? Maybe it would be better to wait and ask all his questions later. Enoch seemed to be in a hurry now. "So we're going to fly to this place?" Billy asked.

"Indeed. And this will be a flight you won't soon forget."

E lam paced back and forth in front of the berm that encircled the village's center. At least a hundred people sat on the stone roads that intersected at the circle, maybe thirty men, forty women, and the rest, children. Every set of eyes followed him, moving back and forth as he paced.

With his wounds aching and still visible on his face, wrist, and through his torn shirt, he wondered if the look of a warrior helped him gain their respect. Maybe. But it would take more than blood and bruises when the time came to fight. What would a warrior chief do? How could he lead a people he didn't even understand? What had he learned during his thousands of years that should have prepared him for this role? What resources did he have?

He paused and scanned the group. To his right, Angel stood near the front, her arms crossed. She seemed cold and nervous as her eyes darted all around. With her knowledge of the people's ways, she could be a great resource, but she seemed to be hiding something. What could it be?

Ashley, sitting in the front row to his left, caught his eye. Now dressed in pantaloons similar to Angel's, her face still flushed from her overheating ordeal, she leaned her head against Walter's shoulder. She, too, would be a great help in battle. Even if she couldn't suffer through healing deadly wounds, her touch alone seemed to do wonders for minor ones. Yet, she still needed time to recover. Her assistance would have to wait for a while.

Acacia sat close by, holding Paili's hand on one side and Listener's on the other. With her fire-starting capability, she'd be a great warrior, but she, too, needed more time to heal.

Near the back, Candle stood next to a muscular man with a dark trim beard and curly hair. This man had the true look of a warrior—confident stance, serious countenance, and riveting stare. Scars on his face and neck gave evidence of past battles, likely real battles rather than skirmishes with muskrats.

Elam heaved in a deep breath. It was about time he said something. "Now that you've all had a chance to think about what happened, let me tell you my ideas on what to do to get Father Abraham back unharmed. Then I will ask for the advice of the experienced warriors and sages.

"I'm not sure how far we can trust Flint or the words I heard him speak, but he has indicated no desire to kill your prophet. Apparently, he plans to hold him for two days. It seems that keeping him away will allow some people Flint calls his allies to come to his side in a potential war. My guess is that if Father Abraham were here, he would know how to stop that army from coming."

"So we must rescue him today," the muscular man called from the back. He clenched a fist and smacked his palm. "We must squash Flint before he is too strong to conquer us."

Elam nodded at the man. "You are a valiant one. What is your name?"

The man bowed low, then raised up, his shoulders squared. "You have spoken my name, Warrior Chief, for I am Valiant, the leader of Peace Village." He again pressed a fist into his palm. "We are at peace because we are strong. The shadow people have raided us only twice since the first eclipse this year, and every one of the dark prowlers has met a fiery death. They know the danger of slinking into our homes, so their burglaries are few."

Several men murmured their agreement. One voice rose above the others with a hearty, "He's right. Flint will not expect us to attack today."

Keeping her arms crossed, Angel stepped toward Elam and lifted her voice. "But can we fight anyone without Father Abraham or Enoch's Ghost to guide us? If we wait for Father to return, I have faith that he will be able to lead us to victory no matter what kind of army Flint is able to gather."

A louder buzz of approval erupted from the crowd, with more women joining in than men.

Elam firmed his lips and nodded. The gender gap was no surprise. Wives and mothers feared losing their men and older boys. The memorial stones he had seen as Grackle flew him toward the village indicated that they had suffered through many costly battles.

"I have a proposal," Angel said, uncrossing her arms to raise a hand. "Let us wait through this day so that you, your dragon, your horse, your healer, and the Oracle of Fire can rest and recover. Your dragon's stitches will hold her wing's membrane, but the break in her mainstay needs more time, and you and your horse lost a great deal of blood. It will be hours before you will be able to fight without fainting.

"Tonight, let Paili, the Oracle's speech-bearer, say her words over the birthing garden. According to the prophecy, this will resurrect a great dragon who will come to our aid. Then tomorrow, we will be at full strength to mount a rescue, and we will recover the Prophet before Flint's army arrives."

A loud "Yes!" broke out from somewhere in the middle of the audience, followed by a chorus of echoed yeses. As smiles spread across nearly every face in the crowd, Angel looked at Elam, crossing her arms again as she added a smile of her own.

Elam nodded at her but held back any other expression of approval. Although Angel's idea had its merits, and the people obviously agreed, rushing into a plan was never a good idea. Something in Angel's expression didn't look quite right. Was it that veiled secret he had noticed before? He shifted his gaze to Valiant. His face remained stoic, neither smiling nor frowning, and his eyes had fixed directly on Angel.

While people continued to buzz, Elam waved his hand and raised his voice. "Excuse me, good people. I would like to hear Valiant's thoughts about Angel's idea."

Every head turned toward the back where Valiant stood. With his thick eyebrows pointing toward his nose, he withdrew a long dagger from a sheath tied to his leather belt. As he held it in front of his eyes, the crowd quieted to a deathly hush.

"I have led every battle Father Abraham has commanded us to engage, and when fighting in the shadows against the dark ones, and splashing through the marshes to repel those who make their homes there, I have learned a very important lesson that no one who never ventures from the safety of his home will understand. If we fail to learn how our enemies conduct themselves, if we assume they will respond the way we would and be true to their words, then we will have lost before we have begun. For we respond with kindness to all, even to those who have offended us. We tell the truth, even at our own cost. And we fight only when we are attacked, when our wives and little ones are in danger. I believe they are in danger now. If we wait and allow our enemies to become strong, we will not be able to resist them."

"Are we to become like our enemies?" Angel asked. "Shall we attack first? Shall we lie just because they deceive …" As her voice trailed off, her head dipped slightly. Then, backing away a step, she looked at Elam. "I apologize. It is not my place to interrupt or question a great warrior."

Elam tried to read Angel's eyes, but she averted her gaze, apparently locking it now on Candle as he stood next to Valiant. Candle gazed up at the tall warrior, his smile of delight as clear as day.

Nodding at Valiant, Elam sat on the berm. "Please continue, and take as much time as you need."

Valiant walked to the front of the villagers, his knife still evident as he clutched its wooden hilt. Angel bent over, scooted to Listener, and sat next to her.

"I will speak but a few more words," Valiant said. "Flint expects us to wait. He believes us to be sheep without a shepherd. The Father of Lights has sent us a new chief for this time of need, and in his infinite wisdom, he has given us one who seems no more than a boy. Flint will not respect him. He assumes that we will cower in fear, or fold our hands, preaching a misguided understanding of grace and forgiveness, until he deems it timely to send Father Abraham back to us."

Valiant leaned over and placed a hand on Elam's shoulder. "Yet, I see in this warrior's eyes wisdom beyond his years. If Enoch sent him to us, then the God of Enoch calls upon us to listen and obey. If he calls us to charge into the marshes, then I will once again raise my dagger and spill my blood in obedience. If he calls me to stay in the village and wait for our deliverance from above, then I will sit in my hut and sharpen my dagger until I am called upon."

Lowering himself to one knee, Valiant laid his dagger at Elam's feet and bowed his head. "Speak, Warrior Chief. I and my dagger are yours to command."

Elam stood and laid his hand on Valiant's curly dark hair. Beginning with the first row, the people rose up to their knees and bowed, each one pressing their hands together in prayer. The shifting bodies looked like a wave upon the sea as the posture of humble submission took shape from front to back. Angel, too, assumed the praying posture.

The sight warmed Elam's heart but also pinched his conscience. With unflinching confidence, these people were willing to lay their lives on the line and follow an inexperienced stranger. The overwhelming responsibility sagged his shoulders.

Walter, Ashley, Acacia, and Paili looked at Elam. Not being villagers, they obviously weren't sure what they should do.

"My friends from the other world," Elam said, keeping his hand on Valiant. "Come and join me."

When they gathered around him, he whispered, "I have no clue what I'm doing, so pray for me with all your might."

Breathing a silent prayer of his own, crying out to God for that wisdom Valiant had mentioned, Elam lifted his hand. "Arise, Valiant, and I will tell you what we will do."

Even as he spoke, Elam shuddered. Somehow those words had spilled out unbidden. What *should* they do? Go to battle now when Flint wasn't expecting it? But some of their best weapons were injured or exhausted. Choose peace and wait for Abraham to return? That would play into Flint's plan. He seemed content simply to hold Abraham for two days and then just let him go.

As Valiant rose, the rest of the people stood as well. Elam shifted his gaze to Angel. She again crossed her arms and kept her head turned.

Elam stared into Valiant's deep brown eyes. He had to give this warrior a vote of confidence, let him know that his courage to charge into danger was appreciated. Yet, Angel's idea had great merit. Could there be a compromise?

"Valiant," Elam said, loud enough for everyone to hear. "I cannot risk going to battle with so many of our weapons in need of rest. Yet, I expect that with our healer's touch, the day will not end before we are ready. As you know, we have been promised another helper, and our speech-bearer will speak the words to provide that tonight."

Valiant's eyebrows drooped slightly, but he gave no other sign of disappointment.

"As you have so wisely suggested," Elam continued, "we should strike when Flint least expects it. So, the moment we receive our helper, we will attack …" He paused for a moment, firming his chin. "We will attack tonight while it is still dark."

215

CHAPTER

ANOTHER PLUNGE

B illy stared at the amazing scene out the copilot's window. After passing over a dense forest, they flew alongside an enormous chasm, so deep there seemed to be no bottom at all. Soaring high above gave him a panoramic view, the blue wall they had left behind far to his right, a series of colorful meadows, rocky ridges, and majestic forests between the wall and the chasm, and the equally magnificent fields and forests beyond the chasm to his left. No artist could possibly set this beauty to canvas; he could never do it justice.

He glanced at Enoch, sitting in the aisle next to Sir Barlow, but he quickly turned back. He couldn't bear to take his eyes off the sheer walls that dropped into nothingness and the grass-covered ledges that promised eye-popping, yet heart-thumping views to anyone who would dare to creep that close. "What is this place?" he asked.

"Zeno's Chasm." Enoch reached forward and tapped Billy's father on the shoulder. "Jared, be sure to stay on this side. When you see a bridge, look for a safe place to land."

"Will do." He pushed Merlin into a slow descent. After a minute or so, they buzzed just over the treetops, watching the uneven contours of the chasm's rocky lip zoom past. Three horses—two roans and a palomino—galloped near the ledge, as if racing the airplane in a wild frolic. A bald eagle leaped up from the pinnacle of a tall evergreen and flew lazily away. In a distant field beyond the chasm's bordering forest, a herd of four-legged animals dashed up to the crest of a hill, but they were too far away to identify.

"What are those?" Billy asked, pointing.

Enoch glanced out. "Unicorns," he said blankly, as if they were a typical sight in the Bridgelands.

Resisting the temptation to say "Wow!" Billy focused on one unicorn at the top of the ridge, looking toward them as if gazing in the same awestruck delight.

As the ridge passed by on his side, Sir Barlow didn't bother to suppress his thoughts. "By all that is holy! I have heard of these beasts. They say to ride one, you must be a maiden of impeccable virtue."

Billy tried to sneak a quick glance at Shiloh sitting across the aisle, but she caught him and gave him a demure smile. Sir Patrick held her hand over the armrest between them. He, too, gazed out the window in wonder.

Soon, another strange scene came into view, a sagging line that spanned the chasm in the shape of a thin smile. With broken boards and frayed rope lining its drooping frame, it seemed old and fragile, and as it swayed precariously in the stiff breeze, it appeared to be unusable, except maybe for campfire fuel.

"That's it," Enoch said from the back. "There should be a suitable field just beyond that stand of trees that borders the oval lake you will see in a moment."

Billy spotted the field. It did seem long and flat enough for landing, a strip of grass that lined a lake so clear, only the ripples on one side proved it to be a lake instead of a hole with a few fish floating in midair near the bottom.

As his father banked the airplane, Billy's window shifted to the chasm. He focused on the point where the bridge attached to rods on the opposite side.

Something moved. A human shape. No. More than one. Several.

"Enoch!" He thrust his finger toward the window. "People."

The old prophet didn't even bother to look. "Not ordinary people. They are Nephilim, and they stand at the edge of the chasm awaiting the opening of the portal." He rose, his back bent to avoid the ceiling, and sat in an aisle seat in the second row, buckling his belt with surprisingly practiced hands. "I will explain the Nephilim after we land."

Billy grinned. This man of millennia past seemed as comfortable with modern technology as he was with ancient legends and fabled creatures. After all, hadn't he already flown with Ashley, disguised as an aging physicist?

A minute later, they sailed over the field and coasted to a smooth landing, the wheels barely jumping at all as they rumbled across the grass.

Enoch unbuckled and scooted into the aisle. "After a brief explanation, I will leave you to your journey. But first, I have something for Jared." He reached into an inner pocket, withdrew a ring with a mounted red gem, and extended it toward Billy's father.

He eyed the stone. "A rubellite?"

"It was your father's. When Devin killed him, he neglected to search for the rubellite embedded between Goliath's scales. Since he was obsessed with the treasure in his victim's regeneracy bed, he merely plucked Goliath's eyes out as his only draconic trophy. When Merlin heard about the slaying, he found the carcass and retrieved the gem. How it came into my hands and then into this ring is another story that I don't have time to tell." Enoch placed it

219

in Jared's palm. "If Goliath had been an honorable dragon, he would have either passed it on to you or given you one of your own when you came of age. I believe the ring is the correct size, and I would like for you to wear it. Yet, if you think such a reminder of his treachery would be too great to bear, I would understand."

Without a second's hesitation, he slid the ring over his finger. Instantly, the gem faded to pink, then white. "It will remind me to be a better man … or dragon … whichever skin the Maker calls me to wear."

"Very well, then, on to my explanation." Enoch returned to his seat and spoke loudly enough for all to hear. "These Nephilim are evil giants from ages ago. They are waiting for an event to occur in Second Eden. If it comes to pass, the chasm's portal will open, and they will be able to enter that world safely, for no evil can enter unless one of the Eden dwellers invites it with an act of corruption.

"Since you have a safe flight conveyance, you may enter now. Fly into the chasm and take the airplane into a steep dive. Such a plunge will test your faith, but I tell you, the steeper the dive, the easier your journey will be. When you arrive, you will do well to find your friends, but I ask you to learn whether or not my friend Abraham has returned to his village. If he is still gone, I implore you to do all you can to get him home with all speed. Many lives depend on his presence when his people call for a warrior's aid in the birthing garden."

"The birthing garden," Billy said. "What's that?"

"You will learn soon enough. Find Abraham. He will tell you all you need to know. But if he is not restored to his people in time, a catastrophe of the greatest proportions will come upon them like a stampede."

Billy opened the back door and extended the airstair. "Any other last-minute instructions?"

220

Enoch looked at the stairs for a moment, hesitating. Finally, he turned toward the front of the plane. "I am almost fearful of asking this, because I know how long the young lady's father suffered while she toiled in misery, but if I could borrow Shiloh, her services would be most beneficial to our cause."

Shiloh shot up from her seat, kissed her father on the forehead, and, sliding her hand away from his, marched to the back. "Father and I have already discussed this possibility, so I am ready to go."

"No questions?" Enoch asked. "Do you want to know where we are going or for how long?"

Shiloh put on her coat and gazed up at him, her face beaming. "No questions at all. I am at your service for as long as you need me." She looked back at her father and waved. He firmed his jaw and waved back without a word.

Enoch and Shiloh descended the airstair and strolled out to the grassy field. Billy closed the door, secured the latch, and walked to the cockpit, hunching to avoid the ceiling. As he passed by, Sir Patrick gazed out the window, his face ashen.

Billy slid into the copilot's seat and looked out. Enoch and Shiloh stood hand in hand, waving. With her braids bouncing in the wind and Enoch's white wisps flying up and exposing his nearly bald head, they looked like grandfather and granddaughter getting ready to go on a picnic.

Billy's father reached over and squeezed his shoulder. "Ready?"

He tightened his buckle and gave his father a thumbs-up. "Let's do it!"

"Indeed!" Sir Barlow said, raising his thumb. "We used this sign back in my day."

Sir Patrick joined the thumb raising. "May I offer a prayer for protection?"

"Of course!" Billy's father bowed his head. When Barlow and Patrick bowed theirs, Patrick spoke in a quiet, respectful tone.

221

"God of Heaven, Maker of all, hear the prayers of your servants. You have called us to bring order to chaos, to divide the world of living sojourners from the wasteland of lost souls. We know that you could do this with a breath, a mere thought, but since you take pleasure in calling your faithful ones to perform extraordinary tasks to build and maintain your kingdom, we humbly submit and place our lives in your hands. We ask you to guide us, protect us, and grant us success. I also ask that you protect my beloved daughter as I leave her in the hands of your mighty prophet to use her in whatever way you command. But if any of us should fall by the sword of our enemies, we ask you to sweep us into Heaven, counting us worthy to stand in your presence because of the character you have created in us through the power of your son, Jesus of Nazareth, the Messiah. Amen."

Amens echoed through the cabin. Without another word, everyone looked forward as the plane rolled down the makeshift runway.

222

Barely clearing the treetops, *Merlin* flew toward the chasm. When the deep scar in the landscape came back into sight, Billy looked down at the giants gathered near the edge, counting them as quickly as he could. He spotted nine, maybe ten, but someone else was down there now, someone small and dressed in red.

"Who could that be?" he asked.

His father banked the plane hard to the right and followed the chasm's channel. "We'll fly pretty close when we dive. Maybe we'll get a better look."

The plane eased into a downward angle. As the steepness sharpened, they dove past the bridge and into the divide. The person in red had flashed by in an instant, but the breeze pressing the cloak against her curvaceous shape made her gender clear.

"A woman," Barlow said. "And I don't like the looks of her. An unsavory hellcat, if you want my opinion."

Sir Patrick spoke up. "Seeing that she is in the company of the Nephilim, I won't argue with your assessment."

"Get ready." Billy's father gripped the yoke with both hands. "We're going to really dive now."

Billy clutched the hand rests. As the plane tipped forward, he watched the readings on the meter dip toward their nosedive target of ninety degrees—one hundred sixty degrees, one forty, one twenty. His body lifted off the seat, but the belt held him in place. As his ears popped, dizziness washed through his head, and black spots filled his vision.

"Time to go for broke!" his father shouted.

Merlin dove almost straight down. The rocky walls on each side blurred, then dimmed until darkness swept across the plane.

As twilight draped the marsh, Abraham returned to his plan. With his ankles looped by a hangman's noose, his wrists bound by the nettle-infested cords, and his body dangling upside down from a gallows with his shoulders and head resting in shallow water, escape seemed impossible. Yet, with darkness approaching, his best hope lay only minutes away. When the time came, he would have to work fast, so he had to get his tool and keep it ready.

He shifted his arms to his side and slid a finger behind his belt, digging into the little pouch he had fashioned years ago. His wounded palm ached, but it couldn't be helped. Yielding to pain wasn't an option.

Pushing farther, he fished for the bone. He touched it with his fingertip, but just as he hooked his finger around it and pulled it up to the outside of his tunic, a woman approached. He opened his hand and pressed the bone against his belt with his palm.

Tall, hefty, and dark-skinned, the woman stooped and tore a morsel of bread from a small loaf. "Hands washed," she said as she pushed the morsel into Abraham's mouth.

223

He nodded a "thank you" and chewed. The bread was still warm and carried the flavor of honey and highlands barley, a rare treat for the people of the marshes. He gave a more enthusiastic nod, trying to show his appreciation for the kindness.

She smiled, but it was a sad sort of smile. "Drink?" She displayed a mug in her thick hands. "Make sleep. No pain."

Abraham swallowed the morsel. "I appreciate the thought, but I need to stay awake. Do you have clean water?"

"Turn head. Swamp water clean."

Abraham blinked, trying to ward away the blurriness that the hours in this position had caused. "You are Greevelow's Eve, aren't you?"

"Mantika." As she mopped his forehead with the hem of her dress, she lowered her voice. "Fear not. My Adam not allow harm to you."

Abraham studied her serious eyes. Even those few words were many for these people, a tribe his own people called "altered," not only because of their speech patterns and aggressive attacks when the dragons flew over, but also because of their ability to produce a child without a birthing garden. Obviously she was stretching her verbal abilities in an attempt to be helpful. "Come closer," he whispered. "I don't want Flint to hear our conversation."

As she leaned toward him with another morsel in hand, he continued. "Flint will not harm me, at least for a while. He only wants to keep me here through the next day and night. I believe a deceiver is in my village. If I am not there to persuade her otherwise, she will utter a lie that will bring a great evil into our land. I believe it is one of my own people, and she doesn't even realize what she is being tempted to do, yet I won't know who she is until I investigate."

Mantika glanced back at her village, a collection of low clay huts on the higher ground. As she shook her head, a frown bent her lips. "Flint kill us."

"That I believe without a doubt." Abraham tried to see if any-one was looking on, but the growing darkness obscured his view. "Greevelow doesn't have to risk setting me free. If both of you go to Flint's home, tell Flint that I have a message for him, that I need to speak to him alone. After we talk, he will return to you. I will cause a disturbance, and when Flint checks on me, he will see that I am gone and that you could not have set me free. When he sends a search party, he will likely include Greevelow, so I ask that you be my guide, because I cannot possibly navigate the marshes at night. Just lead me to the river, and I will find my way home."

Without another word, she rose and marched away, splashing through the water with heavy steps. Seconds later, she was out of sight.

Abraham regripped the bone. Whether or not Greevelow would decide to help wouldn't affect his plan. He had to escape, even if it meant wandering in the marshes for hours and stumbling into nests of sleeping muskrats.

As he looked at the bone, the words of the prophecy came back to his mind.

225

A bone, a stone, meeting atone,
A dragon born in flame;
A shield to wield, marching to yield,
The dragon sheds his shame.

Could this be the bone? If so, what might the stone be? And what dragon could Enoch have been talking about? He let out a sigh. No doubt it would all become clear at exactly the right time.

After several minutes, darkness shrouded his surroundings. He squeezed the bone between his thumb and finger and bent it toward the weeds around his wrists. The tiny thorns dug into his skin. Gritting his teeth, he strained at the bonds, loosening them just enough to force the bone into place.

As he watched for Flint, he sawed the sharp edge against the weed. Pain roared through his arms, but he had to push it out of his mind, concentrate only on the task at hand. It was best only to weaken the bonds, just enough to break free when Flint left … if he would show up at all. Then, he would—

"What are you doing?"

Flint's voice. As a dark form approached from his side, Abraham closed his grip around the bone.

"I am trying to escape," he said in a matter-of-fact tone. "Did you expect anything else?"

Using his shirt to protect his hands, Flint pulled on the weeds. "Still tight enough."

"I noticed."

Flint opened Abraham's fingers on his empty hand. "Are you hiding anything sharp?"

"Do you expect me to answer that?"

"I expect the truth, as always."

"And I will always speak it, but I will not answer every question you conjure. If you think I'm hiding something sharp, feel free to search for it."

"I am no fool. If you had nothing to cut with, you would have said no, and I would have believed you." Flint opened his other hand and removed the bone. "Ah! I thought so."

"Is it a crime that I would try to escape?"

Flint held the bone fragment up in his fingers. It seemed to carry a slight glow. "What is this?"

"A bone, I think. I found it in the tunnel of light, so I kept it."

"Was there an animal carcass around?"

"None that I could find."

Flint slowly rotated the bone, still eyeing it. "It looks like a human finger or thumb."

"Yes, I know."

"Could it be from one of the shadow people?"

"I found it well inside the tunnel, so I highly doubt it."

Flint's voice took on a sarcastic tone. "Oh, yes. You killed all your shadow prisoners at the entrance, didn't you? I should have remembered the last time I saw Father Abraham exercise his tender mercies, a summary execution shortly after we parted ways."

"Have you never stepped on a cockroach?" Abraham asked.

"We will not renew this tired old argument." The bone disappeared into his closed hand. "Why did you send for me?"

Abraham tried to detect any tone that might give away Flint's mood, but with his face shrouded and the bone enveloped, he had nothing to go by. He would just have to dive straight for the heart. "If you succeed with my imprisonment and thereby gain your army, we might never have an opportunity to speak again, so I waited for your people to settle for the night, hoping you would take the time to at least show me the kindness of conversation. No one is around to impress with bravado."

"Bravado?" Flint's voice carried a note of surprise. "Is that what you call my actions?"

"To stab my hand, threaten a boy with a spear to his heart, and imply savage advances on a girl?" Abraham tried to nod, but he only managed to budge his head an inch. "Yes, I would call it bravado, because these actions weren't necessary to gain what you wanted. You rule by fear and intimidation, but your underlings are not around right now. You know those tactics are ineffectual when only my life is at stake."

Flint paused for several seconds. Finally, his dark form stooped, and his voice lowered. "What do you want to talk about?"

"I want you to return to us, son. If you will only confess your wrongdoing, we will all welcome you with open arms."

His voice took on an irritated growl. "I did nothing wrong. You don't own the people, and you don't own me. We have

227

autonomous minds, and I am the only one brave enough to stand up to you."

Abraham kept his voice perfectly calm. "I claim no ownership of anyone. The people freely submit to me."

"And you kick them out of the village if they don't bow to your every whim."

"I offer them a choice," Abraham said.

"Of course you do. Death by stoning or life in exile. Those options are rather limited, don't you think? If that's what you call freedom, I want no part of it."

"I established our villages, and God gave me the rules of governance through Enoch. I have no choice but to follow them. If one person rebels, keeping him in fellowship not only spreads rebellion, it affirms the practice. If you found approval because you were able to stay in our community, you would never change your heart, and your spirit would be doomed."

228

"We are again covering well-trodden territory, Father. I have heard the sermon too many times."

"I ask you to hear it one more time. You have power over me right now. You could kill me with the stroke of a blade. Yet, I still ask you from the heart of a father to heed my call to return to our love, to submit to our ways, and you will be able to leave this place of exile. That is the third option, and you never considered it."

Flint splashed the water with his foot. "You never offered it!"

Abraham blinked at the spray and held his tongue. He had already said too much.

"It makes no difference," Flint continued. "I am in control of my own life here. Why should I go back to a place that offers only chains?"

Abraham held up his bound wrists. "No one in our village wears chains. Every man, woman, and child is free to come and go as they please. Yet, even if I had to wear chains, it would be better to wear them as a servant of the Father of Lights than as a slave to my own passions."

"Passions?" Flint set his heel on Abraham's shoulder. "It is control over my passions that keeps me from killing you. Slitting your throat and setting the people free would satisfy my passion for revenge and justice, but I have long-range goals."

"To rule this world."

"With justice rather than your tyranny."

"By force?"

"If necessary."

Abraham sighed. "And take freedom away from others, the very freedom you say you cherish, as you have taken away mine."

Flint didn't answer. Only the chirps of a few mud crickets broke the silence.

Abraham strained to see him, but the darkness was now complete. If not for Flint's breathing, Abraham wouldn't have known he was there. Yet, an odd glow caught his eye, the dimmest of lights in the shape of a clenched fist, hanging in the air at the place Flint's hand would be. Abraham squinted. Could the bone somehow be causing it?

Finally, something tugged on Abraham's hand, and the binding weeds fell loose. Then, a snick sounded, and Abraham's feet flopped down into the water.

"There you are," Flint said. "You are free. I leave you to your god and to the muskrats. You had better hope they are more merciful to you than you have been to me."

Abraham pushed up to his seat and rubbed his swollen wrists. A dim light arced toward him and fell on his lap. "Here's your bone. Get out of here before I change my mind."

Cupping the bone in his hand, Abraham pushed up to his feet. He wobbled on his stiff, tingling legs but managed to stay upright. He was about to say "Thank you," but the sound of fading splashes announced Flint's departure.

229

He opened his hand and stared at the glowing bone. What could it mean? Did the fire from the tunnel leave a phosphorescent residue on it? Did Timothy's sacrifice cause a reaction that could generate light?

He tucked it back into his pocket and hobbled toward a spot of firelight in the distance, raising and lowering his feet as quietly as his heavy legs would allow. Being set free was a true gift from God, but he needed another gift, a guide. Without someone who knew the marshlands better than he did, he might wander for days.

A dim glow spread across the area. Pegasus had peeked above the horizon, allowing him to see this island in the marsh. Several one-story huts dotted the grassy mound, making an incomplete circle around a plowed field, a rectangle of perhaps three acres.

Spotting the largest of the homes, he continued his painful march. The ground changed to moist earth, then to dry grass. He passed a few stalls housing a mule and a horse, then a cow tied to a wooden fence. He patted the cow on the rump. "Would you care to help me create a distraction, old girl?"

The cow just stared at him and chewed her cud. Keeping his eye on Flint's house, Abraham picked at the knot that held the cow in place. Soon, the rope fell loose. He scooped a handful of feed from a bucket and led the cow toward a pen that encircled a herd of sleeping pigs, perhaps ten or so. Reeling out the cow's lead rope, he climbed over the waist-high log fence and tied one end to a fat, sleeping hog. Then, he gave the hog a slap on its hind quarters and lunged back toward the fence.

The pig squealed and tried to run, but the rope held it fast. Abraham scrambled over the fence, but his injured leg gave way, and he tumbled to the ground. As he crawled through the mud, the pigs dashed around in a frenzy of grunts and squeals. The fettered hog lunged. The cow pulled back, bellowing. Lanterns flashed on. People rushed from their huts shouting in their thrifty sentences.

"Get cow!"

"Untie pig!"

Abraham scuffled toward the marsh as fast as he could. When he reached the downhill slope, he rolled into the water and waited in darkness, watching the ghostly forms hurry from place to place.

Soon, two shadows approached, hunched over as they skulked down the hill. They each grabbed one of Abraham's arms, hoisted him to his feet, and helped him walk deeper into the marsh. Now shielded by a wall of reeds, he nodded at his two helpers.

"Thank you, Greevelow. And thank you, as well, Mantika."

"Must go." Greevelow pulled Abraham's arm, and, leaving the lantern glow behind, the three waded into knee-deep water, pushing thick stalks to the side. With his eyes adjusting and Pegasus now in full view, his surroundings took shape. They seemed to be walking in a narrow channel bordered by short trees that stretched their boughs overhead.

"Muskrats sleep," Greevelow said. "Must not wake."

Abraham nodded. "So we stay away from dry ground."

As they waded, Abraham's body ached. The water stung his leg wound, and the hole in his palm throbbed. If infection had set in, he would have to get Angel to concoct her anti-bacterial salve, but would there be time to roast the boscil herbs and cook down the broth? He had to deal with the deceiver first, whoever she was.

After a quiet half hour, the channel widened and grew shallower. A rush of water sounded in the distance, a sure promise that the river lay ahead. The trees slowly thinned out, as did the reeds. Soon, as the river's song grew louder, they walked upslope onto an alluvial plain. The channel fed the main stream, and the merging created a deposit of fine sand. As tiny crystals sparkled in the moonlight, acorn-sized black shapes skittered around, fisher crabs that always came out after floods to sweep through the debris in search of any tasty morsels the receding water left behind.

Abraham bowed. "Greevelow. Mantika. I thank you with all my heart. I can follow the river now and find my way home."

231

Greevelow held up a hand. "Wait." He waded into the marsh again, pushing aside a thick clump of reeds. Then, a few seconds later, he returned, lugging something flat behind him. With a thrust, he slid it across the sand and yanked on an attached rope, stopping it near the river's edge. "Raft," Greevelow said.

Abraham stooped and touched one of the twine knots that bound the roughly hewn logs together. No larger than a floor mat, the raft looked sea-worthy enough, but its size gave him little comfort. The river, still engorged by the highland fountains, roared just a few feet away.

He stood and shook his head. "Thank you, but I think I'll walk. The river is too wild right now for a raft this size."

Mantika pointed at Abraham's leg. "Blood call muskrats."

Abraham looked down. A thin stream ran from the wound in his foreleg. Mantika was right. The muskrats would come in droves. They would smell his blood, even in their sleep.

Nodding, Abraham picked up the rope. "As they say in a land I know, 'Bon voyage.'"

Without another word, Greevelow and Mantika walked into the channel and, seconds later, disappeared in the darkness of the marsh.

Abraham grabbed a branch on a bitternut tree and broke off a five-foot section. After trimming the slender end and ripping away the leaflets sprouting from the side, he jabbed it into the sand and leaned on it. It would do.

He waded into the shallows. With ice chunks bumping against his legs and frigid water numbing his skin, he pulled the raft into the current and sat on it. He lifted his legs slowly, balancing as he shifted his weight. Then, pushing his steering pole against the sandy bottom, he launched the raft into the swifter flow.

At first, water lapped over the sides, nearly swamping the makeshift boat, but as it accelerated, it kept up with the current and rode higher. Abraham gripped both sides, keeping the pole pressed against the logs. Since the raft was surprisingly buoyant, he hurtled along, having to push against the shoreline at the sharper bends to keep from running aground.

After several minutes, the river slowed and widened, signaling his entry into Nimrod's Basin, the lower plains where the more courageous hunters sought game. Now safely out of the marshlands, he could hike the slow climb through the meadows to get home, but with his leg in such bad shape, a longer ride on the river seemed appropriate. It would take him in his village's general direction for a while longer, though at a lower elevation and not at the pace his mind demanded. Haste was called for. His people needed him. They would never be able to identify the deceiver without him.

He looked up at Pegasus. A gray haze floated across its cratered face. Could it be smoke from a fire in the highlands to the north? Maybe. He took in a long breath through his nose. There was no scent of wood smoke in the air, but the hunters often kept their campfires blazing well into the night, so it wouldn't be unusual. Still, this smoke seemed darker than what the highland timber emitted, and few hunters ventured out the day before or after an eclipse.

233

As the raft slowed even further, he pulled his knees close to his chest and folded his hands on top. He rubbed the finger that once bore his rubellite ring, still unaccustomed to its absence after twenty years. Maybe someday it would come back to him. Or perhaps its new owner would learn to live in the integrity the gem symbolized. That would make its loss far more than worthwhile.

He pushed a finger into his pocket and withdrew the bone fragment. Earlier he had thought it to be part of a thumb because it was so short, but without the rest of it, who could know? Maybe it was a finger. And if a finger, maybe it was his son's ring finger. Why not?

He held it higher to examine its gentle curve. Might Timothy's ring still be in the cave? If so, could it have survived the fire?

Obviously he would have to go back and search for it. He had noticed Timothy's ring while he was alive, but since it carried a white gem, he hadn't mentioned it, not realizing that it was a trans-formed rubellite. Of course, Enoch later told him it meant Tim-othy had lost his dragon essence and had become fully human.

He rubbed his finger again. Then why had his own rubellite, the one he was already wearing when he took his first breath in Second Eden, remained as red as blood?

When the raft reached a sharp bend, the current pushed the edge onto shore. Abraham shoved his pole into the sand, rose to his feet, and sloshed to the grassy beach. After pulling his craft into a flood basin and tying it to a shrub, he looked out over the dark terrain, a grass field that sloped upward as it faded in the distance. Flickering lights illuminated the horizon—his village.

He tried to count the tiny yellow spots, but there were too many. Something was wrong. At this time of night, only the street lanterns and the garden watchmen's torches should be ablaze.

Pressing the pole into the ground again, he set off, glancing between the lights and the dimly lit ground as he leaned on his crutch with every other step. In the plains, he had few worries— stepping on rabbits, moles, or ring-tailed foxes. Yet, there was one predator that could be lurking just about anywhere. The prairie lions were known to hunt at night when the moon had passed eclipse phase, hoping to snatch any vermin the rising river flushed out of the marshes. With his wounded leg, a lion could easily run him down, but at least his pole would give him a fighting chance.

He felt for the bone in his pocket. It was still there. He pushed ahead, forcing his aching leg to walk faster as he waded through belt-high wild wheat. For Makaidos's sake, and for the sake of every soul on the planet, he had to make it home in time.

14

CHAPTER

THE HIDDEN PORTAL

Flint led his mule up the final steps of the steep switchback path and paused at the mouth of the cave. A brisk wind nipped at his cheeks. The elevation allowed for no trees or hillocks to block the ever-present breezes, but he was prepared. With a layer of rabbit fur under his tunic and in his boots, the wind could chill only his face and hands, but he would soon have to shed the warm clothes. The throat of Mount Elijah awaited.

He ducked under the cave's low arch and pushed down on the mule's load—two sheaves of reeds and a bundle of sticks. When he cleared the entry, the ceiling vaulted into a high funnel, the inside of Mount Elijah's cone. A shallow basin lay at the center of the floor, about as wide as a normal man could leap, and perhaps knee-deep if filled with water. A collection of large rocks covered the basin's curved bottom, a cap Abraham had jammed into the volcano's throat to keep curious children and small animals from falling into the deep gorge below. Since scaling the mountain was easy compared to some of the other summits, many fathers and

sons from Abraham's village hiked the trail as part of their initiation journey. A peek into the bowels of a volcano was surely a great
temptation for young and old alike.

Flint took in a deep breath. Even with the cap, sulfur fumes
seeped through dozens of narrow gaps between the irregular rocks,
and heat from the magma river radiated into the granite, making
the edges glow. As he warmed his hands over the rising air, he
looked back at the cave entrance. "Aren't you coming?" he called.

A boy, no more than twelve years old, peered in. Dressed only
in a thin tunic and knee breeches, he tiptoed into the volcano's
cone, his mouth hanging open as his eyes darted from side to side.
"Mountain big!" he cried. As his echo bounced around, he
grinned.

"Didn't Greevelow ever tell you about this place?" Flint asked.

"Father tell." The boy pointed at himself. "Windor stay away."

"You're a good boy, Windor. You're far more obedient than
most of my subjects." Flint pulled a sheaf from the mule's back
and threw it into the basin. As the heat from the rocks dried the
moisture in the reeds, white vapor rose into the funnel above and
seeped out the top and into the sky. Sizzles and pops rebounded
from wall to wall, making the room sound like a cookhouse with
twenty pans frying muskrat bacon.

Flint heaved the second sheaf next to the first and scattered
the kindling sticks over the reeds. "Did you bring the starters?" he
asked as he peeled off his outer clothing.

Windor produced two stones from a pouch tied to his leather
belt and looked at Flint with wide eyes. "I light?"

Flint nodded. Windor knelt and struck the stones together
next to the edge of a clump of reeds. After several tries, the grass
ignited, and the flame crawled over the sheaf, spreading out and
puffing strings of black smoke along the way.

Soon, the kindling crackled and burned. The smoke thickened
and shot through the conic chimney of stone in billowing plumes.

Flint pulled the final item from the mule's back, a broad leaf as wide as his body and nearly as long. He handed the edge to Windor and spiked his voice with excitement. "Now run around the fire and fan the flames!"

Windor sprinted around the basin, jumping while whipping the leaf as if it were a dragon's wing. The rising smoke twisted. The flames exploded into an inferno and spun with the smoke and Windor's unabated dance. Soon, the bonfire looked like a tornado, undulating as the top crept closer and closer to the cone's exit.

Soon, Windor slowed down, panting in the raging heat. Flint lowered himself to his knees, folded his hands, and gazed at the flaming cyclone. After clearing his throat, he spoke, careful to enunciate each syllable.

> Arramos, dragon king, lord of my life,
> Come to my flames I pray.
> Grant me the pleasure of hearing your words;
> Show me the bountiful way.

Three tongues of fire jutted from the tornado. One shaped itself into the head of a dragon, the second into its body, complete with a spiny ridge and wings on its back, and the third into a long tail. When all three parts combined, the fiery dragon animated. As the rest of the fire swirled through the body, the wings flapped slowly, and the tail swayed back and forth. Sparks flew from its mouth, then a crackling voice.

"Why do you call upon Arramos?"

Windor halted. His jaw dropped open, and he backed toward the perimeter wall.

"He is a friend," Flint said. "Don't be frightened." Staying on his knees, he focused on the dragon's eyes, two red spots in the midst of the flames. "Abraham has escaped, but I doubt that he will get back to his village in time to spoil your plans. Earlier, I wounded his leg to ensure his immobility, and I pierced his hand to prevent his use of a weapon. Two of my people guided him to the river, so he won't die."

Arramos growled, but it seemed more of a thoughtful rumble than a snarl of anger. "His escape is not exactly what I planned, but all is well. From what I see happening in his village, we need not worry. He will never arrive in time."

Flint glanced at Windor. The boy crouched near the cave entrance, trembling as he watched.

"I brought you a gift," Flint continued. "Pledge for pledge."

"So soon? I have not delivered the woman to you yet."

Flint shook his head. "It is a matter of opportunity. The boy's parents are the ones who helped Abraham. Of course, it brought no harm, but it was still an act of rebellion that must have consequences. Otherwise, my rule will crumble."

238

The flames congealed around the dragon's body, making him look solid, though his scales remained undefined and shimmering as if made of molten gold. "I am pleased with the offering, and I find it amusing that you wield such an iron fist. Are you not the man who himself rebelled because of the iron fist of another?"

Flint tensed his jaw but kept his voice calm. "All *humans* have autonomy, not these beasts of burden. It was because of my rebellion that they were able to enter our realm in the first place, so I am their master."

As the fire's spin slowed, Arramos laughed. "I was the first to suggest different classes of humanity, so I have no quarrel with you. I merely suggested that it was amusing."

Taking a deep draw of the sulfur-tinged air, Flint rose to his feet and turned toward Windor, who still cowered in a crevice. "Let's hope you stay amused long enough to give me what I want."

As he walked toward Windor, the boy's eyebrows shot up. He scuffled his feet against the floor, trying to scoot farther away, but the wall blocked his escape. Flint grabbed his wrist and dragged him toward the fire.

Windor kicked and slapped Flint's hand. "Not burn!" he shouted. "Not burn!"

Flint jerked him to the edge of the basin and held him upright with both hands on his thin biceps. Windor stiffened his limbs, but his body trembled, shaking his dark curly hair just under Flint's chin.

"Get on with it," the dragon growled. "This portal will close soon, and I am in no mood to open it again."

Flint pushed, but the boy grasped his wrist, pulling Flint with him. They both flailed their arms as they teetered on the edge of the basin. Windor regained his balance first. He jerked Flint away from the fire, then bolted out of the cave.

Flint toppled to the floor, scraping his elbows. Heat flamed his cheeks as he pushed himself up to his knees. "Stupid little monkey!" he shouted. "I'll have you in flames before this day is over!"

Arramos roared with laughter. "Seeing you so humiliated is worth the loss. The lamb becomes a savior for his crucifier. How poetic!"

Leaping to his feet, Flint pointed a stiff finger at Arramos. "Just get Angel for me. She must be mine!"

"All in good time. When the childlike ark calls for the dragon, he will be able to enter your world and do as he pleases. We will soon make Abraham's children learn how to suffer, beginning with the pangs of childbirth." As the fire's spin continued to slow, Arramos faded. "Take care not to awaken this portal too often. If one of the Oracles of Fire discovers it, she will be able to use it to call upon Earth, Hades, and even Heaven. We don't want to open that door, do we?"

Flint shook his head. "All would be lost."

As the fire's spin slowed, the dragon melded with the flames and disappeared. Flint turned, grabbed the mule's rope, and stalked away. After ducking under the cave's mouth, he emerged into the night air and glared at Pegasus. He grumbled under his breath. "I will have that wench. When Abraham sends her away, she will forget about her love for him and cling to me. When she bears my child, my victory will be complete."

B illy peered into the darkness, searching for a light or any kind of landmark that would help him figure out where they were. But only the plane's signal lights blinked in his field of vision. Even those seemed to be swallowed by the pure blackness that surrounded them, and the propeller buzz had dampened in this strange airspace. It felt as if they were floating in the midst of nothingness, much like the inner core of the candlestone. He had wondered if the engine would stall with such a dive, but even in this odd atmosphere, it kept running without a hiccup.

His father turned up the cabin lights and stared at the instruments. "The meters aren't working," he said as he tapped one of the gauges. "It's like we're in outer space."

"And no more g-forces," Billy added. "We must not be falling, but if we finally come out into open air at a ninety-degree angle, it won't be easy to pull up." He swung back to the passengers. Sir Barlow twitched his mustache and stared at him, but said nothing. Sir Patrick looked out the window, but if he saw anything other than darkness, he wasn't letting on.

Billy turned to the front. It was like a state of suspended animation. Every movement felt awkward. Even talking seemed to take more effort than usual.

His father clutched the yoke. "Something's happening!"

"Yeah. I feel it." Billy tightened his belt. "We're dropping again."

"I'm getting an altitude reading," his father said, "five thousand feet, but we're at a level angle." He pointed at the dashboard. "Our descent's slowing. The wings must be catching air."

240

As Billy leaned over to have a look, a light in his father's window caught his eye. A huge yellow disk came into view just above an uneven horizon. "Is that a moon?"

Sir Barlow unbuckled and pushed into the cockpit. "It is, to be sure, William, but it is like no moon I have ever seen. The face is quite different."

"It is larger," Sir Patrick said, now sitting in Barlow's place. "By about 15 to 20 percent. The features are quite different. In fact, I can't see any *maria* at all, though there are a number of significant craters."

"*Maria?*" Billy asked.

"Lunar seas. It's a Latin term. Obviously this is not the moon we know."

"We're no longer dropping," Billy's father said. "But what we're flying over, I can't say."

Barlow leaned so far into the cockpit, he blocked Billy's view of his father. "I see flickering lights on the ground," Barlow said, "and they're moving."

Billy peeked over Barlow. "People carrying lanterns?"

"I believe so," his father said. "That field they're in would be big enough for landing if they weren't on it. We'll have to find another place."

They flew over a small forest, then a village illuminated by more lanterns. From above, the modest huts looked like clay models, but the stream of people funneling toward the field proved it to be a little town alive with activity.

Soon, they found another field on the opposite side of the village and landed. The moment Billy's father cut the engine, a jet of ice sprayed over their windshield.

Billy lurched back in his seat. "Where did that come from?"

"Strange weather in this world," Barlow said. "That was a sudden storm, indeed."

241

Something struck the tail, giving the plane a jolt. As the passengers rocked back and forth, Billy's father hustled to the rear exit door. "This is no storm."

Billy followed and stood behind his father as he threw the door open. Outside, two red eyes hovered in the black air, wavering from side to side like a snake ready to strike. Then, as the eyes moved into the light emanating from the plane's interior, the creature's surrounding form became clear.

Billy's father held up his hands. "We are not enemies, good dragon. I am Jared, and I have come here in peace."

The dragon reared up on its haunches and let out a whistle but nothing more. It blinked, its red eyes glowing like fire.

"He's white," Billy said. "Do you think he even understands our language?"

The dragon whistled again, then spat out a stream that splashed into the cabin in a spray of ice crystals.

"Was that a yes?" Billy asked.

The dragon spat another frosty stream, this one smaller than the first.

"I think he understands. He just can't speak." Billy shrugged his shoulders. "So what should I say to a dragon from another world?"

A new voice piped up. "Tell him you'll rub his belly." A pig-tailed girl holding a bright lantern walked below the dragon's forelegs and pointed a metal tube at his underside. "Albatross has a soft spot right about there." She set her lantern down and pushed her fist into the dragon's stomach, twisting it as she pushed.

Albatross let out a long, warbling whistle. "My name is Listener," the girl said, smiling broadly. "I saw you through my spyglass before you got here, so I hid behind Albatross. I've never seen a mechanical dragon, so I wanted to be sure it wouldn't try to freeze me."

"Nice to meet you, Listener." Billy extended the airstair and climbed to the ground, followed by his father and Sir Barlow. Sir Patrick looked on through the doorway. After Billy introduced

242

everyone, he touched a spine on Albatross's tail. "I've never seen a white dragon. Where I come from, they're either reddish or light brown." He nodded at the jumper the little girl was wearing. "The light brown ones look sort of like your dress. And they breathe fire instead of ice."

Sir Barlow patted Albatross on the neck. "He is a fine dragon, to be sure, young lady, but I am wondering why a child like you is out here by yourself in the middle of the night."

"I'm not by myself." She lifted the spyglass and looked at the moon. "Albatross is here, so I came out to watch Pegasus. It eclipsed last night, and it's always brightest the next night."

Billy wanted to ask a million questions about this new world, but he settled for the one at the forefront of his mind. "Have you had any other visitors lately? I'm looking for a boy my age named Walter and a girl named Ashley, who's a little older."

Listener nodded but kept the spyglass over her eye. "They're at the birthing garden with all the others. Another girl from their world is getting ready to call for a warrior, but everyone is nervous about it because Father Abraham isn't here."

Billy pointed at her. "That was my next question. A prophet named Enoch told us to find Abraham."

She lowered her spyglass, her eyes now wide. "Enoch spoke to you?"

"Yes. He said if Abraham was missing, I had to bring him back to his people. Nothing's more important."

She swung around and extended her spyglass toward a line of mountains in the distance. "Flint is holding Father Abraham prisoner in the marshlands. Our soldiers are going to rescue him as soon as the warrior comes."

Billy grabbed his father's sleeve. "That's too late. Enoch said Abraham has to be there when the people called for the warrior."

"They are already gathering," Listener said. "The ceremony will begin soon."

243

Billy's father grabbed the airplane's fuselage and vaulted inside. "I'll rev it back up!"

"Do you know how to get to the marshlands?" Billy asked Listener.

"They're easy to find." She pointed at the landing gear. "Can your dragon land in a swamp?"

As the engine roared to life, Listener and Albatross backed away. Billy had to shout to compete with the noise. "Maybe in real shallow water if there aren't any trees or high grass around."

Shaking her head, Listener raised her voice. "You can't tell what's shallow or deep when it's dark."

Billy's father returned to the doorway. "I'm ready whenever you are."

"Dad, Listener says we won't be able to find a place to land in the swamp."

She turned and set her palm on the dragon. "Albatross can take us there. When we land, we can point out a safe place."

"You want us to follow the dragon?" Billy asked.

"If you and I ride him together, one of us can hold a lantern for your mechanical dragon to follow."

Billy pointed at himself. "You want me to ride?"

"Sure. Haven't you ever ridden a dragon before?"

"Yeah." Billy grinned at his father. "It was a pretty wild ride."

She reached for the ground and lifted a leather strap. "If you'll help me get his seats on, we can leave right away."

"I will help you, lass," Sir Barlow said as he picked up another strap. "I wish we had used these when I had to ride Legossi. She once launched so fast, I fell off and nearly broke my leg."

Billy and his father pitched in, and, following Listener's directions, they had the seats on in a matter of a few minutes.

Still shouting, Billy touched Listener's shoulder. "I assume the garden is where we saw those lights. We should warn them to wait for Abraham."

She tilted her head to the side and rubbed her cheek against his hand. "You can if you want to, but everyone's already really scared. If any more strangers come, I'm not sure what they would do, especially strangers who fly in a mechanical dragon."

"But Walter and Ashley will vouch for us," Billy said. "They know who we are."

"Valiant, our best warrior, is suspicious of everything, especially Ashley and her dragon, but you can try. The men can go and warn them while you and I find Abraham, but I don't think we're strong enough to defeat Flint by ourselves."

"We'll all go," Billy's father said. "Finding Abraham is our first priority."

Sir Patrick climbed down the stairs. "I will find the gathering. Perhaps an old man entering their midst alone will not raise too much anxiety." He turned and strode toward the village lights, his shoulders sagging as he faded into the dim surroundings.

Listener pointed at Billy's sweatshirt. "That won't be warm enough." She picked up a heavy coat from the ground and slid her arms through the sleeves. "It's much colder up there. I brought my coat in case a shadow person came around. Albatross is so protective, he would've flown me a mile in the air. He can heat up his scales for us, but it's never enough."

"I will get your coat." Sir Barlow lumbered up the stairs and returned within seconds holding the coat and a scabbard, the hilt of the Excalibur replica visible at one end. "This first, William. You can wear it at your waist instead of on your back."

As soon as Billy had attached the scabbard, Barlow helped him put on his coat. "Find a place for us to land," Barlow said, "and I will fight at your side." He clambered back up the stairs and disappeared in the belly of the plane.

When the door closed, Listener pursed her lips and let out a short whistle burst. Albatross lowered his head, creating a stairway with his neck. Listener hustled up the spiny ridges and took her

245

seat in the front. "Albatross isn't the easiest dragon to fly. Since he knows me, I'd better guide him."

Billy picked up the lantern and followed. He had to stretch his legs to step around Listener and reach the backseat. With the lantern swinging in his hand, the sword dangling at his side, and a cold breeze biting his skin, the process was tedious, but he finally managed to settle in the leathery chair and tie the harness around his waist.

"Give us as much heat as you can," Listener called.

Within seconds, a wave of warmth rose from the dragon's scales. Billy set a hand closer to its body and let the heat radiate into his skin. If the little girl was right, he might need all the warmth he could get.

As *Merlin* taxied into position behind Albatross, Listener whistled again, louder and longer this time. The dragon stretched out his wings and leaped into the air. Billy grabbed the back of Listener's seat and hung on. Although Albatross lifted with great strength, the flight seemed far rougher than when Billy rode atop Clefspeare. This dragon dipped and rose abruptly with every beat of his wings, but he seemed to know what he was doing as he flew low over a farm at the outskirts of the village.

Looking back, Billy caught sight of the trailing airplane. He lifted the lantern and waved it, but when the buffeting winds nearly blew out its flame, he propped it on the back of his seat.

Merlin closed in, then kept pace, staying about a hundred yards behind Albatross's swinging tail.

"We'll pass over the grasslands first," Listener shouted. "We can fly low enough to see what's down there, but when we get to the marshes, we'll have to go higher to stay away from Flint's archers."

Billy shivered as he tried to hold the lantern while watching the endless field of grass below. With the moon casting a yellowish-white glow, the wind made the heads of grain look like sea foam being tossed about by churning waves.

As he scanned the landscape, it seemed that shadows appeared and disappeared, as if painted and then instantly erased by an indecisive artist. After a few minutes, one shadow stayed constant, a low, sleek profile that cut through the grass like a living scythe.

Billy pointed at the shape. "What's that?"

Listener leaned over at a precarious angle. "A prairie lion. I think he's stalking something."

"There!" Billy pointed again. "A man! The lion's chasing that man!"

"Hang on!" Listener slapped Albatross's neck and kicked him with her heel. The dragon plunged and banked at the same time. He swooped between the lion and the man, swiped at the lion with his tail as he zoomed past, and slid across the grass on his belly until he came to a stop.

Pulling out his sword, Billy leaped to the ground and sprinted through the waist-high grass. About fifty feet ahead, the man held a stick with both hands, pointing it at the lion. He pivoted and aimed his stick at another shadow, a second lion that approached from the other side.

Billy leaped in front of the closer lion, whipped out his sword, and shouted, "Get back!"

The man sidestepped toward him. "I appreciate your kindness, stranger, but these lions are not easily frightened. They are obviously famished and desperate. I fear that we might have to strike an offensive posture to ward them off."

"I'm on it." Billy took a step toward the first lion and raised his sword.

"Father Abraham!" Listener ran toward them, still clutching her spyglass, but stopped when she saw the lion again. "Uh oh." As she backed away slowly, the airplane skidded to a quick landing not far from Albatross. The lion spied Listener and lowered itself into a crouch, ready to pounce.

247

Billy charged, but the lion sprang toward her before he could reach it with his sword. Suddenly, a stream of ice shot through the grass, knocking the lion on its side. Billy slipped and fell on his back, but he kept his grip on the sword's hilt.

Albatross scooped up Listener with his wing and roared at the lion, spewing a flood of ice over it and Billy.

Billy scrambled to his feet, slipping and sliding. The other lion pounced at Abraham. Its paws struck his chest, and its body snapped his feeble stick as it knocked him to the ground. Billy leaped toward them, but a stinging pain swept across his back. He toppled forward, spinning as he fell.

The first lion lunged at him, its teeth bared and its claws outstretched. He thrust out his sword hand, but the lion flew off to the side, ripped out of mid-flight by a huge man with two muscular arms wrapped around its body.

"Barlow!" Billy leaped back to his feet. "Great tackle!"

"Get the other cat!" Barlow rolled with the lion, holding its mouth closed with one hand while fumbling for his sword with the other. "I'll take care of this little kitty!"

Billy rushed toward Abraham. The cat straddled the man, growling and snapping as he pushed against its chest with bloody hands. Rearing back with the sword as he ran, Billy lunged. With a hefty swipe, he sliced into the lion's chest, then shoved it away with his foot.

The cat fell to the ground and writhed in the grass but quickly righted itself before slinking away into the darkness. Billy braced Abraham's back as he helped him sit up. "Are you okay?"

The moonlight revealed several gashes across his face, each one streaming blood. "I believe so, but I will need medical attention. There is a doctor in Peace Village who—"

"Here's a first-aid kit!" Billy's father dropped to his knees on the other side of Abraham and opened a white metal box. "Billy, get everyone inside *Merlin*. I'm sure the dragon can find his way home."

"Yes, sir!"

Billy rose to leave, but Abraham grabbed his pant leg. "No need to tend to me here. Help me into your airplane. I must get back to my village immediately."

Billy and his father lifted Abraham to his feet. As they helped him hobble past Barlow, now standing over a dead lion with a sword in its belly, Barlow gave them a nod, blood oozing from scratches on both sides of his face. "This cat just spent the last of its nine lives." Barlow touched his cheek, wincing. "Somehow I doubt he thought I was his pajamas."

When they reached Albatross, Abraham signaled for them to stop as he addressed the dragon. "You have done well, my friend. You may release Listener and fly home."

Albatross unfurled his wing, revealing Listener crouching at his flank. She rushed toward Abraham, extending the spyglass. "I saw my mother! She's standing in front of the birthing garden with everyone in your village looking at her. I think she's getting ready to say something. Elam is standing next to her, and he seems really cross."

Abraham touched the spyglass. "You saw Angel with this?"

She nodded.

"What color was her companion's light?"

"I didn't see her companion, but it likes to stay in her hair."

Abraham's body drooped. Billy and his father grunted as they held him up. Even in the dimness of moonlight, his face had clearly turned pale, shades of corpselike gray under ribbons of red. "We must hurry!" Abraham said, trembling as he tipped forward.

They hustled him into the airplane, and as soon as everyone was seated and buckled, Billy turned back to the passengers. Barlow leaned over Abraham and dabbed his wounds with a cotton

249

swab. Listener sat alone on the other side of the aisle, looking out the window with her spyglass. "Albatross is on his way home."

"That's good," Billy said. "No offense to the dragon, but I'd much rather ride in here than out there." The increasing buzz of the propeller forced him to raise his voice. "I think you'll like it, too."

As the plane rolled over the bumpy field, Abraham reached across the aisle. "Listener, have you seen your mother again?"

She lowered the spyglass. "Not yet. I see far away things only once in a while."

"Let me know if you do." When the plane lifted into the sky, Abraham leaned back in his seat. "I have seen aircraft through my ovulum, but I never imagined that I would fly in one."

Sir Barlow smeared a line of antibiotic ointment along one of Abraham's deeper wounds. "I, too, was unaccustomed to modern conveyances when I emerged from the candlestone after over a thousand years of being trapped in that accursed gem, but it didn't take me long to, as the modern idiom says, 'learn the ropes.'"

250

"I see." Abraham patted Sir Barlow's forearm. "We have a few minutes. Let us tell each other our stories as quickly as possible. Afterwards, there may be very little time even to breathe."

15

CHAPTER

THE SEED IS PLANTED

Elam stood near the edge of the birthing garden, his arms folded across his chest as he waited for everyone to be seated in the grass. With Pegasus still barely over the horizon, lanterns abounded, illuminating the fragile expressions of the villagers. The younger children wore smiles and wide eyes that gave away their awestruck amazement at this new and exciting event. Deep lines furrowed the brows of many of the adults. Obviously they knew this gathering wasn't a social ceremony. Somehow it would change their lives forever.

In fact, no one knew for certain what all these signs portended—the young warrior chief coming to their village without Father Abraham; a white-haired girl with fire in her hands and hair; two strangers from another world, one a healer and the other a warrior with a magnificent sword; a talking dragon in search of a human daughter; a strange buzzing machine flying in the air that disappeared over the trees; and a little girl who was supposed to speak words that would call a prophesied helper from yet another realm. To them, it must have sounded like a fairy tale, yet now they had come together to witness what they had heard about in bedtime stories ever since they had emerged from this very garden.

Angel sat cross-legged at the front, while Ashley and Walter stood far to Elam's right where Thigocia had found room to lie in the grass. Valiant stood near the middle of the pack, Candle clutching his hand at his side. Listener, however, was nowhere in sight. She had asked to go to the dragon launching field to look at Pegasus through her spyglass. Since Albatross was there, she would be safe from any lurking shadow people, and his scales would keep her warm if need be. Angel had said Albatross was the most protective dragon she had ever seen, so if it was all right with Listener's mother, Elam decided it was all right with him.

When everyone had settled, Elam gestured toward Acacia and Paili. "Is she ready?"

"She is ready." Acacia took Paili by the hand and joined Elam. "We have been preparing for this moment for years."

Angel jumped up and gave Elam a brief curtsy. "May I interrupt with a question?"

Elam nodded. "You may."

She spoke loudly enough for everyone to hear. "Since you and all who are involved with this ceremony are strangers to our people, you might not be aware of our ways."

"Are we violating a custom?" Elam asked. "Please let me know, and we'll try to do this the right way."

Angel glanced back at Candle. Valiant crossed his arms and stared at her quizzically. As she looked at Elam again, she intertwined her fingers, her voice trembling as she continued. "You are not breaking a custom. It is a matter of priority. Father Abraham should be here to oversee this sacred event. He is the keeper of Enoch's Ghost, but now even that is gone, so we have no guiding hand with which we are all familiar."

"Are you saying that we should wait? I thought you wanted to bring our helper as soon as possible."

"Oh, we must continue, but I wanted you to know what Enoch said to me. Since Father Abraham is not here to relay the message, I must give it for him."

"You received a message when you looked into Enoch's Ghost?" Elam asked.

A wave of gasps crossed the seated crowd. Angel's face twitched, but she kept her eyes focused on Elam. "Enoch spoke to me."

Elam tried to read Angel's expression. Why the twitch? Why did the people react the way they did? He looked over at Valiant. The warrior's face had turned stony. He obviously didn't like what he heard. Something strange was going on. "What did Enoch say?" Elam asked.

"We all know that the girl, Paili, has come to speak a prophecy over our garden. Our understanding is that she is to call upon Makaidos to rise from the dead. I am asking that she change the song and say 'the dragon' instead of 'Makaidos.'"

253

Elam pondered her words. Her odd facial expression raised a warning in his mind. Dealing with Morgan and Naamah for so long had shown him deception in many of its manifestations, and Angel's stance and tone brought back nightmarish memories of his slave mistresses' lies. She had crafted her response precisely and avoided a direct answer, one of the hallmarks of a deceiver. But could he accuse her of lying? Who was he to level such a charge when he was a stranger in this land?

"Your hesitation troubles me," Angel said as she lowered herself to her knees. Pressing her hands together, she bowed her head. "I humbly thank you for hearing the request of your servant. I, of course, will abide by your decision. If you choose not to change the words, then let us proceed without any alteration."

Elam took a step back. Seeing Angel's contrite posture brought to mind Naamah's lament when she begged for forgiveness. He had decided to believe that deceiving temptress, and his faith in her was rewarded to the point of saving the world. How could he doubt this woman who had never told a lie in her life?

He lowered his hand. She took it and allowed him to raise her up. "Did Enoch say why Paili is supposed to change the words?"

Averting her eyes again, Angel shook her head. "He gave me no explanation."

Elam looked over at Ashley. She stood near Thigocia, a hand on the dragon's neck. If she could really read minds, would she be able to help? Would it even be right to ask? Or should he rather just trust Angel and hope his faith would eventually be rewarded no matter what the outcome?

He nodded at Acacia. "Please bring the word-bearer to me."

Acacia guided Paili to the edge of the garden and turned toward Elam. "Is there a problem?"

"Maybe." Elam looked back and forth between Acacia and Angel. The difference in their postures and expressions was like night and day. Acacia's eyes, wide and bright, shone without a hint of secrecy, while Angel's seemed like a stone wall. "Is Makaidos part of her song?" he asked. "Can Paili change it as Angel has requested?"

Acacia touched Paili's head. "She is to call upon Makaidos, Elam, but we aren't comfortable with making the change. Enoch's instructions were clear. He made sure Paili knew the words precisely."

Elam nodded. No doubt Acacia was right to feel that way. Still ... "Is it possible that Enoch changed his mind?"

"Of course, it's possible. When a storm arises, only a fool refuses to alter his course."

He scanned the crowd. Many shifted restlessly, while some of the younger ones pranced around or battled with wooden swords. Leaving Candle behind, Valiant eased his way toward the front, his eyes set on Angel, but he seemed in no hurry.

Elam set his jaw. The people were getting restless. He had to make a decision. "Abraham is gone," he finally said. "I think that qualifies as a storm. Please ask Paili to make the change."

"Very well." Acacia whispered to Paili but too quietly for Elam to hear. He looked at Angel again. A breeze blew her hair back from her shoulders and ears. He searched for her companion, but, unless it was buried in her hair, it wasn't nearby. Squinting, he continued his search. He had to be certain. He needed something more than one of her oblique answers.

Paili set her toes at the edge of the garden, while Acacia stood behind her. Just as she spread out her shimmering blue cloak, Elam raised his arm. "Stop!"

As every head turned toward him, he gestured for Angel to come forward. She walked to the front, her eyes darting more frantically than ever. He grabbed her arm, turned her toward the crowd, and lifted his voice. "I just want to make sure everyone understands what's going on. The great prophet Enoch gave the little girl words to speak to bring us a warrior dragon to help with a coming battle. Angel asked her to make a minor change to the words." He turned to her, but she wouldn't look him in the eye. "Angel, did Enoch tell you to do this? I want a straight answer."

Her eyes flared. She trembled in his grip, and her chest heaved over and over. Elam looked down at her pocket. Her fingers clutched something through the material, something that wiggled violently.

Elam stared at her. Had she stifled her companion? If so, why? That couldn't be normal behavior for the people here, but should he dare to challenge her, one of the most respected citizens of this world? Abraham had said that if a woman could possibly live as a saint without need of a companion, Angel would be that woman.

Slowly turning, Angel looked into the birthing garden. Her eyes locked on something well beyond the influence of the lantern lights.

Elam followed her gaze. A movement disturbed the backdrop. Was it a shadow? A branch blown by the wind?

Then, as if buoyed by the whispers of a friend, she straight-ened her body, turned back to the crowd, and lifted her voice, loud and strong. "Elam asked if Enoch commanded the change to the prophecy. He wanted a straight answer. I am now ready to give it."

When she took a breath to speak again, a shout sounded from somewhere in the crowd. "Excuse me!"

Elam scanned the field and spotted a gray-haired man weav-ing through the seated villagers. "One moment, please!" the man called, a finger raised as he made his way toward the front. "I would like a word with you."

Elam blinked. Could it be? He could barely speak the name. "Patrick?"

As the man strode past the front row, he pushed his hair back and tried to catch his breath. "Yes, yes, of course. I'm glad you rec-ognized me. A fellow by the name of Cliffside detained me at the garden entrance for several valuable minutes, but I managed to convince him that I knew you."

Elam embraced Patrick. "What are you doing here?"

"I have not yet figured out all that is happening, but you should know that Billy Bannister, his father, and Sir Barlow are here. A young girl named Listener is leading them on a mission to find Abraham. I hope they return—"

The buzz of an approaching airplane interrupted him. It flew directly overhead and headed for the dragon launching field on the other side of the village.

Patrick nodded toward the sky. "They are here. I assume they will be with us in a few moments."

"We can't wait!" Angel cried. "We don't know if they found Father Abraham or not, and the moon will be too high before they can walk over here. Remember the prophecy." She changed her voice to singsong and chanted part of the poem Abraham had recited not long ago.

While shadows dress the virgin soil,
Before the moon gives light,
The girl calls forth the garden's fruit,
Then day will rule the night.

As soon as she finished, she stared at Elam, breathing rapidly.

Elam looked up at the moon. Rising above the tree line, its shadows had retreated, now barely covering the garden. "She's right. We have to press on."

Her body shaking, Angel tiptoed toward the crowd. "I'll get out of the way and—"

Elam grabbed her arm again. "Not before you finish what you were about to say."

She looked at Elam's grip, then back at Elam. Her expression sagged, and tears formed in her eyes. "Why do you doubt me, Elam? You are treating me like an ignorant child."

Grimacing inwardly, Elam released her. What had he done? He was a stranger in this land, an alien ready to project the lying ways of his own world onto the citizens of innocence. Even if he was sure Angel was lying, how could he possibly assume a judge's chair and be her accuser? Only Abraham could do that. And what if she was telling the truth? Of course it was possible. Maybe she was acting strangely because she was so unsure of herself. After all, she was taking Abraham's role by communicating the commands of Enoch. The people were obviously surprised that she had even spoken to Enoch, so stepping into the Prophet's shoes had to be a very uncomfortable act.

"Elam?" Angel said, her voice trembling pitifully. "What do you want me to do?"

Elam heaved a deep sigh. "Just tell us all what Enoch said. I will believe you."

"Very well." She turned toward the crowd and, still clutching her pocket, she shouted, "Enoch commanded the change to the prophecy! He said we must call for the dragon!"

257

As soon as the words spilled forth, she clutched her chest, gasping. Her knees buckled, and she dropped to her seat. With frantic fingers, she dug into her pocket and withdrew her companion. It lay in her palm, a faint light strobing within its dull glass. She stared at it, then touched it with her fingertip, but it didn't move.

While the crowd fell silent, Elam stared at Angel. Had she lied after all? He clenched his fist so tight, his fingers ached. If only Abraham were here! He was the only one with the authority and wisdom to judge his people, and even he had said that once the lie was uttered, there was no turning back.

Valiant stepped up to Elam and gripped his forearm. "I advise you to proceed, Warrior Chief. If the harvest of wheat must be shaken to filter the chaff, then so be it."

Elam gazed into Valiant's deeply set brown eyes—sincere, honest, resolved. Finally, as every gaze in the crowd locked on him, Elam let out another sigh and turned toward Paili. "Sing your song, and change the words as Angel has requested."

Billy scrambled down the airstair, followed by Sir Barlow. They reached up, each grabbing an arm as they helped Abraham to the ground. When Billy's father joined them, Abraham grasped Billy's sleeve. "Run ahead of us. With my injuries, we will be too slow."

"Sure." With a quick jerk, Billy tightened his back scabbard. "Which way to the garden?"

Abraham pointed toward the village. "Do not go directly through, or Cliffside will delay you with many questions." He then drew a loop in the air. "Go around to the left, climb over the rock wall, and stay low as you run between the thornbush hedges. Then you will climb through the gap created by two stately fir trees and come out of the forest on the west side of a field that lies between the birthing garden and the village. On nights when

Pegasus rises full, that gateway is not well guarded, so, if you keep your head down, you should be able to get into that part of the field undetected."

Billy gave a firm nod. "What do I say when I get there?"

"Tell them I will be there in mere moments, but if the ceremony has already begun, you must simply wait. Once the Oracle approaches the portal, we cannot stop what has been set in motion. I will have to see what I can do when I arrive." Billy's father and Sir Barlow each put a shoulder under one of Abraham's arms and began helping him limp toward the village.

Billy took off to the left in a full sprint. Within seconds, a waist-high stone wall came into view. Leaping from one foot, he vaulted the wall, landed on a stony path, and kept running, barely breaking stride.

Hedges bordered the path with thornbushes rising to his shoulders. He lowered his body, checking the hilt of his sword as he continued his awkward dash. After about a hundred yards, the hedges ended, and the path changed to hard dirt. It led into a forest of tall evergreens that blocked the way with low bushy branches.

Knocking the branches aside as he slowed his pace, he burst into a clearing and stopped. A vine-covered fence stood in his way, too high to leap over. He searched for the tall firs. Just to the right, two enormous trees served as support posts for the fence. He dashed toward them and stopped again just a few feet away. The trees grew so close together, their trunks were joined in a single mass near the ground, and they allowed just a foot or so of space between them as they reached toward the sky.

He turned sideways, set his foot into the "V" where the trunk split, and squeezed into the gap. After scraping the sword against the bark, he pushed through and rushed out into a meadow about the size of two football fields.

Flickering lantern light covered the grassy expanse, illuminating at least a hundred people kneeling or sitting cross-legged in

259

orderly rows, each one looking toward Billy's left where a flat section of land with plowed furrows dominated the area. A dark form rose from the ground halfway between him and the crowd. It stretched out a long neck and slowly curled in its wings, making its identity clear.

Billy burst into another sprint and slid to a stop near the dragon. "Thigocia!" he whisper-shouted. "It's me!"

Thigocia whipped her neck, bringing her head toward him. "Ashley! Walter! It's Billy!"

Walter appeared from around Thigocia's body. "Hey!" He leaped toward Billy and wrapped him in his arms. "Great to see you! You're just in time!"

"Super! What's happening here?"

Ashley appeared from the shadows, her arms crossed and her brow bent low. "Something sinister."

"Yeah," Walter said. "Elam's trying to sort things out, but without Abraham, the village leader, it's hard to know what's up."

Billy jerked his thumb toward the forest. "Abraham's coming. I have to tell Elam before the ceremony starts."

The lanterns faded all across the field. At the front of the crowd, two girls, one of them wearing a cloak and carrying blue fire in her uplifted hands, walked into the garden.

Walter dropped to a crouch and lowered his voice. "Elam's the young guy at the edge of the garden, the one who looks like he's in charge, but I think you're too late."

"You mean the ceremony's already started?"

Walter nodded toward the cloaked girl. "She's got her fire going, so I'm pretty sure it's under way."

"Then we'll just have to wait. I guess Abraham will figure out what to do when he shows up."

Ashley stared straight ahead. "I sense an evil presence, a powerful mind. It feels strange, as if it's close, yet something is blocking its entry. It's like a madman chopping at the door with an axe, but he can't seem to break it down. I can tell, though, that his heart is set on murder."

Thigocia reared up to her haunches. "I sense danger, as well, growing stronger every second."

Billy pulled his sword from its scabbard. "We'd better get ready."

Walter drew Excalibur. "I can't get it to work here."

"Let me try." Billy and Walter swapped swords. As Billy wrapped his fingers around Excalibur's hilt, he sucked in a quick breath. It had been a while since he last held the great sword, and he had longed for the feel of its warrior heart. Flexing his biceps, he willed the blade to flash to life, but its dull silvery metal merely reflected the moon's yellow glow.

Loosening his grip, he peeled back his fingers and looked at the hilt. Two gems gleamed, crystal clear, about the size of dimes. He flipped the sword over and felt for the depression. As the professor had indicated in his journal, the red gem was missing.

"When we're done here," Billy said, handing Excalibur back to Walter, "I'll have to tell you about something Prof discovered. Maybe it will explain why it's not working."

"I think it's because we're in the Twilight Zone. Everything's crazy."

Billy looked at the garden again. One of the two girls backed out, while the other stayed and began singing a song.

"Whatever's supposed to happen," Billy said, "I think it'll be any minute."

Thigocia lowered her head, creating a staircase with her neck. "Everyone get on. We might need to fly into action at a moment's notice. I think my wings will last."

While Billy climbed aboard, Ashley stooped near Thigocia's head. "Mother, I sense another mind, someone ... familiar."

"Familiar? Who?"

261

She straightened and turned toward the garden. "I'm not sure. It's just an impression, but it's out there somewhere. Someone friendly. Someone who's also trying to get here."

Standing on tiptoes, Walter leaned toward the rows of shadowed plants. "I can't see anything."

Ashley bent over and skulked down a row. "You two go with Mother," she called back. "I'll follow my nose."

"You're not going in there without me!" Walter rushed to join her, and the two faded into the shadows.

As Thigocia turned her head back toward Billy, her red eye-beams swept across his chest. "Get your sword ready, warrior. The greatest danger I have sensed in my thousands of years is building to a crescendo. As Ashley said, murder is on someone's mind."

16

THE SEED BEARS FRUIT

E lam held his breath. Not knowing if he had made the right decision was maddening. If they had waited to see if Abraham had arrived on the plane, which was extremely unlikely, it might have been too late to perform the ceremony at all. Still, Angel's claim seemed to hang in the air like a foul odor. Yet, if he wanted to heed Abraham's warnings, he couldn't stop the proceedings. A simple word change wouldn't do much damage, would it? As he watched Paili approach the garden's edge again, he murmured, "I guess we're about to find out."

Her countenance grim, Paili faced the rows of plants. Acacia stood behind her and flared her cloak. Shadows veiled the little girl as she lifted her hands and called out, "Let everyone extinguish their lanterns, and I will begin when the last light fades."

Across the field, flickering lights waned and then died out. When all was dark except for the rising moon, Acacia let go of her cloak and raised her hands, her fingers slightly curved as if she were holding two balls. Blue flames sprouted from her palms, sparkling and alive with effervescence, rising and swelling until they looked like two bowls overflowing with iridescent soup.

Paili began to hum in a rhythmic beat as the two walked single file along one of the garden's furrows. The blue glow expanded and coated their bodies as it illuminated their way. When they reached the edge of a nearly vacant section of ground, they stopped. Like a transparent shroud, the radiance bathed the circular area, making everything within its influence pulse with an eerie light. A single birthing plant at the center of the loose soil throbbed, alternating shades of light brown and bright red. Scattered bones emanated a frosty white incandescence, as if painted with a luminous dye.

Acacia waved her uplifted arms in a tight circle. The bowls of fire spun and twisted, lengthening vertically into twin columns of rotating blue flames. Leaning back, she threw the two columns into the vacant section. As soon as they touched the ground, the flames spread out and crawled along the circular patch, covering the soil until it looked like the garden had sprouted thousands of tiny glittering sapphires.

When the fire reached the edges, the outer flames stopped and began to rise, curving back toward the center and making a head-high dome over the single plant. The bones inside sizzled and popped. As the flames ate away at their pale coats, their white glow transformed to blue.

Acacia backed away, then turned and joined the mesmerized crowd, leaving Paili standing alone, a mere arm's-length from the curved edge of the flaming dome.

She lifted her hands and began to sing, her voice deepening to the pitch of a young woman, a lovely, haunting alto that carried across the field.

When phantoms knock on doors of light
To open paths to worlds beyond,
A friend replies, "Insert the key
To leave the dark and greet the dawn.

"The key is light, the words of truth;
No lie can break the chains of death.
A whispered word of love avails
To bring new life, the spirit's breath."

So now I sing a key for you,
The phantom waiting at the door;
We call for you, the dragon who
Will join us now in holy war.

As soon as her last note died away, another shout sounded from the back of the crowd, Abraham's voice ringing across the field. "Elam!"

Every head turned. The moon revealed two figures helping a third walk toward them. When they arrived, the two men helped Abraham stand on his own. Elam recognized both men, Jared Bannister and Sir Barlow.

Acacia lifted a lantern. "Give me light!" she called.

The wick flashed and burned brightly, revealing deep scratches in crisscross patterns on Abraham's face.

Elam grabbed Abraham's forearms. "What happened to you?"

"Never mind me! What happened here?" Abraham looked down. Angel sat near his feet, gazing up at him with tear-filled eyes. Her mouth hung open, and her companion lay motionless in her palm.

He dropped to his knees and set his hand under hers. "Dear Maker in Heaven! What has she done?"

Suddenly, the ground trembled. Elam spread out his feet and braced himself. The moon peeked over the surrounding trees and cast its light on the garden. A dark shadow rose near the center, growing taller with every second, as if pushed out of the soil by the quaking earth. Soon, the trembling eased, and the shadow stopped growing. Bending and stretching, it slowly took shape.

Elam whispered to Abraham. "Is that the warrior? Could it be Makaidos?"

"I sense darkness," Abraham replied. "I sense disaster."

Angel rolled her fingers around her companion and rose to her feet, her voice spiking in a pitiful squeak. "Dragon? Is that you?" She stumbled into the garden, barely missing one of the plants as she staggered along a row.

Acacia waved an arm across the crowd and called, "Awake, every wick!" More lanterns flashed to life, and as the villagers lifted them, their light washed over the entire garden.

Angel stopped in front of the dark form. It morphed into a human shape, and its ebony coat melted away, like black wax dripping down a candle. Soon, a man's face appeared, his eyes shining.

"Dragon!" Angel leaped toward him, but her arms passed through his body. Without the expected catch, she fell forward and hit the ground with her knees, chest, and face. Valiant jumped into the garden, brushed by Dragon, and helped Angel to her feet. Valiant propped her up, and the two stared at the strange specter.

A smile spread slowly across his ghostly face. "Since you have called me into this realm, you probably expect me to feel sympathy for your little tumble." Shaking his head, he sighed a "tsk, tsk, tsk." "Soon all your people will learn that the dirt on your face is exquisitely appropriate." He walked to the edge of the garden and nodded at Abraham. "You knew I was coming, didn't you?"

Abraham straightened his body and looked the newcomer in the eye. "I expected you, but not in this form."

Dragon's smile widened. "I am showing you this projected image to demonstrate how I was able to convince one of your wisest citizens to do my will." As he stretched out his hand, a fruit appeared on his palm, an applelike spheroid with a single bite missing from its flesh. "You thought that keeping your people from the knowledge of good and evil would protect them, that my master would never be able to corrupt your land. Flint proved you wrong, but that wasn't enough to persuade you, because my master was still blocked from entering your realm and spoiling your dictatorial rule. Now that I have plucked an Eve from your Garden of Eden, we will leave your village and populate this world with people who will have true knowledge and freedom."

The sound of steel sliding on steel made Elam turn. Sir Barlow was drawing his sword and sidestepping toward the garden. He nodded at Jared, who began to make his way to the opposite side of the ghost.

Angel pulled away from Valiant and tried to caress Dragon's hand, but as her own hands passed through, she could only intertwine her fingers. "I don't understand," she said. "How will we populate the world if we leave the village? This is the only birthing garden."

"Is it the only one?" He lowered himself to a crouch next to one of the garden's plants. He wrapped his fingers around the thick supporting stem, and as he tightened his grip, his hand transformed into a dragon's clawed forefoot. "What is this?" he asked.

Angel stooped with him. "Why do you ask that, Dragon? It's a baby, probably three months from harvesting. You have seen your own children come from—"

"No!" Abraham shouted. "Don't!"

The man's sleeve morphed into scales, completing a dragon's foreleg from his humanlike shoulder down. He flexed his muscles and ripped the plant out of the ground.

Loud gasps erupted from the crowd. Elam leaped toward him, but the man threw the plant high into the air. Angel lunged for it but tripped and fell, then lay still in the dirt. Elam positioned himself underneath the plant, but when it fell into his arms, a sickening crack sounded from within the pod. The leaves fell to the side, revealing an ovular sac covered with a gauzelike mesh. He tried to look within, but as fluid leaked over his fingers, he screamed, "No! How could you do this?"

267

Valiant crouched over Angel, his dagger raised. "Attack! I will protect her!"

Jared and Barlow rushed toward the garden, but the newcomer suddenly swelled in size, his skin hardening and turning red and scaly. His face and nose stretched into a toothy snout.

Jared grabbed Barlow and pulled him back. "It's Goliath! We can't fight him with our bare hands."

Barlow waved his sword, his face blood red. "Then he will feel the wrath of my bare steel!" He charged, but Goliath slapped the sword away with his tail and shot out a narrow stream of fire. Barlow dropped to the ground. The flames flew over his head and splashed against another plant. He shuffled to it on his knees and brushed the flames off the pod with his hands, then, covering it with his body, he yelled, "You cowardly snake! Killing babies to save your worthless hide!"

"A cowardly snake, am I?" Goliath stepped out of the garden, turned toward it, and laughed. "I am merely extinguishing my enemies before they rise from the dead."

Elam gave the broken sac to Abraham, charged to the edge of the garden, and ran up the scales on Goliath's back. He grabbed the scaly neck and tried to jerk it to the side, hoping to throw off his aim, but Goliath raised his tail and swatted him away.

After flying through the air, Elam landed feetfirst beside the nearest row of onlookers. As his momentum threw him back, several hands caught him and propped him up.

Goliath drew in a deep breath and aimed his snout at the remaining plants. A tawny dragon swooped down from the sky and smashed into him. The two dragons tumbled to the ground near the onlookers, snapping and clawing. As the people scattered, a rider flew off the attacking dragon, a drawn sword in his outstretched arm. He fell on his bottom, flipped into a backward somersault, and landed on his seat again.

Elam ran to the fallen rider and helped him up. "Billy Bannister?" Elam asked.

"Yeah." Billy brushed a clod of dirt from his face. "Sorry about the fall."

"It's okay. We have to help Thigocia, she looks—"

"Billy!" Jared's voice rang out. He and Valiant were helping Angel walk, one on each side, but her feet barely touched the garden soil. Her eyes darted all around, and her mouth hung open. When they laid her next to where Abraham sat, she curled into a fetal position and wept.

Jared raised his hand and called again. "Billy! Barlow! Elam! Rally to me!"

Elam and Billy sprinted past the fighting dragons and stopped at Jared's side. Along with Valiant and Barlow, they formed a circle. "Dad," Billy said, "Did you say that dragon is Goliath?"

"Yes." Jared swung his head from side to side. "Where are Ashley and Walter? We're going to need Ashley's healing power."

Billy pointed toward the garden, breathless. "Just before I took off, she and Walter went somewhere in there. I haven't seen them since."

"We have two swords and a dagger," Barlow said. "If we all charge together, we should be able to save Thigocia."

"The smaller dragon is losing the battle," Valiant said. "Let us attack at once!"

Jared thrust his arm toward the struggling dragons. "Now!"

All five men charged, three with weapons raised, but before they could get to Thigocia, Goliath clamped his teeth around her neck and tossed her body to the side. With a mighty snort, he shot a blast of fire directly at them. They dove out of the way, three to the left and two to the right.

When they landed, Elam and Billy banged their heads together. Sitting up, Elam rubbed his head. "We have to try again."

Billy grabbed his arm. "Wait until Dad and the others are ready. I can't see them, but maybe they'll signal for us to attack."

Thigocia struggled to her feet, flapping her damaged wings to keep her balance as she glared at Goliath. "You will not carry out

269

what you whispered in my ear," she growled. "It is obscene. I will die before I let you singe one more leaf."

"How convenient," Goliath said. "I will grant your wish and then kill every weed in the garden."

Thigocia's voice lowered to a plaintive call. "My son, do not let the spirits of the Nephilim control your mind. You are stronger than they are. Listen to the voice of your mother and come back to me."

For a moment, Goliath's eyes dimmed. His head tilted to the side, and he whispered, "Mother?"

"Son." Thigocia shuffled toward him. "Fight them, Goliath. Fight them with all your heart. Come back to me. Help me find your father, and we will be a family again."

Goliath's eyes flashed red. "My father!" A torrent of flames stormed from his mouth and nostrils and splashed into Thigocia's face. He flew at her, his jaws snapping. She toppled over and let him fly past. In a flurry, he swung back around and tried to land on top of her, but she swatted him with her tail, forcing him to touch down between her and the human onlookers.

Barlow charged from behind, but Goliath slapped him away with a wing, sending him rolling. He came to a stop next to Abraham and moved no more.

"That's a good enough signal!" Billy shouted.

He and Elam both lunged toward Goliath, but Jared dashed in front of them and pushed them back. "No! He's too powerful. You'll just end up like Barlow or worse."

Billy jerked away, his cheeks flaming. "Why did I give up my dragon powers? I could use my fire breathing right now!"

His own cheeks matching Billy's, Jared lowered his voice to a growl. "What's done is done. Don't you think I want to be Clefspeare right now? We both have to live with our choices. We won't defeat anyone if we lament the past!"

Goliath let out a guttural laugh. "Go ahead and bicker amongst yourselves. I have work to do." Spreading out his wings, he launched himself toward Thigocia, his claws extended.

Thigocia dodged again, but as he passed by, Goliath wrapped his tail around her neck and jerked her to the ground. He flipped her on her back and pressed his clawed foot on the soft part of her underbelly. The old wound gaped under the pressure, and blood poured around the edges of the larger dragon's foot.

Goliath's eyes flashed. "It is time for you to meet the Maker you love so much."

Elam pulled away from Jared and rushed toward them. Goliath shot out a river of fire, but a scream filled the air, making him turn his head skyward. A dragon carrying two riders swooped down, clawed at his eyes, and slapped his snout with its tail.

As the new dragon zoomed away, Jared pointed. "It's my—It's Roxil!"

Goliath swayed to the side, dazed. His eyes dimmed again, and sparks dribbled from his mouth.

That was just the opening Elam needed. He scaled Goliath's back once more, wrapped an arm around his neck, and pressed a hand over his eyes. Goliath swung his head back and forth. Elam's legs flew, but he squeezed his torso tightly against the sharp spines. They stung and ripped his clothes, and his wounds throbbed, but he had to hold on long enough for Thigocia to escape.

"Roxil!" Elam's voice rattled as he rode the wild dragon. "Pick up your mother!" He had no idea where Roxil had flown; he could only hope that she had stayed within range of his voice.

Billy, Jared, and Valiant rushed into the melee. Goliath dropped to his belly, covering his soft spot. Valiant hacked at the dragon's scales with his dagger. Billy jabbed his snout with his sword. Jared ran up Goliath's flank and bent back one of the longer spines.

In a gust of wind, Roxil landed at Thigocia's side. Walter and Ashley scrambled down, Walter brandishing Excalibur as he jumped toward Goliath. He stabbed the dragon just above his hip joint. The great sword was so sharp, it pierced the armor and penetrated several inches.

Goliath flew into a wild rage, flapping his wings and slapping his tail all around. He bucked Jared off. Whipping his neck, he slung Elam to the ground. Then, beating his wings, Goliath leaped over his attackers, snatched up Angel in one of his claws, and landed back in the garden. He threw her to the ground at the center. With the moon bathing her in yellow, she rolled to a stop next to the single plant that had been the only one in this section. Its leaves had peeled to the side, and its inner sac lay on the ground, ripped to shreds.

Goliath lifted his head and roared. "Now is the time! Let my army come to my aid!"

A clap of thunder shot across the sky. The earth quaked violently, tossing every human to the ground. Elam tried to get up, but as he pushed with his hands, the shock waves knocked him flat. He rolled to his back. His bones rattled, but he managed to brace his hands against the grass and watch Goliath.

The dragon roared again. "If anyone takes a single step toward me, I will kill this woman instantly and incinerate every precious weed in your garden."

Black liquid poured from the darkness above and splashed over Angel's body. Thicker than tar, it pinned her in place, and as more spilled down, it piled up in a flexible column that rippled with every shake of the earth. After a few seconds, the column tilted. A stair step formed next to Angel, and, one by one, more steps cut into the column until the stairway reached out of sight.

Angel struggled to get up, but the sticky goo held her fast, covering her body from her knees to her neck as though she had become the doormat for whatever might descend from the heavens. For a moment, the earthquake stopped. Then, a loud boom sounded from high above, then another and another, each one closer than the one before.

With the ground now stable, Elam struggled to his feet and joined Billy, Walter, and the others as they gathered in front of Thigocia and Roxil. Most of the people had run back to the village, and a few men were already returning with crude swords and shields. Abraham sat with Sir Barlow, touching a wound on the knight's head. Acacia stood with her back to Listener and Paili, her hood over her head as she spread her cloak to shield them.

Breathing rapidly, Thigocia touched Roxil with a wing. "My daughter, how did you become a dragon again?"

Roxil blinked at her outstretched wings. "I do not know, but I think this is no time to try to find answers."

"Yeah," Walter said, holding Excalibur out in front. "Something creepy's coming down the steps. It has to be the Nephilim we saw at the top of the chasm."

Roxil stepped in front of Thigocia and Ashley and spread out her wings. "I will protect both of you. Goliath would not dare attack. I know my mate's weaknesses."

As more thumps sounded from above, Valiant flashed his dagger. "I must save Angel!" He bent over and ran into the garden, well away from Goliath, and disappeared into the darkness.

Billy held up his sword and stood next to Walter. "Let's run interference, or he's toast."

"But didn't he say he'd kill her?" Walter asked.

"I don't believe him. I think he needs her."

"Okay, but we'd better be fast, or we'll get a hotfoot."

"Or a hot something else."

The thumps continued, echoing across the land like gunshots. Goliath stood still. He looked up the staircase, but he kept glancing back at the villagers as they drew nearer with their weapons.

Jared touched Elam's arm. "Come with me. We'll check on Barlow and get his sword."

"And assemble our soldiers," Elam added. "I don't think they have much experience battling dragons." He was about to add, "and neither do I," but thought better of it.

273

Ashley pulled Elam's shirt, drawing him back. "Can you send Acacia over here?"

Tears streaming down her dirty face, Ashley pressed the heel of her hand on Thigocia's wound. Blood oozed over her skin and dripped to the grass. "I have to try to heal my mother," she said. "I hope it's not too late."

Elam nodded at Roxil. "Can she provide the fire?"

Ashley raised her other hand. A red welt blistered her skin from her wrist to her knuckles. "We already tested it. Her flames burn."

"Okay. I'll get her as soon as I can." He patted Jared's back. "Let's go!"

Billy and Walter hustled to the edge of the garden, while Jared and Elam skulked over to Abraham, both bending low.

Jared sank to his knees and propped Barlow up. "Is he all right?"

"He is alive," Abraham said, "but he is no more fit for battle than I am."

Barlow blinked at Jared. "Help me up, my good fellow. As long as I have breath, I will fight. I will teach that dragon some manners he will never forget."

"You're staying put." Jared touched a gash on Barlow's head and rubbed a smear of blood between his thumb and finger. "That wound goes all the way to your skull."

"I use my sword, not my skull. I will—"

"You have to rest!" Elam snapped. "As warrior chief, I command it."

Barlow heaved a sigh. "If I must stay, I will help the Oracle defend the young lasses."

"Right," Elam said. "The Oracle." He scooted over to Acacia. "Ashley needs you to help her heal Thigocia."

She lowered her hood, revealing her snow white hair. "Who will protect Abraham and the girls? I cannot defeat Goliath with fire, but at least I can fend him off."

Jared picked up Barlow's sword. "Send Roxil over here. She and I can hold them off."

"Them?" Abraham asked. "Are you familiar with who is marching down the stairs?"

Jared lifted the sword's point toward the sky. "If they're the ones we saw at the top of the chasm, we're in for a long night."

"The night is not so long." Abraham looked toward the horizon. "Something is terribly amiss. Day is at hand, far sooner than normal."

Elam followed his line of sight. The sky had turned a light shade of violet, and hints of orange colored the tops of the mountains in the distance. "With all your people coming with weapons," Elam said to Abraham, "should I organize—"

"No. Stay here. I have another job for you."

A loud cry sounded from the garden. Billy leaped toward Goliath, hacked at his scaly flank with his sword, then jumped away. Walter did the same at the other flank. As Goliath swung his neck back and forth and spat fireballs in both directions, the two boys continued to lunge and dodge, unable to land solid blows.

Behind Goliath, Valiant crawled up to Angel and began cutting away the hardened black gunk that held her down. She had stopped struggling, apparently unconscious now as he dug his dagger into her prison wall.

Thump! The newest footfall, closer than ever, shook the ground. Billy and Walter glanced at the stairs, but they kept playing their cat and mouse game with Goliath. The light from the rising sun cast yellow rays across the sky. Human forms took shape high on the staircase, huge men marching downward single file, carrying long spears with silvery blades that glinted in the light.

Valiant carved a long slice in the black floor mat, slid Angel out, and hoisted her over his shoulder. As soon as he disappeared with her in the shadows, Walter and Billy sprinted back to the field, leaping from side to side to dodge Goliath's spewing fire. When they reached the others, they turned toward the garden, both breathing heavily. Walter laid a hand on Billy's shoulder. "Great to fight with you again, buddy."

"Yeah." Billy leaned over and rested a hand on his knee. "But let's not tackle a huge dragon too many more times, okay?"

"I wouldn't count on it." Walter turned toward the side of the field. "I'm going to check on Ashley."

Goliath again looked up to the sky. The tromping feet had come within a hundred yards, carrying at least seven or eight giants, maybe more.

"They'll be here any minute," Acacia said, turning to leave. "We'll need another healthy dragon."

"Wait." Abraham grabbed her cloak and pulled her back. "Doesn't the prophetic ark have more words to sing?"

"She does, but how can she sing now? I don't think it was supposed to happen this way, and I have to save Thigocia."

276

Abraham shook his head. "Enoch commanded the ark to sing all her verses and for you to conduct her to her stage. We must obey."

CHAPTER 17

THE UNDERBORN REBORN

Acacia looked toward the edge of the field where Ashley still pressed a hand on her mother's wound, but she quickly turned back and, with her gaze low, said, "I will do as Enoch commanded." After raising her hood over her hair, Acacia took Paili's hand and guided her toward the edge of the garden. Her cloak flared in the breeze, its brilliant blue now sparkling in the growing sunshine.

Jared raised the sword and stood in front of Abraham, Barlow, and Listener. "If the giants attack, I'm not sure we can hold them off, but we'll do our best."

"My guess," Abraham said, "is that the dragon will want to hear the prophecy. He knows it will carry vital information." He reached out a hand. "Please help me up."

When Jared pulled him to his feet, Abraham rubbed the white gem on Jared's ring. "Were you once a dragon?"

He nodded. "I was Clefspeare, grandson of Makaidos."

Billy held up his hand, showing the white gem on his ring. "And I'm his son. I was an anthrozil. I could breathe fire before I gave up my dragon traits."

Abraham pushed both of them along. "Go with the ark and guard her well. Stand in the soil with her as she sings, and let us hope with your swords and Acacia's fire, you will be protected from this devil's onslaught." Abraham then pulled Elam closer. "You guard Acacia's back."

Jared and Billy ran ahead, caught up with Acacia, and moved in front of her, one on each side of Paili, their swords in ready position. Snatching up a fallen sword, Elam trailed them.

Acacia raised her hands and called out, "Give me light!" When flames appeared in her palms, she whipped them into a shield around Paili and her two protectors. As soon as they reached the garden soil, she backed away to the grass and stood next to Elam.

The fire crawled along the ground, and once again, the bones at Paili's feet radiated an iridescent light. The bones seemed to pull the fire across the soil and into themselves, energizing their white coats.

As the first giant set a foot on the ground, Goliath glared at Acacia. "Do you think your feeble shield can stand up to my army?"

"I dare say it can." She pointed at the giant, a nine-foot-tall man with a blackened face, a missing eye, and six fingers on each hand. "Chazaq used to be a tiny spawn that ate mashed worms. Although he is now a muscular brute, and his face is scorched, I still know him well from when he pulled us laborers up and down an elevator shaft. Since he is really a mere plant, he fears my flames. I can see terror in his only good eye."

As a second giant reached the ground, Chazaq pointed his spear at Acacia and laughed. "I remember you, little squirrel. If you think I am frightened by a mere candlewick, you will soon learn what it means to be snuffed out."

Acacia set her hands on her hips. "Your words spew false courage. Your own knees give you away. I saw them knock together when my flames appeared."

"Nonsense! I tremble because I am not yet accustomed to the cold here. Maybe I will warm up by chasing down a certain squirrel and stomping her flat."

"More bluster from an overgrown houseplant." Acacia half closed one eye. "Haven't you heard the law of the Oracles? Whoever spills my blood will surely die. Ask Nimrod about that, or Anak, one of your own kind. They both died by merely scraping Sapphira's skin."

A third giant tromped down to the ground and slapped Chazaq on the back. "The little squirrel scolds you now." He made his voice squeak. "Don't spill my blood! Don't spill my blood!" He laughed out loud.

Chazaq narrowed his eyes. "I won't spill her blood." He raised a hand and tightened his fingers into a fist. "I will just crush her bones."

Goliath let out a rumbling chuckle. "Well, go ahead, Oracle of Fire, and let your little songstress sing her heart out. Perhaps I will learn something valuable in her words." He extended his neck and brought his head within a few feet of Paili. "Yet, I am surprised at her stature. She seems very young to be a mother."

"They told me stories about being a mother," Paili said, "but I don't remember them."

"I heard those stories as well, but now I think they must have lied to you. No girl your age could possibly be a mother and not remember." Goliath chuckled again. "It seems to me that you are doing the bidding of liars. But, after being a slave to Morgan and Naamah for so long, you have likely grown accustomed to that. I hear that you were the most gullible of all the underborns. In fact, you were such an imbecile, you could barely speak at all. Ask Acacia. She will tell you. That is, if she will now tell the truth."

279

Paili looked back at Acacia, a pained expression on her face.

As a fourth giant joined ranks with the others, Acacia glanced at Elam. She whispered, "What do I say?"

"I have an idea." Elam stepped into the garden and crouched behind the fiery shield. With Billy and Jared still standing at each side and the flames warming his skin, he gazed into Paili's puzzled eyes, still the same after all this time. Whether she looked at him as a dirty slave girl or as an elegant wife to Sir Patrick, those sincere brown eyes held a blend of youthful joy and emotional scars—the everlasting pleasure of freedom mixed with the memories of toil and bondage.

He glanced into the mass of villagers but couldn't locate Sir Patrick. With his gray hair, he should have been easy to find. Maybe he had gone to help with Thigocia. Turning back to Paili, Elam kept his voice low. "You remember me from a long time ago, don't you?"

"Of course, Elam." She grinned. "You were the mouse who kept eating the bread crumbs Sapphira and I threw at the hole in the wall."

"That's right, but do you remember how we used to sit in an underground tunnel and sing 'The Lord Is My Shepherd' to a little boy who was dying of cancer?"

Paili looked upward for a moment. "I remember that. I held him in my arms, and he looked at me with those big, sad eyes and …" As her voice faded, a tear inched down her cheek. "I'm too small to hold a boy that big."

"That's right. You were a grown woman." Although he ached to wipe her tear away, he didn't dare try to penetrate the fiery shield. "You see, there are many things about your life that you don't remember, but we once spent many years together in your home. For now, just sing the words Enoch has given you, and we'll defeat these monsters. After this is over, I will tell you as much as I can."

Paili looked at the growing army, now seven giants strong. "Okay," she said, "but this is scarier than the last time."

Elam rolled his hand into a fist. "You can do it. I know you can."

Taking in a deep breath, Paili nodded and turned back toward the center of the garden. She lifted her hands and began to hum a beautiful trilling melody.

Backing away, Elam kept glancing at the giants as they congregated, now up to eight in number, but they seemed to be waiting for everyone to arrive before attacking. Paili's song would have to be short and effective.

She lowered herself to her knees and picked up one of the glowing bones. Then, looking skyward, she began her song.

Pattering feet to clattering claws,
The dragon resurrects;
Fiery eyes and fiery breath
Humanity rejects.

The garden breathes new life to those
Now trapped without their scales,
In human skin or pits of death,
They burst from fragile jails.

The one who treads on soil made hot
By bones of dragon kings,
Restores a coat of scales and claws,
Renews the gift of wings.

A day will come when peace will rest
On Second Eden's land,
But wars will rage for times unknown
Till Prophet takes his stand.

281

The liar lives in exile where
She's promised as a wife.
Redemption comes at kingly cost;
The price is life for life.

O Abraham, the Adam who
Refused the devil's fruit,
O will your sandals toil and tread
On Second Adam's route?

The wars will rage, the battles roar,
And dragons there will find
The rubellite that bears their mark
Restores the form in mind.

282

The fiery shield collapsed. Flames scattered across the garden, sparking for a moment as they passed by each bone in the soil. Then, they vanished. All was quiet except for the cool breeze that wafted across every creature, human and dragon alike.

Paili stayed on her knees, her eyes directed upward. Still brandishing his sword, Billy reached over Paili and nudged his father. "What do we do now?"

"I'm not sure. Maybe there's more to the song. Let's keep guarding her until she's ready to get up."

The last of the Nephilim stepped off the staircase and joined the others. As soon as his foot left the final step, the black column evaporated into thick smoke and rose into the air.

Now ten spear-wielding giants stood shoulder to shoulder behind Goliath, apparently not caring where they set their feet. Some had trampled plants, crushing a stem or pod as they arranged themselves in a line.

Still standing with Acacia, Elam clenched his teeth. The giants were murderers! But what could he do? Lead an attack against them?

That seemed unlikely. Acacia was able to hold them off with the promise of a barrage of fire, but in her weakened state, could she really battle that many giants? And with Thigocia hurt, could Roxil keep Goliath from slaughtering the villagers with a tidal wave of fire?

Elam shivered in the cool breeze, but more from fear than from cold. He was supposed to be the warrior chief, but so far he had messed everything up, and the situation was getting worse every second.

He waved his hands toward Thigocia, still resting at the far side of the field. "Everyone to the wounded dragon! Hurry!"

The villagers who had returned, many now armed with swords and daggers, rushed that way. Dikaios trotted up and lowered his head. "Put the wounded on my back, and I will carry them."

Elam and Acacia helped Barlow and Abraham mount Dikaios. Abraham rode in back and held Barlow upright as the knight laid a hand against his head. "Don't worry about me, my good fellow," Barlow said. "I was practically born on a horse." Dikaios struggled into a trot and followed the hurrying crowd.

Acacia took Listener by the hand and stood at Elam's side. "Should I create a fiery diversion so you can strategize with the others?"

Glancing for a second at Billy as he and Jared continued to guard the kneeling Paili, he focused on his group of potential warriors, both dragon and human. "A diversion might help, but I'm not sure—"

"The prophetess has finished her song and is now stalling," Goliath roared. "Kill her! Four of you capture the Oracle of Fire! You others, join me. We will attack the crowd and capture the uninjured dragon."

"Gotta run!" Billy yelled as he scooped up Paili. Lowering his head, he sprinted along a garden row and rushed into the field.

Jared followed, but as soon as he touched the grass, his shoes split open. Claws replaced his feet and pushed into the ground. His pants split from ankle to hip, exposing muscular, scaly legs. He stopped and called out, "What's happening?" As his shirt ripped open, sparks flew from his lengthening nose. "I'm changing!"

The Nephilim rumbled out of the garden. One knocked Jared down with an elbow as he rushed past. Jared writhed on the ground. His body swelled. Lines crawled along his hardening skin, separating it into scales. Still carrying Paili, Billy sprinted back to him and knelt at his side.

Elam reached for Listener, but Acacia kept hold of her hand and ran toward the forest. "Go to your army," she called. "I'll protect her!"

Lowering his body, Elam lunged in front of one of the Nephilim, rammed his shoulder against his knees, and pushed himself upright again. The giant flew through the air, flailing his arms and legs, and landed face-first in the grass. With his head half buried in the impact trench, his body fell limp.

Elam pumped his fist. That was one down, but the others had already raced by. He ran in their wake, watching Acacia as she closed in on the forest. With Listener still in tow, and those giants striding on long legs, she would never make it back to the village before they caught up.

Just before she reached the line of trees, she dropped down and spread out her arms. "Give me light!" she shouted. Instantly, bolts of lightning shot out from her palms and raced around her and Listener, creating a radiant aura, more like rays of sunlight than fire.

The remaining three giants swarmed around her. Chazaq tried to thrust his spear into the aura, but it sprang out of his hands. He then pounded his fists against the surface while the other two kept watch, their spears ready. With each blow, her fire seemed to shrink and fade. She was already tired. How much longer could she hold out?

Elam dove for the legs of the closest giant. Barely sliding under his stabbing spear, Elam tackled him around the knees and dug his toes into the grass, pushing and thrusting until the Naphil top-pled over. Elam tried to jump back, but something smacked him in the head, sending him rolling to the side.

As he rose to his knees, pain throttled his senses. He tried to find the giant, but with dragon roars and human screams echoing all around, he couldn't get his bearings. The giant he had tackled climbed to his feet. Blood covered the blunt end of his spear.

Elam felt the side of his head. Warm wetness matted his hair, but he couldn't gauge the depth of the wound.

The giant turned toward Acacia and hurled his spear. This time, the point shot through the weakened aura and pierced Acacia's wrist. She fell on her back, clutching her arm. The shield vaporized. Listener screamed and threw herself over Acacia's body.

Just as Chazaq reached a meaty hand toward the girls, a torrent of fire blasted his face. Another river of flames rocketed across the field parallel to the first and poured over a second giant. Both giants, their clothes ablaze, rolled on the grass trying to snuff the flames, while the third dove under another surge of twin fiery jets.

Still on his knees, Elam looked for the source. Waving a sword, Billy rode with a woman atop a great red dragon that half ran and half flew toward Acacia. "Surrender!" Billy called, smoke rising from his mouth, "or you'll get another taste of fire from Clefspeare and me!"

All three giants scrambled to their feet and ran into the forest, one with his pants still on fire. Another faltered, then fell face-first against a tree. He collapsed in a heap next to the trunk and lay still.

Clefspeare wheeled around toward the opposite side of the field where Goliath had attacked with the other Nephilim. With three dragons fighting, fire spewed all around. Goliath launched a stream at Ashley, but Thigocia, now upright and hobbling, stretched out a wing and blocked it just in time. Roxil answered with a fireball that smacked Goliath's face. Smoke engulfed the

285

area, and giants stabbed wildly with their spears, some landing in human flesh and others striking only air.

Elam pointed that way. "Go, Clefspeare! I can take care of Acacia!"

"I'm fine, Elam." Acacia, now sitting up, held a hand over her wound, while Listener watched the forest with her spyglass. "Leave Ruth with me. The people need their warrior chief!"

"Ruth?" Elam looked up at the woman riding with Billy. Paili had transformed into her adult self, Sir Patrick's lovely wife, Ruth Nathanson, now wearing a long-sleeved cloak and clutching it closed in front.

Elam grinned. "Wait'll Patrick sees you!"

"No time for reunions," Billy shouted. Taking Ruth by the hand, he lowered her down Clefspeare's side until Elam could reach her. Elam kissed her cheek, then vaulted high on Clefspeare's tail and ran up his spinal stairway.

As he took a seat behind Billy, he pointed at the smoky battle. "Let's go!"

Clefspeare launched toward the melee. As they closed in, the details clarified. Walter, Valiant, and Barlow fought alongside the villagers, but the giants' superior size and strength seemed overwhelming. The men of the village fought bravely, thrusting with their homemade swords and parrying fireballs with their leather-coated shields, while their companions zipped all around, their inner lights flashing wildly. The barrage forced the villagers to backpedal toward a bordering stone wall. If they retreated any farther, they would be doomed.

Sir Patrick, now riding atop Dikaios, weaved in and out of the fray, jabbing and hacking with a sword, while Dikaios bit the giants whenever one was in range.

Clefspeare sent a barrage of fireballs at Goliath, while Billy heaved a torrent at one of the giants.

The moment Clefspeare slowed down, Elam leaped to the battlefield and, ducking under the firestorm, sneaked into the villagers' ranks. He grabbed a sword from the ground, raised it in the air, and shouted, "Press forward! We have reinforcements!"

Jumping toward one of the giants, he swung the sword and whacked off his thumb. "Follow me!"

Barlow hacked Goliath's leg and drew a spurt of blood. "Take that, you viperous villain!"

Fire splashed against Goliath's back. Smoke billowed all around. With a loud roar, Goliath beat his wings, clearing the haze. "Retreat! Survivors climb on me!"

Two giants leaped on Goliath's back. His body sagged for a moment, but, letting out a hefty grunt, he pushed into the air, flapping madly to gain altitude.

Clefspeare, Roxil, and Billy each launched volleys of fire. One slapped Goliath's wing, another ignited a Naphil's shirt, and the third streamed under Goliath's belly, lifting him higher.

After getting past Clefspeare and Billy, Goliath landed about a hundred feet away. The Nephilim leaped to the ground and ran. Goliath took to the air again, picked up one of the wounded giants in his claws, and soared ahead.

"After them!" Elam yelled. He raised his sword and broke into a sprint. Although his head ached, he had to make sure the Nephilim didn't stop to bother Acacia or the others.

The giants, one stripping off his flaming shirt, rushed into the forest, while Goliath disappeared over the treetops. Elam hurried to the forest's edge where Acacia sat with Listener and Ruth, a dim aura surrounding all three.

As she lowered her hands, the shield faded away. Blood oozed from a gash near her wrist, her cloak lay shredded near a flat rock, and long grass stems tangled her hair.

"Are you okay?" Elam asked.

"Nothing serious." She nodded at the fallen Naphil next to the tree. "He paid the price for shedding my blood."

The village's army filtered into the area, Walter first, then Valiant and Sir Barlow, followed by a dozen or so wounded and

287

weary townsfolk. Trailing the others, Dikaios loped toward them, Patrick riding tall on his bare back.

Elam smiled. It would be a minute or so before Patrick arrived. He could hardly wait.

Sir Barlow sat on the rock and used a scrap of Acacia's cloak to dab his head wound. "That was a battle for the ages. If we had wanted to engage in closer combat, we would have had to get behind them."

Elam reached for Acacia's hand. "Can you get up?"

"I think so." She rose with his pull. "How are Thigocia and the others?"

Walter shook his head. "Not good. At least five villagers are dead, several others are hurt, Thigocia lost a lot of blood trying to fight, and Angel's unconscious." He pointed with his thumb. "Abraham is back there with her. He says she's the best doctor they have, so that's also not good. Clefspeare and Billy are checking on the wounded."

"Does Ashley feel up to trying a healing?" Acacia asked. "I'm not sure how strong I am, but I'll do what I can."

Walter gave her a thumbs-up signal. "She'll want to try whether she feels like it or not."

Acacia rose to her tiptoes and kissed Elam on the cheek. "I saw you take command over there. You really are a warrior chief." With a smile, she turned and hobbled toward the battle site.

Warmth flooded Elam's skin. It was a good warmth, like sunshine breaking through the clouds after a cold rain. He took in a deep breath and straightened to his full height. "Do we have any doctors or nurses at all?"

Ruth stepped forward. "I have medical training in—"

"Ruth!" Sir Patrick jumped off Dikaios and ran the rest of the way. When he came within a few steps of her, he stopped and stared. Lifting a trembling hand, he caressed her cheek, still smooth and youthful, the skin of a thirty-year-old. He then touched his own cheek, wrinkled and weathered.

With her cloak now tied at the waist, she extended her hand and combed her fingers through his gray hair, then pulled her hand back and pushed through her own brown tresses. "My memory has been restored. I know who you were to me."

"Were?" His voice shaking, Patrick took her hand in his. "I have kept my vow. I neither took another wife, nor sought one."

She smiled. "Then what you were is what you still are."

"I have grown old since you went away, likely too old."

"Not so old." Her eyes sparkled with tears. "In fact, I am older than you are. Our outer shells have changed—mine between little girl and grown woman and yours between dragon and noble knight. I am still an underborn who has been reborn, and you are still a dragon who has shed his scales."

"Do you mean, even though I'm so withered and—"

She laid a finger over his lips. "Yes, my husband. I also said 'till death do us part' to complete our covenant veil." She lowered her hand, tipped her head up, and kissed him tenderly on the lips. As she drew back, she smiled again. "Let that be the seal that proves my recommitment. I am your wife, for better or for worse, till death takes one of us away."

As they embraced, Elam wiped a tear from his eye. "Okay. We have medical help. Anyone else?"

One man raised his sword but then let it droop at his side. "I have some experience, as does my Eve." His companion floated near his ear and flashed a dim pale light. It seemed as tired as its ward.

"What's your name?" Elam asked.

"Steadfast." He trudged close and propped himself with his sword. "I will do what I can."

"Do you know how to set up triage, Steadfast?"

289

He nodded. "My hut is close by. Listener knows where it is. She could send word to Pearl, my Eve, while I examine the wounded."

"Good." Elam looked down at Listener. She was once again peering through her spyglass. "Go to Steadfast's home and tell his Eve we're bringing the wounded."

She lowered the spyglass. "I will, but I need to tell Father Abraham what I just saw."

He stooped next to her. "What did you see?"

She pointed the glass at the sky. "Goliath was flying toward the marshlands. It looked like he was going toward Flint's village."

Elam stared in that direction for a moment. The sky, now fully brightened by morning sunlight, revealed nothing but a blue canopy. "I'll be sure to tell him." He clasped her shoulder. "Please go to Steadfast's home now. People are hurting."

"Yes, Warrior Chief." Listener's pigtails tossed about as she ran toward the village.

When she disappeared among the trees, Elam blew out a long sigh. "Time to bandage our soldiers."

"True enough." Sir Patrick patted him on the shoulder. "But we had better find more soldiers as well, draconic ones, if you get my meaning."

"More dragons? How?"

Patrick rubbed his thumb across his ring finger, though no ring was there. "It is clear to me that the garden has become a regenerating field. After the first song, this fellow named Dragon became Goliath and Abigail became Roxil. Note that both were dead on Earth and, before the first song, were never in this realm outside of the garden, as if the song gave them new life.

"After the second song, Jared became Clefspeare once again, and Billy regained his dragon traits. And now Paili's adult memory and body have been restored. Those three never died on Earth, so it seems that the second song brought about a way for those already alive to regain a form they now need for their purposes here. I assume that the same might happen to me."

Elam looked at his own finger where the rubellite ring Karen had given him still resided. He had promised to take it to its rightful place, but he wasn't sure yet where that might be. "Do you mean that you'll go into the garden and—"

"I will try soon. For now, we need to find a way to call the other former dragons here. If Flint is able to complete his army, we'll need all the firepower we can get."

CHAPTER

TO KEEP A VOW

E lam leaned against the table that once held the Enoch's Ghost ovulum and yawned as he looked over the interior of Abraham's humble home. With the front door wide open, light flooded the room, illuminating Abraham, who sat in a wooden chair just a step or two away from the table.

To their left, Walter wrung out a sponge over a basin and mopped Ashley's cheek as she lay on Abraham's cot next to the wall. With Barlow, Angel, and several others receiving medical care in Steadfast's home, Ashley had insisted on going elsewhere. After all, she wasn't really injured, just overheated and exhausted by her latest healing episode. Acacia had again covered her with flames in a successful attempt to seal Thigocia's wound, so she had to cool down, and trying to recuperate in a crowded hut would have made things worse.

Sir Patrick, of course, had stayed with Ruth to help with the patients, while Valiant flew away on Grackle to survey the marshlands from high above. He hoped to bring back a report on any troop movements. Although most of the villagers, as well as the visitors from Earth, had gone without sleep through the night and the morning hours, the escalating danger kept them on their toes.

"While we're waiting for Valiant," Elam said, "let's talk strategy. Abraham, do you have any idea what Listener's discovery means?"

"I do." Slumping his shoulders as he applied a cloth bandage to his leg, Abraham spoke in a low tone. "Goliath and his giants are likely to join Flint. You see, soon after Flint rebelled, Greevelow and the others arrived in our lands. Mantika was the only female, and when she procreated with Greevelow according to the ways of your world, Flint witnessed the birth of their son, Windor. Flint was horrified at the painful procedure and banned further procreation. Of course, such a ban would eventually bring an end to his followers, so apparently he now seeks to build his army another way. Combining the Nephilim with the marsh folk and the shadow people will create a considerable force."

294

Elam lifted a hand and began counting on his fingers. "We have two healthy dragons, a third who is healing, thanks to Ashley and Acacia, a fire-breathing boy with lots of experience, and an assortment of other fighters, including an Oracle of Fire, a super genius healer, and a bona fide knight, Sir Winston Barlow."

"I fear they won't be enough," Abraham said. "Goliath and the giants will likely conduct hundreds of shadow people out of the valley, and if they attack at night, they will swarm over us like a dark disease. We would need a dozen fire-breathers to have any hope at all."

Ashley blinked her eyes open. "Maybe we could get them."

"Are you still in a daze?" Walter asked. "The dragons here spew ice, not fire."

Pushing herself up, Ashley swung her bare feet around and set them on the floor. Wearing only pantaloons and a white T-shirt, she laid a hand on her forehead and grimaced. "Oh, what a headache!"

"You got up too fast," Walter tried to push her back down. "We need your head in good working order."

"I'll be all right," Ashley said, swatting his hand away. "I had a thought, more like a picture, but it just kind of flew away."

"That's not like you." Walter touched the side of her head. "You must have really gotten zapped this time."

"No, it's not that. It's like I got the thought from somewhere else."

"Are you reading minds again?"

"Maybe." Ashley turned her head slowly toward Elam. "I see it again. It's coming from you."

"The garden?" Elam asked.

"Yes, why are you holding it back?"

Elam slid up to the table and sat on it fully. "I didn't want to raise hopes for no reason."

"Go ahead and spill it," Walter said. "At this point, I'd rather have false hopes than no hope at all."

"Okay. Actually, Sir Patrick suggested it first, and it makes a lot of sense. You saw how the birthing garden gave Roxil, Clefspeare, and Billy their dragon traits. He was wondering if it could perform the same miracle for the other dragons."

"You mean Hartanna, Legossi, and the others who are still alive?" Ashley asked.

"Right. Maybe the combination of the bones and the prophetic song made the garden into a dragon regenerating factory."

"And a humanity regenerator," Abraham added. "Your story about Paili's life as an adult was fascinating."

"But how would we get the former dragons here?" Walter asked. "Thigocia used a firestorm to create a portal, but she's in no shape to do it again."

"That's the part that made me hold back the idea," Elam said, "but now I'm wondering if Roxil could do it. If Thigocia made one, why not Roxil?"

295

Walter looked at Ashley. "What do you think? Could *any* dragon do what your mother did?"

"Who knows?" Ashley rubbed her hands up and down her arms. "Let's ask them."

Walter grabbed a sweatshirt from the foot of the cot and handed it to her. "Okay, that's one potential portal maker."

"Acacia could open one that's already there," Elam said, "but the only existing portal I know about is the tunnel where we came in, and that's in enemy territory."

"And the chasm," Walter added. "I think we must have fallen several miles, so getting back that way might be impossible."

Elam looked at Abraham. He had rolled his pant leg back down and was now rubbing thick gray salve into his hand wound. "Do you know of any other portals?" Elam asked.

"Only one." Abraham pulled another strip of cloth around his hand and used his teeth to tie it in place. When he finished, he studied the knot. "There is a portal inside Mount Elijah, an unpredictable volcano. It hasn't erupted in a long time, but it still spews smoke and ash. Enoch told me the cone's magma pipe is a portal. I plugged it with rocks, because the peak is quite accessible, so I didn't want anyone falling in, but I also hoped I could somehow mask the presence of a portal."

"Did Enoch say where the portal leads?" Elam asked.

Abraham slid the basin closer with his foot, reached for Walter's sponge, and wrung it out. "It leads to an underground cave in the depths of Hades itself, and there is no way out. Anyone who used that portal would just have to come right back or be trapped forever, unless, of course, he knew how to open other portals."

"And that's the key." Elam stood and began pacing on the creaky wooden floor. "Maybe it's part of the underground mine tunnels in Hades where I used to live. We had portals there, so it could be the same place."

296

"Maybe," Walter said. "But testing it would be dangerous. If the portal didn't open up, the test pilot is toast."

"True, but Acacia would know if it's open or not before anyone jumped in. In the meantime, we'll see if Roxil can either fly up the chasm or else create a portal with fire." Elam stopped pacing and set his hands on Abraham's shoulders. "You have been very solemn, good Father. Is something else troubling you?"

"Very much so." Abraham patted Elam's hand. "You are thinking wisely. Your plan to add firepower to our numbers could be the only option."

"Okay … So what's on your mind?"

"The words on my mind are from a song I used to teach my dragon children soon after Adam and Eve were banished from the first Eden. When Flint rebelled, I translated it into English. One of the verses says, 'When those he calls will not obey, the Maker finds another way.'"

"I like that," Elam said. "But there's something more. Something's troubling you."

"True enough, but the song is relevant." Abraham gazed again at his bandaged hand. "I am grieving over Angel. Her lie brought this crisis upon us, and I have to deal with her appropriately. Yet, my heart aches at the thought of punishing her."

"You punish liars?" Walter asked. "In our world we elect them to public office."

Abraham gave him a thin smile. "Thank you for trying to uplift me with your humor, Walter. I know it must seem strange to you, since you live in a world of overwhelming corruption, but this is the first time any of my people has lied. In fact, only one other has ever rebelled in any way." He ran trembling fingers through his thick dark hair. "I see every one of my people as my own child, and losing two is a tragedy beyond measure. I took Flint into my home, and ever since Angel's husband died, I gave her emotional support and tried to be a father to her children. I

297

was closer to her than I was to most of my people. In fact I had even entertained the notion that …"

He stopped suddenly and looked straight at Elam. "I apologize. My tongue moved faster than I should have allowed it."

"You are among friends." Elam waved for Ashley and Walter to join him. When all three stood around Abraham, each one laying a hand on him, Elam continued. "I don't need Ashley's mental powers to know your thoughts. You have lived here for untold centuries without an Eve, and you thought Angel might be the one God had finally granted to sleep at your side. But in your grief, I hope you will remember your own words. 'When those he calls will not obey, the Maker finds another way.'"

Elam paused. Ashley pushed her fingers into Abraham's shoulder, massaging it deeply. A tear trickled from her eye. Walter laid his hand on top of Ashley's and allowed his fingers to move with hers.

Taking a deep breath, Elam continued. "You don't have to hold back emotions when you are among people who love you. Tears will only give us more reason to pray for you. They will anoint your countenance with the holiest of water. They will cleanse your soul."

Abraham buried his face in his hands, his fingers still trembling. Soon, his head began to bob up and down. Abraham, the father of Second Eden, wept.

Ashley moved her hand to the top of his head. "I see this in your mind, Father Abraham. You have put Angel on an island all alone. You plan to exile her to keep her influence away from the rest of your people." Her brow arched down. "But there's more. A great fear. Angel looks like she's——"

"Don't say it!" Abraham lifted his head and grabbed Ashley's wrist. "Beware," he said as he pulled her hand down. "Your gift becomes an intrusion when you use it to probe private thoughts."

Ashley slid her hand away and looked down at the floor. "I'm sorry. You're right. This is all so new to me."

Elam stooped next to Abraham and spoke softly. "Will you send her out on her own or have someone conduct her to a place of refuge?"

"When I banished Flint, I knew he would survive, because he is a skilled hunter. Angel has many talents, but battling muskrats or prairie lions would—"

"Father Abraham!" Listener ran through the doorway, waving her spyglass. "I saw a red dragon and a rider flying toward the birthing garden!"

"Through your spyglass?" Abraham asked.

She nodded. "I can't see the dragon without it, but I'm sure it's coming. Clefspeare, Roxil, and Thigocia are already there lying in the sun, so it couldn't be one of them."

Pushing against the chair, Abraham struggled to his feet. Elam and Walter balanced him from each side. "Ashley," Abraham said, a new flush in his cheeks, "since you are well enough to walk, would you go to our infirmary and see what you can do? Even without fire, your healing touch might be of great help."

Ashley glanced at Walter, then pulled her sweatshirt on. "Yes, Father Abraham."

"Walter, you may escort her there and stay if you are so inclined."

"Uh ... sure." Walter let go of Abraham and shifted toward Ashley. "If that's where you want me."

"Elam," Abraham continued, "run to the garden and warn the dragons. I will be there soon."

"Dikaios is at the drinking trough." Elam grabbed a scabbard belt and strapped it around his waist. "He'll be glad to carry you."

"Very well." Abraham pointed at the door. "Go with all speed."

Listener rushed outside. Elam followed and, pushing into a full sprint, caught up with her just as they reached the forest. He scooped her up, barely slowing down as she wrapped her arms

299

around his neck, still hanging on to her spyglass. After navigating the narrow path, he ran out onto the field. The scabbard dragged the ground at his side, but he ignored it and ran on.

In the distance, Clefspeare sat on his haunches, apparently standing guard while Thigocia and Roxil basked in the sunlight. Billy sat with his back against Clefspeare's leg, his eyes open.

When Elam came within earshot, he was about to sound the warning, but Clefspeare spoke first. "I sense danger, and it is getting closer."

"Me, too," Billy said, rising to his feet. "I almost didn't recognize it."

Roxil lifted her head and sniffed the air. Her brow wrinkled, and her eyes flashed. "It is Goliath. I slept at his side too long to forget his scent."

Turning his gaze upward, Elam scanned the sky. Cloudless and deep blue, it seemed close enough to touch, as if a person could reach up and scoop a fingerful of blue frosting. The surrounding trees and stone wall blocked his view of the horizon, so he tuned his ears to listen for the sound of beating wings.

"He is here," Roxil said as she lifted her body. Her eyebeams turned on, and she aimed them at the sky above the village.

Elam swung that way. A dragon appeared and bent into an orbit over the field, flying high enough to stay out of range of spears and arrows. A single rider sat at the intersection of Goliath's neck and back, waving a white flag.

Galloping hoofbeats sounded from the forest, Dikaios carrying Abraham into the field. When they arrived, Abraham slid down, apparently much stronger now, and focused on the circling dragon. "Flint is riding Goliath," he said. "He is waiting for us to signal that he may land without confrontation."

Clefspeare extended his neck toward the sky. "My danger sense tells me that their intentions are foul. This meeting is for their benefit, and theirs alone."

300

"He cannot be trusted," Roxil said. "He allowed Devin and Palin to murder my father and me, though I was his mate. For our race, he invented treachery."

"But he can't fight," Elam said. "It's three dragons against one."

Thigocia struggled to her feet. She stretched out her wings, revealing the long, jagged stitching that held the torn membrane together on one and the tight bandage that bound the mainstay on the other. "We have two and a half dragons, but you are right. Goliath would not even be able to fight Clefspeare in a one-on-one battle, so he is not likely to instigate a conflict."

Clefspeare blinked at her but said nothing.

"Can it hurt to hear what he has to say?" Elam asked.

Glaring at him, Roxil thumped her tail. "Would you listen to an offer from the devil?"

"If I could use the information against him, definitely. Maybe we can get a clue to what we're up against."

"Very well." Abraham took a few steps away from the others, closed his eyes, and spread out his arms as if awaiting an embrace. He stayed in that position for several seconds, then returned. "That is our sign of vulnerability. Flint will understand."

As Goliath swept lower, Clefspeare unfurled his wings and positioned himself in front of the humans and Dikaios. Thigocia and Roxil joined him and formed a wall. Staying on Goliath's back as they landed, Flint wadded his white flag and tucked it into his waistband. "To whom shall I make my petition?" he asked. "It seems that foreign dragons have taken over this realm, and the humans are cowering behind wings and scales."

Abraham gestured for Elam to follow and stepped around Clefspeare. "You may speak to me," Abraham said. "I have not yet abdicated my seat."

Flint arced his glance around Abraham. "I assumed a true warrior chief would have taken command, but I see that I was right.

He is but a lad who lacks the confidence or experience to lead your ragtag children."

"You have come here under a white flag," Abraham said. "Speak your mind and be off."

Flint patted the scales on Goliath's neck. "My new friend has told me that you have a liar in your midst."

Flexing his wounded hand, Abraham paused for a moment before replying. "What concern is that of yours?"

"Something you taught me, Father Abraham. Justice. I learned from the first day that I could sit in one of your classes that corruption breeds corruption, so I know the liar must be sent away. I am here to ensure that her exile is not too difficult to bear. I will take her with me, and she will be safe from the creatures of the wild, safe from exposure and hunger, and safe from the temptation to fill the minds of your people with deceit." As he resettled himself on Goliath, the dormant companion swayed at the end of the chain around his neck, still as dark as before. "Surely you will agree, Father Abraham. While justice and the protection of your people demand that you send her away, mercy insists that she be allowed a place of safe refuge. When that is accomplished, I expect you to fulfill your obligation to preside over the ceremony we discussed earlier."

Elam whispered to Abraham, "Is he being serious, or is this a ploy?"

"Both, I'm afraid. He speaks the truth, yet he hides his primary motivations."

"Do you have any options? Can you refuse him?"

"I can let Angel decide, but I cannot let the sun set before this justice is done." Abraham turned and peered through the gap in the dragon wall. "Billy? Would you please take Dikaios and fetch Angel from our infirmary?"

Dikaios ambled into the clear, Billy already mounted on his back. "Sure thing," Billy said.

"And bring Valiant, if he has returned, and Angel's children, as well." Abraham's shoulders drooped and his voice along with them. "We will need witnesses."

As soon as Dikaios galloped away with Billy, Elam leaned close to Abraham and whispered more urgently. "You're going to let Candle and Listener see their mother being shamed and sent away?"

Taking quick breaths, Abraham squeezed out his words. "The lesson ... will be tragic ... but it will ... never be forgotten." He breathed in deeply and finished stronger. "And I must make sure they are cared for."

Elam felt a knot forming in his gut. This would be too painful to watch. How could he send a mother away in front of her own children? How could Abraham be so callous?

Abraham picked up a palm-sized stone and squeezed it in his hand. "If my people would follow the light, no one would ever have to suffer. In your own world, you might remember how the apostle Peter dealt with liars, both male and female. I am adhering to the same principle."

Elam shifted his gaze to Flint. Earlier, he rode with a straight back and square shoulders, but as soon as Abraham picked up the stone, he sagged noticeably.

Flint slid down Goliath's side and stooped in the grass. "I understand your gesture," he said. "There is no need to remind me of your warped views of justice and mercy."

Spewing twin lines of smoke, Goliath thumped his tail on the ground. "While we wait for the deceiver," he said with a growl, "hear *my* petition. Abraham and the warrior chief must understand who I am. As the firstborn son of Makaidos, I am the true king of the dragons. The one who poses as Arramos is not who he says he is, and Makaidos is gone forever, so as the primary heir of the king, I assume my rightful position and command all dragons from my world to submit to my authority."

303

Thigocia snorted. "Your pride blinds you, Goliath. You speak as though you have forgotten who I am. As Makaidos's surviving mate, I have the authority to choose the next king and queen, and I chose Clefspeare as heir to the throne long ago."

"A king without a queen? Clefspeare has no dragon mate. Will you violate the sacred tradition in order to satisfy your prejudice?"

Thigocia glanced at Roxil, then turned her flashing red eyes back on Goliath. "What exactly is your petition?"

"I am here to take back my mate," Goliath said. "With her at my side, I am the only dragon who can rightfully claim to be king."

Roxil backed away a step, her pupils pulsing scarlet. "I died and rose from the dead as a human, then I was reborn yet again and resurrected in this world. Death breaks our covenant, so I am no longer your mate."

"I, too, died and rose again as a human, a man named Dragon in this world. Is it any surprise that my companion would recognize my dragon nature and assign me such a name in this world? Is it any surprise that the same companion would so easily attach to Timothy, who was also a dragon at one time? And is it any surprise that once that companion was gone I would be able to shed its brainwashing power and return as the dragon I was before?

"Now that I have been resurrected in the same way you have, we are once again mates. We bypassed the words of the traditional covenant veil by substituting our own ceremony. You agreed that making our private vows stronger than what tradition called for gave us the right to consummate our union. Have you forgotten what we sealed with blood on that fateful night?"

Elam looked back at Roxil and imagined the covenant veil that dragons created to sanctify the wedding of two of their own kind. They would pass between two or more dragons who spoke the vows for the potential mates, and if the intention of their hearts didn't match the words of the covenant, they wouldn't be able to pass through.

Roxil's wings trembled. She backed away another step. "I was a fool. When I said that our union would survive our deaths, romantic notions addled my brain. I did not really think that—"

"That we would survive death?" Goliath turned on his eye-beams and drew scarlet letters on the ground. "Shall I quote your own words?"

"I remember them. You have no need to remind me."

"Then I will humor myself." Goliath breathed out a ring of smoke that hung in the air, unmoved by the suddenly calm winds. "The covenant veils of the dragons who went before us were no stronger than the flesh of the humans we despise. Like those vermin, so easily roasted in our flames, the unions of other dragons perished with the fiery trial of death. Yet, our union will survive even the end of our mortal lives, for we will rise again to new life, and whatever world we find ourselves in, I will still be yours forever. As long as I have the strength to breathe in air and light, I will stay at your side."

Roxil averted her eyes. Her tail twitched back and forth as the slimmest of smoke trails rose from her nostrils.

"Did you speak these words or not?" Goliath asked.

Roxil's tail stopped twitching. "I spoke them."

"Did you also say that covenant veils were for unfaithful dragons whose words could not be trusted?"

"I said that."

"Will you then be one of those dragons whose words cannot be trusted, or will you instead honor your vow and come to my side once again as my mate?"

Thigocia thumped her tail so hard, she gouged out a divot. "Roxil, you made that vow before you knew he was a murderer. Just hours ago he killed a human baby, and he bared my vulnerability, ready to kill me, as well. His own mother!"

Roxil blew out two plumes of black smoke. "Does that change my vow? I am not a faithless dragon! I must honor my words, or I will be a liar and a hypocrite!"

Clefspeare shuffled close to Roxil and laid a wing over hers. "Mother, it has been a very long time since I have been able to call you by that name, but I am honored that I can do so once again. Will you hear the words of your son?"

She extended her neck and touched her cheek to his. "Of course, my son. If I had listened to your counsel long ago, I would have avoided a lot of heartache."

Clefspeare drew his head back and looked her in the eye. "Goliath is mounting an army in order to fight and kill each one of us. Do you mean to join him in that effort? In your passion to prevent personal hypocrisy, will you become an accessory to the murder of your mother and your son?"

Roxil stepped to the side, pulling herself from under his wing. "I ... I do not know what to say. I would never want anything to happen to you or Mother, or ..."

"Or our other youngling," Goliath said.

"What?" Roxil whipped her neck toward him. "We have no other younglings."

"Come with me, and I will tell you about a dragon who has never known a mother."

Her eyes flashed. "Impossible! I would know if I gave birth."

"Normally, yes." Goliath's teeth showed through his widening smile. "Yet, I have information that I will share if you will keep your covenant."

"Liar!" Roxil swung her tail and turned her back. "I am no fool! How dare you try such a ploy!"

Elam tugged on Abraham's sleeve and whispered. "I have an idea. Will you trust me?"

"Of course. You are the warrior chief."

Picking up a stone, Elam strode toward Goliath and Flint. "You know what the law of this land calls for when someone lies or rebels, don't you?"

Flint glanced at the stone. "Yes, I know it all too well."

306

"Then why are you still alive?" Elam asked, tossing the stone toward him.

Flint caught it but kept his eyes on Elam. "Because the law also allows for exile if the judge so deems."

"Then the decision is not up to Roxil. If she stays, she will be a liar who must either be stoned or sent into exile. If she leaves with you, then we could consider her a traitor to our cause. Either way, she will never be able to live among us."

Thigocia lowered her head and growled. "Elam, why are you doing this? When they gather all their forces, we cannot defeat them without Roxil."

Elam picked up another stone. "If I am to be warrior chief, I need to know that I am leading an army of holy warriors. If we don't keep our integrity, then we cannot count on God's help against any army, no matter how evil our opponents are." He strode toward Roxil, extending a finger directly toward her snout. "If this dragon stays here, then she will be a handicap, not an asset. I will not tolerate having a liar in my ranks."

As he drew close, he whispered, "Roxil, trust me and listen carefully to my next words."

He spun dramatically and pointed at Goliath, raising his voice. "Now go with your mate. It is better for us if you are there than here."

Roxil tilted her head, then, one eye squinting, sniffed the air near Elam. After a second or two, she scuffled toward Goliath, a growl spicing her voice. "I will go. Since these humans no longer want me here, my choice is an easy one."

LIFE OR DEATH

Hoofbeats sounded from the forest. Angel rode atop Dikaios with Listener seated behind her. Billy, Valiant, and Candle followed, jogging in a row. As soon as they arrived, Elam helped Angel dismount, while Billy carried Listener to the ground.

Listener, clutching her spyglass, as usual, beamed as she surveyed the host of dragons. Her companion buzzed all around, flashing with rapid pulses of blue light. Angel's shoulders drooped, and her glazed eyes focused on nothing in particular.

Elam searched for Angel's companion, but it wasn't in sight. He shifted his gaze to her hand. Her fingers loosely clutched something, but if her companion was in her grasp, it showed no signs of life.

Taking her by the hand, Elam led Angel to Abraham. She stood in front of him, her chin low. Wearing a loose-fitting brown frock that looked more like an altered potato sack than a woman's dress, she folded her bare arms over her chest and trembled.

Valiant stooped next to Elam and put an arm around each of Angel's children, whispering something to them as he nuzzled their ears. His expression seemed a cross between curiosity and concern, but no hint of anger shaded his face.

Listener pointed her spyglass into the air and gazed through the eyepiece, apparently unaware of the solemn assembly's tragic purpose. She lowered her glass and looked up at Elam. "I see something strange."

Bending over, Elam whispered. "What?"

"Smoke in the sky, so thick all of the prairie grass would have to be on fire."

Elam looked up. The sky, still as blue as Sapphira's eyes, gave no hint of smoke, and no burning smell tinged the air. He whispered, "Show me after we're done."

She nodded and lifted the spyglass to her eye again.

When everyone fell silent, save for the whistling wind, Abraham glanced between Flint and Angel. After heaving a great sigh, he spoke with a loud, somber voice. "Angel, I have called you here to answer a charge that I am bringing against you in the presence of witnesses. You claimed that Enoch asked you to relay his desire to change one of the prophecies that Paili sang in the garden. Is that true?"

310

Without lifting her head, Angel replied softly, "Yes, Father Abraham."

The sky dimmed. Elam jerked his head upward. A gray cloud had drifted in front of the sun, part of a thicker, darker bank that streamed from the horizon. He scanned the others. Valiant's eyes had trained on the cloud bank. Candle stared at it as well, while Listener kept her spyglass aimed in that direction.

Abraham and Angel, however, seemed to pay no attention. "Did Enoch actually ask you to communicate that change to Paili?" Abraham asked.

This time Angel's head shifted slowly back and forth. "No, Father Abraham. Enoch made no such request."

The sky grew darker. The clouds boiled, and the wind shifted, gusting and swirling. Valiant turned his gaze toward the ground.

The stiffening breeze tossed his curly dark hair and buffeted Candle's dreadlocks. Listener lowered her spyglass again. Tears welled in her eyes as she stared at her mother.

Billy eased up to Elam's side and whispered, "I just wanted you to know. The dragons and I sense danger."

Elam nodded. "Thanks. I'll keep my eyes open."

As Abraham's pant legs flapped, he folded his arms, clutching his biceps. "Then do you, Angel, admit that you lied?"

She looked up at him, finally meeting his gaze. Tears streamed down her cheeks. Her voice grew so strained, it barely survived the wind's buffeting. "Yes, Father Abraham. … I lied."

A rumble sounded from above. Dark clouds raced across the sky, washing the blue with sooty gray. Nickel-sized raindrops splattered here and there. One splashed on Abraham's face, but he didn't flinch as he raised his voice to compete with the howling wind. "Can you tell us if the lie was for the purpose of saving a life, or was your motivation selfish in nature?"

Angel's chin trembled, but her voice stayed serene. "I could claim that I wanted to save my Adam's life, but that, too, would be a lie, for he was already dead. I wanted to fill my aching arms with his presence and give a father back to my children. If these are selfish motivations, I leave that conclusion to your wise judgment." She held her hand out toward him, her palm exposed. A crystalline egg lay there, motionless and dark. A raindrop splashed on its surface, but it had no effect. Angel's companion seemed no more than a lifeless glass bauble. Her voice shook so hard, she could barely speak as she sobbed through her words. "But I know… the answer. I … I have no excuse. … My companion tried to tell me. … But I didn't … I didn't listen. Now … now when I try to talk to it … it won't answer. I think … I think I killed it."

A tear trickled down Abraham's cheek, joining another raindrop as it dripped from his chin. His voice, too, trembled as if

311

shaken by the wind. "Your confession has been heard by these wit-nesses, and we all know the penalty for your crime." He reached down and picked up the stone he held earlier. "Since I cannot change the laws handed down to me by Enoch himself, I can only offer you the mercy of exile. Flint has said he will take you to his domain where you will have food and shelter. If you wish to go with him, you may do so now."

Flint took a step toward Angel and held out his hand. Goliath gazed at her, his eyes a softer red than the flaring beacons he had flashed during battle.

Turning toward her children, Angel wrung her hands together, weeping. Candle just stared, his mouth half open. Listener let her spyglass droop to the ground. She sniffed and squeaked, "Mommy?"

Angel fell to her knees. Dipping her head, she spread out her arms and cried, "Father, I commit my body to your judgment. If my only options are stoning or going with this man into exile, then I choose to bear the weight of every stone you might hurl, for it is better to bleed and die by your righteous hands than to live in shame in the arms of a rebel."

Abraham set his feet and lifted the stone higher. "Valiant," he said. "You know what we have to do."

"The children have served as witnesses to her crime," Valiant replied, his eyes wide with alarm. "Will you have them also wit-ness her execution?"

Abraham squeezed the stone tightly. "It is essential that they see how justice is carried out. No crime of this magnitude must ever go unpunished."

Elam swallowed down a lump. He scanned the onlookers. Billy had turned his head, as had Clefspeare and Thigocia. Even Goliath looked away, though perhaps he did it to conceal a glee-ful expression. Only Roxil maintained her stare. An irritated scowl twisted her scaly face.

The raindrops thickened. Lightning flashed. A loud clap of thunder shot across the sky. Candle and Listener covered their heads with their arms and shivered.

As Angel bowed lower, rain drenching her hair, a recent memory roared into Elam's mind. Naamah had struck this exact pose when he held a stone over her, ready to strike her down at Dikaios's command. She had deserved to die, yet he had offered her a hand of mercy.

Although Abraham's arm stayed flexed, ready to throw, tears continued to stream down his face. "This is rain," he cried out, "a weeping of the skies, the first in the thousands of years I have been a shepherd of this realm. It testifies against you, for you have brought the Nephilim into our land, and, as God sent flooding rain to Earth because of the evil they provoked, he is doing the same here."

Valiant picked up a stone, though smaller than Abraham's. He, too, wept as he drew his stone back. "Give the word, Father. I await your command."

Flint stepped closer. He uttered no words, but his face spoke volumes. He was conflicted. Obviously he hoped for a wedge to drive between Abraham and his people, and this could well be the opportunity he was waiting for. Yet, a hint of sadness sagged his features.

Raising his stone higher, Abraham shouted, "Let mine be first, but strike well, for there is no need to make her suffer!"

Lightning ripped into the birthing garden. Arcs of electricity ran along the ground, making the bones glitter and the soil glow. A gunshot clap of thunder shook the earth, and, as the garden's glow faded, rain poured, heavier than ever.

Abraham stared at the garden's residual light, his arm lowering with the weight of his saturated sleeve. The light cast a rainbow over him, a short arc that seemed to drape him from shoulder to shoulder. At each end, a tiny light flashed inside an egg-shaped

313

crystal at either side of his neck. Red pulsed from one, blue from the other, back and forth, as if arguing. Abraham's glance shifted between them, yet so subtly, Elam almost didn't notice.

Angel lifted her eyes and cried out, "Let the rain be a rain of stones upon my head, Father of Lights, for I am the guilty one! Do not bring a flood to purge the land! Do not punish my children for the sin that is mine alone!" She bent her body forward. Now only her head and back could be seen as sheets of rain drenched every inch of her sackcloth shroud.

As she waited, shivering violently, Abraham brushed his shoulder as if shooing away an annoying bug. Then, lowering his arm to his side, he shook his head. He dropped his stone and ripped off the bandage, exposing the palm that Flint's arrow had pierced. A trickle of blood still oozed from the wound.

Elam swallowed again. Would his act of mercy with Naamah be replayed in front of him? Would he witness a living echo of what he had done in the Bridgelands? But why? How could his action, seen by only the accuser, the accused, and a horse for a witness send its ripples into another world?

Abraham touched Angel's head. She gasped and jerked up. With rain plastering her hair across her eyes, she blinked at Abraham.

He extended his wounded hand. She took it and allowed him to pull her to her feet. With his lips thinning out, he nodded toward Candle and Listener and spoke quietly. "Go to your children."

When she pulled away, the companion in her grip fell out and landed in the wet grass, still lifeless. She snatched it up, pushed it into her pocket, and reached for her children. Candle and Listener leaped into her arms. Weeping harder than ever, she smothered their cheeks with kisses. "Oh, my children! Oh, my sweet children!"

Flint stomped toward Abraham. His boots splashed as he stopped in front of him, nearly nose to nose. "By what right or law can you show her this mercy? You showed me none!"

As the rain eased to a steady drizzle, Abraham looked him in the eye. "It is not my duty to explain our laws to you. You chose exile, so you have no right to know."

"Are you saying that you would have forgiven me if I had chosen stoning?" His words sprayed into Abraham's face.

"I am saying nothing of the sort. In fact, I have no intention of saying anything more to you at all."

Flint raised a fist. Elam grabbed him by the collar and jerked him away. "You made your petition," Elam said, drawing his sword and setting its point against Flint's chest. "Now go back to your swamp."

Goliath reared up, but Clefspeare shot a jet of fire that glanced off Goliath's face. "If you dare to attack," Clefspeare said, "we will destroy you." Billy blew a stream of fire at Goliath's feet, a punctuation mark on his father's warning.

Stretching out a wing toward Flint, Goliath growled. "We have Roxil. Let us gather our winnings and return to our army."

Flint grabbed the wing and hoisted himself up. As he climbed Goliath's neck, he scowled but said no more.

While keeping an eye on Roxil, Goliath beat his wings. "Come," he said. "Fulfill your vow." He then leaped into the air and caught the damp breeze with his powerful red wings. Within a few seconds, he was circling overhead in a low, tight orbit.

Roxil glanced at Elam, then launched into the sky. After making a single circuit, she caught up with Goliath. As the larger dragon made another pass, he swooped low, caught Angel in his claws, and bent back toward the sky, shouting, "If you follow us, Clefspeare, I will kill her."

With the back of her dress snagged in the dragon's grip, Angel reached out her hands. "No! My children!" As she zoomed upward, the wind smothered her voice.

Clefspeare rose to his haunches, but Roxil tapped him on the head with her tail as she swept past. "Do not doubt Goliath's

315

word," she called, swinging her head back toward him as she flew. "He has no fear of man or the Maker." She lifted higher and followed in Goliath's wake.

Candle and Listener just stared at the shrinking dragons, their mouths hanging open. Valiant withdrew his dagger and clutched it so tightly, the muscles in his forearm rippled. "Will the noble horse take me to Flint's village?"

Dikaios trotted up to Valiant and nudged him with his nose. "I am ready, brave warrior."

"Can you take us both?" Abraham asked. "She is my responsibility, and I know Adam's Marsh, and Flint, better than Valiant does."

Dikaios bowed his head. "For the lady and her children, I would carry a dragon into battle."

"Take my sword," Elam said as he removed his scabbard belt. "I will get another one."

Pushing the sword away, Abraham embraced Elam and whispered, "We will go through the village first and tell the elders that you are in command, to respect you as they have respected me. If I do not return, then appoint Valiant as my successor, for I see this journey as one that will demand more than the blade of a sword can provide."

As their embrace lingered, Elam felt Abraham's trembling hands against his back. Elam whispered, "Do you *intend* to return, Father Abraham?"

"I think I have discerned the meaning of a prophecy, but there are still many questions. First, there is something I must do, and whether or not I return depends on the decisions of another." Abraham drew back and looked Elam in the eye. The rain, now just a sprinkle, had matted down his hair and traced the few wrinkles in his face, making him look older than his earlier thirty-something appearance.

Abraham held out his hand and collected several raindrops in his bloodstained palm. "This rain signals a revolution, Elam. You and I have lived for thousands of years, and even though our faces have stayed the same, our eyes have witnessed countless changes over the centuries, yet likely nothing compares to what will soon take place. It is time to fully assume your role. I believe every pain you have suffered will be revealed as merely the blow of a chisel on the warrior God has sculpted through the ages."

Elam grasped Abraham's shoulder. "If I cannot fight at your side, I will fight in your name, with your wisdom as my guide, your courage as my inspiration, and your love as my motivation."

"Thank you for your confidence in me," Abraham said, "but there is something else I would like for you to do first."

"What?" Elam tightened his grip. "Just name it."

"Be sure to call my sons and daughters … my dragon sons and daughters. Tell them my world needs their help, for I don't see how we can defeat Flint's army with our current soldiers. I'm not sure how you can do this, but the volcano portal might be a way."

"I will move mountains if I have to." Elam let go of Abraham and mopped his brow with his sleeve. "Anything else?"

"Get some rest. Tell my people to rest, as well. I think Flint is waiting for me, and he will not soon attack our village." Abraham turned to Candle and Listener, who stared at him with longing gazes, as if searching for a reason to hope. He stooped and gathered them into his embrace. Forcing a strong, vibrant voice, he spoke. "There is no need to fear, my children. The Father of Lights will always provide."

Listener pulled away. "Will Mother come back today?"

"I cannot make that promise." Arching his brow, he touched her playfully on the chin. "How do my little ones show their faith?"

She sniffed hard and puffed out her chest. "No tears, no fears."

"That's right." He raised his hand and showed his palm to both children. Candle pressed his darker hand against Abraham's, and

Listener joined in with her slender pale hand over her brother's. "Say it with me."

The three spoke in singsong, Abraham's deeper tones harmonizing with the two thinner voices, all three strengthening as they continued.

> With jaws of steel we face our fears;
> With eyes so bright they shed no tears.
> The night will end, the sun will rise;
> Our troubles fade when darkness dies.

He kissed each child on the forehead and limped to Dikaios. With help from Valiant, who had already mounted, and from Elam, Abraham swung his leg over the horse's back and settled in. Then, without another word, the two rode Dikaios toward the village.

Smiling at the children, Elam clapped his hands. "Do you want to help your mother?"

Candle's eyes widened. "Yes! How?"

Giving Candle a wink, Elam turned to Billy. "Billy Bannister! Would you like to go on an important journey?"

Billy hurried to Elam's side. "You name it!"

Refocusing on Candle, Elam creased his brow. "Father Abraham mentioned a volcano called Mount Elijah. Do you know where it is?"

Candle nodded vigorously. "In the highlands. It's pretty far, but my father took me there on a hunting trip. I could find it again."

"Billy," Elam said, patting him on the back, "there's supposed to be a portal within this volcano's cone. Acacia will know for sure, so I would like you to take Acacia and let Candle guide you there. Abraham said the portal leads to a dangerous place, but I have an idea that we might be able to use it to recruit a few more dragons into our army. If Acacia can get through safely, have her try to call for the former dragons. Tell them the real Arramos calls for them to join him in battle. I'd send a dragon with you, but with two healthy ones in the enemy camp and only one healthy one here, I can't afford to lose that firepower … or icepower from the local ones."

"How about Walter? He could go with us. We make a great team."

"I saw that. I was impressed." Elam suppressed a grin. Had Billy even noticed that his old buddy Walter had become a self-chosen protector of all things related to Ashley Stalworth? It wouldn't be a good idea to ask Walter to go and make the poor guy agonize over the decision. "No," Elam said. "I really need him here. He and Ashley make a good team, too, in case you haven't noticed."

"Yeah, I picked up on that." Billy set a hand on Candle's shoulder. "It's all good. We can do it without him."

Candle rubbed Billy's hand with his cheek. "I will take us to my village first and make supply packs."

"I should go, too," Listener said. "I can see things through my spyglass that no one else can. Maybe I could see through the portal."

Candle reached for her hand. "May I take her with us? We've been on long journeys in the highlands before."

"I don't see why not," Elam said. "With an army of giants breathing down our necks, she'd probably be safer with you out on the trail than here. But take enough food and water, just in case something happens and you're gone longer than you expect."

Listener bounced on her toes. "Let's take ginger sticks! And blister beans! And berry bread!"

"Just bread and water," Candle said. "It's less than a half day's journey each way, but if something happens, there are enough berries and nuts on the trail to last a long time."

319

Billy cocked his head toward the village. "We could fly in our airplane. I just need a long, flat place to land."

"Through the air?" A wide grin spread across Candle's face. "I would love it, but I don't think I could see the trail markers from the sky, especially the ones deep in the woods."

"Turn left at Wolf Hollow," Listener chimed in. "Follow Singer's Creek upstream until it bends to the right. Then take the crooked trail that goes around—"

"I get the picture," Billy said, laughing. "We'll walk."

After saying good-bye to his father, Billy set out with Candle and Listener to gather Acacia and their supplies. Now only Elam, Clefspeare, and Thigocia remained at the threshold to the birthing garden.

Clefspeare's ears twitched as he scanned the garden. "Something is amiss."

320

Elam stood at his side and surveyed the area. Many healthy plants remained, though several damaged ones had been propped up by stakes and tied in place, victims of the giants' trampling feet. In the center, where the staircase had landed, a large section was still void of life except for the open pod from which Roxil likely had experienced her rebirth. Crushed and charred bones lay around the pod as did strips of tarlike goo that had trapped Angel at the foot of the staircase.

Thigocia's ears mimicked Clefspeare's, a second pair of miniature satellite receivers tracking an unseen source. "I believe you are sensing something far beyond this realm. If this garden gave new life to Goliath and Roxil, then it is a doorway for both good and evil."

"Who else do we have to worry about?" Elam asked. "Morgan?"

With the aid of his wings, Clefspeare lumbered to the edge of the garden. Elam followed and stood next to the mighty dragon.

"Walter witnessed Morgan's entry into the Lake of Fire," Clefspeare said. "She will never escape, but there are many other evil beings still lurking in our world. If they were to come here, the odds against us would climb even higher."

As the clouds gave way to the sun, Elam looked out over the garden. "Then we will post a constant guard. If anyone shows up, we'll know right away."

"If Arramos were to come, I am the only one powerful enough to face him, and even then, I doubt that I would be able to defeat him. Contain him, perhaps, until help arrives, but it is impossible to be certain."

"Then what do you suggest?"

"First, we should ask the Oracle of Fire to see if a portal exists in the garden. If so, perhaps she or Listener's spyglass can pierce the veil and tell us what lies beyond."

Elam nodded. "Good. We can do that. Anything else?"

"Gather whatever jewels and gold the people can spare. Thigocia and I will make regeneracy domes here, and we will sleep at danger's doorstep. If the threat escalates, we will awaken, and if the jewels do their work, perhaps we will be better equipped to face whatever is beyond that door."

As Elam trained his gaze on the open pod at the center of the garden, something glinted in the emerging sunlight. "Be right back. I see something." Keeping his eye on the spot, he jogged along one of the furrows until he reached the central circle. He knelt next to the open plant, now tipped to the side, exposing a small cluster of roots. A crystalline egg, much like one of the companions, lay nestled in the roots' tendrils.

Using his fingertip, Elam gave the crystal a light prod. As fragile as the thinnest of eggshells, the outer casing cracked, revealing a tiny red bead inside. He coaxed the bead out with his finger and laid it in his palm. Sparkling like a ruby, it was clearly a jewel of some kind, yet it was smaller than the rubellites he had seen, and it had a rubbery feel.

"What is it?" Clefspeare called.

321

"I'm not sure." As he let the bead roll in his palm, a scene from long ago played in his mind, actually the memory of a story Merlin had told him during their last meeting. Sapphira had planted a seed in the sixth circle of Hades, a red-and-white-striped bead that grew into the plant that kept Shiloh alive for forty years.

He pinched it and held it close to his eyes. Could this red bead grow? If so, what would come from it? There was only one way to find out. He dug a shallow hole with his fingers and dropped the bead inside. Then, after covering it up, he smoothed the dirt on top and laid the wilted plant over it, whispering, "When those he calls will not obey, the Maker finds another way."

322

20

CHAPTER

THE UNDERBORN RETURNS

Sapphira held out her dim lantern, searching the stone wall for the familiar hole. Several sections of the tunnel system had caved in, destroying the usual landmarks. Still, the hot springs survived, so this tunnel should lead them to … Yes. There it was, the drawing of Yereq as a spawn Paili had etched with a hunk of limestone so many years ago. The hovel wouldn't be far now.

She looked back at Bonnie, Irene, Shiloh, and Gabriel trailing by quite a distance as they stepped over rocks that littered the floor. Gabriel stretched a wing around Bonnie and pulled her close, both smiling as they chatted happily.

And why not? He had been her invisible guardian angel for years. She had even seen him during one of his rare moments of semitransparency. Bonnie was five or six years old, a weeping child whose heart had been broken by her father's cruel name-calling. In many ways, he had restored a little girl's faith in angelic protectors, though he wasn't really that sort of angel.

Now, they were together, able to relive those tender moments, as well as another fateful event, a snowy December night when Palin came to call in Bonnie's bedroom, ready to slay her as she slept. Somehow, Gabriel's prayers for her protection were miraculously answered, and Palin simply walked away.

Gabriel stretched out his other wing and pulled Shiloh in. Although she hadn't even been aware, he had also acted as her guardian angel. Both laughing as they talked, it sounded like he was now revealing his failed attempt to keep her safe that terrible day when Morgan kidnapped her at the Glastonbury Tor and took her to the sixth circle of Hades.

Sapphira turned her attention back to her task, searching the tunnel walls for her hovel. After a couple of minutes, she spotted the low opening. "I found it," she called.

When the others caught up, Sapphira ducked under the chest-high opening and dropped the two feet or so to her hovel's floor. Bonnie joined her and, cinching up her backpack, extended a hand to help her mother. Shiloh, also wearing a backpack, hopped down without a problem, but Gabriel had to scrunch his wings to squeeze through. Soon they all stood in front of two cubbyholes in the wall.

Sapphira set her lantern on the floor. "I thought Bonnie and her mother could sleep here. That way they'd be surrounded by rocks, and maybe the slayer wouldn't be able to find her."

Bonnie crawled into one of the cubbyholes and lay on a thin mattress, poking a finger through a ragged perforation in the side. "How long did you stay here?"

Sapphira looked at Bonnie's finger. A strip of dark tape covered her rubellite ring. "Part of the time," Sapphira replied, "I lived in the museum room, but if you count it all together ..." She shrugged. "Somewhere between four and five thousand years. I lost track."

"Five thousand years?" Irene touched Sapphira's cheek. "You poor girl! How could you stand being in this dark place for so long?"

Sapphira sat down on the floor and hovered her hand over the lantern's outer glass. "When you're born in darkness, and it's all you know, it doesn't seem so bad. You don't really even notice it. But once you've been in the light, darkness is the worst place in the world." She breathed in deeply and smiled. "At least we won't be here that long this time."

Gabriel stretched out his wings, nearly filling the small chamber before pulling them back in. "This place isn't exactly the Holiday Inn, but it's ... uh ... cozy." He looked up at the entrance hole. "Where are the rest of us going to sleep?"

"I thought Shiloh and I could use the pair of hovels in the next chamber, but it doesn't really matter who sleeps where, except for you, Gabriel. You can go to Elam's old room."

"Elam's room?" Gabriel hugged himself and spoke in mock horror. "You mean where that slave-driving giant used to beat Elam mercilessly, eat all his food, and drink himself to sleep?"

Thoughts of Elam's tortures still stung Sapphira's mind, but she knew Gabriel wanted to set up a joke, so she obliged with a big smile. "Yep. The torture capital of the underworld. If Nabal's still there, he can break you in with the whip tonight."

"Sounds perfect. You girls should bring some popcorn and watch." He nodded toward the hovel's exit. "Should I wander around in darkness until I find it?"

"No, silly. I'll show you in a minute." Sapphira reached toward the wall and set her finger in the fist-sized hole at its base. "It's right through there, so we can communicate." As she pushed her finger through, her mind drifted back thousands of years to the time she pushed handfuls of stew through this hole to feed Elam on the other side. Even now her fingers tingled as she imagined

325

Elam licking the stew from her skin, an invisible boy so starved that he had to get every drop of precious nourishment. "Maybe Shiloh and I should take this room after all."

She pointed to the curved bone in Irene's hand. "Is that the one Enoch said I was supposed to take?"

"Yes." Irene handed it to her. "Do you know what to do with it?"

"Not yet, but I'm sure I'll find out soon."

Once Sapphira had settled everyone in their hovels, she and Gabriel walked together in the tunnel. Sapphira paused at a side corridor where the sound of falling water sent an echo all around. Although the source was no more than a six-foot-wide stream, the tunnel magnified its sound into that of a hundred cascading rivers.

"You can take your bath now," she said, extending the lantern. "Girls will go in the morning. No worries about running out of hot water here, but you'll have to drip dry. Maybe Yereq can get us some towels the next time he brings supplies."

"Not a problem." He took the lantern and let it swing from his finger. "But how will you find your way in the dark if you're not allowed to use your power?"

"With this." She withdrew the ovulum from underneath her shirt. As it rocked back and forth on her palm, it cast a red aura all around. "I think Enoch is ready to talk to me, so I'm going to find a quiet place to listen."

"Sounds good. I guess no one will bother you down here."

"Not likely. I shouldn't be gone too long, so when you're ready for me to show you your bed, set the lantern on the floor here, and I'll know it's okay to come back."

She turned to walk away, but Gabriel grasped her wrist and pulled her gently toward him. He lowered the lantern to the floor, then pushed a strand of hair out of her eyes as he whispered, "Can I be completely honest with you?"

The lantern's light flickered in his face, reflecting in his sparkling tears. His touch sent chill bumps across her skin. She gave a shrug, trying to hide her embarrassment. "Uh … sure. I mean, we're going to be stuck together for quite a while. We should be honest with each other."

He kept his eyes locked on hers. "I'm not trying to be forward or anything, but I wanted to let you know that you're the most amazing girl I've ever met. You saved my life. You saved Bonnie's life. You saved Shiloh's life, too. And you did it all after suffering alone for thousands of years."

As a wave of warmth pulsed through her body, she lifted a finger. "It was a team effort. You helped me rescue Bonnie."

He laid his palms on her cheeks. They felt cool against her hot skin. "Learn to take a compliment. You are an amazing girl, Sapphira Adi, and I want you to know that someone appreciates all you've done." He kissed her on the forehead. "Now go talk to Enoch, and tell him I said, 'Howdy.'"

He picked up the lantern and walked into the side corridor, slowly fading as darkness swallowed his form. With the sound of tumbling water again dominating the tunnel, she stared at the residual glow. Her cheeks still flamed. Prickles coated her skin. His gentle touch and soft words brought Elam to mind.

She sighed deeply. Oh, how she ached to be with him again! Would they ever get together? Would she ever have a chance to whisper the words she had longed to say to him for centuries?

As she walked toward the museum room, guided by the ovulum's glow, she shook her head. Maybe she and Elam would never be together. They were separated by more than just miles. She was once again trapped in the depths of Hades while he fought against demonic enemies in another realm. Would he survive? Would she ever leave this place once and for all? Maybe they both had been called by God to suffer and die without ever fulfilling their own dreams, just like many faithful saints of times gone by. As children, they had lived as slaves to Morgan, suffering for many years under her cruel hand. Now they served God, but their suffering continued.

Sapphira passed the old portal room, the chamber that housed the spinning column of light Morgan had used to send her and Mardon to the upper world. That first time in the land of Shinar had been the most wondrous day of her life—her first glimpse of the sun, her first conversations with unshackled humans, and her first view of dance, a man and woman spinning and leaping in gorgeous costumes bearing every color of the rainbow. Up to that point, the colors in her life had been brown, gray, and orange, and each one of those muted by the darkness of the underworld. Yet, even as wonderful as that day had been, it soon crumbled into the worst day imaginable. After the dragons toppled Nimrod's tower, she had to return in shame to her slavery.

She squeezed past a fallen boulder and entered the final tunnel. All of life had been like that. She would witness an amazing miracle and experience God's tender love and care, but the miracle would soon be followed by a tragic collapse, and she always ended up back in the same place ... the mines. She had outlived Morgan and Naamah, Nimrod and Mardon, and most of the whip-bearing Nephilim. Now she was queen of the caves, the empress of emptiness, once again marooned and wandering alone in the midst of the loneliest place in the universe.

As she approached the opening to the museum room, she slowed her pace. Ahead lay the massive chamber where she had spent so many hundreds of years alone watching the world above through a portal screen. She extended her hand, allowing the ovulum's red glow to illuminate the area. Directly in front of her, the museum looked like it always did, yet now, shrouded in a scarlet cloak, it seemed more sinister than ever. At one time it had served as the lower third of the great Tower of Babel, a pitiful excuse for a stairway to heaven, but now it stood as a blood-drenched prison guard, a warden who once loomed over her, marking off year after year of solitude as the only witness to her sufferings.

The portal screen that had always given her glimpses of worlds beyond was gone. It had been the only window to light and freedom, but someone slammed it shut, boarded it over, and made this prison darker than ever.

The ovulum's light slowly brightened. Enoch's familiar voice emanated from within. "Why are you so troubled, my child?"

She let her sad smile stay in place. "The mines remind me of so many bad things. I thought I would never have to come back."

"Yet, so many good things happened here, as well. It was here that you watched Bonnie and gained the kind of faith she has in the Messiah. It was from here that you were able to leap into the Great Key and create the covenant veil that ushered the residents of Dragons' Rest into Heaven. It was here that you learned how to suffer in darkness so that you could bring comfort to your friends who are now called to do the same."

"I know. Keep reminding me." She brought the ovulum closer to her eyes and tried to find Enoch within, but red mist veiled the center. "How long am I going to be here?"

"I expect that it will be quite a long time, but it depends on how events transpire in Second Eden. Your friend Elam will help determine both the destiny of that land and the timing of your departure from this place."

"Will I ever get to be with Elam? I mean, I know I'll get to see him in Heaven when we die, but I wanted to someday ..." She paused and bit her lip.

"You want to be united with him through the covenant of marriage." A warm, gentle laugh flowed from the ovulum. "Yes, I know, dear child, but I cannot answer that question. I simply have no idea. God's purposes are often fulfilled through the sacrifice of our personal desires."

She nodded. "So I have more sacrifices ahead of me?"

"That remains to be seen." The mist billowed for a moment, then settled. "Now let us go into the museum room. I want to

329

remind you of another wonderful event that happened in one of these underground chambers."

With the ovulum's glow as bright as ever, she had no problem finding her way through the museum's broken door. She walked to the center of the room and stopped at the edge of the circular planter where the tree of life still stood. Although greenery covered most of the branches, it bore no fruit and seemed to be the same height as before.

She looked around. The magnetic bricks she had placed to give light to the tree no longer emitted their colorful beams. Apparently the lack of energy played a part in stopping the tree's fruit production.

Still, the tree felt like an altar, a place to come for meditation and prayer, a place of silence. She raised the ovulum to her lips and whispered to Enoch, "I'm here."

"Do you have the rib?"

She lifted it close to the ovulum, still whispering. "Right here."

"Kneel at the side of the tree's planter and lay it in the soil near the trunk."

Balancing the ovulum in her palm, Sapphira lowered herself to her knees and set the bone on the cool, dark earth. As she looked at the soil, the contrasting shades of white on black sharpened. Tiny pores in the bone's surface magnified, enabling her to see minute grains of dirt embedded within, and her emotions sank even further than before, two sure signs that a portal was near.

"Where does this portal lead?" she asked.

"To a place that is not ready to receive you yet. You must not attempt a passage until I give you permission."

"Okay. I put the bone by the tree. Anything else?"

"Did you bring the soil Yereq collected in the Bridgelands?"

Sapphira dug into her jeans pocket and pulled out a handful of dirt. "I've got it."

"Sprinkle it evenly on top of the tree's bed."

Holding her fist over the soil, she opened the gaps between her fingers while scooting around the planter on her knees. When she finished, she brushed her hand on her jeans. "Okay. That's done."

"Now set the ovulum down, call a hot fire to your hands, and rub the bone's surface. Pick it up to make sure you massage the entire bone, but keep your hands over the soil."

After setting the ovulum gently at the edge of the planter, Sapphira raised her hands, her palms pointing upward, and whispered, "Ignite. And make it hot." Fire leaped from her hands. White and at least a foot tall, the flames seemed hot even to her fireproof skin. She picked up the bone and wrapped her fingers around both ends, then, pushing it through her grip, she coated the entire surface with her blaze.

As she rubbed, the bone sizzled and popped. Radiant white drops spilled to the soil, and sparkling smoke rose toward the upper reaches of the tower. The bone began to shrink in her grip, becoming more slender with each second. "Enoch!" she called. "It's melting!"

The mist in the ovulum swirled. "When it completely dissolves, spread the residue around and cover it over."

Sapphira continued to massage the bone. Within a minute, it shrank to the width of a straw and then vaporized. She blew on her hands, extinguishing the flames. Using one finger, she touched the white powder and mixed it into the soil. Soon, no trace of it remained on the surface.

Still on her knees, she straightened and looked at the ovulum. "Anything else?"

"No, my faithful child. You have done well."

"But what did I just do?"

"You have fertilized our little garden. A time will come when fire will energize the soil, and any dragonkind, whether still with dragon essence or not, will have his or her dragon traits restored."

"You did this for Bonnie, didn't you?"

"Again you have guessed my purposes. Since I am unaware of her current state, I devised this plan to restore her traits if they are gone."

"I thought she was given a choice," Sapphira said. "Why would you take it away now?"

"If she chose to give up her traits before, and she wants that choice to go on, my plan will not work. But I suspect, with the current danger, she will want her wings whether she has them now or not." The ovulum's glow faded. "Now you must go back to the others and wait."

Sapphira slumped her shoulders. Wait? The word weighed down her heart. If only she knew how long the wait might be, it would be tolerable, but this would be like walking down one of the underground passages without a lantern. Nothing but gloom as far as the eye could see. No light at the end of the tunnel.

As she picked up the ovulum and rose to her feet, every limb felt like lead. Why would Jehovah make her suffer so? Centuries ago at the hot springs, as a slave girl with a dangerously infected wound, she met Jehovah, knowing him as Elohim at the time. He had healed her with a touch on the shoulder and asked her to dance with him, and he provided the light she needed, the strength to go on.

She closed her eyes and relived that night, pretending the spring was a fountain in a ballroom. In her imagination, when the touch on her shoulder flooded her skin with warmth, she turned and pointed at herself. *Me? You want to dance with me?*

She painted the face of her invisible partner, giving him Elam's features. He smiled and nodded. *Of course, my love. I want to dance with you.* As he took her hands, music filled the air. They stepped in time with the lovely tune, performing a waltz as elegant as any that had ever graced a dance floor, and when he spun her around, tiny droplets sprayed her skin with soothing coolness.

As she drank in the pleasure, she opened her eyes, but instead of the museum's dark inner chamber, she saw a ballroom filled with light. A real fountain shot sparkling water into the air, raining droplets over her and her dance partner. She gave his hands a gentle squeeze. Real flesh! She was really dancing with ... Elam?

Enoch himself stood next to the fountain, holding an open book in his hands.

"Enoch?" Sapphira called, her voice quaking, "What's happening?"

Elam tilted his head. "Why are you calling for Enoch?"

His voice barely loud enough to overcome the music, Enoch spoke through the fountain's misty shower. "It is a gift from Jehovah, my child. It is the light at the end of the tunnel."

"Do you mean this is what will happen to me? Is it a wedding festival?"

"I do not know. It is Jehovah's gift, not mine. Enjoy what he has provided, and dance with your beloved."

The tree blazed with fire and disappeared along with the ovulum. Elam, now dressed in a radiant white tunic and trousers, his hair perfectly brushed and smelling of wildflowers, leaned close. "Yes, it's a wedding festival," he said. "Why do you find it hard to believe?"

She pressed her cheek against his chest. "Hold me! Just ... just hold me!"

As he wrapped his arms around her, he swept her back into the dance. Barely able to move her feet with his, she cried into his shirt. The music rose to a crescendo, and the song she had heard so many centuries ago, when Elohim healed her body and soul, now returned, this time in the voice of Elam.

> So dance, my child, and feel my love
> In rain, the healing drops of life.
> Forsake your cares, your toils and pain,
> The wounds and scars of slavish strife.

333

O cast aside the chains of grief
And reach for heaven's grace above;
Sapphira Adi, dance with me!
Enfold yourself in arms of love.

She pulled him into a tighter embrace. His heart thrummed in her ear, beating faster and faster. The fountain rained down. Droplets joined the tears on her hot face. Even as her aching shoulder had found relief so long ago, now the water soothed her aching heart. Someday all of this suffering would end. Someday she would be with her love forever.

But for now, she had work to do. She had to communicate this gift, the joy of Jehovah's presence, a healing salve that would soothe hearts that ached to be with loved ones. No matter how long they had to wait in caves of darkness, someday they would emerge into the light, and they would learn that Jehovah's purpose, the reason for their suffering, would not be in vain.

"I have to go now," she whispered.

"I know." Elam drew back.

"I have something to tell you, something I've been wanting to tell you for hundreds of years." Smiling, she took in a deep breath. "I lo—"

"No." He made a shushing noise. "Wait."

Her heart sank. "But why?"

"I don't want to hear those words until this dream comes true." As he released her, he lifted his hand and wiggled his fingers. She waved back in the same way, smiling again as her tears flowed.

Elam, the fountain, and the dance floor all faded, and the inner sanctum of the museum reappeared. Sapphira drew her hand to her mouth and kissed her fingers. "Someday, my love. Someday."

Sitting on the mobility room floor, Yereq rested his back against a pile of boulders. So far, though clouds blocked the sun, and cold air filtered into the pit, all was peaceful. After all, who could possibly rappel thousands of feet into this hole? And if anyone did, would he be ready to face a Naphil bearing a sword?

Yereq pushed his hands behind his head. Even if a slayer could get past him, he still had to move the boulders, another unlikely feat, and find his way through the maze of tunnels. Yes, everything seemed safe enough. He could even leave on an occasional expedition for food, making sure to come back before anyone had time to dig through the rubble.

He had already killed and salted a deer and then left its hide and some meat at a farmer's doorstep, ample payment for the vegetables he had gathered from his garden. Yereq chuckled at the note Bonnie had written to the farmer, an eloquent missive that explained her plight as a teenager hiding from a stalking murderer. She begged him not to tell the authorities, lamenting that the murderer had friends in high places and would surely track her down.

The gentle farmer, an elderly man who lived alone, had left a reply on the same doorstep, assuring her that she could have all she needed. He had only one request, that she would write to him regularly. Since he was all alone, except for three cats, he had no one else to talk to. Bonnie, of course, was delighted and promised to do so.

As Yereq pondered how long his haul of supplies would last, an odd whipping sound drifted to his ears. He shot to his feet and searched the sky. A helicopter glided into view as it descended into the pit.

Grabbing his sword, Yereq ducked into a crevice he had chiseled out for himself and watched the small helicopter. As it drew closer, its details clarified. The pilot, wearing sunglasses and a long-billed baseball cap, was unfamiliar. Yet, there was no mistaking the passenger—Mardon, his former master, older, to be sure, but his ovular head and piercing eyes were unequalled.

335

The helicopter landed, raising plumes of dust and sweeping much of the gritty remains of the mobility room to the walls. When the blades slowed, Mardon jumped out and began to search the floor, brushing away pebbles with his shoe. The pilot, now brandishing a machine gun, stood at the side of the helicopter.

Something on Mardon's shoulder sparkled red. He looked at it and spoke, but he was too far away to hear, especially with the helicopter engine still running. The glint appeared to be a crystalline egg, smaller than a normal man's fist.

Mardon pushed his hands into his pockets and walked along the edges of the floor, looking up and down the walls. When he reached the pile of boulders, he stopped and picked up one of the smaller stones.

Yereq tightened his grip on his sword. Should he strike? If Mardon escaped to the helicopter, he would know for certain that his prey had hidden somewhere behind the rubble. Then he would return with an army if need be to attack the giant who had vainly tried to kill him. If the pilot ripped into Yereq with a volley of bullets, they could take their time and enter the tunnel whenever they pleased.

As Yereq tried to decide what to do, Mardon spoke. "You don't sense anything?"

The egg flashed red.

"I followed the rope as far as I could. It's just too thin, and we'd have to walk."

The red light faded and pulsed a steady, heartbeat rhythm.

"This was your idea," Mardon said. "Hiding here is really too obvious." He dropped the stone and kicked it across the floor. "Try again. If you don't sense anything, I'm not about to ferry an army of workers down here by helicopter to dislodge this mess."

The egg strobed so brightly, Mardon blocked it with his hand. "Save your rants and think logically. Of course there's a pile of stones here. The tunnel to the mines collapsed. As I said, if you sense her presence, I'll do whatever is necessary to get inside. Otherwise, we would be better off using your powers to locate the other dragons."

The egg's light dimmed and changed to a softer hue.

"We will follow that lead immediately. If we capture Legossi, we are free to destroy her any way you wish."

Now a blue light pulsed from within the egg.

Mardon turned and ambled back to the helicopter, his voice fading. "Don't worry. I'll have someone check this place daily for any sign of life."

Soon, with Mardon again aboard, the helicopter rose into the air and flew out of sight. Yereq emerged from his hiding place, gripped the edges of a boulder, and pulled it away from the pile, revealing a hole, the waist-high doorway he had fashioned to allow the refugees an easier way to come and go if necessary.

As he bent low to enter, he pushed his sword inside. He had to alert Sapphira and the others. They would want to know his new information. Perhaps they could risk using a bit more light energy.

Now, of course, he would have to hunt at night to avoid detection, but that wasn't a problem. He would do anything for Sapphira, including stumbling through a dark wilderness chasing yearlings up and down forested slopes.

Once inside, Yereq picked up his sword and hurried through the tunnel, bending over to keep from banging his head on the ceiling. Yes, nothing had really changed. Unless the news gave Enoch reason to alter his orders, they would stay put. And maybe the prophet could help them understand why Mardon was now a dragon slayer.

337

21

CHAPTER

MOUNT ELIJAH

H ey, Elam. We're taking off now."

Elam shot up, blinking his eyes. After a few seconds, Billy came into focus, standing at the door to Abraham's hut. "Taking off where?" Elam asked.

Billy held up a walking stick. "To Mount Elijah. You asked me to tell you when we were leaving. The kids and I got a good nap, so we're raring to go. Did you have something else you wanted me to do first?"

"Give me a minute." Elam pressed his hands against the sides of his head. Had he fallen asleep? The dream had pushed out every thought of Second Eden, his mission as Warrior Chief, and the looming war with Flint, Goliath, and their army. Oh, and what a dream! Dancing with Sapphira at their wedding, holding her close as a fountain sprayed cool water droplets over their heads. It was heavenly. Yet, it ended all too soon and was already fading from his mind.

Trying to grasp the fleeting images, he caught a vision of Sapphira's face. Tears of joy ran down her cheeks as she wiggled her fingers at him. Yes. That would be it. He would hold that keepsake image and never let it go.

He focused on Billy again. "Did Acacia find a portal in the garden?"

"Sort of. She couldn't look through it, though. She doesn't know why."

"Thanks." Elam rose from Abraham's cot and rubbed his eyes. "Report to me as soon as you get back."

"You got it." As Billy walked out of sight, three others trooped behind him. Although he couldn't see their faces, Elam nodded as he scanned them—Candle, Listener, and Acacia, each one hiking with lively steps. They seemed no worse for the wear after the big battle, though a bandage wrapped Acacia's forearm, the only sign of injury.

"Speaking of injuries." He threw on a cloak and hustled outside. As soon as the breeze struck his face, he bundled the cloak together and fastened a belt at his waist. One of the villagers had said colder weather was coming, something about a season of death. But would frigid temperatures help or hurt their cause?

When Elam reached the infirmary, Walter met him at the door, closing it behind him. "They're trying to keep it warmer in there," he said, pointing at the hut with his thumb.

"Can't blame them for that." Elam bounced on his toes, trying to ward off the chill. "Anyone hear from Abraham or Valiant?"

"Not here. I thought you'd be keeping track of that."

"I kind of fell asleep." Elam looked around the village, but only a few people milled about. "Have you seen Patrick?"

"He's inside with Paili ... or Ruth, or whatever her name is now." Walter shook his head. "It seems like everyone's either changing their names or going from dragon to human or back to dragon again."

Elam pointed at Walter. "Except you. You never change."

Stretching his arms, Walter replied with a yawn. "Maybe not, but I'd like to change into my warmest clothes and go to bed."

"No rest at all?"

Walter angled his head toward the door. "We've been sleeping in shifts. I got a couple of hours. I'm okay."

"Feel up to joining a new military division I'm considering?" Elam rubbed his hands together, trying to generate some warming friction. "It'll be cold and dangerous."

"Dangerous, as in 'the likelihood of dying by any number of horribly painful methods is well above the risk that any normal human being would be willing to take'?"

"I suppose that's one way of putting it."

Walter shrugged. "Sure. Why make today any different from the last few days I've been through?"

"I know what you mean. Anyway, I had a dream about Sapphira. You know her, right?"

"Snow white hair, blue eyes that'll knock your socks off, and fire shooting out from every pore?" Walter leaned against the wall and looked up at the sky. "Never heard of her."

Elam wanted to laugh, but he let only a smile come through. It was time to get serious. "Just before the dream ended, I saw Enoch standing by a fountain. He said something very strange, and the meaning didn't dawn on me right away."

"Enoch has a way with words, that's for sure. I met him on an airplane going to London, and he kind of shook me up. Ashley, too."

"Well, this time he said, 'Let the Father find his way. You must prepare your army. They need to learn to fight from the air.' I got the impression from Abraham that he thought this was a suicide mission for him. Since this is his world, it really isn't any of my business, so I didn't do anything to stop him. Enoch kind of confirmed my guess, and now I think he wants me to create an air force."

"Dragon riding?" Walter asked. "I'm up for that."

"That's what I was thinking. We can ask Clefspeare, but he can't take too much time away from watching the birthing garden, and Thigocia's too injured. I'm not sure how equipped the native dragons are for warfare, but there is another option."

"The airplane?"

Elam nodded. "It would be perfect for shuttling troops, patients, supplies, and maybe even attack runs if we can make bombs. But the most experienced pilot is a dragon now, and the other is on his way to Mount Elijah, so we'll have to wait for him to get back."

"Ashley's flown it. Well, at least she's taken off in the Bannisters' old plane, *Merlin II*. She never had a chance to land. It met kind of a fiery doom at the hands of a demon."

"So we could take off, but we might not be able to land." He laughed under his breath. "I think we'll wait for Billy."

"Let's ask Ashley what she thinks. Maybe she can fly it." Walter pushed the door open and breezed inside. Elam stepped in and guided the door with his back until the latch clicked. With several lanterns flickering throughout the spacious single room, undulating orange tongues snaked over every detail.

Two rows of eight cots each lined the floor from wall to wall, leaving just enough space in between for people to walk by or tend to the wounded. Three cots lay empty, one in the far corner had been shoved to the side, a table of sorts for bandages and other supplies, and the rest held mostly male patients, each one covered with a thick blanket. Dark IV bags hung from makeshift wooden poles that stood near several of the cots, looking like small potato sacks dangling from coat trees instead of the typical sterile plastic and metal in Earth's hospitals.

Ashley knelt at the side of a younger man, barely more than a boy. With his blanket pulled down enough to expose his bare shoulders, she held her fingers over a wound just below his throat. Although the young man seemed unconscious, Ashley spoke to him as she lightly massaged his wound, her words too soft for Elam to hear. Two others tended patients at separate cots, Steadfast and Pearl, checking the IV apparatus and bearing worried looks.

Walter walked straight to Ashley and stooped at her side. While the two chatted, Elam searched the room for Patrick. He sat on the floor with his head against the back wall, holding the hand of a woman sleeping in a cot that had been pushed away from the others. Although it was too far to tell for sure, she had to be Ruth, taking her turn to sleep.

Catching his gaze, Elam nodded at Patrick, who gave a weary nod in return. With most of the patients asleep, maybe he could grab a few winks with his newly restored wife.

Walter returned with Ashley. She picked up one of the villagers' cloaks and pushed her arms through. "Let's talk outside," she said.

343

When they had gathered on the street, Ashley shivered in the strengthening wind. "I'm glad you mentioned the airplane. We really need it, but not just for training." She looked back at the infirmary. "The villagers told me about a hospital in the sky, a metal tubelike thing that stays up by some kind of magnetic force. It's warmer than this place, a lot better equipped, and safer, at least once you get inside. A few of these patients could die really soon if they stay down here, but they tell me it's probably too cold to fly them up there by way of dragon."

"Is there a landing strip?" Elam asked.

Ashley shook her head. "Not a traditional one. They have a docking station for dragons, but it doesn't sound big enough for an airplane."

"Then how do we transport patients?"

"They said the hospital is constantly moving. An airplane could stay level with the docking station and fly alongside." She flattened her hands and set them side by side to illustrate. "If we could hold the plane steady enough, we could wheel the patients across on a ramp."

"Sounds risky." Elam stroked his chin. "Maybe too risky."

"I think an expert pilot could do it," Ashley said, "and that would count me out."

"That means Billy." Elam flicked his thumb toward the far side of the street. "And he's heading for Mount Elijah."

"And I'm not even sure he could do it," Walter said. "He knows how to fly the plane, but keeping it steady enough to wheel patients through a heavy breeze with thousands of feet of empty air underneath?" He shook his head. "Not to say anything bad about Billy, but that might be more than he can handle."

344

Ashley raised three fingers. "Well, three of my patients are going to die if we don't get them up there. Their hearts are failing, and they might not make it through the day. The sky hospital has a heart machine we could haul down here on a dragon, but only Angel and Abraham know how to set it up. Steadfast can operate it, but he's afraid if we disconnect it, we wouldn't be able to get it running again." She let her fingers droop and pushed her hand inside her cloak, shivering again. "I don't want to lose them. One of them is a young man about my age, and another is a little girl. Both are way too young to die at the hands of that monster."

"Agreed." Elam nodded toward the birthing garden. "Let's ask Clefspeare if he thinks Billy can do it. If he gives the go-ahead, we can send someone on a dragon to pick Billy up. One of the villagers ought to be able to find the way to Mount Elijah by air."

"Let's do it now." Ashley began marching toward the garden, raising her voice as she walked. "It's a matter of life and death.

Once Clefspeare realizes that, maybe he'll go and pick up Billy himself."

Billy hiked up the steep, narrow trail, Excalibur's scabbard hanging from his belt. Since Walter had opted to stay and help with the wounded, he had insisted on trading swords.

"I won't need Excalibur," Walter had said. "Not if we're just twiddling our thumbs waiting for an attack from overgrown plant creatures who might never show up. Maybe your dad and I can roast some marshmallows and make s'mores, that is, if they have marshmallows here ... or chocolate bars ... or graham crackers. Then again, maybe he can teach me how to fly your airplane. I can't get into any trouble doing that, right?"

Billy grinned. Picturing Walter flying *Merlin* while Clefspeare flew at his side shouting instructions almost made him laugh out loud. His mind sketched Ashley barking orders at Walter from the copilot's seat.

When the image faded, Billy looked up at the peak of Mount Elijah. A thin string of gray vapor rose from the cone, like smoke from a chimney. Nothing alarming. More inviting than ominous. Near the top, an arched opening cut into the mountain's face, a cavelike entrance that reminded him of his father's cave back in West Virginia. This opening was quite a bit smaller but had the same kind of semicircle shape.

He looked back at his fellow hikers, Candle pushing a walking stick against the rocky path, and Listener, hanging on to her brother with one hand and her spyglass with the other. Each wore burlap bags on their backs tied over their shoulders and around their torsos. Bundled up for the cold breeze—woolen hats with flaps that covered their ears and scarves around their necks, and heavy coats of rabbit fur—they looked like marching bunnies with human faces.

To their right, the mountainside dropped sharply, a plunge of at least three hundred feet if they happened to stumble that way.

345

Fortunately, the path was wide enough for two people to walk side by side with room to spare.

Acacia trailed the children, now wearing a pair of low-top boots donated by one of the doting mothers back at the village. With her cloak no longer available, she had borrowed a child's robe of thick khaki linen, tied at the waist by a leather belt. Since it was likely an ankle-length garment for the child, and Acacia was not much taller than many of the village children, the bottom hem brushed her calves. Her long white dress, protruding a few inches from underneath the robe, flapped in the cold breeze. She carried a wide, rag-topped stick and used it for balance as she labored up the path.

Billy stopped and pointed toward the peak, glad for an excuse to rest. "Is that our destination? The cave up there?"

"That's it!" Candle looked back at Listener who was now staring at the peak through her spyglass. "See anything, Sister?"

Listener lowered the glass and shook her head. When Acacia caught up, she pulled her belt tighter, shivering. "This portal must be an unusual one. I can already sense its presence."

"Really?" Billy asked. "What does it feel like?"

"My eyesight sharpens, and I feel a sense of sadness, like something tragic has happened … or is going to happen."

"On that uplifting note …" Billy withdrew Excalibur and continued the march. When they reached the top, he paused at the cave's arched entry and leaned into the mountain's shadow. As his eyes adjusted, the scene inside took shape—a depressed basin at the center of a chamber with a high roof, a mini-cathedral of stone.

"Looks safe enough." He stepped across the rough lava rock that coated the floor and stopped at the edge of the basin. Ashes lay across uneven stones that seemed jammed into the volcano's throat. Gray smoke seeped through the gaps and rose toward the ceiling, an inverted funnel that released fumes into the sky.

Billy sniffed, then coughed. Sulfur permeated the acrid air, coating his tongue with a bitter film. "Come on in," he said, "but you might want to hold your nose."

Filing in one by one, the remaining travelers joined him, Acacia first, then Candle and Listener. Acacia held out her stick. "Shall I light our torch?"

"Not if these fumes are combustible."

"They aren't." Acacia took in a deep breath. "I know this odor. It smells like my old home." She nodded at the stick and whispered, "Give me light." A flame erupted from one side of the rag and spread quickly over the top of the torch. She lowered it toward the bottom of the basin, but it didn't quite reach the smoldering ashes.

"Can you see anything with your souped-up eyesight?" Billy asked.

While Listener trained her spyglass on the basin, Acacia lowered herself to her knees and set the torchlight close to one of the larger gaps between the stones. "There is a magma river far below, very much like the one in my Hades home."

"Could it be the same one?" Billy asked. "I mean, could you be looking through a portal into another world?"

She rose to her feet. "I don't think so. There is a portal here, but we always needed a swirl of fire to open one."

"Did you see the tree?" Listener kept her spyglass pointed at the basin. "It's kind of small, but I can see it."

"A tree?" Billy leaned over. "May I look?"

Listener passed the scope to him and held the large end in place, steadying the tube. "If you point it between that charred weed and the gray rock and look through the crack, you can see it."

"I don't see anything but the rocks." He handed the spyglass back to her. "Maybe you're the only one who's meant to use it."

Acacia stooped and pushed Listener's pigtails behind her shoulders. "Did its leaves look sort of like stars?"

347

Listener nodded. "Dark green ones, and it's growing from a circle of dirt that's surrounded by stone."

Acacia rose and, keeping the torch pointed at the basin, turned toward Billy. The orange flames danced in her brilliant blue eyes. "If Listener is describing what I think she's describing, this portal leads to the underground mines, my old home in Hades."

"How can we find out for sure?"

"Let's see if we can have a look." Acacia extended the torch over the basin and waved it in a wide circle. The fire swirled. A ribbon of flames reached out and stretched around the basin as if tracing its perimeter from five feet above. As she continued her motions, the ribbon extended itself downward like an orange curtain drawing a theatre act to a close.

Soon, a rotating cylinder hovered over the volcano's throat, semitransparent and dazzling. Fingers of light flickered on the chamber walls and on their clothes.

Giggling, Listener batted at the dancing lights as if they were hyperactive fireflies alighting and then jumping away. Candle kept his stare fixed on the cylinder, mesmerized.

Acacia pushed the end of the torch into the cylinder wall, creating a gap in the flames. "Look inside and tell me what you see. Hurry, the viewer won't last long."

Billy peered into the furrow. Inside and below the basin, a tree stood in the midst of a dim room lined with shelves. Objects that looked like rolling pins were piled in cubbyholes, some sticking out haphazardly, but only the top of the tree reached into Mount Elijah's cave, making it impossible to judge its size. "Is that the museum you told me about on the way over here?"

"The very same." Acacia drew back the torch, closing the gap. The fiery spin slowed and soon evaporated, leaving the basin as it was before. "Did you notice that you couldn't see the floor?"

"Yeah. What's up with that?"

She pointed the torch. "The portal extends downward. In order to enter, we would have to unplug the volcano's throat and jump in."

"Right into the river, huh?" Billy peered at the cracks between the rocks again. "Kind of risky, to say the least."

"I assume we would pass through the portal before we struck the magma."

"Assume?" Billy tapped Excalibur's point near Listener's sandals. "Maybe you and I could risk it, but not Candle and Listener."

"Then I should go alone," Acacia said. "If it's safe, I can come back and bring you three with me."

Billy nodded. "I guess you're the only option. If I went alone, I couldn't come back."

"Not unless you suddenly became an Oracle of Fire."

Billy touched one of the rocks with his blade. "If you went through it, would you be able to get out of the mines, I mean, to the Earth's surface? If we want to get the other dragons over here, we need a path from there."

"I'm not sure. A lot of the portals closed for good, and since Hades merged with Earth, everything might have changed. When I get down there, I'll look around for a way out."

"Okay, let's see what happens." He slid Excalibur into a gap. One of the rocks shifted but didn't break free. Gripping the hilt with both hands, he pushed with all his might, using the sword like a lever. Both rocks gave way, and the rest tumbled into the volcano's throat. A few seconds later, a new cloud of gas erupted and streamed to the escape hole above.

Billy batted at the hot, smelly air. "When you try to come back up to this level, won't you just fall into the river?"

"Good point." She peered into the opening. "But if this leads to the mines, I know where to get a rope. Be ready to catch it and pull me up."

"You really have a lot of confidence in me, don't you?"

Rising to tiptoes, she kissed him on the cheek. "Complete confidence." Then, with a spin toward the volcano's throat, she waved the torch again and recreated the portal cylinder. "I'll be back as soon as I can."

Billy pushed Excalibur into its scabbard and grasped Listener's hand. "We'll be waiting."

After setting the torch on the ground and tightening her belt, she stepped to the edge of the gaping hole, still visible through the wall of fire. Then, taking a deep breath, she leaped into the flames.

Abraham patted Dikaios's neck. "We will have to stop here, good horse."

Valiant slid to the muddy ground and helped Abraham dismount. "How is your arrow wound, Father?"

Shifting his weight to his injured leg, Abraham nodded. "Much better, though I hope to avoid running."

Valiant drew his dagger from a sheath on his belt. "Nightfall will soon arrive. Should I sneak into the village and see where they are holding Angel? We can come back afterward with darkness as our ally."

"I will go." He patted Valiant's back. "I'm not sure how the prophecies will be fulfilled, but if Angel comes out, you must carry her home on Dikaios."

"I am strong," Dikaios said, "but carrying three passengers through this marsh would be impossible."

Abraham raised a pair of fingers. "You need only carry two. If events transpire as I expect, I will not be coming back."

"Not coming back?" Valiant thrust his dagger to its sheath. "What do you mean to do?"

"Do you remember the restoration prophecy?"

Valiant looked up toward the darkening sky. For a moment he hummed, as if remembering a song. After a few seconds, his brow dipped low. "Are you the man who lost his scales?"

Before Abraham could answer, Dikaios breathed through his flapping lips. "Is this a prophecy I have heard?"

"I sang it earlier, my friend, but I will recite the relevant lines." Abraham reached for Valiant's dagger and withdrew it from its sheath. As he touched the blade's edge with his thumb, he spoke the poem, this time without a tune.

> And only one can save her life,
> A man who lost his scales.
> A sacrifice to win his wife,
> If love is to prevail.

He pricked his finger with the point of the dagger. "With the exception of Flint, I have never told our people that I was once a dragon. In fact, I was the very first dragon on Earth, and after I died in the flood, Michael the archangel transported me here to create a new world."

351

Valiant stared at the blood oozing from Abraham's fingertip. "You were a dragon?"

"As you have seen, dragons were not the beasts you know. On Earth, they were equal to or greater than man in intelligence, and often far surpassed him in wisdom. But they, much like mankind, fell from grace, though, unlike man, not all followed the path of the first to go astray. Goliath's father, Makaidos, was also reborn here, and he sacrificed himself to rescue his daughters. Now I must do the same for this daughter."

"Daughter?" Dikaios said. "The prophecy says, 'his wife.'"

"It does, but it could mean Flint's wife. I think he plans to force Angel into marriage and bring Eve's curse upon her, the pain of childbirth in the manner of women on Earth. I suppose his plot is a twisted way of gaining revenge against me, even though he chose his path."

"But Angel chose stoning," Valiant said, "and yet you dropped your stone."

Abraham grasped Valiant's muscular forearm. It felt as tight as a tree limb. "I tell you this, my faithful warrior, in confidence. There is always a third option, but I have never revealed it, for I would never be able to judge it rightly if the rebel or liar knew about it beforehand."

"Repentance," Dikaios said. "You waited to see her bear the fruit of true sorrow."

"Indeed." Abraham let a drop of blood fall to the water. "As it says in Elam's Scriptures, 'love believes all things.'" He handed the dagger back to Valiant. "And greater love has no man than this, that he lay down his life for his friends."

Valiant sheathed his weapon. "You are wise and good, Father. I am grateful that you are in command of our hearts while I am merely in command of our army."

Abraham drew closer and lowered his voice. "Yet, I have told you these things so that you can take my place. I know of no other who is qualified in strength, wisdom, and honor." He kissed Valiant on both cheeks, and, with a heavy sigh, turned and padded slowly toward Flint's village ... alone.

352

ALONE

Sapphira sat cross-legged and set a lantern on the floor in front of her. "Considering what Yereq told us, I think we can risk a little underground sunshine." She blew a breathy whisper toward the wick. "Give me light."

A small flame crawled along the wick, growing to a half inch in height and illuminating the cramped sleeping area. Shiloh sat across from her, while Bonnie and her mother looked on, lying on their sides in the two cubbyholes. With a small stack of journals in front of her, Bonnie opened the top one and poised a pen over the page. "Just enough light to enter what happened today."

Sapphira knocked on the wall behind her with the heel of her hand. "Gabriel, can you hear me?"

A muffled voice replied, drifting into the room from the mouse hole at the base of the wall. "I'm here ... wherever here is. I don't have a lantern."

"I'll bring you one when it's time to wake up." Sapphira folded her hands in her lap. "We might be in this place for a very long time, so we should get to know each other better. I could tell you stories that would fill up years of waiting, but I'd like to hear more about you." She scanned each set of eyes. "Who would like to go first?"

"I suppose I will," Shiloh said. "I've never been known as the shy sort." She set her folded hands on her backpack, now crumpled in her lap. "My father is Patrick, a former dragon named Valcor, who became fully human over fifty years ago. Gabriel was involved in Valcor's transformation, so I'll tell that story first. You see, Morgan was threatening to kill my mother, a beautiful woman named Ruth, who also had a very interesting life, but I'll get to that later. Anyway—"

"Hello?"

Everyone turned toward the sound, a soft voice coming from the tunnel. Sapphira hissed at the lantern, "Lights out!" As darkness flooded the hovel, she jumped to her feet and felt her way toward the exit.

"I saw a light," the voice said. "Is anyone down there?"

Now close enough to look through the exit passage, Sapphira craned her neck, trying to find the source. The voice seemed oddly familiar—feminine, cautious, maybe even nervous.

Suddenly, a light flashed into the hovel, so bright it blinded Sapphira. She staggered back, rubbing her eyes. Several hands caught her and held her up as she refocused on the exit hole.

"Are you okay?" Bonnie whispered.

"Fine. Shhh."

Within the shaft of light, two boots slid down, followed by two bare legs with a cloak and white dress riding up toward the girl's hips. She then dropped to their level, one hand holding a ball of white flame, illuminating her equally white hair.

Chill bumps ran along Sapphira's skin as she took a step toward her. "A ... Acacia?"

"Sapphira?" Acacia's chin quivered. Her flame dwindled to a bare spark.

Sapphira spun toward her lantern, pointed at it, and shouted, "Ignite!" A bright yellow light flooded the room. She spread out her arms and squealed, "Acacia!"

They rushed into each other's arms. Crying so hard she could barely speak, Sapphira massaged Acacia's back. "Oh, my dear sister, I can't believe you're here! Flesh and bone, and not a phantom!" She wept, burying her eyes in Acacia's cloak.

Acacia pulled back and set her hands on Sapphira's cheeks. Tears flowed down her own cheeks as her bright blue eyes danced. "Dearest, darling sister, so much has happened, but there is no time to tell you the half of it."

"How ..." Sapphira swallowed through a lump, trying to steady her voice. "How did you get here? Did Yereq let you in?"

Acacia shook her head and let her arms fall to her sides. "I came from Second Eden through a volcano portal that dropped me off at the tree in the museum room. Elam sent me to—"

355

"Elam sent you?" Sapphira grabbed Acacia's wrists. "Where is he? How can I get to him? Can I go through that portal?"

Acacia laughed. "Calm down. All in good time." As she swept her gaze across the other girls, Acacia's eyes brightened. "Ah! Bonnie and her mother are here. I have seen both of you through portal viewers." She shifted to the final girl. "And you must be Shiloh, Bonnie's duplicate."

Shiloh grinned. "I believe she is *my* duplicate, if you don't mind me saying so. I was born first."

Irene stepped forward and set a hand on each of the Oracles. "You two are identical! Now we have two sets of duplicates."

"Hey!" a muffled voice called. "Let a guy in on what's going on over there."

Shiloh picked up the lantern. "I'll go fetch the male of the species."

"Are you sure you can find his chamber?" Sapphira asked.

"Not a problem. I found his pad when I searched for the water closet. He pointed me in the right direction." Shiloh climbed through the hole and disappeared.

As the light faded, Acacia ignited a new flame in her palm. She stared at the others through its shimmering glow, shadows now covering her eyes. "Second Eden is in great danger. The dragon Goliath has come back from the dead, and he has allied himself with a rebel in that world. They are gathering an army that will attack Abraham's people."

"Abraham?" Irene repeated. "Are we supposed to know who that is?"

Acacia shook her head. "He was once Arramos, the very first dragon and father of Makaidos. When the devil stole his body during the flood, God put the soul of Arramos into a human body and set him in Second Eden to begin a new world." She took a deep breath. "Are you with me so far?"

"This is just too much to take in," Irene said, "but keep going."

"I really can't tell the entire story. I have no way of knowing how much time elapses there while I'm here, so I have to hurry. What you need to know is that we are asking all former dragons to come to Second Eden to protect the people from an attack. There is a garden there that will regenerate you and make you into a dragon again. It's already worked for Clefspeare and Roxil. It even gave Billy his fire breathing back."

Irene looked at her ring and rubbed the white gem with her thumb. "I see."

Sapphira glanced at Bonnie, but she gave no hint as to how she felt about that revelation. She just looked on with wide eyes.

"So," Acacia continued, "we need to contact the others and call them to the portal in the museum room."

"What if they don't want to come?" Sapphira asked. "Maybe they don't want to be dragons again. And can they revert to human form once the crisis is over?"

"We haven't figured that part out yet, so the risk of staying in dragon form is very real. Of course, the choice to go to Second Eden will be up to them, but it is the real Arramos, the king and father of all good and noble dragons, who calls for their help. When they realize that, I don't think they will refuse."

"I will go," Irene said. "I see no other option."

Bonnie took her mother's hand. "Count me in, too."

"To get new wings and fly?" Acacia asked. "Or do you still have them?"

"I've been instructed to keep that a secret, but …" She dipped her head and smiled. "Billy's there. I'm not going to let him fight Goliath without me."

"Now it all makes sense," Sapphira said as she picked up Shiloh's backpack. "Enoch will want Shiloh to go with you."

"As a decoy?" Irene asked.

"That's what I'm thinking." Sapphira propped the pack on her own back. "If someone thinks she's Bonnie, she would make good slayer bait."

"But it could be very dangerous," Irene said.

"Somebody call me?" Shiloh slid into the hovel and pointed at herself with her thumb. "Dangerous is my middle name."

Gabriel dropped down beside Shiloh, the lantern in his hand. "Dangerous is right. She tripped over me and burned my leg. That's why I'm carrying the lantern."

Acacia blew out the flame on her palm. "Did you hear what we were talking about?"

"I heard enough," Shiloh replied. "I've already done the decoy bit once when I tricked Morgan into thinking I was Bonnie. I'm a pretty good actress if I do say so myself."

"So how do we let the others know?" Sapphira asked. "I'm not sure if Enoch would want any of us to go to the surface."

Gabriel raised his hand. "I wasn't drafted. I'm just a subterranean volunteer, so I leave whenever I want. Just let me know

357

how I can find everyone, and we'll see how many dragons want to join the party."

"Wait a minute," Sapphira said. "This is all moving way too fast. Let me think." As she looked at the pairs of eyes staring at her, she tried to remember the reasons each person was there. For one thing, the slayer was topside, hunting for Irene and Bonnie. She and Shiloh were there to comfort them in the lonely darkness, but wouldn't that mean Enoch expected them to stay for a long time? Gabriel could have been chosen to go and get the other former dragons, so that made sense. Since Devin probably wasn't having much luck finding Irene and Bonnie, he might be hunting for the others now, so the underground mines could be a good hideout for them, too. Maybe the time it would take to gather the dragons together, perhaps several weeks, equaled the time Enoch expected them to stay. Then they could all go to Second Eden together.

358

"Okay," Sapphira said. "Let's send Gabriel out to call the former dragons to Second Eden. He can visit Mrs. Bannister and give her an update, and maybe she and Larry can help him find everyone. Acacia, you can go back and tell Abraham that we're gathering his troops. When we're all ready, we'll go through the portal together."

"Bonnie and I could go now," Irene said. "She … I mean, we would be out of danger from the slayer, and maybe we could help Second Eden right away."

"And me, too," Shiloh said. "We might as well plan our decoy maneuvers. Why wait?"

Sapphira looked at each face again. Enoch had said that she, herself, wasn't allowed to use the portal at the tree, but he didn't say others couldn't. Then, if Irene, Bonnie, and Shiloh went with Acacia to Second Eden, and Gabriel flew away to search for the other dragons, that would leave only one person in the mines, the one person who could open the portal from this side to lead the dragon troops to the battlefront. That one person? Sapphira

Adi. … Alone. … Again. But that didn't matter, did it? Her own feelings weren't important.

She let out a long sigh. "I think that might be the best plan."

"There's only one problem," Acacia said. "We will appear in Second Eden in the magma pipe of a volcano. I'll need a rope to throw to Billy when I get there. It'll be tricky, but if I can do it, the others probably can, too."

"The rope in the old elevator?" Sapphira asked.

"That's what I was thinking, but we'll have to cut it."

Gabriel pulled a dagger from his belt and handed it to Sapphira. "You can use this."

"Morgan's dagger?" She reached it back to him. "I … I don't know about that. It's a murder weapon."

He held up his hands, blocking the dagger. "Use it. It's just a knife. Jared Bannister killed Naamah with it, and I stabbed one of the Nephilim, so obviously it can be used for good."

As she held the gnarled hilt and passed her finger over the primitive stone blade, her skin tingled, almost as if the dagger vibrated, but it had to be her imagination. "I guess it'll be okay, as long as we're doing what we've been told to do."

"Exactly. It should be perfectly safe." Gabriel bowed. "Since you ladies have everything under control, I'll head for the exit tunnel and see if Yereq will move the stone for me."

Acacia handed him the lantern. "You'll need this more than we will."

"And Walter's cell phone." Sapphira dug it out of her pocket and gave it to him. "It's useless down here. Even if I could get a signal, the battery won't last more than another day or two, and I can't plug it in to recharge it. "

"Got it!" Keeping his wings tucked, he crawled out, taking the light with him.

Acacia snapped her fingers and created a new ball of flame in her palm, this one pale blue. "Ready to go, Sister?"

359

Sapphira stared at the dagger—a staurolite blade, Merlin had called it. Tiny crystals glittered in the stone, looking like little crosses burning with blue fire. "I guess so, but there's no use wasting your energy." She reached into her sweatshirt pocket and withdrew the ovulum. Its red glow mixed with Acacia's blue and bathed the room in violet.

Acacia extinguished her light. "Then we'll let Enoch lead the way."

All five climbed out of the hovel and hiked to the old elevator shaft, Sapphira in front with the ovulum in one hand and the dagger in the other. When they arrived, the platform they had stood upon when calling for Chazaq to lift or lower them to their destination was no longer there, just a rope dangling from the darkness above.

"I'll try it," Shiloh said. She stepped past Sapphira, grabbed the rope, and, after testing her weight against it, swung out to the middle of the shaft. Then, yanking the rope, she jerked her body up and down. "Seems strong to me," she said as she swung back.

Acacia knelt by the shaft and peered down. "I see plenty of rope. Pull up about twenty feet. That should be enough."

"Let's get more, just in case." Shiloh reeled the entire length of the rope and coiled it on the stone floor. "That should do it. Let's cut a fifty-foot section and leave the rest."

Sapphira lowered herself to her knees, set the ovulum next to the coil, and pushed the edge of the blade against the rope. She forced her arm to stay steady. Were they really doing what they were told? Enoch obviously wanted something to happen with the tree of life before they could go anywhere, otherwise he wouldn't have asked her to dissolve the bone and cover everything with the Bridgelands soil. Yet, maybe what he wanted to happen already took place and she didn't realize it. Still, in the past, anything associated with the tree of life always took longer than she had hoped.

360

When dealing with Enoch, waiting seemed to be a way of life. Why would this be any different?

"Is something wrong, Sister?" Acacia asked.

Sapphira jerked the dagger back. "I … I'm just not sure about this whole plan. I don't know what Enoch wants us to do."

"The ovulum is here." Acacia pointed toward it with her foot. "You could ask him now."

Sapphira picked up the ovulum and again held it in one hand and the dagger in the other. As she stared at the billowing mist inside the egg, a river of thoughts rushed through her mind. Why should she ask Enoch? Hadn't he already given his instructions? Wouldn't he be disappointed that she couldn't follow the simplest commands without bothering him with trivial details?

After all, going to Second Eden was for a noble cause, to save lives, so Enoch would be delighted that they would risk their own lives for others. And besides, she certainly wasn't helping Irene and Bonnie and Shiloh leave for her own sake. She would be all alone again, forced to stay there to wait for the other dragons to arrive. This was a sacrifice, not self-serving at all. Wouldn't insisting that they stay with her be the most selfish act possible? Why should she bother Enoch with such an easy question?

She set the ovulum down, pushed the dagger's edge against the rope, and cut through it. "There." She threaded about fifty feet of rope through her hand and sliced again. "Now go," she said, handing one end to Acacia. "And please hurry."

Acacia took the rope. "Are you sure? You'll be all alone."

"I know." Still on her knees, Sapphira drooped her head, trying to hide her emerging tears. "Please. … Just go. I'll be okay. I'm sure Gabriel will be back soon enough."

"I'll have to make at least a little light." A candle-sized flame rose from Acacia's fingertip. She stooped and kissed Sapphira on the cheek. "I'm sure we'll be together again soon."

As Acacia rose, she waved to the others. "Come on, girls. I think she needs to be alone." She brushed her lips across Sapphira's cheek and whispered, "I love you, Sister."

Sapphira blinked but didn't look up. Other hands patted her back or squeezed her shoulder, and soon, the scratching and pattering of shoes on stone quickly faded. Then, as Acacia had said, Sapphira Adi was alone.

Sitting now with her head between her knees and her arms locked around her legs, she let the dagger dangle from her fingers. Then, it slipped away and clattered to the stone.

The ovulum's glow strengthened, sending ribbons of red across the floor. She lifted her head and stared at the pulsing egg. What did Enoch want to say? Scold her for using the dagger, something she knew had been a murder weapon? Give her a tongue-lashing for sending Bonnie and Irene away, the very people she was supposed to watch over in the mines? Rebuke her for giving in to pressure? Everyone seemed to think they should jump at the chance to do something that was obviously good and noble, yet wasn't exactly in line with what they had assumed to be true. Should she have listened?

Now with the light washing over her, everything seemed so clear. Her decision was stupid. She was the one who heard Enoch's commands. She was the one who should have stood her ground and said no. And now she was getting exactly what was coming to her.

An ignorant slave girl deserved to be whipped, but a child of God who should have known better deserved to suffer even more. And she would suffer, separated from friends and from God in isolation, loneliness, and silence. That was the worst part of all, the silence.

Sapphira began to weep. Did anyone really understand? Had anyone ever suffered so much? No one in history had to live alone, day after day after day, with no one to talk to except herself and an invisible God she so desperately tried to believe in as another thousand sunsets passed by in the unreachable land above.

As she etched marks in the stone for every lonely day, wondering if her perception of day and night even mattered, she had watched her skin grow pale, and had wandered through the dark tunnels in hope that someday, if she ever did again see the sun, her muscles wouldn't be so atrophied that she would have to crawl.

Yes, it was true. No one could ever understand her suffering. Nothing was worse than centuries alone—not disease, not torture … not even death.

A strange scratching noise perked her ears. She tipped to the side and, bracing her body with one hand, looked at the ovulum and dagger sitting on the floor, almost touching.

The scratching seemed to come from the dagger, increasing in volume and taking on a static-filled voice, like an announcer on a too-distant radio station.

"Mara, daughter of the Earth."

She shifted to all fours and peered at the stone blade, awash in the ovulum's glow. In the red light, the crystals now appeared as crisscross-shaped droplets of blood.

"Enoch?" she said. "Is that you?"

"No, Mara." The voice grew louder and clearer. "Pick me up. Hold me close. If you want to escape loneliness, I will tell you what you must do."

She slid her hand under the hilt, now as warm as one of the rocks in the hot springs, and held it close to her chest. "Like this?"

"Closer."

She pressed the flat side of the blade against her body. Its warmth penetrated her shirt and radiated across her skin. Yet, instead of bringing the soothing relief of the spring's steamy bath, it raised a cascade of shivers from her shoulders to her waist. "Is that better?"

"Turn my point toward your heart and press it against bare skin. Only then will I be able to communicate my message."

She pulled the collar of her shirt down and set the tip of the blade against her bosom. As the stone radiated cold into her skin, her fingers trembled around the grip. "Like this?"

"Very good." The voice became crisp and clear. "Now you can listen to the words of truth, words you cannot deny. You were born a slave in this God-forsaken mine, and you are destined to die here. God used you for his purposes over and over, only to send you back here to suffer alone. You helped save the race of dragons, ended the schemes of slayers, and rescued Bonnie Silver from exposure, and each time you returned to this dungeon." The dagger's voice softened. "You know that, don't you?"

As she closed her eyes, Sapphira's face twitched. "Yes." Her voice spiked high. "Yes, I know. But I deserve it. I'm just a—"

"A slave girl. A foolish slave girl who thought she could rise up on the wings of faith, yet she was dashed to the lower realms time after time." A "tsk, tsk" sound emanated from the blade. "Long ago King Nimrod wanted to give you to the men of the temple. Do you remember that?"

She nodded, tears now dripping. "I remember."

"And you know what they would have done, don't you?"

Again, she nodded. With the dagger shaking in her hand, the blade pricked her skin, but not deep enough to draw blood.

"You ran away, of course, and to where? The same place you toil now, your only refuge from those who sit high and mighty on royal thrones, who wish only to use you for their pleasures and cast you to the ground when you have outlived your usefulness. Now that you have violated Enoch's trust, you can never be trusted again. And since you took from the tree of life, you cannot die of natural causes. You will stay here forever.

"Forever alone. Forever without Elam. And Elam will forever be without you, which is all for the better. You don't deserve such a brave, obedient warrior, and he would be better off without you. He will take Acacia into his heart, the sister you betrayed so long ago, the only Oracle who has truly been faithful and—"

"Stop it!" Sapphira wailed. "Stop it! I know it's all true. Why do you torment me like this?"

The dagger's voice lowered to a snakelike hiss. "Because I want to help you end your suffering. Because of the curse on those who would spill your blood, only you would be willing to take your life, but I will be your instrument of destruction. Plunge me into your heart. You will escape this dungeon, and you will never, ever have to come back. Elam will marry Acacia, and he will be happy forever, safely in the arms of an Oracle who never betrayed anyone, neither you, nor Enoch, nor God. If you will complete this final act of unselfishness, everyone you love will be happy and fulfilled, and you will never be alone again."

Still sobbing, Sapphira heaved shallow breaths. Every spasm drove the blade's stinging point deeper. As she watched the staurolite dagger against her pale skin, its embedded crystals sparkled like scarlet mirrors, spattering reflections of themselves across her chest. A hundred tiny crosses, each one bloody red, wavered over a sea of white.

365

"Do it now, Mara. Plunge deep and quick. Your pain will soon be over, and the world will be rid of this daughter of the Earth, this faithless betrayer who is unworthy to draw another breath."

The ovulum's glow blossomed, sending brighter and brighter light across her body, magnifying the crystalline images on her skin. As the largest cross remained steady at the center of her chest, a memory flashed in her mind. Standing at the edge of a precipice, she stared at death, the magma river below, ready to cast herself into its fiery clutches. She had held aloft a flaming cross, the same cross she had carried for years, lighting her way through so many dark times.

Just before jumping, she had pressed the cross against her bosom, bringing its flames into her heart and killing forever the daughter of Earth that she once was and resurrecting her as a daughter of the King. The searing heat purged her eternal loneliness, the same empty feeling that had now crept back in like a crafty serpent. Words eased into her mind, Gabriel's beautiful phrases spoken in a dim echoing tunnel. *"You are an amazing girl, Sapphira Adi, and I want you to know that someone appreciates all you've done."*

She jerked the dagger away and slammed it to the floor. Shaking violently, she rose to her feet. She pressed her hand against her chest and shouted, "I am Sapphira Adi! A child of Jehovah!" She kicked the dagger across the floor. "I already died once, and I don't ever have to die again!"

She scooped up the ovulum and stroked its glass. Inside, the red cloud swirled faster than ever, as if dancing with delight. Parting her lips, she breathed over the surface, frosting the crystal with a coat of white mist. The cloud slowed for a moment, then spun again, as if responding to her delicate touch. She rose to the balls of her feet, spread her arms, and swirled in a circle of her own, dancing with the holy presence within her grasp.

She didn't have to speak. She didn't have to try to explain her mistake. Jehovah knew her heart. Frightened and confused, she had done the best she could. Her loving God had searched her soul and found no shadow of selfishness. Her choice to let them go through the portal, a decision manipulated by the presence of a vile deceiver, had done nothing to drive a wedge between her and her eternal dance partner.

Slowing her spin, she drew the ovulum close and pressed it against her chest. Warmth flooded her body, and, this time, her soul. Every chill flew away. Every doubt vanished. She would never again allow an accuser to hold such sway over her mind.

As her tremors eased, Sapphira gazed down the dark tunnel. It was probably too late to run to the museum and stop them from using the portal. Her best choice now would be to dispose of the dagger and return to her hovel. Yes, return to her hovel and wait. For how long? It didn't matter. Even if she had to wait for years, she would never be alone. Not this time. Sure, Gabriel would eventually return, bearing news of his efforts and perhaps leading former dragons into the mines, and he would be a welcome addition, but now she would never again forget that she always had someone at her side, Jehovah-Shammah—the Lord is there.

She stuffed the ovulum under her shirt and snatched up the dagger. Now it was time to put the deceiver in his place. After tying the loose rope to the dangling piece in the shaft, she clamped the dagger between her teeth, wrapped her arms and legs around the line, and slid down. Since she had to descend only one level, the remaining rope would be long enough … she hoped.

The dagger buzzed in her teeth, the voice again whispering its static-filled words, but she just hummed a tune, nothing in particular, just something loud enough to drown out the viperous tongue.

367

When she arrived, she swung into the new tunnel, pulled out the ovulum, and gripped the dagger's hilt in her fist. Once again she traveled the path to the precipice, but this time marching like a soldier, with new purpose, no hesitation, no dread. She was the bearer of the dagger, and she would take this deceiver to its appointed doom.

She strode out to the ledge. As the heat from the magma river rushed upward, she pulled her arm back, threw the dagger as far as she could, and, not bothering to watch it fall, marched back through the tunnel, Enoch's ovulum leading the way.

Still walking with purpose, she let out a long, satisfied sigh. The demon was gone, vanquished. Now she would go back to the hovel and wait patiently for the next step, no matter how long it might take.

Sitting on the floor near the back of *Merlin*, Ashley reeled in a long run of twine and wrapped it around her hand, her makeshift measuring line. "We can fit three cots, but no more. Since they'll be on wheels, we can probably adjust them once we get them in."

"That is," Walter added, "if Cliffside gets the wheels done in time." Sitting cross-legged with his back against the closed cargo door, he pointed at the seats. "If we had his tools, maybe we could remove those to make more room."

"No time, but at least we can fit the sickest ones. Since it's going to be so dangerous, it's better to limit our patients to the three who would die anyway."

"So those three are going," Walter said, "and you, Billy, Steadfast, and his wife make seven."

"Right." She scrunched her eyebrows. "Are you sure you're okay with staying at the magnet station?"

"I'm okay. I'd rather be bouncing around the sky with you and Billy, but I don't mind being your translator."

Ashley pushed her hand against his and intertwined their fingers. "We said we'd be together for the rest of these adventures, but …" She sighed. What else could she say? She had already explained why he had to stay at the magnet station. Cliffside couldn't learn their lingo fast enough to make the proper adjustments to turn or to change the speed of the sky hospital, and if Walter flew with Billy, he wouldn't be able to adjust the Cessna's radio if something went wrong.

Finally, she pulled away and set her hands in her lap. "We can do this. We *have* to do this. Even if we're not together."

"If you're trying to read my mind again," Walter said, "I think you're tuned into the wrong frequency. I'm really cool with the idea. Don't worry about it." He withdrew his MP3 player from his pocket. "Speaking of frequency, we still haven't tested it long range."

Ashley pointed at the player. "You said your radio might come in handy. You can say 'I told you so' if you want to."

"Yeah, you read me right that time, but I wasn't going to say it." He scooted around her and jumped out the passenger door. "I should be at the station in about three minutes. Give me a holler."

Ashley rose to her knees and looked out the door. Walter sprinted across the dragon-launching field, his arms pumping in the cold wind. He was such a great guy—polite, courageous, virtuous, and, of course, funny.

As she walked to the cockpit, she caught another view of him out the front windshield, shrinking in the distance as he crested a hill. Yes, he was all she could ever ask for in a young man, but he was so young … too young. And it would take years, maybe five years or more, before the gap in their ages would seem narrow enough to allow anything more than a close friendship to develop.

She sat in the copilot's chair and slid the headset on. Since she had taken the airplane's radio out of the dashboard and left it hanging, she could tweak the frequency if necessary, but she would have to secure everything before takeoff.

She glanced at the sky. No sign of Clefspeare. He had no idea how long it would take to find Billy at Mount Elijah and then fly back. With Mother the only one watching the birthing garden, the entire village lay at greater risk. And who could tell about Flint and his army? When would they feel strong enough to attack?

After guessing that three minutes were up, Ashley called on the radio. "Walter, I'm broadcasting on one-oh-seven-point-nine. I know you can't answer, but I'll keep talking for a while to make sure you've had time to get to the station. Since you're not even a mile away, this might be an inadequate test. We'll have to fly at ten-thousand feet. Now, I don't mean to insult you, because I know you can do the math, but that's just under two miles … well, one point eight nine and change, in case you want to know, and because of the angle between the central magnet and where we

369

happen to be flying at any given time, the distance would be even greater.

"Of course, since they use a magnet that's not ferromagnetic, I'm not completely sure that my calculations are correct, but that's all for the better. If they used magnets that attracted iron and steel, our airplane would be affected in unpredictable ways. The whole concept is super cool, but it has its drawbacks, including taking a full day to land the thing if they wanted to pick up people with life-threatening injuries. Maybe I can figure out a way to improve that process. Anyway …"

Ashley kept chattering, still glancing from time to time at the sky, hoping to see a returning dragon. As soon as Billy arrived, they would have to get the patients to the airplane in a hurry. No sense loading them ahead of time, not in such cold weather. She would just have to wait and trust that God would keep those poor villagers alive long enough to get them safely to the hospital.

Finally, she stopped talking and pulled off the headset. As she laid it in her lap, she looked at her palms. There was no trace of the deep wounds that had once gouged her skin, the holes the pennies bored there when she surrendered her gifts to God. And now with her healing gift restored, she felt useless. Yes, she could still do a healing, but the last episode took so much out of her, it nearly killed her, and she was exhausted for hours. Somehow her powers were crippled in this place, sort of like how Excalibur had lost its ability to send out its destructive beam. Obviously she and Walter would have to count on others to do what they couldn't do themselves.

Looking into the air again, she whispered, "And that means you, God." She lifted her hand, exposing her palm to the sky. "It's all yours. Use this hand however you will. I, Ashley Stalworth, give it to you again today … and forever."

23

CHAPTER

CLIMBING BETWEEN WORLDS

Acacia stood next to the tree of life, carrying a lantern that had been one of the museum's window lights for hundreds of years. Now burning the last bit of oil in its reservoir, it illuminated the curved inner walls, revealing a few dusty scrolls lying on shelves. Leaning against the shelves, wooden ladders, some with broken or missing rungs, climbed high into the dark upper reaches. The rope from the elevator shaft lay in a coil at her feet.

"Hold this, please." She handed the lantern to Bonnie. "Here's the plan. I'll create the portal around everyone, and as soon as I can see the volcano in Second Eden, I'll throw the rope to Billy and climb up. That way, we'll be sure it's safe to pass from here to there. Then, from the volcano level, I'll keep the portal open for you to join me." She scanned each face. "Who'll be next?"

Irene raised her hand. "They need a dragon up there. We'd better make sure they get one." She pointed at the two girls in turn. "Then Bonnie, and then Shiloh."

371

Acacia picked up an end of the rope. "If you don't have the strength to climb, I'm sure we can pull you. Billy and Candle and Listener are all there to help."

Looking up, Acacia peered through the darkness. Her enhanced vision acted like a telescope, allowing her to see the beams that crossed just under the museum's domed top and a hint of light from an unseen source. Could it be the other realm? "This must be a very thin portal," she said, waving for everyone to gather around. "It shouldn't take much to open it."

When all four drew into a tight huddle, Acacia raised her hand and called out, "Give me light!" A white flame erupted from her palm. She swirled her arm, creating the usual circle, then a descending curtain. Within seconds, the twisting fire swept around their cluster and enveloped the tree, as well. The leaves fluttered, and the soil in the planter glowed white.

Soon, the volcano chamber materialized above their heads. Half in one dimension and half in another, they seemed firmly planted in the museum room while floating in the volcano's throat. The fire passed right through the cave's semitransparent floor above, unhindered by the solid stone, and made a wall that encircled the upper hole.

Billy, standing next to Candle and Listener, held his hands up, as if blinded by the fire, or maybe warding off the heat.

Acacia lowered her hand and let the portal vortex spin on its own while she wound the rope into a loop. Then, tossing it through the flames, she yelled, "Catch!"

Billy snagged the rope, wound it around his waist, and backed up slowly. "Let's go!"

As the rope slid against the side of the volcano chamber's floor opening, Acacia gripped the line, riding the pull as she struggled to help by climbing hand over hand. It took only a few seconds for her to reach the lip of the hole. About a foot or so of stone floor lay between her hand and the encircling wall of flames. When she stretched one arm and pushed her hand through the wall, Candle and Listener grabbed it and dragged her the rest of the way out.

She leaped to her feet, faced the portal, and waved her arms. "I have to keep it open. Irene is next."

Candle pointed at the rope. "It's catching fire."

"The fire is real," Acacia said as she stamped out the embers. "If we keep the rope moving up and down, maybe it won't burn up."

Billy took a few steps forward and reeled the rope back down. "Okay! Let me know when to pull!"

As Acacia peered into the fire, Irene grabbed the rope and began to hoist herself up. "She's got it," Acacia said. "Pull!"

Billy heaved backward again. The rope tightened. Several fibers broke free, blackened and smoking. When Irene's head appeared above floor level, Acacia leaned into the flames and grabbed her by an arm. Then, while lifting, Acacia raised her free hand, waved it around, and shouted, "Increase!" The curtain of fire crept outward, allowing Irene room to stand.

"Now Bonnie!" Acacia called. As the rope lowered again, she looked into the museum room. Bonnie clutched the line, but the flaming wall down below had contracted, forcing her and Shiloh to squeeze close together.

"The tree's on fire!" Shiloh yelled.

Suddenly, the mountain began to shake. Pebbles drizzled from above, pelting Acacia's head. She swung around to Billy. Smoke rose from the rope between them. More fibers snapped. "Pull!" she shouted. "Now!"

Billy backed up a step. The rope broke away, sending him stumbling toward the outer wall. As the line whipped toward the hole, Acacia grabbed it and hung on. More rocks fell, bigger ones crunching on the cave floor.

A stone as large as her head plunged into the museum room, striking Bonnie's shoulder. She collapsed to the floor in a heap. Shiloh leaped over her body, and they faded out of sight.

Acacia looked up. The cone's entire opening crumbled. She yelled, "Extinguish!" and threw herself and Irene through the dwindling wall of fire.

Candle and Listener jumped to the cave's outer wall just before the chamber's roof collapsed. Tons of rocks crashed down into the volcano's throat, some falling through while others plugged the hole and piled up in a heap.

Acacia, Irene, Billy, Candle, and Listener pressed their bodies against the side wall, watching the rain of boulders, rocks, and dirt. Soon, the breeze swept the dust away. The volcano top was now just a flat stony platform with a surrounding circular wall and a heap of stones in the center.

Billy leaped for the pile of rocks and began slinging them to the side. "Bonnie and Shiloh!"

As the castaway stones tumbled down the slope, Acacia and the others joined him. "I don't sense a portal," Acacia said as she pushed a stone to the side. "It might be gone."

Irene dug into the grit and pebbles with both hands. "My daughter's hurt! We have to get it open!"

In spite of the frigid wind buffeting their faces, beads of sweat speckled each brow as they grabbed, clawed, and tunneled. Soon, only a cluster of rocks remained wedged at the top of the volcano's throat. As before, Billy pushed Excalibur into one of the gaps and pried a stone loose. When it gave way, the obstruction broke apart and tumbled into the void. A new stream of sulfur-laden fumes rushed upward and dissipated in the wind.

Acacia knelt and peered into the darkness, while Listener pointed her spyglass.

"I think I see magma," Acacia said. "My eyesight is normal now, so the portal is probably gone." She looked up at Billy. "The other realm is out of reach."

"Can't you open a new one?" Billy waved his arms in the air. "I mean, like you did before. Just make the fire spin and open it up again."

Acacia shook her head. "I open portals that are already there, and I have moved portals from one place to another, but creating a new one requires more firepower than I can generate."

"I see someone," Listener said. "Two girls who look exactly alike."

Irene dropped to her knees and looked down. "Bonnie and Shiloh!"

"They're lying close to a burning tree. Too close, I think, and ..." Listener's brow furrowed. "And now they're gone."

"If she can still see the other realm," Acacia said, lifting her arms again, "I'll try to open it. I'll give it all I've got."

Acacia followed her usual portal-opening procedure, shooting more flames than ever into her cyclone, but the museum room never appeared. Of course, she could have jumped into the hole anyway just to see if it led to the mines, but the leap would have been suicide if reality matched what her eyesight told her.

She lowered her arms and let the spin of fire die away. "It's no use. There's no way to get down there now."

Billy clenched his teeth. "I can't believe this! Bonnie's hurt, and now we can't help her!"

"She'll have help." Irene wrapped Billy in her arms and leaned her head against his. "Sapphira's still there. She and Shiloh can take her to Yereq." A sob broke through, shaking her words. "I'm sure ... she'll be all right. Remember the prophecy."

He patted her on the back but said nothing. His facial expression said it all—a blend of anxiety and determination in his wrinkled brow and steeled jaw.

"There's nothing more we can do here," Acacia said as she huddled with the two children. "We'd better get out of this cold wind."

Pushing Irene back, Billy added, "And get you to the garden. We need another dragon as soon as possible." He took off his coat and gave it to her, leaving only a thick sweatshirt for himself. "Let's get going."

After hiking down the side of the volcano, they crossed a field of rippled lava, black and crumbling. Tree-studded slopes rose on each side to rocky peaks, lining this valley of basaltic stone. A few puffy clouds raced overhead, riding the numbing breeze that swept down and funneled through their channel, making their passage a wind tunnel. Fortunately, it streamed in from behind, cold, to be sure, but helpful as it pushed them speedily along.

As usual, Listener gazed through her spyglass from time to time, always on the lookout for any oddity, announcing every sighting of clouds that might bring another rainstorm, or birds that might be carrying shadow people. Finally, as they approached a thin forest, she grabbed Billy's shirt. "A dragon! A red one!"

Billy looked in the direction her spyglass pointed. "I see it. It's coming this way!"

"Could it be Goliath?" Acacia asked.

"It's not Goliath," Irene said. "Look at those powerful wings. I would recognize them anywhere." As the breeze tossed her blond locks, a smile spread across her face. "It's Clefspeare."

A few seconds later, Clefspeare landed on the dark field, his red wings a striking contrast to the black lava residue.

Billy ran to his side. "What's up, Dad? Why are you here?"

"An important mission." He heaved large gulps of air. "Life or death."

While they waited for him to catch his breath, Candle scooted closer to Billy. "I wonder how he found us without a guide."

After a final deep breath, Clefspeare pulled in his wings and settled to the ground. "I apologize for my lack of endurance, but I flew here as quickly as I could, and I fought a ghastly wind all the way." He lowered his snout toward Candle. "One of your people gave me general directions, and once I sensed Billy's presence, I followed my nose."

"Dad," Billy said, nodding toward Irene. "Look who's here."

Clefspeare shifted her way and bowed his head. "You are a welcome presence, Irene, but we have no time for pleasantries. I must take Billy back immediately for a vital flying mission. With no healthy dragon to watch the birthing garden, the villagers are vulnerable."

Billy hooked his arm around Irene's. "Can you carry both of us? That way we can get another dragon right away. Candle knows how to lead Acacia and Listener home."

"Let us take Listener as well," Clefspeare said. "With the wind in our favor, I will be able to carry three." He lowered his head to the ground, allowing Billy, Irene, and Listener to climb his neck and settle on his back, Billy in front, then Irene and Listener. "Come as quickly as you can," Clefspeare said to Acacia. "If what we have in mind for Billy to do doesn't work, Ashley will want to try a fiery healing. Although Elam believes she needs to rest further, she will not be persuaded easily."

Acacia nodded. "I understand."

Clefspeare spread out his wings and beat them furiously, raising black lava dust in his wake as he rose into the sky. Within seconds, he and the three riders disappeared over the treetops.

Acacia took Candle's hand. "Know any shortcuts?"

"I was hoping you'd ask that," he replied, grinning. "Listener's scared of them, so we went the long way coming up here."

"I'm glad to hear you're so sensitive to her fears."

He half closed one eye. "Are you afraid of skunk lizards?"

"Skunk lizards!" Acacia brushed lava dust off her tunic and tugged down on the hem. "Well, I'm not sure what they are, but with a brave young man at my side, I'm sure I can manage."

"You sound so much like my mother, I think …" Candle's smile suddenly wilted. His companion pushed under his dreadlocks and nestled against his ear, pulsing a soft blue light.

As tears welled in his weary brown eyes, Acacia laid a hand on his shoulder. "I used the right words for you. You really are a brave young man. You remind me of Valiant."

377

Candle tilted his head and rubbed her hand with his cheek. "Do you really think so?"

"I know so. And your mother knows, and your sister knows. And I'll bet even the skunk lizards know." She gave his back a gentle push. "Now lead the way, valiant soldier. I'll be right behind you."

Valiant pushed a clump of tall reeds to the side. Across a wide, shallow gulley, the land sloped upward to high ground where at least thirty huts encircled a field of crops as well as a modest collection of pigs and goats. Some of the beasts were tied to hewn logs that had been pounded into the mud, and some were corralled within waist-high wooden fences. "Father Abraham's trail leads here," he whispered. "But I cannot see him."

Pushing his nose past Valiant, Dikaios looked through the gap. "Nor I. Perhaps I can pose as a witless horse and be taken in."

"Father Abraham said that the people have already heard you speak."

"Flint did not hear me, and knowing Greevelow, I doubt that a man of such few words would ever volunteer to tell him. As far as Flint knows, I am merely a faithful horse who sought help for Abraham. He has no idea that I am able to act as a spy."

"Very well. I will wait here and watch."

Dikaios strode into the clearing, then paused and looked back. "If they decide to tie me up like some kind of senseless farm horse, I should be able to free myself, but if not, I will be glad of your help."

Lifting his dagger, Valiant smiled. "Easily done, my friend."

Standing at the edge of the garden, Elam looked out over the plants, his sword arm drooping. After only an hour of training with Sir Barlow and their new army, his muscles had rebelled. Still, although he had given everyone a break, they would all have to go back to work as soon as he finished overseeing this important task.

With Thigocia using this opportunity to get her wings checked out at the dragon launching field, and Clefspeare taking off to collect Acacia and Candle, he would have to stick around until at least one of them returned.

Irene, whom Clefspeare had recently dropped off, stood at his side, gazing at the garden in wonder. "There are living babies within those leaves?" she asked.

"That's how they procreate here." Elam stepped into the garden and crouched near one of the plants. "They didn't tell me how long it takes."

She pointed at the soil. "Are those white things the bones Clefspeare told me about?"

"They are." He picked up a short bone. "We think they're what made this place into a dragon regeneration garden, but we're not sure how it works. Jared just walked in there and walked back. As soon as he stepped out, he turned into Clefspeare. When Patrick tried, it didn't work, but I'm hoping he's just unique for some reason."

She took in a deep breath. "I'm ready."

"Let's do it." Elam stepped back from the garden.

As Irene walked along one of the furrows, glancing from side to side, Elam watched her progress. Somehow everything seemed different. Without the brilliant aura around Paili and the energized bones, would it work at all?

Irene reached down and petted one of the plants. "Is this far enough?"

"Maybe. Come out, and we'll see."

She hurried back to the edge and stopped. "Okay. Here goes." With a dramatic stretch, she stepped out of the garden and onto the grassy field. Then, standing upright, she set her hands on her hips. "I don't feel anything."

379

"That's because nothing's happening." Elam looked up at the sky. "Clefspeare should be back any minute. I hope he found Acacia. We'll need her fire to energize the bones."

"Would Billy's fire work? He's at the infirmary. I could go get him."

"His fire is different." Elam set his hands as if holding a ball. "Acacia's aura is a lot like her portal opener—"

"There they are." Irene pointed at the sky. "I guess I'm about to see for myself."

Soon, Clefspeare landed, Candle riding tall in front and Acacia clutching his waist. After Elam sent Candle to find his sister at Abraham's house, he guided Irene and Acacia to the garden. "Let's try it again, shall we?"

Irene took three steps along the row and turned around. "I'm ready."

380

Acacia raised her hands. Fire sprang up in both palms. As the breeze flapped her cloak and white hair, a foul odor assaulted Elam's nose. "What's that smell?" he asked.

"Skunk lizard." Acacia said blankly. "I'll explain later."

As she had done with Paili, Acacia fashioned a flaming blue aura around Irene, leaving a couple of feet of space between her and the surrounding fire.

"Now walk to the plowed area and back," Elam said.

Irene obeyed. The aura floated along with her. With each step, the bones along her path sizzled and popped, glowing bright white. When she returned to the edge, she stopped and looked at Elam through her veil of shimmering blue. "I feel something this time."

Acacia waved her arms and whispered, "Extinguish." The flames immediately evaporated in a puff of blue smoke.

"Now step out of the garden," Elam said. "That is, if you're ready."

"I'm ready."

While Elam, Clefspeare, and Acacia moved back several paces, Irene again stepped out of the garden. This time, as soon as her athletic shoe touched the grass, it swelled, splitting the leather sides. The swelling spread up her leg, ripping her jeans. Beginning at the ankle, her skin dried out and changed to a scaly coat, darkening from pale to light brown.

When her other shoe touched the grass, the process repeated, just seconds behind the other leg. With her waist now expanding, she reached for the snap in her jeans.

Elam turned his head. Better now to listen than to watch. As the process continued, rips, pops, and grunts sounded from the regenerating dragon. Soon, everything was quiet.

Something leathery touched his cheek. "You can look now, Elam."

Turning, he pushed a huge dragon wing away from his face and smiled. "Process complete, I see."

"I am now Hartanna once again." She spread her wings and let the wind billow them like a pair of sails. "What is your command, Warrior Chief?"

Elam waved Acacia and the two dragons together. "I need one dragon to patrol this garden and the other to help Ashley and Walter with their mission at the sky hospital."

"I will go with them," Hartanna said. "I am anxious to fly again." She turned to Clefspeare and blinked her fiery eyes. "That is, of course, if you agree, Clefspeare."

The red dragon bowed. "I agree."

Hartanna extended one of the "fingers" on her forefoot. "Well, look at this!"

Elam and the others looked at the finger. Shimmering gold scales encircled it, and a red gem had been wedged between scales at the top.

"It looks like a ring," Elam said.

"That's what I thought. It's exactly where I wore my rubellite."

381

Clefspeare raised his foreleg. "I have the same markings where my ring used to be, and a gem as well. I had not even noticed."

Hartanna picked up her torn jeans. After pushing a claw into the pocket, she retrieved a ring. "Enoch gave me this one," she said, extending it to Elam. "He said a time will come when I will be able to give it to Makaidos. I would be grateful if you kept it. I have no place to store it."

"Gladly." Elam slid it into his pocket. "Now that we have two healthy dragons, we have many more options, but first things first. Hartanna, go with all speed to the field on the other side of the village. You'll find Ashley and the airplane there."

She bowed her head. "I will."

As she launched into the air, Clefspeare flicked his tail toward Elam. "Warrior Chief, I think we should teach your finest soldiers how to ride into battle on a dragon as soon as possible. If you will bring some to this field, we can begin their training."

"My finest soldiers?" Elam asked, giving him an uneasy grin. "With Valiant gone, I have no idea how to choose."

"A simple test of courage will provide your answer. Allow them to volunteer. Then have Barlow tell them about his flying adventures. If they still want to fly after hearing those harrowing tales, then they will be our test pilots."

A shley pointed out the airplane's front windshield. "There it is. I see the sun glinting off its metal surface."

"Right. I got it marked." Billy guided *Merlin* into a sharp turn. "I'll just point our nose in the direction it's going. It shouldn't be too hard to catch up with it."

"If it's as big as Cliffside described, it's probably about a mile ahead of us."

As Billy completed his turn, a heavy crosswind buffeted the plane, making everyone bounce. Ashley leaned around her copilot's chair. In the back, beyond the seats, Steadfast knelt between two cots, clutching their sides, while Pearl, a tall, big-boned woman with curly blond hair, leaned over a third, holding it down while the plane rocked back and forth. Their companions zipped from shoulder to ear and back to shoulder again, as if excited by the new adventure.

An unconscious patient lay in each cot. One heaved fast, shallow breaths—Mason, a muscular man, a builder and the father of two little girls. Something had broken his sternum and bruised his heart. Another patient groaned with each lurch of the plane— Willow, a young artist who had been impaled by one of Goliath's spines. Apparently it speared his heart. How he had survived this long, no one could tell. Finally, the third patient lay quietly ... too quietly—a little girl named Onyx, less than two years old and as dark and beautiful as her namesake. With a punctured lung and internal bleeding, she would have to be the first one out.

Another sharp lurch shook Ashley back to attention. "How's it going?"

"Pretty rough," Billy said. "The direction we're heading will keep us jumping like crazy, and we can't fly as slow as the hospital."

Clutching her armrests, Ashley bounced in place, her voice shaking with the jolts. "I see what you mean. A tailwind would be better, but we have to wait for Hartanna to land before we can speed it up."

Billy sat up higher and looked out his side window. "Any sign of her?"

"Not yet." Ashley leaned as far forward as her seat belt would allow. Near the top of her view through the windshield, a dark spot appeared, bouncing in the sky and closing in on the hospital platform, a small concrete circle that protruded from the side near the front of the tube. "There she is!"

In a flurry of wings, Hartanna landed heavily on the platform. Striking belly first, she rocked forward, but her outstretched wings kept her from somersaulting into the main body of the flying tube.

When Hartanna settled into an upright position, Ashley adjusted her headset and spoke into the microphone. "Walter, the dragon has landed. Now we need to turn the hospital ninety degrees to the left and keep it there. Speed it up. I'll let you know when you're at the right velocity for us."

The silver metal tube, at least five times as large as the fuselage of a jumbo jet, slowly turned. Billy steered to match and picked up the tail wind, kicking them to a faster speed.

Ashley kept an eye on the instruments. Soon, they were flying even with the hospital, both in elevation and velocity. Wind still jostled the plane, but now it felt more like a ride on a bumpy road rather than on a rampaging bull.

"This'll work," Billy said. "See if Walter can hold it."

Ashley pushed her microphone closer to her lips. "Keep it right there, Walter. Since it's about five-point-two miles until we pass the focal magnetic plane, we'll be able to stay on course for fourteen-point-two miles total. Billy will watch the distance and let you know when we're getting close to the drop dead point for turning back."

"Try to think of a better term," Billy said.

Ashley arched her brow. "Would you prefer 'minimum webers of magnetic flux'?"

"Never mind. Drop dead will do."

As the airplane edged closer to the docking platform, Ashley shook her head. It looked smaller than a helicopter landing pad. "This is going to be really tough."

Billy glanced between his instruments and the hospital. "You're telling me! When I get right next to the tube, I'm not sure what the effect will be on the air currents or the magnetic field. We might create a weird cushion of air that'll really make us rock."

"Yeah, but I'm sure you can handle it." Ashley raised her hands to her headset. "Walter, I'm going to help unload the patients. Just keep it steady. Billy will talk to you now." After

384

whipping off the earphones, she hurried toward the back. "Let's make it quick, Steadfast! The magnetic field has a nine-mile range, so Walter and Cliffside have to turn it back in less than four minutes. We don't want to ride those crosswinds while we're wheeling our patients out."

She reached for the latch and pushed open the upper half of the cargo door. Freezing air rushed across her body and into the cabin. The plane bounced erratically, jostling everything not bolted to the floor. Steadfast and Pearl pushed down on the sides of the cots, while Ashley leaned against the gusts and set her hand on the lower latch.

"Don't open the other door until I get us right up to the dock," Billy shouted. "We had it modified to open down like a ramp."

Ashley half closed her eyes, forcing herself to brave the bone-chilling wind so she could survey their destination. Tears streamed back across her temples as she read the lettering on the side of the hospital's wall—*Healing in His Wings.*

Soon, their left wing extended over the platform. With the plane rattling as it rode out the bumps, they eased even closer, bringing the cargo door within a foot of the platform's outer edge. The gap seemed like a chasm, every bit as dangerous and impossible to cross as the chasm spanned by the rickety bridge. One wrong step, and a plunge through thousands of feet of freezing air would follow, then a bone-crushing smash in a remote forest where no one would ever find her rag-doll body.

Ashley bit her bottom lip. *Okay. Gotta stop thinking like that. This is going to work.* She looked at Billy. "Ready?"

"Okay!" He shouted. "Now!"

She opened the latch and pushed the door with her foot. The howling wind pushed back at first, then a downdraft slapped it to the platform's surface.

Hartanna lumbered to the edge and set a forefoot on the ramp. As the airplane continued to bounce, the door jiggled up and

385

down on its hinges. She extended a wing toward Ashley and bel-lowed, "Roll the first one to the edge! I will block the wind!"

"Okay!" Ashley called. "Here goes!" Grabbing the head rail of Onyx's cot while Steadfast guided the other end, she backed toward the door and set her foot down gingerly. The ramp held firm. As she lifted the cot's wheels over the bumps, Hartanna's wing billowed at her left, redirecting the howling wind. The plane's engine and propeller droned, adding to the cacophony of confus-ing sounds.

Holding her breath, Ashley took the remaining two steps to the platform and backpedaled until Steadfast also reached firmer ground. With Hartanna's wing and body still blocking the wind, Ashley pointed at the double doors to the hospital. "Take her in! I'll get Willow!"

While Steadfast wheeled the cot away, his companion tucking itself under his collar, Ashley ran to the airplane. She hesitated for a moment and took a deep breath. Then, ducking her head, she leaped back inside. Pearl caught Ashley's arm and pulled her to a stop.

Ashley turned to the front and panted through her words. "Billy! How much time till we have to turn?"

"Probably just under two minutes!"

Ashley nodded at Pearl. "Let's go!" She grabbed the head rail of Willow's cot and backed toward the door, this time with more confidence. When she set a foot on the platform, the plane bucked and tossed the cot into the air, slinging Willow into Hartanna's webbing. The door shot upward and slammed in front of Pearl's face. The cot flew over the edge of the platform and tumbled end over end behind them.

With a jerk of her wing, Hartanna made a pocket for Willow and lowered him gently to the floor.

Now buffeted by the wind, Ashley leaned into every step until she reached Willow. "Can you carry him to the door?" she shouted. "I have to get Mason!"

"I will," Hartanna said, "but Pearl will have to open *Merlin*'s door for you. Billy can't leave the pilot's chair."

"I can do it. The upper door is open, and the lower door has a latch on the outside."

"As if it weren't already dangerous enough out here." Hartanna scooted toward the hospital entrance. "I won't be able to shield you from the wind until I return."

"I know." Ashley hurried back to the plane, leaning to her left to battle the wind. Through the pilot's window, Billy pointed at his wrist, obviously indicating that they were out of time. They would have to make the turn.

She walked as close to the edge of the platform as she dared and shouted into the open upper door. "Pearl! Tell Billy to tell Walter to make a full one-eighty degree turn! A headwind will be easier than a crosswind."

Pearl nodded, and as she made her way toward the front, her profile, bending low to avoid the ceiling, passed by each window. Ashley leaned out and grasped the door handle. It would be better to try to get inside before the turn than afterward. Who could tell how rough it would become?

She tried to twist the handle, but it wouldn't budge. As she used her weight to try to muscle it open, the plane eased away. Ashley lurched forward and slung her arms over the top of the lower door. Her head leaned into the cabin as her feet lifted off the platform. She tried to scream, but her "Help!" sounded more like the croak of a frog.

Merlin slid farther from the dock and then dropped. With the sudden fall, Ashley felt almost weightless. She kicked and pulled, then finally tumbled into the cabin. After rolling to a stop, she lay on her side and gasped for breath.

As Pearl rushed down the aisle, Billy shouted from the front. "Are you okay?"

Ashley coughed. Her stomach boiled inside. She clutched her abdomen and dry heaved, unable to control the spasms.

387

Laying a hand on Ashley's side, Pearl called to Billy, "It is probably just temporary nausea due to extreme stress. Go ahead with the turn."

As Ashley curled into a fetal position, the plane dipped, slid, and banked as if batted about by the hand of a spiteful giant. Obviously they had turned back into the crosswinds. Gusts hurtled in through the open upper door and swirled throughout the cabin.

Closing her eyes as she tried to find a distraction from the horrible nausea, she listened to the propeller buzz and Billy's sharp commands. "We're at exactly ninety degrees now, Walter. Keep turning left. I'll give you a countdown. Because of the headwinds, you might have to kick up the speed when you make the turn. I'm not sure how much. I'll just have to let you know."

After nearly a minute, Ashley let out a long breath and sat up. Pearl stared, her companion sitting on her shoulder, its tiny eyes blinking. "There is medicine in the hospital for your stomach," Pearl said. "You will be fine very soon."

While the plane continued to buck wildly, Ashley rubbed her abdomen. The muscles felt like knotted steel. "Let's worry about me later. We have to get Mason inside." With Pearl's help, she rose to her feet, then clutched the head rail of the last cot. Mason's shallow breaths came faster and faster. His face grimaced with every bounce.

"Let's do it, Billy!" Ashley called.

"Two seconds!" Billy barked into his microphone. "That's it, Walter! Hold her there!"

With a turn into the headwind, the bucking eased a bit, but not enough. Mason continued to hyperventilate. His lips turned blue and his face ashen.

"We're losing him!" Ashley reached for the handle. "I'm opening the door."

"Go for it! We're steady."

As before, she opened the lower hatch and pushed it down with her foot. Hartanna, now near the center of the platform, shuffled toward the plane. Turning her back again to the door, Ashley grasped Mason's cot.

Pearl tugged on Ashley's arm. "I will go first this time. You stay here."

Too sick to resist, she switched places with Pearl. As soon as she put her hands on the cot near Mason's feet, his gasping breaths stopped.

Ashley's stomach knotted twice as hard. "Go! Go!"

As soon as Hartanna created her wing shield, Pearl backed onto the ramp. Her blond hair flew into a swirl over her head, and her tunic and trousers slapped against her arms and legs. Grunting with every inch of progress, she finally set the front wheels on the docking floor.

Just as Ashley picked up her end of the cot to lift it over the final bump, a shout of "I'll get that!" pierced the rushing wind. Steadfast was running toward them from the other side of the platform.

Pearl turned toward him. The force of Ashley's lift thrust the cot into Pearl's legs. Pearl toppled backward, flailing. The cot slipped from Ashley's fingers and ran over Pearl's body.

Hartanna shifted her free wing to scoop Pearl and Mason to safety, but the wind breezing underneath her shield swept them over the platform's side. Hartanna leaped after them and disappeared.

Steadfast dropped to his knees and stared. Ashley backed up to the opposite side of the plane, dashed forward, and jumped to the platform. Landing on the run, she rushed to him and stooped at his side, breathless. "Hartanna ... will catch them. ... I know she will. ... She is fast ... and powerful."

Still staring straight ahead, Steadfast could only say, "Perhaps one of them. Catching both would take more than a miracle."

389

Billy pulled the plane away from the platform, waving from the window. Ashley returned his wave, then hoisted Steadfast to his feet. "We can't wait. We have two patients who will die if we don't do something right now. I know your companion gave you that name for a reason, so let's move!"

Poking out from under Steadfast's collar, his companion flashed a soothing blue light. Without another word, he laid a shaking arm over Ashley's shoulders, and the two leaned against the wind as they hurried inside.

24

UNITED FOREVER

Dikaios eyed the village, a collection of modest huts, some with angled thatched roofs, others with flat tops or domes of brown grass. Since most of them had been constructed with crudely sawn logs, it was easy to spot Flint's home, the only brick-and-mortar structure in the area and the only one with a second floor. Positioned well away from the other homes and close to the water, apparently Flint felt himself superior to his neighbors.

Easing one hoof in front of the other, Dikaios crept toward Flint's house, listening carefully. Someone chopped wood nearby, yet out of sight, and the breeze provided the usual background hum, but nothing else stirred. Why was no one around? Were they all inside their homes? Out hunting? Did they have children? If so, why were there no sounds of playing or laughter?

As he approached the wooden door, he let out a whinny, then blew through his flapping lips. Surely that would be enough to attract attention. Humans always had a strange habit of running toward a horse's natural sounds when they didn't expect such a noble creature to be in the area.

After several seconds with no response, he stomped a hoof on the hard dirt. What would it take to get Flint to notice? Maybe if he snorted, but he would resort to that only if he truly had to. That would be a rather rude way to make his presence known.

Finally, the door swung open, revealing Flint. Dressed in black trousers and a sparkling black tunic tied at the waist, he smiled. "Well, what do we have here? Did Abraham's horse follow his scent?" He patted Dikaios on the nose. "This is an unexpected addition to our catch today, a fine stallion indeed."

Now Dikaios wanted to snort. The typical pat on the nose. Such condescension! But at least Flint was a good judge of horse-flesh. He scanned Flint for a weapon and spied a sheathed dagger fastened into his belt.

Flint touched Dikaios's chest. "What happened here, boy? Did the muskrats try to have you for a meal?" He blew a shrill whistle into the air. "Windor! Come here!"

Within seconds, a skinny boy ran from around the house. Wiping sweat from his brow, he slowed as he approached, his head down. Wearing an animal-hide tunic and breeches ripped at the knees, he shivered in the cold wind.

"Have you finished chopping wood for the bonfire?"

"Yes," came his weak voice in reply.

"Take this horse to the stalls and secure him. Give him a good bath and put salve on his wounds." As he again set his fingers near Dikaios's cuts, he smiled. "We will use Abraham's horse for our wedding processional. With his coat decorated by the stripes of defeat, his presence will be poetic indeed."

Windor stroked Dikaios's mane. "Horse needs rest. Not carry you."

"Did I ask your opinion?" Flint grabbed a shock of Windor's hair and jerked his head up. "If you do what I say and care for him well, I'll forget about what you did at the volcano."

Windor gulped. "I … I saved life."

Flint released him, then slapped his cheek with the back of his hand. The boy staggered back but held his tongue.

"Whether you saved my life or not," Flint said, "you rebelled against me." He pointed across a garden area toward the stalls. "There's a rope over there. Get it and tie him securely."

While Windor ran for the rope, Flint clutched a handful of Dikaios's mane. Even though such a grip exemplified the worst kind of manners, just as it did when he grabbed the boy, Dikaios resisted the urge to break free. Better to play dumb and get all the information he could.

He peeked through the open doorway. Inside, Abraham sat on the floor with his hands in his lap, but they seemed unbound. Angel stood next to him, wearing a silky white dress that fell to her feet, simple, yet shimmering, and a garland of white flowers decorated her neatly braided hair. They both kept their gazes on the floor, apparently not paying attention to the horse watching from outside. A giant of a man sat against the back wall. Carrying a long spear, he stared at Abraham, but he seemed bored rather than menacing.

Dikaios blinked. So they're planning a wedding. Could that be why the villagers had stowed away in their huts? They were probably making ready for a big event, maybe cooking or preparing their best clothes ... if they had any best clothes. Judging from the state of the houses and Windor's torn breeches, they seemed to be toiling in poverty.

He scanned the area for the two dragons. One trail of dragon tracks scarred a section of mud, ending abruptly near Flint's house. Tilting his head to the side, he searched the sky, now decorated with puffy white clouds, too small to conceal a dragon for long, yet there was no sign of either of them. And where could the other Nephilim be? They, too, would have a hard time hiding in this village. Had they gone to the Valley of Shadows to gather their forces?

393

Windor returned with a rope and pushed a loop over Dikaios's head. Now that he knew where Abraham and Angel were, Dikaios followed the boy obediently, loping along rather stupidly as many of the common horses did. As soon as the boy left him alone, he would go back and work out a rescue plan.

As Windor tied the other end of the rope to a corner fence post, Dikaios surveyed the other animals. Within the fenced area, pigs slept or wallowed, a rather foul-smelling lot, but what could he expect? They were pigs. A small herd of long-haired goats grazed in another fenced section, picking at the sparse grass within. A cow stood in one of four stalls, tied by the neck and eating some sort of green hay, its hindquarters facing him through the open door, not exactly the best view.

One stall lay empty. Perhaps its former resident had become dinner recently. A mule occupied stall number three, his handsome head facing out, but he looked bored and stupid, not exactly a good candidate for conversation. And some kind of four-legged animal stood behind the closed door of the fourth stall. Only the lower third of the creature's legs were visible in the gap between the bottom of the door and the ground.

Lowering his head, Dikaios tried to get a better look. Could it be? Horse hooves? Whoever this was, his head should have been visible over the door. Maybe he was eating hay from a bin at the side of the stall. In any case, this horse had fine reddish-brown forelegs, obviously a superb runner. He would be of great help if he could be persuaded to aid their escape.

Clapping dirt off his hands, Windor nodded at Dikaios. "Tight. No run away."

Dikaios blinked at the boy. With a welt growing on his dark cheek and a sad smile emerging on his dry lips, he seemed so pitiful. What would Flint do to the poor kid when a certain "fine stallion" escaped? This was a delicate matter, indeed.

"Good horse." Windor patted Dikaios on the neck. "Get food."

As soon as the boy left, Dikaios turned to the stall and let out a short whinny, a friendly greeting in horse language, or at least he thought so. It had been so long since he had used it.

The other horse's head rose above the stall door, its ears perked. Chewing a mouthful of hay, it stared at Dikaios, its nostrils flaring.

Dikaios stared back. Could this be a mare? The look in her eyes would say so. He dipped his head in a polite sort of way and pawed the hardened mud beneath him. This also communicated friendliness … he hoped.

She just kept staring, neither frightened, nor amused.

Windor set an oaken bucket on the ground, half filled with some kind of grain. "River oats," he said as he patted Dikaios again. "Back soon."

Just as he turned, Dikaios grabbed his shirt with his teeth. Windor spun back around, laughing. "No go?" he asked, pulling away.

"I prefer that you stay for a moment," Dikaios said.

Windor's eyes grew wide, and his mouth fell open. The mare dropped her hay and kept her stare fixed on Dikaios.

"Close your mouth, Windor," Dikaios said, keeping his voice low. "Such a gaping expression is unbecoming in a human."

Windor's mouth snapped shut.

"Good. I am sure you are aware of the prisoners Flint is holding. Is that correct?"

The boy nodded, his eyes still wide.

"And am I right in assuming that you are not fond of Flint?" Again, he nodded.

"Excellent. Then if you will help me set those prisoners free, I will take you to Abraham's village where you will be properly cared for."

Windor swallowed hard. "Mother? Father?"

"I see," Dikaios said. "Familial relations." He looked at the various huts surrounding the garden, the closest of which lay about three horse leaps beyond the pigpen. "Where is your home?"

Windor pointed. "Chimney house."

With a quick scan, Dikaios spotted the only house with a chimney. A thin curl of smoke rose from within. "If your parents are willing, we will carry everyone to safety."

"We?" Windor asked.

"The mare looks strong enough to carry two. I will take whomever else I must. Do you think your parents will want to join us?"

He nodded. "But they at wedding."

"Ah! The wedding. Where is it to take place?"

"Flint's house." Windor pointed that way. "In back."

"Will the entire village attend?"

Windor shook his head. "Feast after."

Dikaios scanned the area once again. "I have a warrior friend hiding in the marsh," he explained, nodding in that direction. "But if I summon him too soon, I fear that our opportunity to spirit our friends and relations away by stealth will be gone. If not for the giant, I think the two of us could manage, but I have no idea yet how to avoid him."

Windor pointed at himself. "I do."

"Really? What is your idea?"

"You see." Without another word, the boy dashed away toward his house.

Dikaios flattened his ears. The boy had left a bit too quickly. He could have loosened the knot and saved a lot of trouble. Still, what boy could be strong enough to tie a knot so tightly that a warrior horse couldn't pry it loose?

As he reached toward the rope with his teeth, the mare blew through her lips. He raised his head and eyed her. Her expression seemed softer now as she continued staring at him over the stall door.

Dipping his head again, Dikaios spoke with a gentle tone. "Good lady, although I doubt that you can speak, your noble brow and sparkling eyes suggest that you possess a great deal of intelligence. Therefore, I am assuming that you understand spoken words. Am I correct?"

When she bobbed her head, her lower jaw hit the top of the door. She shook her mane and snorted, obviously annoyed at herself.

Dikaios suppressed a laugh and continued. "Will you assist us in the escape plan I outlined for the boy?"

Again she bobbed her head, this time backing away enough to protect her jaw.

"Very good." Dikaios bit the knot at the fencepost and pulled. It was tight, indeed, far tighter than expected. No matter. He set his neck against the post and pushed the loop up over his head. Then, after sliding the stall latch open with his teeth, he bowed. "You are now free, my lady."

The mare nudged the door with her head and trotted out. After circling back to Dikaios, she let out a little whinny.

Dikaios butted her gently. "Quiet, please, or you will alert your owners."

She backed away, her ears pinned low, a clear sign of shame.

"I am not angry," Dikaios said. "I am merely being cautious. I appreciate your enthusiasm, yet silence is of the utmost importance."

Her ears perked up again, and she began prancing in place.

Dikaios chuckled inside. This young lady had a lot of spirit. "Since you seem ready to get started, may I suggest that you hide in the rushes just beyond the border channel? There you will find a human warrior named Valiant. He is very wise and will understand that I have sent you to him as a vessel to carry our escapees."

The mare took a step closer and nuzzled him, cheek to cheek. Then, with a quick spin, she cantered toward the marsh, her tail swishing with her gait.

As he watched the muscular sorrel cross the shallow channel, Dikaios let out a low, "Hmmm." Obviously she was smitten, but he couldn't allow her emotions to get in the way of their mission. It was time for action.

Turning, he spotted Windor. The boy, his shoulders hunched and both hands carrying a steaming mug, disappeared around the corner of Flint's house.

Dikaios trotted to the house, and as he circled toward the rear, he slowed. The sounds of human speech reached his ears. Halting at the back corner, he peeked around. Green grass covered the spacious backyard, hemmed in by a low wooden fence. A gate at the far end opened to the area beyond the fence, a muddy strip of land that bordered the marsh. There, a head-high pile of dried reeds lay next to a shorter pyramid of split wood. Beyond that, bulrushes and scrubby trees lined the swamp.

Flint walked toward the gate, followed by Abraham, Angel, Greevelow, and a stocky woman who seemed to have many of Greevelow's features, a kind face, yet just as stoic. The giant stood at the house's rear entrance, holding the spear at his side and sipping from the same mug Windor had carried.

Pointing at the ground, Flint spoke clearly and without emotion. "Then we will dismount the horse at this point." He took Angel's hand and guided her to his side. "And Father Abraham will stand in front of us and conduct the ceremony while Greevelow and Mantika watch as the two witnesses."

Still dressed in her shimmering white gown, Angel held Flint's hand loosely while the breeze flapped her hair and the flower garland, apparently woven into her locks tightly enough to keep it in place. In spite of the cold wind, she didn't shake at all, though her garment seemed made only of multiple layers of thin silk. A slender belt of white satin encircled her waist and fastened a satin pouch at her side. She stared at the ground. Her lips moved, but if she said anything, Dikaios couldn't hear her words.

Abraham stood at the spot Flint had indicated. "If you plan to follow the ways of the people on Earth, then do you have a ring to give her?" Although his voice seemed strong and lively, his drooping face and shoulders gave away his sadness.

"A ring?" Flint blinked at him. "Why a ring?"

Abraham drew a loop in the air with his finger. "Since a ring makes a circle, it is the symbol of an eternal bond. On Earth, the groom gives it to the bride as part of his vow."

Flint looked at his own hand. "The only ring I have is the one you gave me years ago."

"That will do." Abraham held out his palm, still marred by his earlier wound. "May I?"

While keeping his narrowed eyes on Abraham, Flint slid off the ring. "I kept this, because I thought it might have some kind of power, but I now think it's nothing more than gold metal and red glass."

"Whether or not it has power, I cannot say. I have never seen it display any." As soon as Flint laid the ring in his hand, Abraham enclosed it in his fist. "Shall I use the traditional Earth vows?"

"Yes. Of course." He turned toward Angel and let his gaze move slowly from her head to her feet. "Everything will be as it is on the Earth."

"I see." Abraham paused for a moment before raising a finger. "I hope you realize that a vow of eternal fidelity includes a promise not to harm Angel in any way."

Flint's cheeks reddened. "That is not an issue. Once we are united, I will want to keep her safe. I cannot start a new race of free people without her."

"That is agreeable." Abraham's features sagged further. "I assume, then, that we should proceed."

399

Dikaios turned and soft-stepped toward the front. Whatever Abraham had planned, it sounded like a last resort. Obviously Angel was being forced into this marriage. It was time to sweep the bride away and leave the groom standing at the altar.

When he reached the main door, he gave it a hefty kick with both rear hooves, then hurried toward the back again. He arrived just in time to see Flint and the giant running into the house.

Dikaios loped into view and stopped next to the fence. "Abraham!" he hissed. "Let us fly!"

Raising his hand to keep Angel from following, Abraham limped toward him and whispered, "Wait through the ceremony. You will know when it is time to escape." He reached a finger behind his belt, withdrew a bone fragment, and showed it to Dikaios. "Pray that Flint's distrust of me will work to our advantage."

Just as Dikaios hid himself again around the corner, Flint walked into the backyard. "Look who was pounding on the door. The little wood chopper." The giant followed, dragging Windor by the hair. The boy, carrying an axe, grimaced, but he didn't cry out or even whimper.

Mantika took a step toward him, but, with a quick hand, Greevelow held her back. "Flint kill," he said.

The giant snatched the axe away and slung Windor to the ground, sending him sprawling. Flint shook a finger at the fallen boy. "Why did you knock at the door and run? And the horse is missing. Did you let him go free?"

Cringing, Windor raised his hand, apparently to block an expected blow, but said nothing.

Flint shoved him with his foot. "Stupid boy! Just go home and wait for the feast."

As Windor struggled to get up, Abraham stepped forward and helped him rise. "May I suggest, Flint, that the boy stay and be our third witness?"

"A third witness? Why?"

"The tradition calls for two or three witnesses." Abraham raised a trio of fingers. "With three, no one could ever doubt the veracity of this ceremony."

Flint maintained his doubtful glare. "I get the impression that you're engaging in stealth."

"Is that so? What stealth could be behind wanting the fine young man to stay here with us?"

He aimed a finger at Abraham's face. "As usual, I know you won't lie to me. Do you have a plan that is designed to subvert my intentions?"

"I assure you," Abraham said, laying a hand on his chest, "that I will do everything in my power to stop this wedding, but since I have no such power, I am at the mercy of the Father of Lights."

"If there *is* a Father of Lights." Flint eyed Abraham for a few more seconds, then swatted Windor on the back of his head. "Go home until the feast."

Windor dashed out the back gate, around the fence, and right by Dikaios without offering a glance or a word.

"Since we no longer have our stallion," Flint said, "everyone stand in their places. We will conduct the ceremony before Father Abraham's doubtful deity can stop us." He took Angel's hand and faced Abraham, while Greevelow and Mantika stood at the side.

Abraham's eyes darted all around, pausing for a brief second in Dikaios's direction. "Because of your hurry," he said, "I will dispense with formality and speak only the essentials, at least as well as I can remember them."

Flint glanced at the sky, now fidgeting. "I am in agreement."

Dikaios looked up. What was Flint worried about? Ah! Dark clouds in the distance, coming this way.

Abraham raised a hand, his palm toward the bride and groom. "Do you take Angel to be your lawfully wedded wife, to have and to hold, in sickness and in health, to love, honor, and cherish as long as you both shall live?"

401

After a short pause, Flint asked, "Am I supposed to say something now?"

Abraham nodded. "I do."

Dikaios studied the great prophet's face. He wasn't even looking at Flint. He was staring straight at Angel. Why would that be?

"I do," Flint repeated.

Keeping one hand closed in a fist, Abraham handed the ring to Flint with the other. "Put this on her finger. I will give you the words to say."

Flint took the ring. "I expected her to speak vows similar to mine."

"Her vows will follow the ring ceremony. The order is unimportant." Abraham reached for Angel's hand, grasped it for a moment, then drew back. Even from where Dikaios stood, he could tell that Abraham had slipped something into her grip.

Abraham nodded at Flint. "Put the ring on her finger."

A scowl bent Flint's brow. "What are you plotting?"

"Plotting? I merely gave Angel a symbolic token. She will know what it means."

Flint grabbed Angel's wrist. "Open it! Let me see what it is!"

As soon as she opened her hand, Flint snatched its contents and held it up, a small white object that glinted in the sunlight. "Is this the bone you found in the tunnel?"

"I consider it a keepsake," Abraham said. "I wanted Angel to have it."

Flint looked at his hands, first at the bone in one, then at the ring in the other. "There is stealth in your mind, Father Abraham. Tell me what your plan is."

"If you ask me a question, I will tell you no lie, but I will keep all secret counsel to myself."

"We will see about that." Flint shoved the ring and bone into Abraham's hands. "Hold the bone while putting the ring on. I want to see what happens."

402

Abraham shrugged his shoulders. "Very well." He slid the ring over the index finger of his right hand. When the ring slid down as far as it could go, he moved the bone to the ring hand and balled his fist. "I am the very first dragon," he said with an air of nonchalance.

"I already knew that." Flint tilted his head toward the sky. The cloud had boiled to a dark and menacing storm, covering the descending sun and rolling toward the village. "Why do you bring it up now?"

As a shadow drifted over them, Abraham gave him a weak smile. "I am the father of a race that has suffered greatly and has also caused the suffering of many."

Flint's lips twitched. Still glancing at the darkening sky, he shifted his weight from one foot to the other. "I think we should proceed. I don't see how this is relevant."

A rumble sounded from above. A flash of light shot through the clouds, followed by a clap of thunder.

Flint ducked his head, as did Greevelow and Mantika, while Abraham and Angel stood tall.

"My words are relevant," Abraham said, "because my life on Earth ended too soon to stop the suffering there, but I will sacrifice everything to prevent my children from going through the same tragedies." He spread out his arms as if to embrace Flint. "As a dragon, I wait for the Father of Lights to make me a flame."

Lightning crashed down from the sky and struck the top of Abraham's head. Flint and Angel fell backwards. Greevelow and Mantika dropped to their knees. Dikaios flinched but kept watch. Too much was at stake to do otherwise.

His arms still spread, jagged arcs of current snaked all over Abraham's body until he became as bright as the sun itself.

Flint slid away on his seat. Angel tried to look at Abraham, shielding her eyes with her arm. Suddenly, his clothes burst into flames, then his face and hands. As tongues of fire melted away his skin, he turned to Angel and said in a pain-streaked voice, "Your time of widowhood has expired."

Clutching her dress at her chest, she gasped. "I ... I don't understand."

"I have already spoken my vow to you," he said, extending a flaming hand. "If you wish to become one with me, I would be honored. I might not have enough fuel to finish my journey."

"Fuel? Finish your journey?" She scooted back. "Good Father, you speak in riddles."

"If you do not understand, then you are not ready to join me." With his face now completely engulfed, Abraham turned and walked out the back gate, leaving a skinny trail of fire in his wake. As he passed by the piles of reeds and split wood, they ignited and exploded into a huge blaze. After circling the fence, he strode by Dikaios, seeming to float across the ground as he called out from the midst of the flames. "Make haste! Get Angel and go to my village immediately. Do not even take the time to look back!"

With a mighty kick, Dikaios vaulted the fence and landed in the backyard. Biting the back of Angel's dress, he jerked her to her feet. "Mount and hang on as tightly as you can," he said, lowering himself to his knees. "Whoever else seeks safety, follow me!"

Flint shouted, "Where is my giant?"

Dikaios looked at the back door. The Naphil lay sprawled on the ground, the mug again in his grip.

Just as Angel lifted her leg to mount Dikaios, Flint withdrew a stiletto from its sheath and dove for her. "No!" he shouted, grabbing her ankle. "You will stay!"

Angel pulled against the prostrate Flint, but she couldn't budge. Greevelow pounced. He threw his body over Flint and jerked Angel free. As she leaped onto Dikaios, Flint threw Greevelow to the side, rolling him face up with the stiletto protruding from his chest. Mantika rushed to Greevelow's side and knelt. With a cry of anguish, she wept over his lifeless body.

Flint yanked his weapon out and stalked toward Angel. Just as he lunged with the blade, Dikaios jumped out of the way, taking Angel with him. Flint wheeled around, grabbed Mantika from behind, and held the blade to her throat, panting. "If you do not stay with me ... before this creature draws five breaths ... she will join her mate."

With his eyes darting, he began a rapid count, matching Mantika's frantic respiration. "One, two, three ..."

Mantika held her breath. Angel whispered to Dikaios, "What should I do?"

"Pray." Dikaios swung around and aimed his rear hooves at Flint. Should he risk a kick? Or would Flint slice her throat before he fell unconscious?

Flint swatted Mantika's head. "Breathe, you fool!"

Suddenly, Flint arched his body. A long dagger protruded from between his shoulders. As his arms drooped, another horse leaped over the fence and charged into the yard. A rider reached down, snatched Mantika up by her clothes, and dragged her away. "Let us fly!" the rider shouted as the horse slowed to a stop.

"Valiant!" Angel cried.

Windor jumped down from behind Valiant and helped his mother to her feet.

As Flint wobbled in place, Dikaios kicked him in the back, knocking him headlong. "Valiant, help the boy remount! I will take his mother!"

When the two had climbed aboard, Dikaios galloped ahead and leaped over the fence. Listening to the pounding hooves behind him, he followed Abraham's fiery trail. With the failing light of evening dimming his vision, he plunged through the channel, then into the shallower marsh. Flames crawled up and down the reed stalks and crackled at the ends of skinny branches on nubby trees, illuminating the path. Soon, the fire grew brighter, the flames healthier. Was this a sign that they were catching up with Abraham?

405

Finally, in the distance, a striding column of fire came into view, surging through the marsh like flames following a trail of lamp oil. When Dikaios caught up, he slowed and trotted at the side of the column.

"Abraham?" Dikaios called, breathless. "Is that you?"

A raspy voice replied. "It is I … or what is left of me."

As the sorrel mare galloped to join them, Valiant shouted, "Father! What are you doing?"

The voice, weaker than before, sounded again. "Protecting my people. You will understand soon enough."

The column of fire turned and began a new course. "The boundary starts here," Abraham continued. "Remember it well. My journey will take all night. If I have enough fuel, I will enclose the Valley of Shadows. Goliath, Roxil, and the Nephilim are there."

With every inch he pressed forward, his body of fire seemed to shrink ever so slightly. Now, instead of dying out, the trail of flames behind him grew into a towering wall, rising higher and higher until the top reached out of sight. Reeds and trees crackled. Water boiled and sizzled, shooting plumes of steam into the sky.

With heat singeing his hide, Dikaios backed away. "Valiant!" he shouted. "What is your counsel?"

Valiant stared at the rippling orange wall, his eyes wide and gleaming. His voice was barely audible over the crackling fury. "We must obey Father and return to the village."

"Then let us go." Dikaios turned, but before he could leap away, something splashed at his side and jerked a passenger from his back. Angel's white gown swept past his eyes, clutched in the arms of a mule-riding man.

Dikaios and the mare turned as one and gave chase. The mule galloped to Abraham's flaming form, and the rider dismounted with Angel still in his arms, his stiletto again in hand.

Abraham stopped and turned toward them. His flames illuminated their faces. Flint, his teeth clenched, pressed the dagger against Angel's throat. Her eyes wide with fear, she stayed silent and kept her body stiff.

"Flint!" Valiant shouted as the mare came to a stop. "If you harm her, I will feed your flesh to the muskrats."

Dikaios joined him. "If there is any left after I trounce you to pieces."

"I will not harm her." Flint eased the dagger away. "She only needs to complete the vows."

"Is a forced vow a true one?" Valiant splashed to the ground and marched toward them. "Give her back to me now, and I will let you live."

"Stop!" Flint again pressed the dagger, this time drawing blood. "I will accept a forced vow. I want her womb, not her devotion."

Valiant halted within three steps of Angel, his fists clenched, but he said no more.

"Flint!" The crackling voice came from the leading edge of the fiery wall. "Let Angel stand freely, and I will finish the ceremony."

Flint glanced between Angel and the fire. "If Valiant gives us room."

Patting Dikaios on the flank, Valiant backed away. "Let Father Abraham do what he must."

When the two horses and their riders had retreated a distance of fifteen horse lengths, Flint released Angel but kept the stiletto flat against her back.

The flames spoke again. "Angel, it is time for you to make your vow."

"Father Abraham?" She lowered her head. "My time of widowhood has expired, and I do not wish to die, so it seems I have no choice."

The head of the flaming figure dipped a few inches. "I am in agreement."

407

"I now understand what you said earlier, but if I make the vow you request of me, who will care for my children?"

"Mantika will be welcomed into our village, and she will love Candle and Listener as her own."

"Very well. I have seen the heart of a mother in her eyes." Angel withdrew the dead companion from the pouch at her side and threw it underhand toward Valiant. When it splashed near his feet, he reached down and plucked it from the water.

Keeping her gaze on the wall of fire, Angel straightened her shoulders. With tears streaming, spasms punctuated each word. "I take you ... to be my lawfully wedded husband ... to have and to hold ... in sickness and in health ... to love, honor, and cherish ... as long as we both shall live."

She buried her face in her hands and sobbed.

After a moment of silence, Flint pushed his stiletto into its sheath. "Is that it? Are we married?"

"That depends." The flames crackled louder than ever. "To whom was Angel speaking?"

Angel lifted her head. She looked at Flint, then at the fire. Finally, she leaped ahead and ran. "To you, Abraham! My forever Adam!" She collided with the wall, her arms spread wide.

In the midst of the flames, Angel's form ignited from the garland of flowers in her hair to the hem of her silky dress. As arms of fire wrapped around her, she and the wall became one. The inferno billowed and brightened, and dozens of fireballs shot out and arced to the ground.

Flint dropped to his knees, his mouth agape.

A new voice emanated from the flames, now sounding like two in perfect harmony, a blend of male and female. "Flint, if you leave now, Valiant will allow you to go home without harm."

Flint rose slowly, his legs shaking as he looked at Valiant. He jumped aboard his mule and slapped it on the rump. With firelight dancing on their forms, the mule trotted off toward home, making a wide berth around the edge of the flaming wall.

As they faded in the darkness, Valiant slid his feet toward the raging fire. "Father." His voice faltered. "What shall we do?"

Again the blended tones rose above the crackling flames. "You and the warrior chief must make ready for the greatest conflict our world has ever seen. We will try to keep the enemies hemmed in long enough for you to prepare a mighty army."

Valiant backed away. As the warrior's tears dripped down his cheeks, his voice strengthened. "We will do your bidding, Father. Every able man will fight, and every woman and child will lend support. We will truly be as one."

"Then you honor us well." The fire marched on without another word.

Valiant remounted and extended the dead companion to Mantika, still seated on Dikaios, with Windor now standing at the horse's flank. "Will you care for her children?" Valiant asked.

With tears sliding down her dark cheeks, she took it and gave him a quivering smile. "I care."

He used his thumb to wipe away one of her tears. "Angel passed the authority over her children to you. Take her companion to them in remembrance of their beautiful mother."

Reaching for Windor with one hand, she raised the crystal egg to her lips and gave it a tender kiss. "We remember."

THE CALM BEFORE THE STORM

Sapphira carried the ovulum through the familiar tunnel, allowing its light to lead the way. The museum chasm lay ahead, as always. Of course, no one would be there. Bonnie and Shiloh and Irene would all have gone with Acacia, and the only voices within would be her own and any echo that cared to answer.

Still, maybe they left a note, a farewell of some kind. With nothing else to do, why not have a look? It certainly wouldn't hurt anything, and maybe she could kill some time perusing some of the old scrolls she hadn't read in the last hundred years.

As she neared the end of the tunnel, a strange light flickered in the distance. Did they leave the lantern behind? How could it still be burning after so many hours? Could one of them have come back and lost her way?

Sapphira tucked the ovulum under her shirt and ran. When she burst into the chamber, she stopped. A fire blazed at the center of the museum room, so bright, it washed out everything else inside.

She hurried ahead and stopped again at the museum's broken doorway. Flames covered the tree of life, licking the trunk, branches, and leaves, yet they emitted no smoke at all or even the slightest crackling sound. Between her and the fire, two bodies lay amid scattered stones, pebbles, and sand, one body wearing a backpack.

Sapphira pushed her way into the room, fighting wave after wave of hotter and hotter air. After passing the two bodies, she stopped and raised her arms. "Extinguish!"

The flames continued unabated.

Turning her back to the fire, she tried to shield the victims. She grabbed a backpack strap and turned one body to its side. "Bonnie? Can you hear me?"

Bonnie's smudged cheeks quivered, accentuating her swollen lips, but she gave no answer. Her dry skin was so cracked, it looked like dragon scales. Chalky dust spattered her clothes and made a trail of white that led back to the burning soil. Sapphira stared at the dust. Could it be residue from the bone she had sprinkled in the planter?

She reached for the other girl and turned her on her back. Her lips had also swollen from the heat. "Shiloh! Wake up!"

Blinking at the flames, Shiloh murmured, "Sapphira?"

Sapphira pushed her upright. "Try to crawl! I'll drag Bonnie before she gets heat stroke."

Shiloh rolled to her hands and knees. "Better check her collarbone first. It might be broken."

"Okay." Sapphira set her fingers on Bonnie's collar and pressed down. Bonnie winced but her eyes stayed closed.

"It's either bruised or broken, but we have to get her out of here somehow."

Shiloh squatted and pushed her arms under Bonnie's legs. "You get her back. Let's see if we can carry her out."

After sliding her arms between Bonnie's backpack and her sweatshirt, Sapphira lifted and shuffled sideways, her knees bent.

Shiloh did the same. With sweat dripping down her cheeks and nose, Sapphira grunted. The searing heat stung her skin, and Bonnie's weight made her arms ache, but she had to push on. Bonnie was so dehydrated, she could die at any moment.

When they finally passed the entryway, Sapphira jumped up and pushed the broken door across the opening, blocking the heat.

Shiloh's eyes turned glassy. She leaned her head against the wall and let her mouth drop open. Her tongue pushed out, cracked and swollen.

"I think we have some water left over." Sapphira ran around the museum's perimeter, collected four glass bottles from a pile of empty containers, and filled them from a jug of water she had stored long ago behind a barrel. She dashed back with the bottles in her arms and handed one to Shiloh. Shiloh poured a trickle over her tongue before pressing it against her lips for a long drink.

Sapphira poured another bottle over Bonnie's lips. Then, ever so gently, she opened Bonnie's mouth and let the water trickle inside.

As it drained to the back of her throat, Bonnie gagged, then swallowed, smacking her lips. Soon, Sapphira was able to get her to drink slowly, though her eyes remained closed.

She turned back to Shiloh. "How are you doing?"

Shiloh had already drained half of another bottle. "Much better. How is my twin?"

"I think she'll be okay. She's drinking." Sapphira let some of the water wash over Bonnie's parched skin. As she rubbed it in, the scaly cracks vanished. "What happened? Where are Acacia and Irene?"

"They made it through the portal, and we didn't." Shiloh gave her a shrug. "It's kind of hard to explain."

Sapphira propped Bonnie's bottle as she continued to drink. "I have time. Give it a try."

"Acacia's fire surrounded us," Shiloh said, drawing a circle in the air, "but when she climbed out, it started squeezing us in. A big rock dropped on Bonnie from the other dimension, and she

413

rolled into the dirt under the tree. The tree caught fire, so I had to drag her out, broken collarbone or no broken collarbone. When I grabbed her, she was coated with that chalky stuff, and blue fire burned all over her body. I thought she was a goner, but after I dragged her a few feet, the flames just snuffed out by themselves. I think I fainted after that." Shiloh drained her bottle and set it at her side. "Give me a minute to recover, and I'll try to remember more."

"Take all the time you need." Sapphira pulled back Bonnie's shirt collar, revealing an angry gash. Blood drained down her back, clotting quickly as it ran across her scaly, dirty skin, much of it dusted with the chalk Shiloh had mentioned. What could it all mean? Enoch had said something about the planter becoming a resurrection garden for dragonkind.

She stretched Bonnie's collar a few more inches. Would it be okay to see if she had wings? Even if she didn't before, maybe she had them now.

She eased the collar back into place. No. It wouldn't be right. That revelation belonged to Bonnie alone.

"Bonnie?" she called softly. "Can you hear me?"

"Hmmm?" Smacking her lips, Bonnie opened her eyes. "Sapphira?"

Sapphira couldn't hold back a laugh. "Girl, you really scared us."

Bonnie rotated her shoulder, grimacing. "I think I might've broken something."

"Maybe." Sapphira pulled back Bonnie's collar again. "We'll have to clean this wound right away and then take you to the hot spring for a good soaking."

"That sounds perfect." As she stretched out her arms, her face twisted in pain. "Help me get my backpack off."

Billy slid on his headset, gripped *Merlin*'s yoke, and looked over at Walter as he sat in the copilot's seat. "Ready to give it a try?"

After adjusting the earphones, Walter set his microphone in front of his lips. "Can you hear me all the way over there?"

"Loud and clear. I know it seems stupid to wear these, but they'll come in handy when the propeller gets louder." Billy rolled the airplane along the bumpy dragon launching pad. Outside, Ashley and Acacia waved, while Hartanna basked nearby in the sun, obviously exhausted. Stooping between Hartanna's front and back legs, Pearl rubbed some kind of salve into one of her wings, massaging a wound she had suffered while saving Pearl's life. Unfortunately, she wasn't able to rescue Mason. It was all she could do to snatch Pearl out of the air just before she hit the ground.

Billy sighed. Now another widow would cry out for comfort as she reared her children without a husband ... or an Adam. If this mission failed, he would have to get used to that term. He might have to stay in Second Eden for a very long time.

Fortunately, Onyx and Willow survived, but Steadfast would have to stay in the flying hospital with them, at least for a while. Cliffside was already making plans to bring the hospital in for a landing. With the threat from the altered tribes so low, he saw no reason to keep it up in the air, but since landing was a complicated procedure, he was taking plenty of time to do it safely.

As he throttled up, Billy tried to smile in spite of his anxiety. Since the tunnel portal in the Valley of Shadows was inaccessible behind Abraham's and Angel's wall, and his father had failed to open a portal with fire, this journey represented their last hope. And it could be a dangerous journey, maybe even shakier than his close encounter with the flying hospital.

Walter tossed a packet of peanut butter crackers into Billy's lap. "What's up? You look like you bit into a hunk of earwax."

"Just thinking about all the stuff going on." He picked up the crackers. "Where'd you find these?"

Walter tilted his head toward the back. "There's a stash by one of the seats."

415

"Sir Barlow sat there," Billy said. "He loves peanut butter."

As he unwrapped his own packet, Walter gazed out the window on his side. "I've been thinking, too. The creepiest thing was what Ashley said when she stood near that barrier."

Billy nodded as he replayed the scene in his mind. Hartanna had already tried to breach the wall of fire, but she could neither penetrate it nor fly high enough to surmount it. Then he and Ashley had flown the airplane, trying to find the top, but to no avail. After landing in a dry portion of the marsh, he stood next to Ashley as she faced the flames. *"I sense two minds within the fire,"* she had said, *"one male and one female. They are in pain, more emotional than physical, I think."* After shivering in a blast of cold wind, she added, *"But there is much love within that fire. They are content."*

As he pushed *Merlin* toward top speed and began a wide orbit around the village, Billy added a shiver of his own. A wall of human flames protected the people from a horde of giants, shadow creatures, and an evil dragon. That might just be the strangest of all the strange things he had seen over the last couple of years.

He looked out the window again. Now that they were about to pass directly over the birthing garden, it was time to go for it. The portal was probably directly above where Roxil had transformed. "You might want to wait to eat those crackers. We're going to climb like crazy now."

"Good thought," Walter said in a garbled voice. He swallowed his mouthful and tightened his seat belt. "Let her rip!"

Billy guided *Merlin* into a climb, circling as tightly over the garden as he could. Since Ashley was already concocting a formula for fuel using the oil deposits in the area, they didn't have to worry about running out. And they had plenty of time, so it made no sense to try for a dangerously steep incline. It was better just to take it easy.

"Twelve thousand feet?" Walter asked as he peered at the altimeter. "What does it max out at?"

"Supposedly about forty-five thousand, but I couldn't get past thirty-five when I tried to fly over the fire. The air pressure gradients are different here."

They continued their ascension, both staying quiet. With each orbit, the wall of fire came into view through Billy's window, rippling bright orange and towering out of sight. He studied each wave in the wall. What might Abraham's counsel be? Maybe he would say this mission was pretty much a waste. Since *Merlin* couldn't fly over the wall, what made anyone think it could fly high enough to find the portal? Besides, when they dropped out of the portal, they were at five thousand feet. If there was any way to get back through from the lower end, wouldn't they have reached that point already?

Billy eased out of the climb. "Let's go back."

"What's up?" Walter glanced at the meter again. "We're not at max yet."

"I know." He heaved another sigh and leaned back in his seat. "You ever get the feeling that you just can't do something, and you really can't explain why?"

Walter tapped his head with a finger. "That little voice inside?"

"Sometimes there." Billy pressed his fist against his chest. "And sometimes here."

"Yeah. I know what you mean." As *Merlin* began a slow descent, Walter looked out the window. "I get that feeling more and more these days, especially since I've been hanging around Ashley. She's ... well ... I don't know how to say it."

Billy shifted his gaze straight ahead but kept watching him out of the corner of his eye. "Penetrating?"

"Perfect word." Walter pulled another cracker out of his packet but just held it aloft. "I'm really too young for her, you know."

Billy pushed *Merlin* into a steeper descent. "You're definitely too young right now." He almost added, "When we finally get out of this place you both might be too *old* to get married," but he decided against it.

417

Now flying low, Billy peeked out the side window. In the field next to the birthing garden, Elam and Sir Barlow stood in front of sixty or so men, demonstrating sword thrusts and footwork. Obviously the troops from the other village had arrived, swelling their ranks. While a few were able to follow the moves with precision, the others seemed clumsy and uncertain. It would be a while before this army was ready for battle.

Nearby, Valiant practiced swordplay with Candle and Windor, while Mantika and Listener watched, hand in hand. With his graceful moves and precise footwork, Valiant was every bit as accomplished as Sir Barlow, while Candle, mimicking every step, thrust, and parry, had already surpassed some of the men. Valiant and Candle would soon be a formidable pair.

At the edge of the field, one man climbed aboard Clefspeare's back. Little did this pilot recruit know that sitting atop the greatest dragon warrior of them all was a privilege that few others had enjoyed. He was in for the ride of his life.

After making a swing around the field, he headed for the dragon launching site. He let his shoulders sag. Watching the army hadn't boosted his confidence. Although when Thigocia and Hartanna reached full strength, they would have more dragons than the enemy, the Nephilim and shadow people could easily overwhelm them with numbers. The good guys wouldn't last long, especially if an attack came at night. And even if Abraham and Angel could keep their fire going for months, Flint might have trained an unstoppable army by that time.

If only Patrick could become Valcor again. That would help a lot. But his latest attempt, with Acacia's fiery blue aura surrounding him, yielded only the same gentleman he had always been. Still, he didn't seem to mind. Working in the infirmary with Ruth had brought a bounce back into his step.

As soon as they landed, Ashley opened the rear passenger door and climbed inside. "What happened?" she asked as she made her way to the front.

"We passed the portal altitude and nothing happened," Billy said. "We'd better get used to the fact that we're stuck here for a while. My biggest concern is getting word to my mother about what's going on."

"Well, I've been thinking about that." Ashley stooped in the aisle just behind Billy and Walter and nodded toward the airplane's dash. "I might be able to use *Merlin*'s transmitter in combination with the magnetic field generator and maybe send a signal to Larry. Even if I can't send voice, maybe some bursts of text data would be enough. He can decipher almost anything."

"How long would it take you to set that up?"

Ashley shrugged. "Impossible to know. I have no idea what kind of supplies they have here, but if they can make a magnet-driven flying hospital, they must have some techno-wizardry."

"Maybe." Billy looked out the front window. He could see the ripples in the protective wall even from where they sat. "But the local wizard might be going up in flames right now."

"What about Enoch?" Walter asked. "He knows we're here. Won't he let our families know?"

Ashley laughed. "He might, but he's kind of unpredictable."

As Billy thought about the people back home, Bonnie came to mind. The last he heard, a big rock had fallen on her, and she and Shiloh seemed to be in trouble. Was she alive? How could he find out? And what about Mom? She was probably already worried sick about Dad, and she had no clue that he was now a dragon again. But what could anyone do about it? They all had to press on and be the warriors they were called to be.

"We just have to trust Enoch's wisdom." He set his hand in front of Ashley, his palm down. "Meanwhile, we're in this together, no matter what."

Ashley covered his hand with hers. "You got it. We're a team, come dragons or ugly giants."

"I ain't afraid of no giants," Walter said as he added his hand. "We'll stick together like glue."

419

Ashley withdrew her hand and wiped it on Walter's jeans. "Or like peanut butter."

Marilyn?"

The male voice drifted into her mind from somewhere far away, quiet, yet probing. Was it a dream? It wasn't Larry. Not Edmund, either. Walter's dad?

She shook herself awake, lifted her head from her folded arms, and peered into the darkness. "Carl?"

A switch clicked. Light flooded the computer room, revealing Carl and Catherine Foley walking through the doorway to the hall. Sir Edmund and Shelly entered behind them, each with steaming cups in their hands.

"We just got home," Carl said. "It's almost one in the morning, but I thought it would be okay to bring you some news."

Marilyn waved them toward the scattered chairs. "Yes. Of course."

"Shelly turned off the alarms and let us in." He removed his wet trench coat and draped it over a chair. "Sir Newman's been trying to call you. He finally got hold of me while we were on our way back from the airport."

"Very strange." Marilyn looked up at Larry's main console. "Is our phone on the fritz?"

"I will now play back audio that includes your most recent directive."

A cartoon megaphone appeared on the screen. Larry's speakers crackled briefly, then Marilyn's voice came through loud and clear. "Larry, if I fall asleep, turn off the phone, and don't wake me up, even if the slayer himself breaks in."

Larry's voice returned. "End of recording."

"Whew! I must have been really out of it." Marilyn rubbed her eyes, then looked up at Carl again. "What's the news?"

"It's nothing urgent, so let's sit down first." While Shelly and Edmund passed around the cups, Carl pulled four chairs into a circle with Marilyn's. When everyone was seated, he leaned toward her. "Your research led Sir Newman to a house Palin once owned. It's just outside of London, a small place where an elderly man lives, just him and his dog. He gave Newman permission to search the house and grounds, and with the help of a bloodhound and a metal detector, he located a buried container." He drew a rectangle in the air. "One of those fireproof boxes."

While he took a sip of coffee, Marilyn drummed her fingers on her thigh. Waiting for the bottom line of this story was maddening. "Go on," she said.

"Of course, the box was locked, but it didn't take long to force it open. Inside, Sir Newman found a single sheet of paper and a red gem."

"A rubellite?" she asked.

"Not difficult to guess, was it?" After taking another sip, Carl nodded at Larry. "Sir Newman said he would scan the sheet of paper and email it to you. Did you get it?"

"Affirmative. I am displaying it now."

The screen showed a pencil sketch of a sword, an exquisite rendering of hilt and blade with every detail meticulously included. In the blade's etching, two dragons battled, and on the hilt, Palin had drawn lines radiating from a small circle as if to make the round object sparkle.

"Excalibur," Edmund said. "A fine drawing, indeed."

Marilyn stood and set her finger on the image. "Larry, can you zoom in on this text at the bottom?"

After a brief flash, two lines of neat block lettering filled the screen. Marilyn read them out loud. "Morgan claimed that removing the gem would take a third of Excalibur's power away. Perhaps frustration will cause my master to stop hunting children."

She turned slowly back to the others. "So Excalibur is crippled."

421

"And supposedly," Carl said, taking Catherine's hand, "Walter has the sword in some kind of alternate reality."

Marilyn took her seat and counted on her fingers. "We think Jared, Billy, Ashley, Abigail, Thigocia, Shiloh, Sir Patrick, and Sir Barlow are all over there. At least that's what Sapphira said when she made her last call. She said something about Shiloh possibly staying with her on Earth, but she wasn't sure."

"Maybe I'm crazy," Shelly said, "but if my brother needs that gem to make the sword work better, then I'm all for trying to get it to him. Since they haven't come back, they might be in all sorts of trouble."

"But how do we get it there?" Marilyn asked. "We don't have a way to cross dimensional barriers. We don't have any dragons or Oracles of Fire."

Larry's speakers clicked on. "May I interject an idea?"

"Of course." Marilyn rolled back to the desk and turned up his volume knob. "Go ahead."

The image on the console screen changed to an object that looked similar to an old-fashioned hourglass. A transparent rectangle separated the circular platforms at the top and bottom, and four dowels surrounded it at the corners, obviously supports or places to grasp it.

"This is Apollo. Although it was destroyed in the Circles of Seven, I still have the schematic, including every detail you would need to reconstruct it. If you can locate a portal gateway to Walter's realm, I should be able to analyze the light patterns, use Apollo to create the proper flash, and send the gem through the opening. If anyone has the courage to attempt the journey, we could try to send a human."

Carl raised his hand. "In a heartbeat. Anything to help Walter ... and the others, of course."

422

"How long would it take us to build Apollo?" Marilyn asked.

"Impossible to calculate, but without Ashley's abilities, it could take several weeks or perhaps much longer."

"Several weeks?" Marilyn clenched her eyes shut. "Even if we could build it, only Sapphira can find the right portal, and we haven't heard from her in a while."

"Did Sapphira say where she was going?" Carl asked.

Opening her eyes again, Marilyn shook her head. "Just that she and Gabriel had to go into hiding, somewhere the slayer would never find them."

"Have you tried calling her back?"

"Several times." Marilyn slid her desk phone closer and scrolled through the numbers in her caller ID list. "Want to try again?"

Carl stood and read the number on the tiny screen. "That's Walter's cell phone."

"I guess she borrowed it."

Standing, Carl fished his phone from his pocket, punched a speed dial, and held the phone to his ear. After a few seconds, his eyebrows shot up. "This is Carl Foley. Who is this?" A smile spread across his face. "Gabriel? How did you get Walter's phone?"

He sat back down. "Yes ... Uh huh ... Yes, it's okay to be out of breath. Flying must take a lot of energy. Take your time." He looked up at Marilyn. "He's on his way here."

"Can he tell us where Sapphira is?" Shelly asked.

Carl raised a finger. "Good. ... Yeah, you can't do that on a commercial flight. Listen. Do you know where Sapphira is? ... You do?" Carl gave everyone a thumbs-up. "Good. I'm going to jump in the car right now and head west. You find a safe, warm place to hide and call me to let me know where you are. No sense killing yourself flying at night. ... Yeah. I'll bet." He grinned. "I

423

wouldn't want to fly through a swarm of hungry bats either. Talk to you soon."

Carl closed the phone and pointed it at Catherine and Shelly in turn. "I'll need both of you to help me drive. No sleeping stops until we find Gabriel."

Shelly let out a whoop and shouted, "Road trip!"

"Did Gabriel offer any updates?" Catherine asked. "Does he know where everyone is and how they're doing?"

Carl shook his head. "I'm sure we'll get the lowdown when we find him. He did say something about a hideout being guarded by the last of the Nephilim, but he didn't say what that meant."

"Larry?" Marilyn's words stretched out as she yawned. "Will you please print out the parts list for Apollo?"

"Certainly. It is quite lengthy, but it will be all you need."

Sir Edmund rose to his feet. "Since Mrs. Bannister and I will be the only adults remaining, I will excuse myself and find a place to sleep outside."

"No way," Marilyn said, pointing at him. "You stay in Billy's room, and I'll sleep with the girls. Even an honorable knight such as yourself would agree to that, wouldn't you?"

Edmund shifted nervously on his feet. "Well, since you put it that way, I suppose it will be all right."

"Besides ..." Marilyn pulled one of the sheets from Larry's printer bin and scanned the parts list. "I'll need you to be wide awake to guard the house while I take the girls on a shopping trip to the local cross-dimensional supply store."

Seated on a stone, Semiramis passed her hands around the candle's red flame. A gray bead dripped down the side, hardening as it neared the splatter of wax on the stone table. She inhaled the smoke and closed her eyes as she chanted in low tones.

The time has come to spring the trap
That wisdom once began;
No love or friend or even son
Shall stop my master's plan.

Now come to me, my dragon lord;
The fools have done our will.
Prepare our weapons, honed for blood;
The time has come to kill.

Looking up into the dark sky, Semiramis waited. How long would it take? Her previous summons had taken an hour, or so it seemed. Sitting in this buffer between the worlds always skewed her sense of time passage, worse than the Bridgelands ever could. Yet, this realm served a purpose, an excellent hideaway for clandestine meetings that only the most skilled in Samyaza's arts could enter, the perfect place to hide the anchor points between Earth and Hades.

Finally, after what seemed like twenty minutes, Arramos landed next to the table. As red and shimmering as ever, he stalked toward her, his magnificent wings stretching once, then pulling in.

"Your calling spell would lead me to believe that you have good news." Arramos stopped at the opposite side of the table and extended his neck. As his head hovered over the candle flame, his red pupils throbbed like a beating heart. "Tell me what you know."

Semiramis raised a hand and caressed the dragon's scaly cheek. "Good news, indeed, my lord. The rope is in place, the giants are in Second Eden, and the garden has been fertilized. Although the pathetic children Abraham calls his army have three dragons now, they are guided by the son of Shem, who has never been a general in his life. His only other true warriors are a boy who breathes fire, his wise-cracking sidekick, and an idiom-quoting, centuries-old knight. You might also count one local soldier, a certain Valiant, but his promotion to the role of prophet could well hinder his fighting status."

"Promotion? What has become of Abraham?"

"Abraham has made himself into a wall of flames, thinking his ring of fire will be enough to enclose our army."

"He invoked the prophecy so soon?" Arramos's emerging grin revealed four daggerlike teeth. "We could not have hoped for a better result."

"True, but he had no choice. His misguided love for the lying woman proved to addle his brain more thoroughly than we predicted."

"Then he will burn out soon. Perhaps six months, a year at the most."

"Well … not exactly." Semiramis drummed her fingers on the table, glancing back and forth between the splash of wax and the dragon's fiery eyes. "There is a … a complication, and it will not please you."

Arramos's voice deepened to a growl. "Tell me."

"The woman, Angel they call her, joined the wall of flame. Mardon analyzed the data streaming through our cross-dimensional viewer, and, for some reason, Abraham and Angel together are able to sustain energy far longer than simple mathematics would suggest. The fuel for the boundary could last four years or more."

"Four years?" The dragon's eyes flared. "Can Mardon and the slayer keep the dragons on the run for that long?"

"Not likely. As soon as one of them learns she is being chased by a dead scientist and a floating bauble, she and the rest will come out of hiding, and Second Eden will be flooded with dragons."

"Then let us end the charade." Arramos backed away. "Meet me at the chasm with Mardon."

Semiramis rose to her feet. "Of course, my lord, but may I ask what you're planning?"

"The garden has already reconstituted dragons. I know for a fact that it will also reconstitute a human, and we have one who needs a body."

"But Clefspeare and Roxil had a body already. They merely needed to be transformed. Creating a new body will take more time."

"We have time." Arramos raised a foreleg. A crystalline bauble, semitransparent and glowing, floated above his clawed hand. "Seeds germinate. Seedlings grow. Then the harvest. Four years should be enough."

"What of your plan to hold Bonnie Silver hostage?" Semiramis asked. "Using her finger to chill their hearts was a stroke of genius. It can still be harvested."

A low chuckle rumbled from the dragon's throat. "When that self-righteous little vixen finally enters Second Eden, she will be Devin's first victim. I am sure he will be happy to begin his new war against dragonkind by slicing her apart bit by bit."

"At the risk of testing your patience with yet another question, my lord, what of my son? He has been a faithful servant to both of us."

"We will send him, as well. Someone needs to plant our seed in the garden."

As Semiramis gazed into the candle's flame, she slowed her words. "I told him he could not survive in that world, that being dead on Earth made it impossible for him to leave Hades."

"There is a way. Since you have been watching the proceedings in Second Eden, I thought you might have discerned it by now and tried to go there yourself."

Semiramis folded her hands on the table. "I ... I see once again that I lack your wisdom. I would very much like for us to go to Second Eden together."

427

"There is no need to try to flatter me. I will see to your safe journey there. With both of you living outside of Abraham's wall, we will have the spies we need. Devin will surely rise again."

"Mardon will need an appropriate disguise. The Oracles know him and will not be duped easily."

"I will take care of disguises, as well. Just guide him to the chasm's bridge during Second Eden's next eclipse cycle, and I will arrange the rest." Arramos unfurled his wings, creating a draft that blew out the candle. Now in total darkness, his voice seemed lower and more menacing than ever. "Devin the dragon slayer must live again and stalk the land of Second Eden. And he will need no disguise."

Bonnie sat between Sapphira and Shiloh. With an old journal open over her lap, and their bare feet dangling in the hot spring's bubbling pool, everything was perfect for a nice long reading session. The ovulum, sitting in Sapphira's open palm, gave them just enough light to see each other's faces. It would be fun trading stares and smiles in the wash of red light, especially as Bonnie read out loud about her many harrowing adventures.

She turned the page to a very special entry in one of her older journals. "This is what I wrote right before the dragon slayer killed my mother. Earlier that day, my father had drawn blood from me, even though he had promised so many times never to do it again. After he took it and sent me away, I felt ... well ..." She pulled the journal closer so she could make out her cursive script in the dim glow. "If I just read it, I think you'll understand."

She took a deep breath and began, "I descended into the shadowlands today. A specter of fear wrapped his cold, cruel fingers around my heart and led me into his chamber of treachery, a sanitary cube of torment that once again enclosed my mind in darkness. Can any instrument of torture deliver cruelty as savage as love betrayed? Does a dungeon's rack stretch a body as sadistically as betrayal stretches trust? Can faith endure a traitor's sinister hand as it turns the wheel, each notch testing conviction until the sword of despair separates peace from its rightful habitat?"

As Bonnie read, Sapphira smiled and nodded, acknowledging that she had seen this entry before. Shiloh sat agape, gasping at times, and tearing up at others. With both girls paying such rapt attention, this gathering seemed more like a slumber party than an exile in the underworld.

Finally, Bonnie took in another breath and finished the entry. "And now I see it. I can give you nothing that you have not already given to me. I am purchased, a slave of love. I am your vessel to be used in whatever way you wish. If you make me an urn for ashes, a common earthen jar to bear incinerated bones, leaving me to collect dust in a forgotten tomb, even then, I will be content. For just as you would not leave your son forever in the ground, I know you will raise me up from the land of the dead. You have not ignited this fire in my heart to be wasted in Sheol's pit. Though dead, buried, and forgotten, I will rise again."

She closed the journal and quoted the remaining words from memory. "No matter what happens, I will never forsake you, for you will never forsake me. You are with me, no matter where I go."

"That was so beautiful," Shiloh said, wiping a tear away. "I know exactly how you felt."

Bonnie took Shiloh's hand and moved it to her lap. "After forty years in the sixth circle, I'm sure you do." Pulling Sapphira's hand to join hers and Shiloh's, she added, "And who knows loneliness better than you?"

"I can't argue with that." Sapphira tightened her grip on Bonnie's fingers. "No matter how long it takes, we can do this."

Shiloh tightened her grip, as well. "We'll face dragons, giants, slayers, and even the devil himself if we have to."

Bonnie wrapped her wings around Sapphira and Shiloh and pulled them close. "As long as we're together, we can face anything."

EPILOGUE

Sitting on an egg crate near a wall in an abandoned warehouse, Rebekah held a handwritten letter close to her eyes. Dallas, her aunt, though more like a sister than an aunt, sat on a similar crate, leaning her head close to Rebekah's. With raven locks spilling from under a wide-brimmed hat, dark glasses spanning her eyes, a black leather purse on her lap, and her trench coat collar pulled up high, Dallas looked more like a secret agent than a former dragon.

Rebekah squinted at the hastily written script, angling the page toward a row of dirty windows to gain better light. "I received Valcor's note this morning. The slayer is definitely on the move, so Valcor wants us to locate and warn the others."

Dallas removed her sunglasses and leaned toward the letter. "Does he know where they are?"

"Four of them, but he considered it too risky to write down their whereabouts. Since they lacked fluency in any modern language, he escorted them back to England and settled them into separate hideouts where they could study the culture. He instructed us to go to West Virginia where we will find their addresses in a secure file in a supercomputer named Larry."

"Supercomputer?"

"A new invention. I will have to explain some other time."

"Soon, I hope." Dallas pulled a cell phone from her purse. "I still have to figure out how to use this."

"I will teach you that, as well, but we must finish our business here." Rebekah pushed a strand of blond hair from her eyes and reached for a handbag on the floor. "I started my own list of surviving dragons."

"I know Yellinia went with Valcor," Dallas said. "She and Martinesse."

"A good start." Rebekah pulled a pen and spiral notebook from her bag, opened it to the first page, and silently read the first two lines.

432

Legossi: Rebekah (Boston, MA)
Firedda: Dallas (Boston, MA)

On the next two lines, she wrote:

Yellinia: Dorian (London, England)
Martinesse: Jordan (London, England)

"According to Valcor, we need not concern ourselves about Clefspeare, Hartanna, or your mother." She tapped her chin with her pen. "What about your other sisters?"

Dallas raised two fingers and lowered them as she counted off her siblings. "Sorentine wanted to travel north, perhaps to Canada. For some strange reason, she loves cold weather. And I think Alithia said something about staying with your sister in Scotland."

"I remember that. They must be the other two Valcor took with him." Rebekah jotted down the following lines:

Sorentine: Tamara (Somewhere, Canada)
Alithia: Kaylee (Glasgow, Scotland)
Carboni: Elise (Glasgow, Scotland)

As she imagined the locations on a world map, Rebekah nodded. With four of them in the British Isles, perhaps finding everyone would take only weeks rather than months. Yet, who knew when they would have mailing addresses or cell phones? Even with those in place, open communication would be dangerous. Their deaths in the past proved that the slayer was always vigilant. "I could contact them using older dialects," she said, "but would that help us or make our communication more obvious?"

"I believe we should use modern English and trust them to learn quickly," Dallas said. "Although the rest of us lack your ability to consume knowledge, we are all very adaptable."

"Except for Sorentine."

Dallas sighed. "Yes. Except for Sorentine."

Rebekah pressed her lips together, trying to hold back her tears. It was time to address the subject she had avoided for too long. "Shall we discuss our younglings?"

"*Our* younglings?" Dallas raised her eyebrows. "What do you mean?"

"The very day the slayer killed us, I was going to tell you." Rebekah's throat tightened, but she pressed on in a higher pitch. "I wanted to be sure before I told anyone."

Dallas grasped her hand. "You were … with child?"

Closing her eyes, Rebekah nodded. Now she could barely speak at all. "Three months."

"Oh!" Dallas clutched Rebekah's hand. "I am so sorry!"

Rebekah laid her hand over her abdomen, the very spot Devin had thrust his sword. Could it have been over a hundred years ago? Memories of the horrible pain were still so fresh. As she massaged the point of entry, a sudden feeling of emptiness overwhelmed her. Tears flowed. She couldn't go on.

"You need not speak," Dallas said. "The pain of losing your only child is too tragic for words."

Rebekah nodded her thankfulness.

"I was wondering," Dallas continued, "if *my* youngling might still be alive. Humans rarely live that long, at least not since the times of the patriarchs."

Rebekah pulled a tissue from her handbag and dabbed her eyes. After almost a minute, her throat loosened. "It is possible. When Alithia's son went into hiding, he was over one hundred years old, so your daughter might well be alive."

Dallas squinted at the ceiling, moving her lips as if counting. "Assuming she escaped the slayer and survived this long, Mariel would be ..." She looked at Rebekah again. "One hundred thirty-seven years old."

434

"So our search will include her and ..." Rebekah tapped her chin, trying to remember Alithia's son's name.

"Thomas," Dallas said.

"Please pardon my memory loss, but I seem to remember one other youngling. Did Sorentine give birth?"

"I never heard. She died so soon, I often wondered. At the time of our transformation, she was far enough along in her pregnancy, so she could have delivered before Devin killed her. But delivered what? Was her little one transformed within her?"

Rebekah let a thin smile emerge. "Sorentine was within a week of delivering when Merlin brought the wine to Bald Top. Gartrand was such a proud father, he counted the days."

"Your brother was one to boast—" Dallas held a hand over her mouth. "I apologize. My insensitive ways are not helpful."

Rebekah waved a hand. "No need. I know his folly all too well."

The two women stared at each other for a moment. As Dallas's eyes filled with tears, she sighed. "So many heartaches."

Rebekah read her aunt's face. She knew. Everyone knew. Sorentine had made many judgment errors. Going through the covenant veil with Gartrand had been Sorentine's most obvious blunder, but her lack of care in staying away from the slayer had cost her her life soon after her transformation and had inadvertently given the slayer knowledge that helped him track down the remaining dragons. "Since we have no way to search for Sorentine's youngling, we will confine our efforts to the known dragons and offspring. Agreed?"

Dallas nodded. "Agreed."

Grabbing her handbag, Rebekah rose to her feet. "Have you learned how to drive?"

Dallas's eyes shot open. "In so few days? In Boston? Without a car?"

"Do you remember the silver dollar from our cache the dealer made such a fuss about?"

"Indeed. He was not a skilled barterer, was he? He practically drooled."

"We settled on a payment this morning. I now have a sports utility vehicle and all the supplies we need to go to West Virginia."

Dallas looked at the ceiling again, a coy grin on her face. "What words did they use in that movie last night?"

"Road trip." Rebekah reached for her hand. "Let's hit the road."

435